I0613994

Floods and Drought

ZAHRA OWENS

Dreamspinner Press

Published by
Dreamspinner Press
382 NE 191st Street #88329
Miami, FL 33179-3899, USA
http://www.dreamspinnerpress.com/

This is a work of fiction. Names, characters, places, and incidents either are the product of the author's imagination or are used fictitiously, and any resemblance to actual persons, living or dead, business establishments, events, or locales is entirely coincidental.

Floods and Drought
Copyright © 2012 by Zahra Owens

Cover Art by Anne Cain   annecain.art@gmail.com
Cover Design by Mara McKennen

All rights reserved. No part of this book may be reproduced or transmitted in any form or by any means, electronic or mechanical, including photocopying, recording, or by any information storage and retrieval system without the written permission of the Publisher, except where permitted by law. To request permission and all other inquiries, contact Dreamspinner Press, 382 NE 191st Street #88329, Miami, FL 33179-3899, USA
http://www.dreamspinnerpress.com/

ISBN: 978-1-61372-427-9

Printed in the United States of America
First Edition
March 2012

eBook edition available
eBook ISBN: 978-1-61372-428-6

To anyone who has ever known in their head that something was never going to pan out right, but who did it nevertheless, because they could not forgo following their heart.

And to everyone who braved watching the train wreck happen, just so they'd be there to help you pick up the pieces.

—1—

GRANT JARREAU came bounding up the porch stairs of the largest house on the Blue River Ranch with Matthew on his arm. The child was laughing ecstatically at being tossed around rather roughly by the big cowboy and only complained when Grant put him on the kitchen floor.

"More!" Matthew called out, but Grant ignored his pleas and simply tousled the boy's hair before moving to the breakfast table and kissing his lover.

"You know, if you keep tossing him around like that, he's going to expect all of us to do it as well," Hunter Krause remarked. "You spoil him."

Grant squeezed Hunter's shoulder. "That's because I know how much you enjoy being spoiled; why should your son be any different?" He winked, and Hunter started laughing.

At that moment, the kitchen door opened again and a flood of children came bounding in, closely followed by Christy Marshall, the mother of most of them.

"Calm down already!" She raised her voice. "Be quiet and sit down to eat your breakfast."

Hunter had put out bread, cheese, and lunchmeat and was making sandwiches for all the kids to take to school. Three years ago he and Grant had built their own house on the property, but they ate breakfast at the larger ranch house most of the time because they wanted to see Grant's three kids before they went to school. Everyone had their fixed routine in the morning, which took some of the heat off Christy, who also cooked for the workers who lived at the ranch.

Grant thought the kitchen resembled a daycare center more than a ranch house most mornings, between his kids with Christy and the two little girls playing with Matty, who belonged to Hunter's sister Izzie and Hugh Conroy, the ranch foreman. Danny, Hugh's son with his first wife, Lisa—also a sister of Hunter's—completed the picture. He was old enough to sit with the adults and was pitching in to help Hunter make them sandwiches along with the ones for the school kids when the phone rang.

Grant got up from the table to pick up the receiver. "Blue River Ranch." The kids were making a racket, so he tried to cover his other ear, but he still couldn't make out what the soft voice on the other end of the receiver was saying. By the time he'd rounded the door to the hallway, the caller had disconnected the call.

"Who was that?" Hunter asked as Grant sat down next to him.

"No idea," Grant answered. "Whoever it was didn't wait for me to get to a quieter part of the house so I could hear."

Hunter shrugged. "They'll call back. They probably thought they got a wrong number and had inadvertently called the zoo, or something."

"Well, it certainly sounds like a zoo in here. I feel sorry for the schoolteachers who get this bunch in morning classes," Grant replied with a smile.

"Saddle up, kids. Get your lunch and your books out to the car. Time to leave for school," Hugh announced while Izzie helped the kids find everything and everyone chipped in to get the four oldest children out the door.

As Hugh and Izzie walked down the porch, Tim—one of the wranglers and Hugh's baby brother—came running up to the house.

"Can I talk to you, Hugh?" Tim asked. He leaned in a little closer. "It's not for everyone's ears."

Hugh knew his brother well enough to tell this couldn't wait and exchanged a silent look with his wife, who held out her hand for the car keys.

"Sure, let's go into the office."

Tim followed Hugh to the ranch office, which was located downstairs next to the mud room. This was usually where Hunter did the books and recorded the orders that needed to leave the ranch, but since Hunter was still in the kitchen, Hugh knew they'd have some privacy there.

"Shoot," Hugh said after closing the door behind Tim.

Tim hesitated, playing with the rim of his hat. "Remember Rory?"

Hugh narrowed his eyes and shook his head. "Rory?"

"Drifter who asked for a job a few years ago. Stayed for about three weeks and then disappeared after picking up his Friday night paycheck," Tim explained.

"You expect me to remember every ranch hand who passes through here, Timmy?"

Tim shook his head. "You should remember this one. He's the one who helped Delco steal all those foals that year."

"Right. That Rory. What about him?"

Tim took a deep breath and looked at his brother. "I need a favor, Hugh."

"Will you cut to the chase?" Hugh asked impatiently. "I have a ranch to run, and at this pace it'll be dinnertime before I get around to it."

"I need you to give him his old job back," Tim said determinedly.

Hugh laughed. "You must be joking."

"I'm not," Tim replied calmly. "He needs a job and a place to stay or they won't let him out on parole."

Hugh leaned over the desk. "Let me get this straight. He worked here for three weeks to get inside information on the workings of this ranch, then disappeared like a thief in the night, only to come back with Delco to steal seven foals from us. And you want me to give him a job?" He pushed himself off the desk with some force to straighten his back and then folded his arms in an attempt to look taller, which was easy since he was well over six feet and Tim was at least two inches shorter. "Even you have to realize I'm not *that* gullible, Timmy."

"He's no criminal mastermind, Hugh," Tim answered. "He's just a guy who's been dealt a rough hand. The horse thieving wasn't his idea, it was Delco's. Rory simply had no money for more than a pro-bono lawyer, and that's why he got four years and Delco was out after eleven months."

"Don't you think the fact he had a rap sheet an arm long could have had something to do with the judge's decision?" Hugh shook his head. "The guy's a career criminal. He got off lightly as far as I'm concerned. Other states have a three-strikes law, and he would have been behind bars for life just about anywhere other than Idaho." Hugh leaned closer to his brother again. "Timmy, I know you're the one who always brings home strays, but Hunter will skin me alive if I hire this guy."

"I thought maybe you could talk to Hunter," Tim pleaded. "Rory's been an exemplary prisoner. He's getting out early for good behavior, and he's determined to walk the line from now on. Hugh, please?"

"How do you know all this?" Hugh asked, mellowing somewhat. "Have you been visiting this guy in prison?"

Tim shook his head. "One of the wardens is an old classmate of mine. He's been keeping me up to date."

Hugh nodded. "Fine. I'll talk to Hunter at a moment when he won't bite my head off. Don't expect him to say yes, but if he does, I'm going to suggest that you be responsible for this guy's behavior on the ranch. If anything is stolen or, heaven forbid, we start losing horses again, there's only going to be one guy to blame, and that's Rory. You do understand that, don't you? You're going to be his babysitter, and we're going to shoot first and ask questions later." Hugh sighed dramatically. "We've always run a safe ranch. Nobody locks their doors around here, and I don't want that to change. This guy would have a much easier go of it in a place where they don't know him, Tim. Our old-timers are all nice guys, but I can't vouch for them when it comes to working with a convicted felon. They might not even want to work with him at all, and then what?"

"I'll work with Rory," Tim said with clear conviction.

"You're a wrangler, and as I recall, he doesn't even know how to ride a horse. How are you going to work together? We can't spare you on the range, Tim. Especially not when the foals are born and the mares need to be serviced again."

A smile formed around Tim's mouth. "I always thought we had stallions for that, Hugh."

Hugh rolled his eyes and slapped Tim's head. "You're my brother, Tim. We've lived and worked on this ranch all our lives, and I don't want anything to compromise that."

"It won't," Tim assured his brother. "I just want to give this guy a break."

Hugh sighed. "I know." He put his arm around Tim's shoulders and eased him out of the office and into the light of the bright autumn sky. "Let's get some work done, okay?"

HUGH pondered his brother's request all day. Tim had a big heart; everyone knew that. In fact both dogs that guarded the stables were mutts Tim had found by the side of the road abandoned as puppies. He'd always taken care of them, and although they were both kind-hearted dogs, they only really listened to Tim, who could summon them with a whistle and a click of his tongue.

The not-so-small favor Tim had asked of him definitely fell into the Tim-has-a-big-heart category as far as Hugh was concerned. He tried to recall everything about the horse theft case and remembered that Delco's prison record had been squeaky clean, yet this Rory fellow had had a few things to his name. Nothing major, Hugh remembered—some petty theft and a "borrowed" car came to mind—but he'd been to prison twice before, and so the judge had given him the harshest sentence he could give under the circumstances. This guy sounded like a lost cause, a career criminal who'd have a hard time finding an honest job anywhere he went, and so of course Tim was drawn to him like a moth to a flame. Part of Hugh wanted to protect his baby brother, but Tim wasn't a teenager anymore. Tim carried a lot of responsibility around the ranch, especially around foaling time, when he was the one in charge of keeping vigil over the mares in labor. He had saved numerous foals with his calm demeanor and swift action. Hugh trusted Tim blindly with everything but his big heart. Even after all these years, he still wanted to protect Tim from the evils of the world. And

Hugh felt like a coward when he realized he was turning to Hunter to play the boogieman by letting him have the final word.

For that reason, it took Hugh almost a full week to approach Hunter about Rory. He knew Tim was getting antsy and wanted an answer to his request.

"Hunter, can we talk in private tonight? After dinner maybe?" Hugh asked his brother-in-law as they were helping set the table for Sunday dinner.

"Sure. Business or pleasure?" Hunter asked in a laid-back sort of way.

"Business, I'm afraid."

"Can't it wait until tomorrow then?" Hunter asked.

Hugh sighed. "I should have asked you earlier in the week."

Hunter's face grew serious, and he moved a little closer to Hugh. "You're not leaving us again, are you? Who did you snare this time? Bernie?"

Hugh laughed. He could take the joke because he knew Hunter wasn't serious. Hunter loved to tease him because Hugh had left Hunter's oldest sister, Lisa, for Izzie, his middle one. Bernie was Hunter's baby sister and a force to be reckoned with on the three-day-eventing circuit. In fact, she was probably going to go to the Olympics with a horse that Hunter had bought her.

"Izzie's the girl for me, Hunter, always was and always will be," Hugh answered good-naturedly. "Bernie'll find herself a good show-jumping champion one day."

"So what's troubling you then?" Hunter asked.

Hugh shrugged.

"Dinner's in about twenty minutes, I heard Mom say, so if you want to go down to the office now, we can discuss it."

After telling Christy and his mother where they were going to be, Hunter and Hugh went downstairs.

Hugh had a pretty good idea how Tim must have felt on Monday when he had to come down to the office to argue his case. "I'll cut right to the chase," Hugh told Hunter. "Tim asked me whether we'd consider hiring Rory McCown as a ranch hand."

Hunter's mouth fell open. "Rory McCown? Who stole our horses?"

"The one and only. Well, actually one of the two."

"And why would Tim want us to hire him?"

"Because he was a good worker when he was here, and because he's eligible for parole as long as he has a place to live and gainful employment." Hugh could see Hunter shaking his head in disbelief, so he continued before Hunter could say anything. "Besides, Rory wasn't the brains behind the whole operation. You and I both know that Delco was the one with the contacts to sell the horses and the cunning to devise a way to trick us into thinking we were looking for a cougar instead of a horse thief."

"Yeah, but Delco wasn't the one with the rap sheet all the way to Canada," Hunter intervened.

"That's just because he never got caught. How many people do you know who are interested in buying stolen foals? I for one don't know anyone like that. And I bet you don't either. Delco made the shady contacts. Rory was just stupid enough to get caught."

"So you're telling me we should hire a ranch hand because he's stupid?"

"Don't twist my words, Hunter," Hugh replied.

"So is this guy going to stay longer than three weeks this time?"

"Suppose it's a stipulation of his parole. He probably can't travel outside state lines and needs to stay employed. Not like he's going to find work easily with the jail time he's done."

"Don't suppose he will." Hunter pondered. "So how do I know he's not going to steal more of my horses?"

"You don't. But I told Tim that if you say yes, *he's* going to be the one keeping an eye on Rory."

"Do it," Hunter said.

Hugh couldn't believe what he'd just heard. "But you don't have any guarantees."

Hunter shrugged. "We employ just about anyone who asks for a job around here. I know that makes us seem desperate, but in a sense we are. We don't pay badly, yet it's nearly impossible to find people to work, especially for the low level jobs. Nobody over the age of sixteen wants to muck out stables anymore, so who am I to say no? Besides, we won't need to explain too many things to him. I'm sure he remembers. And we can trust Tim to keep an eye on him, right?"

Hugh nodded his agreement. Hunter was right, of course. At least with Rory they knew what to expect, which was more than they knew about the other drifters walking onto the ranch. Although he certainly had his apprehensions, Hugh almost couldn't wait to tell Tim, just so he'd see his baby brother's face light up.

—2—

TIM never thought Hunter would say yes. He'd even rehearsed what he was going to say to Hunter because he didn't think Hugh would have the nerve to ask Hunter about Rory. But two miracles had come together, and now he was going to call the public defender to tell him that Rory would have a place to work and a roof over his head so he could be let out on parole. He just hoped Rory appreciated the strings he'd had to pull.

While he waited for the lawyers and courts to do their job, Tim started worrying. Had he taken on too much responsibility? What if Rory jumped parole? What if Hugh was right and Rory didn't appreciate the second chance he was being given?

Tim was tempted to visit Rory in jail, but he kept putting it off, afraid that Rory would give him a lukewarm reception. Then suddenly he got a call from Rory's lawyer asking for someone to pick up his client to take him to his new place of employment.

Rory was going to be released within the next twenty-four hours.

"Hugh!" Tim called out, bounding up the porch steps of the main ranch house. "Hugh!" he repeated when his brother didn't answer immediately. The front door was unlocked, as always, and Tim walked into the hallway.

"Where's the fire?" Hugh answered calmly as he came down the stairs carrying his youngest daughter.

"Rory's coming tomorrow. He's being released."

Hugh raised an eyebrow and nodded. "I guess you better get his room ready, then. Read him his rights on the way over here when you pick him up, okay? Ranch hands are to be seen, not heard. I expect him to do his job and not argue with anyone. First sign of trouble, he's out on his ass, and I won't be doing the explaining to his parole officer. That will be you." Hugh poked Tim in the chest and then threw him a teasing smile. "Make sure he knows that."

"I can't threaten him with that on the day they let him out!" Tim argued.

"He should be grateful we're willing to give him a chance. I don't see anyone else doing that," Hugh answered gruffly. "And settle down," he said, taking Tim's arm. "I know you carry a torch for this guy, but life and work goes on. Give him some space so you can both do the jobs you're supposed to do."

Tim nodded as Hugh left him in the hallway to take his daughter into the kitchen. He ran his hand through his longish brown hair and scratched the scruff on his face, hoping it would calm him down. Hugh was right. He had work to do today and would need to crank it up a bit to cover for the next day when he'd be away from the ranch all afternoon to pick up Rory.

Then Hugh's words rang through his head. *"I know you carry a torch for this guy."* What was Hugh suggesting? What was he reading into Tim's behavior? Tim didn't even know why he was so nervous about seeing Rory again. Was it because he feared he'd misjudged the guy he'd hit it off with so easily the few weeks he'd worked on the ranch?

Tim had followed Rory from afar since his arrest. Although at the time the whole ranch had been talking about Delco, since he was Izzie's ex-boyfriend, and how he had been the one behind the horse theft, Tim had been more surprised by Rory's involvement.

THREE years ago, after Hugh had hired Rory, he'd introduced him to Tim, who organized the ever-changing ranch hands. Tim noticed that Rory was taller than most of the drifters who worked the worst-paying jobs on the ranch. He was also lean, bordering on skinny. His eyes were mostly hidden under long, straight brown hair and the rest of his face by an only barely maintained full beard. It took Tim more than a week to see that Rory's eyes were brown too.

Rory didn't talk much, but he knew how to follow orders, and he was kind and gentle with the horses, although Tim had spotted right away that Rory wasn't a country boy. He was a fast learner and a hard worker and always cleaned up after himself. That was more than Tim was used to.

One night during Rory's third week at the ranch, most of the men had taken their dinner in front of the TV because there was football on. Tim noticed Rory eating alone at the large crew table.

"Mind if I join you?"

Rory gestured across the table, which Tim interpreted as "go ahead". He settled across from Rory and watched him eat the beef stew and potatoes with gusto.

"You don't watch football?" Tim asked in an attempt to get Rory to enter into a conversation.

Rory shrugged. "Don't care much for it. Prefer soccer."

"I don't know much about soccer," Tim admitted.

"They don't show it on the local stations," Rory replied resignedly. "Nobody else here watches it anyway, so it doesn't matter."

Tim thought about asking Hugh if he could look for it at the main house where they had cable. He didn't want to promise Rory anything he couldn't deliver, though, so he continued eating.

"Stew's good," Tim remarked, hoping to coax more words out of the other man.

Rory smiled as he wiped his plate clean with a slice of bread. "Best food I've had in a long time. You have a great cook in this place. Most ranches the crew cooks for themselves and the food is edible at best. Not here."

"Yeah, we're lucky," Tim replied. He couldn't stop looking at Rory's mouth and his almost-perfect teeth. He saw one crooked tooth on the left side of Rory's mouth when he ate some bread. Tim had no idea why that fascinated him so. Although he knew he was attracted to men rather than women, he'd never taken notice of a man's mouth in that way before.

"So what happens around here over the weekend?" Rory asked. "Everyone left last Saturday, but I don't know where they went."

Tim realized this was the most words they'd exchanged since Rory had arrived at the ranch. He tore his eyes away from Rory's mouth and looked him in the eye.

"They usually go to The Barrel Run. That's a bar in town where local music groups play on Saturday evening. I don't go unless Jack's band is playing. He's my brother."

"Your brother plays in a band?"

There was that smile again. He really had to stop looking at Rory's mouth.

"Yeah. The Teton Wranglers. Country rock. They're pretty good. Write their own music and all."

"Could you, like, tell me when they're playing next?" Rory asked a little hesitantly.

"Sure. Actually they're playing this weekend. I'll come and find you and you can drive with me."

Rory nodded his thanks and stayed at the table until Tim finished his meal. Without being asked, Rory took Tim's plate along with his own and turned to the sink to wash them. Silently Tim joined him to dry the dishes and put them away. Neither of them spoke, and Tim felt that he didn't really need to.

THE next Saturday, Tim drove to The Barrel Run with Rory in the passenger seat. Since it was foaling season, they'd worked hard all week and hadn't had much rest today so they were both ready for some relaxation.

At the bar, Tim knew what to expect. Whenever Jack's band was playing, the bar was packed, and since he was a native, everyone there knew him. And since he was Jack Conroy's brother and Jack was the local celebrity, Tim's stock went up as well. On top of that, Tim, like his brothers, was tall, dark, and handsome, and he lived in a community where many of the young men had moved away to the city to get better-paying jobs. He practically had to swat the women away, but since he had no real interest in them, he was a deft hand at letting them down gently. Because Rory had come in with him, he too got some attention. Tim was a little surprised to see his rather shy ranch hand smile at the women, then brush them off after exchanging just a few words.

Most of the guys Tim brought to The Barrel Run went home with one of the women, but Rory didn't seem interested. Like Tim, Rory remained near the bar, watching the stage and the crowd with amusement. They each bought their own drinks, and although Tim had a few beers, Rory ordered one beer-with-a-chaser after another, making swift work of each. By the third beer, Tim already felt his head grow light, but Rory, who'd had at least double what Tim had consumed, seemed a little more relaxed, but certainly not drunk yet.

When the band finished their set, Jack came over to Tim and greeted him like brothers do. Tim introduced Rory and stood by as Rory struck up an entire conversation about what guitars Jack played and how they chose their songs. Knowing that talking to Rory was like pulling teeth, Tim was surprised at Rory's easy conversation with a virtual stranger. Jack soon left to talk to some other people, and Tim saw Rory follow Jack with his eyes.

"I better go," Tim eventually said, knowing he'd have to get up early the next morning. "If you want a ride back to the ranch, you can come with me. Otherwise you're on your own."

Rory peeled his eyes off Jack and looked at Tim. "Yeah, sure. I'll come with you. "

Once inside Tim's truck, Rory was still smiling, but the ease with which he'd talked to Jack was lost again.

"Looks like you had fun tonight," Tim remarked.

"Yeah," Rory admitted. "Your brother's really talented. Good looking guy, too. I'm surprised he hasn't been picked up by a label somewhere. They could sure sell him to all those country birds in Nashville."

Tim noticed a Southern twang creeping into Rory's speech. "Are you from around there?"

Rory shook his head. "Georgia, actually, but I lived in Tennessee for a while."

"You don't sound like you're from the South."

Rory shrugged. "I've been traveling for a long time. It pays to sound like you belong everywhere and nowhere in particular."

Tim nodded. The truck was sitting in the parking lot, surrounded by haphazardly parked vehicles, and Tim was wondering how he was ever going to get out of there.

"The women seemed to like you," Tim said, just to try to keep the conversation going.

"Not just me, it seems. They asked about you more than me." He mimicked their behavior. "Did Tim bring you? My friend would like to go home with Tim. Maybe if you come with me, he'll follow her. What do you think?"

Tim smiled. "They should know by now they can't persuade me."

"Me neither," Rory said.

Tim felt Rory's eyes on him and turned toward him, just in time to see Rory move closer. Before he could react, Rory's deliciously curved mouth was all over his and Tim felt the softness of Rory's beard. Almost automatically he grabbed the back of Rory's head and held him there so he could return the kiss in earnest. Rory pushed his sinewy body against Tim's, and Tim felt his jeans grow tight, so he lowered one hand to Rory's ass. At the same time, he felt Rory's hands on him, and he moaned into the kiss when he felt a thigh rub against his groin.

Suddenly Tim heard a bottle crash outside the truck. "Faggots!" Reflexively, he pushed Rory away and looked around. There was just one guy standing in the parking lot. He looked very drunk, and Tim recognized him as a groom from the Hope Ranch in the next county. He hoped the guy wouldn't recognize him. Then the passenger door opened and Rory got out. For a moment, Tim was afraid that Rory was going to challenge the guy, but Rory went the other way.

Tim waited in the parking lot for about another hour, hoping Rory was just a little spooked and would return when the coast was clear, but as more cars drove away, Rory was nowhere to be found, so eventually, Tim drove home.

THREE years later, Tim still remembered what it felt like to be kissed by Rory and how his supple body had felt under his hands.

—3—

RORY exchanged his prison issue jumpsuit for the clothes he'd taken off just short of three years ago. He had to tighten his belt a notch, and his jeans were a little too baggy for his taste, but it wasn't like he'd been let out to go clothes shopping. He had another pair of jeans in his duffel bag, but they were even wider, and the shirt he'd chosen was one that had fewer holes in it than the one he stuffed back in the bag. Luckily, his red plaid coat was fairly warm, and he had a cap with the logo of a garage he once worked at to keep his head warm.

The day before, the barber had trimmed his beard some, but he'd forgone getting his hair cut. He liked it a little long. He liked the scruff, liked the anonymity it gave him.

In less than an hour, he was going to walk out of the place that had been his home for three years. He'd said goodbye to the other guys and signed a few papers, and now he was about to be carted away to another kind of prison.

His lawyer—provided to him by the state, of course, since he had no money to speak of—had joked that Rory should see it as a form of community service. Rory had objected, but his lawyer had made it clear that this was his only chance and he should be grateful for it.

Why anybody in their right mind would hire a horse thief to work on a stud ranch was beyond him, but it beat staying in prison for another year, and Rory was good at keeping his head low. He could tough it out for a year.

Thirty more minutes, and then someone was going to pick him up and drive him to where he would get a place to stay. Then tomorrow he had to check in with his parole officer. He knew the drill. It wasn't like it was the first time he'd had to go through the humiliation of being read his rights as a parolee.

"McCown."

Rory veered up, picking up his duffel bag and the brown envelope containing a few personal items.

"Let's get moving," the warden said. "I never get why you guys aren't breaking down the doors to get out of here on release day," he muttered under his breath.

Rory didn't say anything. He didn't feel like it was expected. Instead he listened to latches opening, doors rolling away and closing again after he walked through. With every door he came a little closer to freedom. Or at least closer to fresh air.

Just before the last door, the head warden turned to him.

"Keep your nose clean. Turn up for work. And don't miss any appointments with your parole officer, starting tomorrow at nine. You know how crowded it is here. You've been an exemplary prisoner, and I don't want to see you back any time soon, you hear, son?"

Rory nodded. He stepped back and let the warden open the final door to freedom.

Rory blinked at the invasion of bright sunlight. He waited for a moment until his eyes adjusted to the low afternoon sun in the wintery sky. There was a truck parked across the road, and a man with a Stetson was leaning against it. Rory shook his head when he recognized the handsome cowboy with the unruly brown hair and the broad shoulders. He didn't even need to come closer to remember the wide-set eyes, the curious eyebrows, the perpetual smile, and those big, strong hands.

Tim Conroy.

It answered a few of Rory's questions, of course. Suddenly it wasn't such a surprise that an employer had crawled out of the woodwork just when he needed one. Then again, it must have taken some pretty persuasion for Tim to convince his boss to take on a man who was not only a convicted felon, but the convicted felon who'd stolen horses off the very ranch he was now going to work on.

Rory felt his confidence wane. Everyone at the Blue River Ranch knew him. Almost all the guys working there were old-timers, and Rory figured most of them would still be working there now. The rest were family of Hunter, the owner, or Hugh, the foreman. Tim fell into the last category, since he just happened to be Hugh's baby brother.

The men at the ranch weren't likely to have forgotten him, and Rory didn't think it mattered much that he hadn't been the mastermind behind the horse thieving. He'd helped enough to get a stiff prison sentence and another notch on his record. And since most of the men had followed the trial, it was no longer a secret that Rory had a far from clean criminal record.

Luckily, he'd grown a thick skin over the years.

Rory swung the duffel over his shoulder, turned away slightly when a long-haul truck kicked up a bunch of dirt, and then walked across the road to the waiting truck.

"Tim," Rory greeted his chauffeur. He kept his voice sounding as neutral as possible.

"Rory," Tim replied, tipping his hat.

Rory wondered if it was his imagination, but he could have sworn he heard longing in Tim's soft, velvet voice. Then again, he'd always found Tim's voice particularly sexy for such a butch-looking cowboy.

"Let's go," Tim said. "It's a long drive back."

Rory threw his duffel in the back of the pick-up truck and got in on the passenger side. Tim didn't say anything as he pulled into the road and drove off. Rory didn't know what to say either, so he just looked at the scenery and chewed on his thumbnail.

It took them a full two hours to strike up some sort of conversation.

"You hungry?" Tim asked out of the blue.

"Sure," Rory replied.

"Bet they didn't have any decent burgers in prison, right?" Tim asked, turning toward Rory with his ever-present smile all over his face as he pulled into the parking lot of a diner.

"Not like Barnaby's," Rory said, reading the sign over the old-fashioned roadside place.

It was fairly crowded inside since it was happy hour, and they each ordered the Early Bird Burger Special and a beer. Rory kept his head low, but nobody seemed to recognize him, not even the occasional guy who nodded in Tim's direction or the waitress who brought their oversized dinners. He didn't even feel that badly dressed, sitting among the ordinary folk and some farmers and ranchers who'd come in early to get a cheap dinner. The only difference between their table and the surrounding ones was that they didn't talk to each other. Rory could feel Tim looking at him from time to time, but he didn't look back. He just wouldn't know what to say if their eyes met.

When their waitress brought the check, Rory snatched it from Tim's hand and got up to pay for it at the register.

"Rory," Tim called after him, but Rory didn't look back. He paid the manager with the money he'd earned in jail and walked outside to the truck.

Tim caught up with him and let him inside.

"You didn't need to pay for my dinner," Tim said, not starting the truck but turning to Rory from his driver's seat.

"You drove two hours to pick me up and two hours back. You probably had to forfeit half a day's pay for it too. Was the least I could do," Rory replied, looking out the window. "Besides, we had the special, and it wasn't that expensive."

"It's not my truck, so the ranch paid the gas, and I worked extra to cover for today. Hunter trusts me, so he doesn't count my hours. As long as I get my work done, Hugh doesn't fret either."

Tim's voice sounded calm and in control, while Rory had the uncontrollable urge to get out of the car and run. He didn't know why that was, but he knew he had to will himself to stay put. That became even harder when Tim put his hand on Rory's arm, and Rory pulled back as if he'd been stung.

"Rory, please. You're wound tighter than a spring. I didn't mean to scare you and—"

"You didn't scare me," Rory was quick to reply.

"Then just look at me?"

"What do you want from me?" Rory said through gritted teeth.

Tim left his hand on the bench between them, and Rory eyed it suspiciously.

"I don't want anything," Tim answered. "No, that's not true."

That made Rory look up at Tim. For the first time in three years, Rory saw the curiously light-brown eyes that always sparkled. Tim couldn't hold Rory's gaze for long, though. So Tim wanted more? Rory clearly remembered a truck very much like this one, and he also remembered kissing Tim inside it.

"I want to give you a chance, Rory," Tim continued. "I don't know what made you end up on the wrong side of the track so many times during your life, but there has *got* to be a better way."

"Who are you to lecture me?" Rory said with subdued anger evident in his voice. "You were born on that ranch. You probably never even got as much as a speeding ticket. You've never had to worry where your next meal came from."

"I know," Tim replied, still sounding as calm as ever. "And that's why I feel I should share my luck. Always have. We have two dogs guarding the stables, and they were both dogs I found tied up by the side of the road, abandoned by people who no longer had any use for them. I brought them home and fed them and took care of them, and now they happily play guard dog. I've rescued horses like that too."

"I'm no animal to save," Rory said, still protesting but feeling calmer already. Tim's easy-going nature and soothing voice had an effect on him, although he would never admit to that.

"I know that too," Tim said with a chuckle. "I'm just saying that life isn't too bad at the ranch if you give it a shot. It's hard work at times, but the guys are great, and the horses make it worthwhile too."

"Only trouble is that the guys know I'm a horse thief. I stole their horses, some of them too young to be taken from their mothers. That's cruelty."

"Then why did you do it?"

Rory shrugged. "Why does anyone turn to crime?"

"Money," Tim said. He wasn't even asking.

"Money," Rory acknowledged.

"And where's that money now?"

Rory bit his lip. "Nothing left. I hope they made that Delco bleed too, because he took the bulk of it. I was just the sidekick. I got handouts."

"I know," Tim said.

"It was a stupid thing to do," Rory said as quietly as he could.

"Yeah, I know that too, but we can't change what happened. We all have to live with the stupid decisions we make."

Rory looked at Tim again. "When have you ever made any stupid decisions?"

"Maybe one day I'll tell you," Tim said teasingly.

"Maybe this one will turn out to be legendary?" Rory said with less humor in his voice.

"This one?"

"Asking your boss to give me a job."

"Doubt it."

"What if another horse disappears? What if something else gets stolen? Fingers will inevitably point at me, and it wouldn't be good to take my side then. These things never pan out right, man."

"That's a self-fulfilling prophecy."

"A self-f.... Whatever. What are you talking about?"

"At least we're talking," Tim said with a smile and a sideways glance. "I thought you'd given up on talking while we were driving all the way over here. The silence was killing me."

"I was never much of a talker."

"I know," Tim said. "I talk enough for both of us."

"I remember that."

"But I'm serious, you know," Tim continued. "If you keep telling yourself things can't go right for you, they never will. You have to believe that you can turn it around."

Rory shrugged Tim's words away.

"I believe you can turn things around," Tim said with clear conviction.

Silence fell between them again, but Rory didn't mind so much now. Night was falling, and the parking lot was still crowded, but with different cars than when they arrived. He looked at a couple waltzing between the cars to go inside and followed them with his eyes.

"Second wife," Tim stated.

Rory felt caught as he realized Tim had noticed him staring. "Do you know those people?"

"No," Tim answered, "but she's at least twenty years younger than him, and she's showing off her knockers."

"Then maybe they're not married yet? Maybe she's his mistress." Rory offered with a wry smile.

"Or his daughter's friend."

"That's disgusting," Rory said, looking like he smelled something foul.

"At least I got you to smile," Tim said with a shrug.

Rory immediately stopped. "I smile about as much as I talk."

"Okay, I'll take that as a challenge. Right next to showing you that walking the line pays off in the long run, I'm going to prove to you that you can get a lot farther in life by smiling than by frowning."

"Good luck with that," Rory said, unable to hide a grin.

—4—

"SHOWER block's through here," Tim said, pointing to the left where an open doorway led to a darkened room that smelled vaguely damp. "Light switch is just around the corner, but it has a fifteen minute cut-off since nobody remembers to actually switch the light off again, so the consensus is that you hit the knob when you walk in regardless of whether the light is already on. That way you have fifteen minutes to shower, and the people already in there get some more time to do their business." He knocked the knob with his fist just to prove his point, and the entire shower block lit up. "Bring your own towel and soap, shampoo, whatever you need, and take it back to your room when you're done. We're pretty relaxed about nudity around here, as you probably remember, but wear a towel or something anyway."

Or not, Tim thought. *But make sure I'm around to see it.* He smiled at his own thoughts. Although the last time Rory had spent only three weeks at the ranch, it had been three weeks of glorious weather, and they'd worked side by side most of that time. During the midday heat they'd both taken their shirts off, and Tim had feasted his eyes on Rory's sinewy body with those nicely developed shoulders and pecs, but he'd always made sure his gaze didn't linger. Having a boss who lived with a male lover was one thing. The men still joked about it behind Hunter and Grant's back, but never to their faces, because Hunter signed their paychecks. Tim didn't think he'd get the same courtesy if they ever found out he was batting for the same team, so he kept it quiet and drove to the next city whenever he got the urge for different hands on his body.

He'd had his feelings about Rory from the first moment, though. Last time his suspicions had only been partially confirmed, but he hoped Rory would be more forthcoming this time. The problem was that the skittishness in the car had continued, so Tim knew it would take time for Rory to get comfortable around him again.

"Your room is through here." Tim continued the tour by walking along the dimly lit corridor to a door along the same side as the shower block. The room it opened into was long and narrow with a single bed to the side, a wardrobe at the end, and a small table and one chair. Tim knew what the ranch hand rooms looked like, but he almost felt embarrassed when he thought about his own room, which, besides being a lot more lived-in, was also more than twice this size.

"It's not much, but you don't need to share," Tim said by way of apology.

"That's nice all in itself," Rory said with a half-smile as he walked past Tim and threw his duffel bag on the bed.

"Clean sheets should be in the wardrobe. I can help you make the bed if you like." Tim knew he was stalling, but he hadn't seen Rory in three years, and it wasn't like he had anything else to do tonight.

"I'm used to making my own bed. I can manage. Thanks."

Tim nodded, understanding he'd just been dismissed. "I'll drive you into town tomorrow," Tim said from the doorway. "Eight thirty?"

"Yes," Rory replied. "Parole officer. Not looking forward to that."

"Worse part is over. You have a place to stay and a job."

Rory nodded as he unzipped his duffel and opened the wardrobe. Just as Tim was leaving the room, Rory spoke again. "Thanks for today. And for this job."

Tim turned around and flashed his best smile. "Don't mention it." Rory's face was soft now, and Tim knew that if he stayed any longer he'd be tempted to kiss him, so he just nodded his goodbye and walked off.

On the way upstairs, Tim remembered he'd forgotten to tell Rory where his own room was. Then again, what was Rory going to do? Sneak in there in the middle of the night and have his way with him? Only in his dreams, for sure. Tim pushed these thoughts away and changed into his work clothes. He was sure he could find some more work to do to keep himself occupied.

THE next morning, Tim got up before dawn and put in a good two hours of work before going back to the house for breakfast. He hoped to meet Rory in the mess room, but it was already deserted, so he grabbed a sandwich and a cup of coffee and walked back into the corridor. He'd just rounded the corner when Rory came out of the shower block, wearing only a towel. He was rubbing his hair dry with another towel, and there was water dripping from his beard. Tim had to remember to close his mouth but couldn't prevent his eyes from wandering over Rory's lean, perfectly balanced body and seemingly haphazardly chosen body art. Tim took a sip of his coffee in an attempt to look casual as he admired the tribal tattoo wrapped around Rory's right bicep as well as the sparse hairs sprinkled along Rory's chest and down from his bellybutton to where Tim could only imagine Rory's pubic hair would be. He tried to look away, but not before imagining licking one of Rory's tiny, pebbled nipples.

When Rory spotted Tim, he wiped the towel over his face and continued, letting the towel pass over his chest as well. "Am I late?"

Tim didn't immediately answer, since he was a little too preoccupied with the fact Rory had caught him staring. "Not really. Have you had breakfast?"

Rory nodded and seemed particularly amused by Tim. He walked by him and grabbed the cup Tim was holding. "Thanks for bringing me coffee." He took a big swig. "Fuck, you take your coffee black?" Rory pushed the cup back into Tim's hand.

Tim smiled. "Yeah, I do. You don't?"

Rory shook his head. "Lots of sugar for me next time, thanks." He let go of the cup and turned away.

Tim watched Rory disappear into his room and could have sworn he was flirting. This was an entirely different side of Rory, and he wondered what had happened between last night and this morning. He took a sip from the same coffee and figured it tasted just right, so he bit into his sandwich and walked back to the kitchen, where he added sugar to his coffee and tasted it again. He had to admit it wasn't bad sweetened either.

Just a few minutes later, Rory appeared with his hair neatly combed back, wearing pretty much the same clothes as the day before.

"Ready to go?" Rory asked.

Tim got up and put his cup in the sink. "Let's hit the road."

"You don't have to do this, you know," Rory said as Tim drove the truck off the property.

"Yes, I do," Tim said. "Your parole officer needs to hear that we stand behind you. Besides, it's a bit early to hand you the keys to the truck."

"Don't have a license anyway," Rory said with a shrug. "They're not going to let you in, you know. At the parole office. What he tells me is confidential."

"Then I'll just wait outside. At least he'll see that someone from the ranch is there."

"You'll miss work."

Tim shrugged. "Like I said, I'm not on the clock. As long as my work gets done, everything's fine. I spent last night oiling tack in the barn. That's work that needs to be done too." He didn't elaborate that it was the perfect chance for him to think.

Rory looked at him, but Tim kept his eyes on the road. It wasn't far into town, and they didn't talk anymore until they got there.

"Want me to go inside with you?"

Rory shook his head. "It's not like I haven't done this before."

"With this parole officer?"

"I bailed on him last time. Reported in with him when I got a job and then didn't show for the follow-up three weeks later."

"Is that why you left us without notice?"

"He's a moron. I didn't want to go back to him, so I skipped bail, only to run into John Delco, who figured I could give him inside information."

"And are you going to do that again this time?" Tim asked with some apprehension.

Rory threw him a pensive look as if he was weighing his words. "Nobody is ever given a second chance, Tim. You gave me one anyway."

"Meaning?"

"Meaning I'll try."

"Try harder," Tim said with a broad smile on his face, hoping Rory would get the gist. He watched Rory walk to the grubby-looking office and saw through the opened blinds how he signed in with the receptionist. He really hoped Rory would try to turn his life around.

TWENTY minutes later, Rory returned with a guy in a suit in tow. Rory didn't look very happy, so Tim rolled down the window and felt the cold air float in.

"This is the man who's responsible for me while I'm working on the ranch," Rory said, clearly not out of choice.

The man stuck his hand inside and shook Tim's. "You're one of the Conroy boys?"

"Yes, sir," Tim replied, not feeling like he should elaborate since the guy didn't exactly introduce himself either.

"McCown here worked for you before?"

"For my brother, to be exact. He's the foreman. I'm just one of the wranglers."

"Then why isn't your brother here?"

"I didn't think it mattered," Tim said, feeling like he was winging it and wondering what the guy was getting at. He just hoped he said all the right things. This guy had clout with the judge, and if he didn't report that Rory was walking the line, then the judge could revoke Rory's parole. "Hugh said all the papers were signed at the house before the judge made his decision. I'm just here because Rory needed a ride into town."

The man stared intently at Tim, to the point where it was starting to feel uncomfortable. For a split second, Tim looked at Rory and saw he seemed annoyed, but he knew he couldn't linger.

"Okay," the man sighed. "I expect you to notify me the very instant this one *forgets* to show up for work." He pointed over his shoulder at Rory. "Not like last time when I had to find out for myself."

"Last time my brother didn't know Rory was out on parole."

The man raised an eyebrow. "Well, he sure as hell knows now."

Tim smiled and instantly felt it might be a little too much. "I'll let you know anything that's worth knowing about Rory," Tim assured him. "Now I need to take him back to the ranch so he can start work."

"Very well," the man said. "Here's my card."

Tim took it without looking at it and tossed it on the dashboard. "Have a good day, sir."

Rory got in the truck, and Tim made a point out of tearing away from his parking space. They were at the end of the road when Rory turned to him.

"You know, I never figured you were a macho man, but I need to adjust my opinion."

"I'm no macho man," Tim said softly. He wasn't. Unless it was called for.

"What did you call that back there then? You stared him down. The way you tossed his card? Man, that was a classic."

"He got on my nerves, that's all. He was treating you like scum. Asking me to report you. Who does he think he is?"

"Well, legally my ass belongs to him," Rory said with a sigh. "But I'd much rather think it belongs to you."

Tim turned sideways to look at Rory, flabbergasted by what Rory had just said. Maybe being a closeted gay man made him hear things that weren't really said out loud, but he could have sworn Rory had just offered him his ass. That was one step past innuendo; that was blatant seduction, and he didn't know Rory well enough to gauge whether Rory had really intended to be that blatant.

A sharp horn honked, and Tim ripped his gaze from Rory's smiling face and turned it back to the road.

"You better watch where you're going," Rory said. "Can we stop at the grocery store? And can you shout me fifty bucks until I get paid on Friday?"

"Sure," Tim replied without really hearing the question. Then he realized he'd just agreed to give a convicted felon more than a day's wage. "We can stop at Calley's. I have store credit there." He was just going to have to trust Rory.

—5—

"HEY, guys," Calley greeted the men.

Rory nodded at her and walked toward the back of the store. When he was out of earshot, Calley leaned toward Tim.

"Who's the drifter? New ranch hand?"

Tim looked to check Rory wasn't too close. "Not that new. Rory McCown."

The thought-lines on Calley's forehead deepened. "Name sounds familiar, but I can't place him. He doesn't look familiar to me."

"He worked at the ranch before, three years ago." Tim paused to let Calley catch up. When she didn't he continued. "He was Delco's sidekick for stealing the foals."

Calley's mouth formed a large O. "Oh. My. God. And Hunter took him on again?"

Tim bit his lower lip and nodded. "He got a much stiffer sentence than Delco, because he's got a record and Delco didn't, but he was just along for the ride." Tim was whispering, and he knew what that would look like to Rory, but he couldn't talk behind his back out loud. "He just needs a break, Calley."

She smiled at him. "So he's *your* drifter. Like the old horses you found on that land that doesn't belong to anyone and like the dogs you spotted tied up by the interstate."

"It's not like that, Calley."

She raised an eyebrow at him.

"Okay, maybe it is, but they let him out on parole yesterday, and I just want to give him a chance to prove to everyone that he can keep his nose clean and work hard. He was a good worker three years ago."

"For all of three weeks, if I recall."

Tim sighed, exasperated. "Calley, it's hard enough to battle everyone else."

Calley smiled at him compassionately. "Well, if anyone can change the world, it's you, Tim Conroy."

"Calley, he says to put it on Tim's tab. You okay with that?" Leah, Calley's store assistant, shouted through the entire store.

"Yeah, that's fine," Tim shouted back. Tim nodded they should walk to the counter, and Calley followed. Rory was standing by the checkout counter, looking at Tim from under his cap. His purchases were already packed into a brown paper bag. "How much is it?" Tim asked as they got closer. "He's got to pay me back on Friday. Out of his first paycheck." He smiled at Rory, both to tell him that he was okay with it and to make sure Rory knew this wasn't a gift. Trusting him to pay back the money was one thing; giving it to him was something entirely different.

"Forty-two dollars and thirty-five cents," Leah answered, writing Tim's name on the bill and slipping it into a little cashbox behind the counter.

Tim turned back to Rory. "So if you're all done, we should get going. There's a lot of work waiting for us at the ranch."

Rory picked up his bag, and Tim heard clanging glass. He wanted to ask Rory what he'd bought and wondered how much of his forty-two dollars was liquor, but he decided Rory was a grownup and old enough to be responsible, so he didn't. He'd make sure Rory did his job, and that was that.

TIM spent the afternoon taking Rory through his paces, making sure he knew what to do and where to find the equipment he needed. Although Tim was a wrangler, he was the one responsible for making sure the stables stayed in good condition, and he had a bunch of ranch hands to do the actual dirty work. Although they had one old-timer who was about sixty—a guy everyone called Mackenzie, but nobody knew whether it was his first or his last name—and who had never done anything other than manual labor around the ranch, most of the workers came and went, but even if they only stayed for a few weeks, Tim always felt that the few hours he spent with the newbies paid off. Explaining everything to Rory wasn't a hardship, although Rory rarely did more than nod to show he understood.

Even on that first afternoon, Rory showed Tim he was a hard worker. Together they mucked out all the stalls for the wranglers' riding horses before they came back from the field and kitted out a birthing stall, although it wasn't really foaling season.

"So you can do this on your own tomorrow?" Tim asked as they were sitting on some bales of hay taking a well-deserved drink of water.

"Sure. It's not exactly rocket science."

"You don't ride?" Tim asked.

"I'm a city boy. Never had much use for it," Rory answered with a shrug.

"Would you be interested in learning?" Tim suggested, looking at Rory sideways.

Rory looked at him as if to gauge his intent. "I'm probably a little old for that."

"Nobody's too old to learn to ride."

"Why?" Rory asked.

"Why do I want to teach you to ride?"

Rory nodded.

"Because being a wrangler pays better, and we're always short of wranglers. And you're good with the horses. You treat them with respect."

"Well, they're kind of big, and if you get in their way, they step on your foot and that hurts. It pays to be aware of that."

Tim laughed. "That's one way of looking at it, but I can tell they like you. They don't like everyone who steps into their stall, you know. Horses are very sensitive to people. They pick up on things other human beings don't."

"Like what?" Rory asked with clear apprehension.

"Like when you have a bad day. Some horses will give you hell if you're not feeling well. Davenport, Hunter's gelding, is one horse you should stay far away from if you're not having an absolutely stellar day. Now Belle, on the other hand, which is a mare Hunter rides even more than Davenport these days, she'll come and console you. She'll nuzzle your back and beg to be scratched and generally act like a lovesick puppy when you're feeling a bit down or when you're in a bad mood. She's a really sweet horse, and she'll make you feel better instantly. And once you're smiling again, she'll leave you to your work. I swear sometimes she can read minds."

Tim saw a smile play around Rory's mouth, and it made him feel good.

"I like working around horses."

"Then you'll like riding them too. Besides, when you're riding you're outside all the time and not cooped up in here, where it smells of manure."

This time Rory smiled for real. "Yeah, but it's a lot warmer in here than out there."

"You need a duster to work outside. And chaps. And it rains quite a bit here, so you do get soaked sometimes, but still."

"I don't have all that," Rory replied with a defeated look on his face.

Tim knew what Rory was getting at. He didn't have any money, and it was unlikely that he could buy things like an oilskin duster on a ranch hand's pay. Tim made a mental note to look through his old clothes to see if he had anything he could give to Rory.

"Why don't we start with riding lessons? During the winter months I have time to teach you, and then maybe you can get some hands-on experience in the spring when we take the horses to the higher fields to graze."

"Sure," Rory replied, but Tim had the distinct impression he was only saying it to keep him from going on about it.

They sat together for a little while, not talking. Eventually Tim checked his watch. "We better get going, otherwise we'll need to reheat our dinner."

Once inside the crew house, they each went their separate ways to clean up. When Tim returned, he found Rory sitting alone at a table while most of the other guys sat together at the other side. He filled up a plate with potatoes, green beans, and pork chops and decided to lead by example and join Rory. The others guys eyed them suspiciously, and some of them didn't hide the fact they had a problem with Tim's support for Rory by leaving the table.

"You should sit with them," Rory said quietly, nodding in their general direction.

"Don't see why I should," Tim replied confidently.

"No use for you to get ostracized as well."

"They'll come around."

Rory shook his head. "You live here, Tim. Don't make life hard for yourself."

"That's right," Tim said. "I live here. I'm part of the furniture. I'm also a wrangler, the crew boss, and the foreman's brother, who happens to be the owner's brother-in-law. They can't afford to alienate me." He said those last words loud enough for the other table to hear him. They grabbed their plates and cleared off.

Rory waited for them to leave. "Tim, don't do this. I appreciate what you did for me, but I'm not your project. I can take care of myself. You live here. You'll still work with these men long after I'm gone."

Tim leaned across the table toward Rory. "You think it'll be easier anywhere else? How long will it take for the men you work with to realize you have a rap sheet? And you won't have anyone there to take your side."

"I don't want anyone to take my side. I'll fight my own battles." Rory got up from his chair and grabbed his half-finished plate.

"Like you've done these past twenty years?" Tim said, raising his voice. "Stealing other people's property?" Tim stood up as well and walked around the table in Rory's direction. "Always on the run from the authorities and in and out of jail?"

Before he could react, Rory pushed Tim against the wall with surprising strength. He saw how dark Rory's eyes were and knew it was anger he saw in them. They stood like that, facing off, for long moments, Rory leaning against Tim, and then Rory stepped back and composed himself.

"If you really want to give me a chance, then let me make my own way," Rory said, his breathing clearly measured. "Being the crew boss' pet only makes life harder."

Tim couldn't argue with that. He'd always been between a rock and a hard place. He wasn't one of the employees because he was Hugh's brother, and he wasn't one of the owners because he was *only* Hugh's brother. He'd always kept his private life a secret, so he didn't really have friends among the crew, and although he had an amicable relationship with Hunter's sister Izzie because they grew up together, that had faded once she started her family with Hugh.

Although that first time Rory had only stayed for three weeks, after he was gone Tim had felt like he'd lost a friend. Now that Rory was back on the ranch, the friendship hadn't returned with him. Maybe Tim just had to live with the fact that his feelings weren't returned. He'd just have to content himself with having done his good deed and hoping that Rory would stick it out until his parole was over.

—6—

WITH the steady downpour of rain, Rory was happy that a lot of his work was done indoors. The only coat he owned sucked up every drop of water until it felt like it was never going to get dry, no matter how close he hung it to the heater at night, and he knew it would take all winter for him to make enough money to buy himself a more weatherproof one. Until then, he darted in and out of barns and stables whenever it wasn't raining too hard and stayed put when it was.

After three weeks of working at the ranch, Rory was starting to feel at home, although he kept to himself and didn't interact with the other ranch hands unless he absolutely had to. Most of the men had become less hostile and sort of tolerated him as long as he just did what was asked, and Rory felt it was as good a stalemate as he could achieve.

Since their argument, Tim no longer sought him out, and Rory figured he deserved that, although he was always happy whenever he could spot the wrangler riding between the stables on horseback or if he could watch him from afar at work in the meadows.

Then one rare sunny but cold day, Rory rounded a corner and Tim was there.

"Old Mac is sick," Tim stated out of the blue. "If you have the time, could you help out with the foaling stalls, please?"

Rory looked into Tim's light-brown eyes and felt himself grow warm inside. At the same time, his hands grew clammy inside his working gloves, and he realized he was nervous.

"Sure," Rory said with a nod. "Is there anything in particular I need to do? You know, something different than with the other stalls?"

"Mac's been sick for a few days, so he's only done some of the work. I'll help out so you can catch up," Tim said, his always-present smile only faint now.

"I'm sure you have better things to do, so I can manage if you can just tell me what to watch out for," Rory replied. He couldn't stop looking at Tim for some reason. "I might not catch up this afternoon, but if you give me a few days, I'm sure I can make them look like new."

"Rory, I'm sorry."

"For what?"

"For the things I said to you."

Rory shrugged it away and walked past Tim toward the stable block where he knew the mares and new foals were housed.

Tim followed Rory. "It's not nothing. If you knew me at all, you would know it's not at all like me to drag the past out into the open to humiliate someone."

"You didn't humiliate me," Rory said, trying to keep the emotion from filtering into his voice. He knew what Tim was getting at, but it was futile to feel bad about Tim's words. Tim was right. There was no reason to think he'd do any better now than he had in the past. "You just stated the obvious."

"So please accept my apology."

Rory stopped to look at Tim's face, hoping to gauge his honesty. Tim wasn't even smiling at him. "Fine. Now can we get to work?"

This time Tim did smile, and Rory looked away, because that small mouth and the way it widened into a smile that made little laugh lines appear around Tim's eyes did things to Rory's insides he'd forgotten about in the last three or so years.

They walked into the barn that housed the breeding mares and their new foals during the cold winter months. Because it was a dry, sunny day, most of them were outside in the paddock next to the stable, which gave the men a lot of room to maneuver. Since the foaling barn was heated, they had both worked up a sweat in less than an hour, and Tim was the first one to take his shirt off. Although Rory was mucking out the stall next to Tim's, he caught a glimpse of naked flesh and couldn't resist stopping to take a better look.

Tim caught his eye but continued scooping soiled straw into the wheelbarrow, a knowing smile on his face. Since Rory was as good as finished in his stall, he moved his equipment to the one opposite Tim's, and since the half doors were kept all the way open, Rory knew he could give as good as he got, so he took his shirt off as well.

Rory could barely keep his eyes off Tim's broad chest and the small rivulets of sweat occasionally running down the ample muscles. He knew he couldn't hold a candle to Tim's physique but wasn't too shy to admit that a life of manual labor had left him with a lean, chiseled frame and nothing to be ashamed of. Part of him wanted to cross the path between the two stalls to show Tim exactly what his little performance did to him, but Rory knew he had too much to lose.

Rory vividly remembered the last time he'd made an overture toward Tim, and how Tim had at first kissed him back with gusto and then pushed him away when they'd gotten caught. In the last three weeks, Rory had noticed nothing much had changed. Tim definitely didn't make his preference for men known around the ranch, and Rory worried that any move he made toward him wouldn't be welcome. It didn't mean that Rory interpreted what Tim was doing as anything else than flirting. He just figured he'd have to find playtime elsewhere.

BY DINNERTIME, the two of them finished the thorough mucking out, and after bringing the dams and foals back inside, they went back to the crew house. They managed to miss each other at dinner and didn't see each other again until it was time for Rory to pick up his weekly paycheck. To Rory's surprise, Hunter was in the office when he entered, and Tim was standing next to him.

"Mr. Krause," Rory greeted Hunter. "Tim."

"Please call me Hunter. We don't really stand on formalities here."

"Hunter," Rory said with a nod, more quietly than before.

"Tim here says you're doing well. Showing up on time, doing an excellent job."

Rory looked at Tim for a moment and then back at Hunter. "If Tim says so, it must be true, sir… Hunter."

"He also tells me you're good with the horses and would like to learn to ride?"

This time Rory's look at Tim lasted a little longer and was a mix of "why did you have to tell him that" and "are you sure?" He turned back to Hunter quickly enough not to let on, though.

Hunter gave Rory a genuine smile, and Rory understood why Hunter was well liked by his crew. "I told Tim it would be a great idea. The horses can always use a little extra riding time. It's a good test for them to be ridden by an inexperienced rider, and if you end up being any good, well, we're just as short on wranglers as we are on ranch hands."

Rory nodded at Hunter. "If Tim can spare the time, I wouldn't mind if he gave me riding lessons. If he wants to, that is."

"That's settled then," Hunter said confidently. He handed Rory an envelope. "Hugh told me you don't have a bank account. Maybe you should consider getting one? It would be safer than carrying all that cash around."

"Maybe," Rory agreed. "Thank you," he said, nodding at both men and taking his leave.

Walking outside, Rory felt restless. He walked from the main building to the crew house and stood on the darkened porch for a while, thinking about what he was going to do tonight. He took a few sips of vodka from his hip flask to stay warm and then walked in the direction of the main barn to do a last check and turn off the lights. When he looked over at the second homestead, which was Hunter's house, he spotted him on the back porch looking out over the darkening fields. Hunter was standing still, leaning on the railing, until another man walked outside. Rory had seen both Hunter and his lover, Grant, around the stables and out in the meadows, but they never acted like lovers there. Not that they hid the fact they lived together, and Rory had heard enough mocking remarks from the newer ranch hands to know for sure that Hunter and Grant were definitely a committed couple, but what Rory was witnessing now certainly wasn't meant for the eyes of strangers.

Grant wiped his hands on a towel before swinging it over his shoulder and enveloping Hunter in a tight embrace. Hunter leaned into his lover's touch, and they exchanged a few words that Rory couldn't make out. Rory was glad he was shrouded in darkness and the porch the men were standing on was partially lit by light coming from what Rory figured was the kitchen, because he couldn't keep his eyes off the two men and the tenderness visible in their touches. Rory knew this sort of exchange between two manly men was possible, of course, but he'd never seen it before, let alone experienced it himself. Up until that moment, he'd also never realized he wanted it too. These two men lived the life Rory had only thought possible if he'd taken a wife, yet here they were—tall, broad men who worked on a successful ranch in redneck country—and they lived together openly.

Rory also had to admit he'd never heard the old-timers make the snide remarks the younger ones made about their bosses. They seemed to be okay with their bosses' living arrangements and even told the young ones to shut up about it if it got out of hand.

Hunter turned around in Grant's embrace, and the two men on the porch kissed. It was a deep, passionate kiss that ended in another embrace and the two of them staring out at the last sliver of light left on the horizon. It all seemed so normal. Did he really think it was normal? At least Hunter and Grant made it look that way.

It made Rory restless. He had to do something tonight. He couldn't just sit in his room again, so he made a beeline for the crew house to get his jacket. He was going to try to hitch a ride into the city. It had been too long since he'd gotten laid.

—7—

LIKE most patrons, Tim parked his truck at the back of The Handle Bar, out of sight of the road. To casual passersby the roadside bar looked like any other, but to get in you needed to show ID, and strangers were let into a small foyer where they could get a drink if they absolutely wanted. If you were a regular, and a man, and you said the right words—something along the line of "this place was recommended by a friend" or "I was told I could find some action here"—you were led into the main bar, which still looked pretty much like any other roadside drinking establishment. The only difference was that there wasn't a woman in sight, and most of the men knew their way to the backroom, which was more important than the fact you could get anything from cheap beer to a variety of whisky, vodka, or tequila to drink.

Since it was quite a drive from the ranch, Tim didn't come every week, but he'd been there enough for the bouncer to wave him through to the main bar without even checking his ID. Of course it helped that the bouncer knew him from more than just the entrance. The man wasn't on duty all night long, and he unwound like everyone else. In the backroom.

Tim walked up to the bar and ordered a beer with a tequila chaser from the leather-clad, bald, and heavily tattooed and pierced bartender. He wasn't a big drinker, but he knew just a little liquor would help him to feel less nervous and a little more confident. Always aware that he would have to drive home again in a few hours, he'd stick to just another beer or two for the rest of the night. He was still waiting for his order when a familiar face appeared next to him.

"Hi, Jimmy," Tim greeted the blond twink leaning on the bar.

"We missed you, Tim," Jimmy replied, trying to give him a seductive look.

Jimmy wasn't Tim's type, but he was eager and willing and had a great mouth and a tight ass. Tim had been on the receiving end of both in the back room, and unless he got a better offer, Tim knew Jimmy would be more than eager to repeat the performance. He had no illusions he'd be the kid's only entertainment tonight, but then, it wasn't like he was looking for commitment. "I'm sure you say that to all the guys," Tim joked.

Jimmy moved a little closer. "What other guys?"

Tim chuckled. "You don't need to pretend with me, Jimmy."

"I know," Jimmy said, backing off. "But you know I'll treat you right, don't you? I'll give you everything you need, Timmy. Gladly." He pushed himself against Tim and grabbed for Tim's crotch. "And boy, do you need it."

Tim knew he wasn't even excited yet. Although Jimmy's hand did stir something, he knew Jimmy was used to a little more response. "Why don't you flirt up a storm with some other guys, and I promise you I'll look you up before I leave."

Jimmy smirked at him. "You might not find me, Timmy. I might have gotten a better offer by then, and you know I can't resist a nice big cock."

Tim smiled at how Jimmy emphasized those last three words. "I know. I'll take my chances."

Jimmy drifted off, and Tim eyed Jimmy as he ambled through the crowd of the slowly filling bar. It was nice to know he always had a fallback in case nobody else interesting showed up.

The next guy to sit next to him at the bar was the opposite of Jimmy and much more Tim's type. He was lean and dark, wore a leather jacket and leather pants, but seemed very nervous. The bartender was pretty busy with so many new arrivals, and the guy had to wait to be served. After a while his eyes locked with Tim's, and Tim smiled at him.

"He'll come this way soon," Tim said to the guy, trying to set him at ease.

"He seems to be ignoring me," the other man said.

"No, he's just one of those guys you can't unsettle. It's easier for him to focus on one patron at a time, but he's making his way over here." That didn't seem to soothe the guy. "What are you having? He knows me. He might be quicker if he sees I need something."

"Thanks," the man answered. "Beer and a chaser?"

"Good choice," Tim replied. "I'm Tim, by the way." He held out his hand.

The other guy looked at it and decided it was safe to be polite. "Bailey."

Tim shook the offered hand and felt how clammy it was.

"Sorry," Bailey said, retracting his hand and wiping it on his white T-shirt. "I guess I'm nervous."

"First time?"

Bailey's mouth turned tense, and then he nodded slightly.

"Don't worry. Relax. We're all in the same boat here."

"Boat?" Bailey parroted.

"In the closet, but in need of some action."

"Ah," Bailey responded. "I've… never… I don't usually go to bars."

Tim clapped him on the shoulder and smiled. "There's a first time for everything, I suppose. This isn't a bad place. Most of the guys here want the same thing you do. Just keep your wallet in a safe place and don't expect the other guy to bring the condoms and you'll be okay."

Tim managed to wave to the bartender and got their order filled: one beer with a chaser and one without. Bailey paid for both. He downed the beer in one big gulp and then the chaser right after that, while Tim watched him with some amusement.

Bailey wiped his mouth with the back of his hand and took a deep breath. "I don't suppose you'd like to…." He gestured at the backroom.

Tim looked at him, trying to figure out if the guy was just very quickly influenced by the drink or playing the innocent virgin as part of his seduction technique.

"Depends on what you have in mind," Tim eventually answered.

The insecurity in Bailey returned for a moment, and then it was gone. "Why don't I show you?" He got up from his stool and took a few steps back.

Tim remained seated. "I like to know what I'm getting. I'm not big on surprises."

Bailey's eyes lowered to Tim's groin. "I'd like a taste of that."

Tim chuckled but didn't respond right away, so Bailey came closer again. He leaned against Tim and whispered in his ear. "I want to suck the cream out of you."

"Fine," Tim said with a smirk, getting up this time after Bailey moved back. "Let's go."

They walked through the crowd. Tim was always surprised at how little attention the other patrons paid them, considering the fact that everyone knew what people were getting up to as they walked past the black velvet curtain. In the dark room behind it, heads did turn, since there were always guys lurking there, hoping to get lucky a second, or third, time. There was no music in the backroom, except for what drifted in from the bar, but the noises there were more animalistic: grunts and growls, moans and groans, the slapping of skin on skin, and occasionally slurping and talking.

Tim was never a fan of public sex, but he took what he could get, and if that meant finding a nook somewhere to lean against a wall while he was being sucked off, he didn't mind having something that resembled a porn orgy in his visual path.

It wasn't too busy yet, so Tim easily found a more secluded space. It wasn't until he'd dragged Bailey along with him into the shadows and the younger man was on his knees that he noticed the couple across the gang path. One guy was leaning with his elbows on the back of the faux-leather couch. His jeans were pulled down around his knees, and a big guy was pounding mercilessly into him from behind. The bottom had his head down, so Tim couldn't see his expression, but the top was clearly enjoying it. When Tim looked down, he saw Bailey unzip him and pull his cock out. Without a lot of finesse, Bailey started sucking him. Tim figured Bailey was enjoying it, and the way he moaned around his cock felt good, but it was the display in front of him that made him hard. Tim could hear the top's dirty mouth and figured he wouldn't do badly in a porn movie.

"Love your tight ass. Do you love my big, fat cock?"

The bottom didn't answer; in fact, he didn't react at all. Then again, he needed all his strength to prevent being pushed into the couch.

"You love it, don't you? You need it so badly, and I'm the one to give it to you."

Tim almost rolled his eyes at the cheesiness of the one-sided conversation. He continued watching the lean bottom, still fully dressed with the exception of his pulled-down jeans.

"Come on, bottom boy, show me how much you like it."

"Just get on with it," a surprisingly deep, raspy voice said. He didn't raise his head, but the voice sounded vaguely familiar to Tim. It wasn't until the top started growling and pushing in with more urgency, shouting as he came, that the bottom raised his head.

Rory.

Tim couldn't move. Bailey was doing a good job, and Tim was close to coming, but he didn't *want* to come now. He pulled away from Bailey and tried to tuck himself into his jeans, which wasn't easy. Tim heard Bailey protest but ignored it since Rory was moving away from the sweaty guy behind him and pulling up his jeans before walking off. Tim didn't think Rory had spotted him, and part of him didn't want Rory to know he'd seen what had happened, but Rory didn't look very happy, and all Tim wanted to do was make it better.

Tim followed him out of the dark room and through the bar, but lost sight of him along the way. He walked outside anyway, into the cold night air, and around the corner to the parking lot, where he practically bumped into Rory standing against the side of the building.

"Always saving the world, aren't you?"

"I didn't follow you, Rory."

"So we just happened to go cruising in the same bar, an hour's drive away from the ranch?"

Tim sighed. "This is my regular haunt. They know me here."

"No kidding," Rory snorted. "That blond twink was all over you."

"You saw that? You knew I was there?"

"Yeah, I saw that," Rory said with eyebrows raised.

Tim didn't know how to react.

"I know you're gay, Tim."

"I know you know. You kissed me, remember?"

"Aaah, have you been pining for me for the last three and a half years? That's so cute."

Tim saw the mockery in Rory's face and felt hurt, but then he saw something else. The mockery turned softer, more tender. And when Tim took a step closer, Rory first looked at his feet and then straight at Tim. Tim closed the gap even more and realized Rory wanted him. He could see it in the way Rory's eyes turned liquid and his body relaxed.

"Can I kiss you?" Tim whispered, now definitely standing in Rory's personal space.

"Always the gentleman," Rory replied softly without bridging the gap. "You know, you should be more forceful. You have the body for it, and guys get off on that."

"Do you?"

"Depends." Rory shrugged. "On my mood."

"And what's your mood like tonight?"

Rory moved a little closer, just enough to let the hair around his mouth caress Tim's lips. This was one of those times he hated being shorter than Rory, so he had to stand tall. Rory didn't kiss him, though, and Tim craved it, wanting to bring back the memory of the crushing kiss they'd shared more than three years ago. He couldn't bring himself to move closer, though. He knew if he did, he wouldn't be able to stop himself, and this time he knew he'd never let Rory go again. Only he didn't think Rory would be able to take it yet.

"Come on, Timmy," Rory whispered.

"There's two of us here."

For a moment Rory hesitated, and then he pulled Tim to him and turned them around until Tim felt his back hit the wall. Tim thought he was going to be ravaged, but instead Rory's kiss was slow and tender. He pushed Tim against the wall with his body, but his mouth remained teasing and soft, even a little hesitant. Tim tipped his head back a little and welcomed the change of pace, but when Rory didn't speed up, his mind wandered to the feel of Rory's body pressed against his.

"He didn't make you come. That guy."

Rory raised his eyebrows. "For that he would have had to try a hell of a lot harder, but he wasn't interested in that. He just wanted to get off."

"And you?"

"I figured I could go home and jack off. At least then I'd be sure it would be good. I don't trust anyone else to do it the way I want."

"So you're a power bottom?"

Rory chuckled. "I know what I like. If that's how you want to label it, be my guest." There were deep lines in Rory's forehead, not from worry this time, but from amusement as he continued with raised eyebrows. "That guy who was blowing you couldn't keep your interest either, I noticed."

"Your show was more interesting," Tim admitted. "I just don't get what you get out of it, if you let a guy use you like that without even bothering to make it good for you too."

"Oh, Timmy," Rory said with mockery in his voice. "Have you ever had a really satisfying one night stand? It's sex. Period. I'll be sore in all the right places and then imagine it wasn't some inconsiderate bastard, but somebody who actually gave a shit. I can get myself off with that thought."

The words were harsh, but the fact that Rory was still pressed against him gave Tim courage. He pushed his hand between them and brushed his knuckles over Rory's hardness.

Rory exhaled audibly, and Tim could feel the warmth against his face.

"I bet I can make you feel good too," Tim whispered.

"I'm sure you can," Rory replied, equally quietly. Rory pulled Tim's hand from between them and pushed his groin against Tim. "Shit, you're as hard as I am."

"It's all your fault."

Rory shook his head, his gaze away from Tim, and then suddenly he kissed Tim for real.

Tim's head was swimming. While Rory's beard was surprisingly soft against his skin, his body was hard and mercilessly rutting against his. Tim wanted it that way; he wanted the hard body and the lust he felt in Rory. Tim's hands were trying to feel as much of it as he could, grabbing at Rory's hips, trying to pull him even closer. Tim was at least as close to coming as he had been in the back room, but this time he wanted to come, wanted to feel the surge of blood, and wanted to feel Rory coming against him. That was the only reason he tried to stave off his orgasm. Rory had to come first. Always. That was just how Tim was wired.

The only thing that felt strange was that Rory was almost completely quiet. His body showed the urgency, the lust, the need, and he was breathing hard, but there was no moaning and no other sound than what Tim couldn't hold in.

"God, Rory, the things you do to me," Tim rasped. Suddenly Rory shuddered against Tim, and Tim held him close as he felt his own orgasm overtake him. They stood panting, arms around each other and finding support against the wall. Tim could smell Rory's sweaty, earthy scent and couldn't get enough of it. He had his face buried against Rory's neck and didn't want to let him go.

"Come home with me."

Rory pulled out of Tim's embrace. His eyes were a little glazed, but he'd gathered himself already. "A ride back to the ranch would be nice. I'll get my coat from inside."

Tim was left standing against the wall, only then realizing just how cold it was. He could actually see his own breath every time he exhaled. He'd left his coat in the truck and was glad that Rory returned quickly, dressed in his ragged old jacket and garage cap.

"We should get you a new coat," Tim suggested when Rory walked up to him.

"Maybe in a few paychecks' time I'll be able to think about it," Rory said blandly.

Tim figured they were back to normal, and he didn't like it one bit.

—8—

ON THE way home, they didn't talk. Rory didn't even know what to say. All he could do was stare out the window, but his mind kept drifting to the encounter against the wall.

Rory knew he couldn't get attached to Tim. There was no way they could have a life like Grant and Hunter and live together openly. If that's what Tim wanted, then he would be out to his coworkers already, but he wasn't. They could sneak around, of course, but Rory didn't think that was something Tim would want to do either. He might be in the closet, but only because he didn't have a boyfriend. And how would it look to the outside world if Tim told them Rory was his boyfriend? He couldn't do that to Tim. Tim deserved better than a convicted felon on parole.

For the entire hour's drive, Rory tried to figure out his feelings for the buff cowboy next to him on the truck bench. He'd lusted after men for as long as he'd known what lust was, but never as much as after Tim. It had been there that first time, three years ago in the truck at The Barrel Run when Rory hadn't been able to control himself, and it was there again tonight. And it wasn't just about sex. It was about kissing, too, and running his hands over Tim's bulky, tight frame, those narrow hips and broad shoulders, those distended pecs. As Rory closed his eyes for a moment, it also became about sleeping next to Tim. Hadn't Tim asked him to come *home* with him? At the time, Rory had reacted to the words, but slowly the meaning was seeping in as well. Did Tim really ask him to come to his home? And by extension, his room?

Rory couldn't do this. He had to keep his distance from Tim. The last complication he needed was for his head to be occupied with someone else.

ZAHRA OWENS

Tim drove up to the crew house. They expected the house to be quiet and dark, but to their dismay, most of the occupants were standing outside, looking at the house.

"What's going on?" Tim asked Johnny, one of the other ranch hands.

"There was a fire. We figure old Mackenzie fell asleep while smoking a cigarette."

Tim ran inside and Rory followed. Although there were no visible flames, water was running over the wooden floors toward the exit, and it smelled of smoke.

"What happened?" Tim asked Grant, who was coming out of Rory's room.

"Old Mac is dead. The coroner's inside, but he thinks it's smoke inhalation." Grant turned to Rory. "Your room sustained water damage, and part of your wall is ruined. I'm afraid your clothes might not have survived this, either." He directed his gaze at Tim again. "Tim. Can you find Rory another place to stay?"

"He can stay with me," Tim replied without hesitation. He looked at Rory, but Rory couldn't return the look because he was afraid it would be written all over his face that he had feelings for Tim. And Grant would certainly be able to read those.

"There are no other rooms available, and I have the biggest room. We'll put up a camping bed," Tim explained, and Rory recognized it for what it was: Tim's way to cover their tracks. Most of the men had seen them arrive together in the dead of night, and who knew how the other workers would interpret that? Rory was sure they would be the talk of the town, and the fire would be forgotten much sooner.

"So there's no structural damage to the house?" Tim asked Grant.

"No, we caught it pretty fast, and the shower was just around the corner, so we had plenty of water nearby. When Hunter and I arrived, the guys had already put out the fire. We just called the cops."

Tim nodded. "Sorry I wasn't here," he mumbled.

Grant clapped him on the shoulder. "Don't worry about it. It's Friday night. You bachelor boys need to spend that paycheck, right?"

Tim looked at Rory for a fleeting moment and then smiled at Grant. "I'm sure you remember those days, old man."

"Wait until you have kids, and then you'll know how quickly a good night's sleep wins over a night on the town."

Rory watched the last of the water being swept out, and then the men from the coroner's office came out of Old Mac's room with a body bag on a stretcher. The coroner sealed off the room with door strips and nodded at the men standing in the hallway.

"I better go see if anything can be rescued," Rory said to Tim.

"I'll go get a fold-up bed from the main house, and we can get you settled in as well. My room's up the stairs and to the left. First door," Tim added. "You can take your stuff in there. Door's unlocked."

Rory nodded and watched Tim leave.

TEN minutes later, Rory knew he didn't even have clean underwear left. His wardrobe stood against the wall that had taken most of the fire damage, and there was a gaping hole crisscrossed with tape where his wall used to be. Everything was either scorched or soaked with water and soot. He'd dropped the clothes that didn't look too damaged in the washer, but he didn't hold out a lot of hope that they would actually be salvageable.

Rory made his way up the stairs, knocked on Tim's door, and entered when nobody answered. It felt strange to walk into Tim's domain, especially because Tim wasn't with him. Even in the harsh light of the bulb hanging from the ceiling, Rory could see the personal effects all around. He smiled when he realized Tim wasn't the tidiest person on the planet, but then again, he didn't think Tim had to share his room with someone else very often. At least, that's what it looked like.

"Sorry for the mess," Tim said, walking in carrying an air mattress. "Johnny beat you to the fold-up bed. Apparently he needs to sleep somewhere else as well. His room is right above Mac's, and it got damaged too."

"That's okay. I've slept on worse than that."

"You could share my bed," Tim said a little hesitantly. He gestured at the large bed occupying most of the room. "I'm not used to sharing, but I'm sure we can manage."

Rory took the mattress from Tim. "This will do. Don't worry."

Tim looked disappointed, but Rory tried not to notice. "Well, if you change your mind, the offer still stands." He started clearing out the space next to the bed so Rory could put down the mattress and sleeping bag.

"I'm going to go clean up a bit," Rory announced, not looking at Tim as he made his getaway. His briefs felt crusty by now, and he didn't have any clean ones, so he would wash them by hand and hope they'd be dry in the morning. He was going to have to ask one of the men for a ride into town to buy some new ones, and he'd have to make do with the pair of jeans and the shirt he had on, but he would for the foreseeable future. At least he had a roof over his head and food on the table this time.

When Rory arrived back in Tim's room, the room was lit by the bedside lamp and Tim was lying in bed, reading. He was wearing a T-shirt and—Rory could only guess—boxers and had the covers pulled up tight.

"Will you be warm enough in there?" Tim asked.

"Sure," Rory said, slipping into the sleeping bag with his clothes on.

Tim looked confused, and then something appeared to dawn on him. "How inconsiderate of me." He got out of the bed and rummaged through his wardrobe. "You don't have any clothes to sleep in."

"That's okay." Rory said. "When you sleep on the street, you sleep in your clothes every day."

Tim held out a folded bunch of grey fabric. "But you're not living on the street. They may be a bit big, but we'll get you some in your size in the morning."

Tim's expectant look gave Rory no other choice than to accept the offering. His reward was one of Tim's stellar smiles, so Rory took off his shirt and replaced it with a soft cotton T-shirt that, like Tim predicted, was more than a bit too big, but it felt nice anyway and smelled of fabric softener and Tim, although that could well be his imagination. Bending over and protected by the oversized T-shirt, Rory took off his jeans and slipped into the boxers.

"Going commando?" Tim asked, giving away that he'd been eyeing Rory.

"I washed out my underwear, since it's now my only pair and I need some for tomorrow," Rory replied, realizing he sounded almost like he was apologizing. Tim was lounging on the bed, head resting on his hand, and Rory had a hard time keeping his eyes off him, so he quickly crawled into the sleeping bag. He didn't need to look to the side to know Tim was still staring at him.

"It's late. Maybe we should get some sleep?" Rory suggested, so Tim turned off the bedside lamp.

The room went pitch dark, and Rory felt cold. He wanted to crawl into bed next to Tim, but he knew if he did that, the last thing they'd do was sleep, so he hugged the sleeping bag around himself and tried to relax.

"How long did you live on the street?" Tim asked in his soft, sultry voice.

"Off and on for most of my life," Rory admitted. The fact he couldn't see Tim's face was a blessing and a curse. Rory could tell himself that Tim didn't care or wasn't shocked. On the other hand, he needed Tim to show him his smile, telling Rory he accepted him unconditionally. Rory figured the truth was somewhere in the middle, and it was best that he didn't know Tim's true feelings.

"Couldn't have been easy. I can't imagine not having a warm place to sleep."

Rory didn't say anything. What could he say?

"You were right about me being privileged," Tim continued.

"You weren't privileged, you were just lucky," Rory replied, turning to his side so he was facing Tim. His eyes were adjusting to the darkness, but he was still glad it was too dark to make out more than shadows.

"I never had to sleep on the street."

"Did you live on this ranch all your life?" Rory asked, trying to take the focus away from himself.

"Yeah," Tim said softly, as if he wasn't happy with it. "I grew up in this house here, before they turned it into the crew house. When my mother died, Hunter's mother took us boys in. Hugh and Hunter were already working on the ranch, and Jack and I were still in school. Jack wanted to go to college, and the Krauses made sure he could."

"You never wanted to go?"

"I never liked school much. I suppose now I wish I'd paid more attention, but then I couldn't wait to start working with the horses. How about you?"

Up until then, Rory had felt quite comfortable listening to Tim talking about his childhood, but now Tim had turned the tables, and he didn't want to burden Tim with the story of his miserable life.

"Are your parents still alive?"

Rory sighed. "I have no idea." Rory listened to the silence that followed.

"You don't know?"

"No, Tim, I don't know," Rory replied. He immediately wanted to take back his words, not because of their meaning, but because of the tone he'd used. "I'm sorry. I just don't feel comfortable talking about them."

"Okay," Tim conceded. "I understand. You like to stay an enigma."

"It's not that—" Rory started to protest, but then he felt Tim's hand brush over his cheek, and he couldn't speak any more. The hand retreated, and Rory wanted it to return, but he didn't dare say anything.

"So you think you can sleep now?" Tim asked tenderly.

Rory really wanted to say "Yes, but I'd rather sleep in your arms." Instead he shook the thoughts out of his head and answered, "Should work. I'm tired enough, in any case." They were silly thoughts, anyway.

—9—

WHEN Tim woke up the next morning, Rory was gone. The air mattress was standing against the wall and the sleeping bag was neatly folded underneath it. Tim didn't see any clothes that weren't his, and even the sleepwear he'd lent Rory was gone. He instantly regretted having slept so uncharacteristically late.

Outside the sun was shining, and after a quick breakfast, Tim went in search of his roommate. He found him near the foaling stables.

"Morning, Rory."

Rory startled and then smiled underneath his garage cap. "Guess you slept well. I've been up for ages."

"I can tell," Tim said, looking at the neatly-swept floor of the stable block. "Mothers and foals give you any grief?"

"Not really," Rory replied. "I hope you don't mind that I put them in the paddock. I figured it was at least as warm as yesterday, and the foals were jumping around like crazy once they realized they had room to stretch their legs."

"It's good. We usually don't let them out this early in the morning when it's this cold, but you're right, you can tell they're enjoying it."

Rory's smile disappeared, and he started sweeping again. Almost immediately Tim cursed to himself. He knew Rory felt like a screw-up, and there he'd put him down for doing his job.

"Rory," he said. Rory didn't turn around, so Tim stepped closer and put his hand on the ranch hand's shoulder. "You didn't do anything wrong."

Rory looked at him and shrugged. "Don't worry about it."

Tim knew he'd hurt the man's feelings, but he couldn't go around walking on eggshells like this. Rory was going to have to man up. On the other hand, he did feel for Rory and hated to see him retreat like that. Tim picked up a pitchfork and started heaving the straw Rory had gathered at the exit of the stall into a wheelbarrow. Rory eyed him for a moment, but Tim pretended not to notice and continued working, at which Rory returned to turning the straw and picking out the soiled patches. Like the day before, they were done in no time, and after checking on the horses, they decided to bring the mares and their foals back inside later in the day.

"How about I give you your first riding lesson?" Tim suggested as they stowed away the wheelbarrow. "It's a great day for it, and there are a few horses that could use a little exercise. We could start in the training corral, and then if you do well, we could take a gander outside. Not too far for a first time. You know, take it easy." Tim knew he was rambling, like always when he was nervous, but he couldn't help himself. He just didn't want Rory to turn him down.

"I don't know if I'll be any good," Rory said matter-of-factly. "I'm sure you have better things to do."

Tim shrugged, trying not to let Rory's lukewarm response get him down. "You won't know until you try. Besides, you heard Hunter. He'd love for you to become a wrangler, which means you need to learn to ride first, and he said it was okay for me to teach you."

"Guess you're not going to let me off the hook for this, are you?" Rory said with a smirk on his face.

"No."

Rory nodded, his hands in the pockets of his threadbare jeans. "Fine. Let's get it over with."

Tim couldn't prevent a smile. "And after that, I'm taking you into town to buy some clothes. It's only going to get colder, you know."

"Right," Rory stated curtly.

Tim knew he'd called Rory on something he didn't feel comfortable about again. This time he decided to ignore it.

"Let's go. I'll teach you how to saddle a horse."

Tim tried to stay upbeat, and Rory slowly warmed up to him again as Tim led him to Chase, one of the older horses, and showed him what to check for before going out riding. The gelding was over twenty years old and looked like nothing could bother him, not even Tim talking incessantly and two men walking around him and prodding him from all angles. Once he wore a bridle and saddle, Tim walked him to the round corral, which was used for breaking in horses. He tied both reins to the horn of the western saddle and then put his foot in the stirrup. With practiced ease, Tim mounted the horse.

"See, just put your foot in here, your hands on the pommel, and pull yourself up as you swing your leg over."

Rory's eyebrows were flirting with his hairline. "You've been doing this since you could walk. Wanna bet it's not quite that easy?"

Tim swung his leg over again and jumped down. "Nobody's watching. If you fail, I'm the only one who'll know."

"Yeah," Rory sighed more than spoke as he moved closer to the horse. Chase wasn't a very tall horse, and Rory could easily grasp the saddle. It took a few tries for Rory to get his foot into the stirrup, and Tim could tell Rory was starting to get nervous. He looked at Tim, and Tim held onto Chase's bridle, although the horse barely needed it. Tim watched as Rory grasped the saddle knob with both hands and pulled himself up while trying to swing his leg around. Unexpectedly, the stirrup lunged forward, and Rory couldn't get his weight over his foot, so Tim let go of the docile horse and came to Rory's aid. As Rory came back down to the ground, he bumped into Tim, who reflexively wrapped his arms around Rory to prevent him from tumbling over, but as soon as Rory felt Tim's presence, he twisted away and out of Tim's reach in a very aggressive manner.

"Hey," Tim called out, trying to keep his voice from sounding too harsh. "It's okay. First time is always tricky."

"Just forget about it," Rory replied blankly.

"No way." Tim moved closer, putting his hand on Rory's shoulder, but the taller man pulled away like a petulant child. "Rory, come on. I'll help you try again. Once you get the hang of it, it'll come naturally."

Rory turned around, his face strained.

Tim smiled at him. "Come on, Grumpy. One more time."

"Grumpy?" A tentative smile wiped away the tension on Rory's face.

"You're no Sneezy, Sleepy, or Dopey. You're too skinny to be Doc. Bashful might suit you, but that's not much of a nickname. And if you prefer Happy, you're going to have to smile more."

Rory was smiling full on now, and Tim took a step closer to him, half expecting Rory to pull away again. When he didn't, Tim took another step, right into Rory's personal space. Rory wasn't looking directly at him, but he was still smiling, so Tim stretched his back and let his lips ghost over Rory's beard. Rory closed the remaining distance between them and kissed Tim so softly a moan escaped Tim's throat.

"I'm sorry." Rory stepped back.

"Why?" Tim asked. Their first kiss had been rather chaste, so Tim didn't want to wait for an answer. He wanted a real kiss from Rory and didn't really doubt whether Rory wanted it too, so this time he grabbed the front of Rory's shirt and pulled him closer before hungrily kissing him. It wasn't until he felt Rory's hesitant hand at the back of his skull that he could actually start enjoying the kiss too.

This time, when they stopped kissing, they didn't pull apart but remained firmly in each other's personal space.

"You make a lot of noise," Rory said with a chuckle.

"I don't."

"Yes, you do. I think the only one who didn't hear you all the way to the next county was that deaf guy who lives next to Calley's shop."

"I was enjoying it," Tim admitted. "And it's a way of showing my appreciation. I can't help myself."

Suddenly Rory twisted away from Tim's hold, and Tim looked around to see why he'd startled. Grant was next to the corral atop Raven, his black mare. Tim thought he looked slightly embarrassed having caught them in their intimate act.

"Grant?"

This time Grant looked straight at Tim. "I wondered if you felt like riding fences with me?"

"I'm giving Rory a riding lesson."

"Oh. Was that what it was? I see. In that case, I'll go rescue Hunter from his paper work. I'm sure he won't mind." With that, Grant turned Raven back toward the main house and galloped off.

"Shit," Rory muttered.

Tim looked at Rory. "You're embarrassed."

"And you're not? He caught us kissing!"

"They know I'm gay, Rory. It's not because I don't flaunt it that I live in the closet."

"But—"

"Grant, of all people, will understand. He didn't have the best reputation when he stole Hunter's heart either. And look at them now. Kings of the manor. Even Mrs. Krause treats him like her own son."

"I bet Grant doesn't have a rap sheet."

Tim put his arm around Rory's shoulders and quickly kissed his temple before letting go and walking back to Chase. "Let's get you up this horse and show you how easy it is to ride a well-trained gelding."

—10—

GRANT rode his horse back to the main house and hung his reins over the side post of the porch before walking to the side of the house and entering through the mudroom. He didn't bother taking off his boots, because he was only going to stick his head inside the office to entice Hunter to come riding with him.

As soon as he entered and saw Hunter sitting on the small couch, he knew that probably wouldn't work.

"What's wrong?" Grant asked as he saw Hunter staring into nothingness with the phone in his hand.

Hunter shook his head.

"Matty down for his afternoon nap?"

Hunter nodded.

"Of course he is," Grant mused, trying to set his lover at ease. "He's like his father. You rub his back, give him a kiss, whisper sweet nothings in his ear, and before his head hits the pillow, he's snoring."

Hunter smiled half-heartedly. "Matty doesn't snore."

"No, but his dad does."

"So does his other dad," Hunter rebutted—without his usual vigor, Grant noticed.

Grant sat down on the armrest of the couch next to Hunter and nudged him with his elbow. "What's wrong?" he repeated, this time sounding softer and more empathic than he had when he walked into the room.

"Miranda's in town."

Grant pursed his lips and tried to sound upbeat. "How is she doing?"

"She wants to see Matty," Hunter answered.

"When is she coming by?" Grant asked, trying to make it sound like she hadn't abandoned her son three years earlier and disappeared into thin air.

"I told her I'd call her back tomorrow. I didn't feel like giving into her demands all of a sudden. Does that make me spiteful?"

Hunter hid his face against Grant's chest, and Grant knew what that meant. His reasonably macho better half was trying to be entirely macho and not show how scared Miranda's call had made him. Grant put his hand on Hunter's head, and Hunter turned to snuggle closer until he was in Grant's arms. Grant squeezed his lover tightly and continued to soothe him by rubbing small circles over Hunter's shoulder blades. "It's okay," he heard himself say. "We prepared for this, remember? We have the letters from the nurses and Matty's doctors stating that she refused to take her son home with her from the hospital. We have the receipts from the personal ads we took out to try and find her. Our lawyer said that would be enough to prove abandonment."

"But what if it isn't enough?" Hunter said after a long pause. "What if she gets her doctor to tell the courts that she wasn't making rational decisions at the time, and that now she's had treatment and she can take care of her son again? I can't lose Matty, Grant. He's the best thing that ever happened to me."

They'd had this conversation before. The rational part of the conversation had been conducted at their lawyer's office in town, but the emotional ones always happened here, in the office or in their bedroom. Usually after they'd put their son to bed.

Matthew was a worry-baby. They'd known that from the start, since he'd had surgery twice before they could take him home with them that first time. He was born with a spinal cord defect, so the first operation was to repair his back where the nerves of his spinal cord had been exposed. The second one was to place a little tube in his head to drain the fluid from his brain, often a side effect from the spina bifida. That first year he was in and out of hospital all the time, and at three, he still couldn't walk, and they had no idea if he ever would. The flip side of that was that Matthew was a ray of sunshine. He'd warmed both men's hearts in his incubator in the pediatric ICU, and he continued to brighten every single day. He rarely cried, he always smiled when anyone gave him even the smallest amount of attention, and he was everyone's friend, including the doctor who examined him or the nurse who gave him the shots he really didn't like.

Although Matty couldn't walk, he did get around, much to Christy's dismay. While her three children with Grant were at school, she looked after Izzie's girls and Matty while everyone worked the ranch and she cooked dinner for the ranch hands who lived in the crew house. The children had a cordoned-off area in the huge family kitchen where they could play while Christy cooked. Matty's favorite thing to do was play Houdini, though, and he often escaped the play area when she wasn't looking. He had his own way of crawling, pulling himself along on his arms while leaning on one of his hips, and had other creative ways of getting into cupboards or under them. He'd never gotten into any serious trouble, but as Christy liked to point out, it was only a matter of time. Nobody could stay mad at him for long, though, and he wasn't just Christy's favorite, but also his grandmother's. When Christy came to live with them, Beth Krause had retired from most of the cooking, although she still helped out preparing the family dinner, and she often took her grandchildren into the living room to give Christy a little time on her own. Although Matthew was a real boy who liked to play rough, the one time he could be found sitting quietly was when Beth read him stories on the living room couch.

For all the heartache Matthew gave his two fathers, they could no longer imagine their lives without him. Matthew was the child they shared and the worry they shared. Although he was only three, and called them both Daddy, Grant knew that to Matty, there was no difference between him and Hunter, even though Hunter was his biological father.

Right after Matthew was born, Hunter had tried to keep Miranda in Matthew's life, in spite of Grant's objections. Grant had always felt that since Miranda had abandoned Matthew at the hospital, returning home without him and without even informing Hunter that he had a son, she had forfeited her rights as a mother. In Grant's eyes, Miranda didn't deserve to be kept in the loop where Matthew was concerned. Grant had softened his stance somewhat in the last three years, though. Now that his own children were finally living close by, he understood the bond a man had with his own flesh and blood and had grown to understand that it would be hard to live apart from them again. He didn't understand how Miranda had just abandoned her child, and now that she had returned, he felt every bit as angry and helpless as Hunter.

Grant hated that it looked like they were going to have to fight for their son.

"Did she say anything about wanting him back?"

Hunter looked up and shook his head. Although his face was dry, his eyes were bloodshot, and Grant knew he'd been holding back tears. "She just asked to see him. I don't see we have any other choice. The last time we saw her, I did tell her she could see him any time she wanted."

"Then let's let her. We'll just have to make it abundantly clear that we're Matty's parents and she's a visitor."

"Who just happens to be his mother."

"Yes," Grant agreed. "Happens to be. To Matty, she's a stranger. There's no way he misses a mother figure. He's got Christy and your mother and Auntie Izzie. Plenty of female carers there."

"I suppose," Hunter conceded. "It still worries me, though. I want to know what she's up to."

"Time will tell." Grant pulled Hunter closer again until he raised his head.

"What's up with you, though? You were pretty happy when you walked in."

Grant rolled his eyes. "I caught Tim smooching with Rory in the corral."

"Smooching?" Hunter raised an eyebrow.

"You know, kissing, holding each other close. I probably missed the juicy part, but I didn't believe Tim when he said he was giving Rory riding lessons."

"You just didn't understand the euphemism."

"Euphe—?"

"Rory riding Tim instead of a horse?" Hunter replied cheekily.

Grant chuckled. "They were both still dressed, but I see what you mean, you pervert."

Hunter nudged his man with his shoulder. "We both know Tim's gay. And I told you he'd been pining for Rory ever since Rory disappeared, back when the horses were being stolen. I'm glad Rory's returning Tim's feelings. Tim deserves a boyfriend."

"Even if that boyfriend is a convicted felon?"

"You think I made a mistake hiring him?"

Grant shrugged. "Rory is a good worker. He's basically replaced Old Mac and still does his own work as well, although I'm sure Tim helps him out. I see Tim wielding a pitchfork more than he should."

"As long as Tim still does his own job, I don't want to talk about it to Hugh. I can't blame Tim for wanting to spend time with his man."

Hunter looked at Grant with a soft smile, and Grant was acutely reminded of how much he loved his own man, so he kissed Hunter with all the tenderness he could muster.

"Maybe putting Tim in charge of Rory wasn't the best idea, since Tim's judgment is obviously going to be clouded," Hunter continued where he'd left off before their interaction had become more intimate. "Then again, maybe it helps. If Rory is as in love with Tim as Tim is with Rory, maybe Rory will have an easier time keeping to the straight and narrow because he doesn't want Tim to catch any heat for him. Then again, if Rory is only using Tim…."

"If you'd seen them together like I did, when they thought nobody was watching and then when they noticed I was there, you wouldn't doubt. Rory pulled away from Tim when he saw I was there. Then he looked at Tim to gauge whether he'd hurt him by his actions. He reminded me of myself in that stage of our relationship. And I knew what I felt for you then."

"Only then?" Hunter asked with a teasing smile.

"It only got worse," Grant answered, pulling Hunter roughly against him and running his knuckles over Hunter's head. "Now let's get out of here to saddle you a horse. I want someone to ride with."

"Well, if you put it that way."

"WE CAN ride past the corral," Grant suggested. "With any luck we'll catch them again, and you can judge for yourself."

"Let's not," Hunter said seriously. "They may be sharing a room at the crew house, but you remember what that was like, right? Paper thin walls, no privacy, and all the ranch hands talking behind your back as if they know your every move. The corral may be out in the open, but it's purposely a secluded place on this ranch, so at least there they shouldn't have to worry about prying eyes."

"Yeah, they should get a place of their own."

Hunter got up and pulled Grant to his feet. "Let's go ride. I wouldn't mind a little privacy out in the open air either."

—11—

RORY was sore that night when he crawled into his sleeping bag on Tim's floor. And it wasn't a pleasant kind of sore.

He'd finally agreed to try mounting the horse again and, with a little help from Tim, had managed to crawl into the saddle with the grace of a hippopotamus. Luckily Tim hadn't laughed, because Rory had felt mortified.

To calm his nerves, Tim had adjusted the stirrups to accommodate Rory's endless legs, and in doing so had let no opportunity go by to stroke Rory's thighs, calves, and lower back, to the point where Rory was getting uncomfortable from the pressure inside his jeans. Of course Tim explained all this was necessary to teach Rory how to sit properly on the horse, and Rory wasn't about to stop him, because it simply felt too good. Even the slow trotting around the corral and the subsequent relaxing walk on horseback around the immediate vicinity didn't help Rory's pressing hard-on or his raging libido. Every time he looked at Tim and his radiant smile, the lust boiled up again.

It hadn't taken much persuasion to get Tim interested in a repeat of their interaction at the back door of the club. Once the horses were taken care of, they'd brought each other off, fully clothed, against the wall of Chase's stall. It had relieved some of the tension, but as two more hours of frantic mucking out had proven to Rory, he wanted more. He wanted all of Tim, wanted to run his hands over Tim's naked skin and bulging muscles and wanted Tim to ravage him, fuck him, possess him.

Tim seemed to feel differently, though.

When Tim arrived at his room, Rory was already in his sleeping bag, and Tim acted like every night, getting undressed without flaunting it and then crawling under the covers.

Rory bit the inside of his cheek and wondered why the hell he'd resisted jacking off in the shower. At least then he would have been able to sleep.

When Tim turned off the light, Rory rolled away from him and tried to relax.

"You awake, Rory?"

At first Rory didn't want to answer. Maybe he should just pretend to be asleep. He didn't feel like talking anyway.

"This is silly, Grumpy."

The use of his new nickname made Rory smile, and he was glad it was too dark for Tim to see him.

"Get off the floor and crawl into bed with me. Nothing has to happen. I promise I'll be the perfect gentleman and won't ravage you in the middle of the night, no matter how much I want to."

"What are you saying?" Rory asked after a long silence.

Tim's answer held no hesitation. "It feels sort of weird that you're sleeping on the floor when I have a big enough bed to accommodate both of us. Surely this bed is warmer and more comfortable than the floor?"

Rory wanted to. Of course he did. But Tim invited him to sleep, and he didn't know if he'd be able to control himself in his current state if he could feel Tim's warmth and smell Tim's scent next to him.

"Stop overthinking it, Grumpy. It's just a warmer place to sleep."

Rory thought Tim sounded sleepy already. Or maybe it was his way of sounding seductive. In any case, it was working.

Rory crawled out of his sleeping bag. His eyes had adjusted to the dark enough for him to see Tim holding up the blankets so he could crawl under them. When Rory did, Tim's hand brushed over his stomach, and despite the thick cotton of his T-shirt, the warmth of Tim's hand made his muscles flutter. He swallowed hard and couldn't stop himself staring at Tim as he tried to relax on the bed. Not while Tim was staring back and slowly moving his hand over Rory's covered chest.

They didn't speak, and the tension was almost unbearable. Then Tim scooted a little closer, aligned himself at Rory's side, and nuzzled Rory's temple. Rory swallowed hard in an attempt to keep some semblance of control.

"I'm sorry," Tim whispered. "I know I promised to be a gentleman, but I don't know if I can deliver."

"I don't want you to," Rory answered, this time without hesitation. "I don't want you to be a gentleman." He turned toward Tim and kissed him, trying to convey how much he wanted to do this. Rory was sure the message would come across. He was rock hard and couldn't prevent his body from seeking friction against Tim's equally hard frame. At the same time, he wanted to touch Tim's naked skin, taste it with his mouth. He remembered from the bar that Tim like to get sucked off, so as he pushed Tim's T-shirt up, he pulled his lips away from Tim's and bent down to lick the exposed skin.

Tim gasped, and Rory stopped as soon as he realized they could be heard.

"What's wrong?" Tim asked. "Do you want to stop?"

"They'll hear you and know what we're doing."

Tim smiled. "We're allowed to bring people to our rooms. This isn't a college dorm or something." When Rory stayed quiet, Tim continued, "Most of the guys bring girls home at some point during the weekend. Some of them have a woman living here almost permanently. You've heard them at night, right?"

Rory nodded. "But it's usually the women moaning."

"The men groan too."

Rory didn't want to go into it. He felt awkward about the noises. It brought him right back to prison, and the last thing he wanted to think about when he was in bed with Tim was what it was like there, so he pulled his T-shirt over his head and dove down to take Tim's cock in his mouth, silencing Tim until he started moaning again. Rory could tell he was holding back, trying to keep the noises low, and suddenly it seemed silly. He sucked harder, using his hand to rub over the shaft and his tongue to swirl around the head, letting the tip of his tongue tickle the slit to taste the cream already leaking out. Rory liked giving head, liked the taste of it and the power it gave him. Even more than when he was letting a man fuck him, *he* was in control of the man's pleasure, and he enjoyed that feeling.

Suddenly Rory felt Tim's hand on his head. Reflexively, he pulled away from the touch, afraid Tim would push his head down.

When Rory looked up, Tim was smiling. "You almost made me come." He pushed himself to sit upright and took off his T-shirt. "Come here." Tim invitingly held out his hand.

Rory crawled higher and let Tim pull him closer. It felt very intimate as Tim wrapped his arm around Rory and kissed him. Tim's free hand caressed Rory's naked skin, and it made Rory shiver, so Tim pulled the covers around them. "Cold?"

Rory shook his head. It felt awkward to lie down inside Tim's tender embrace. It wasn't something Rory was used to. He didn't know how to act, so he leaned over Tim and kissed him.

As their exchange became more passionate, Tim pulled away. "Easy, take your time."

Rory shook his head. He wanted Tim and didn't know any other way to tell him. "Do you have condoms?" Tim nodded. "Then fuck me. I want you to." Rory couldn't keep looking at Tim, so he got up on all fours, pulled his boxers down, and focused his eyes on the old-fashioned carved wood backboard of the bed. At first Tim didn't move, but then Rory heard him open his bedside drawer and take stuff out. It was too dark to see what, but Rory had a pretty good idea. Ever since that time at the bar, Rory had wanted this, had wanted Tim to be the one fucking him. Now it was finally going to happen. He just hoped he could still look Tim in the eye later.

The lube was cold, and Rory expected the touch to be cursory and quick. Instead, Tim took his time, and Rory had to bite back the urge to tell Tim to get a move on. Instead of being lubed up just to facilitate the entry, this was definitely something more. This was meant for enjoyment, and Rory lowered his head into his hands to hide the emotions he was sure would be all over his face. It was also an effective way to mute any sounds bubbling up from his chest. Rory never had a lot of trouble keeping the sounds in, but this was different. The casual brush of Tim's finger over the sensitive spot inside him almost made him gasp. Despite his restraint, Rory knew his body betrayed him, and the repeat of Tim's actions made that clear to him. It was just a matter of time before he'd lose it.

"Tim, please," Rory begged as quietly as he could.

"What?" Tim asked in an almost normal voice.

"Fuck me already," Rory whispered. He heard the ripping of the condom and Tim's soft sigh as he rolled it on. He felt the pressure as Tim softly pushed against him, and he pushed back until he felt Tim slip inside him. Almost immediately, Tim wrapped an arm around Rory's chest.

"I'm sorry, I couldn't hold back. You feel so good."

Rory smiled. "You feel better," he whispered. "Come on, show me what you got."

Tim's movements were restrained, careful, maybe even a little hesitant. As soon as Rory realized he wasn't going to be fucked into the mattress, he reached back to touch Tim and urge him on. Tim seemed to understand as he upped the tempo.

Pretty soon they were moving in unison, and Rory tried not to be too distracted by Tim's noises. It wasn't that he didn't enjoy hearing how Tim couldn't hold back the grunts. It just brought back memories of prison, of men rutting against each other, of sex that was not always consensual. He'd learned to make do, to enjoy the fact he actually liked having a cock buried in his ass as opposed to the men who didn't but let others do it anyway in order to get protection.

Rory shook his head, trying to make the memories stop. He didn't want to make do. He wanted to enjoy it. This time the cock plowing into him belonged to Tim. Sweet, loving, caring, smiling Tim, who was clinging to him, kissing his shoulder, and making him feel so good.

As Tim's thrusts became more powerful, Rory raised his arms to the headboard, bracing himself and pushing back at the same time. Tim was still leaning over him, warming his back, moaning into his ear, and puffing against his neck, and it was turning Rory on like nothing else. Little by little he retreated into his little cocoon, the one he was so used to creating for himself, only now, this secret place included Tim, and Rory had no intention of shutting him out. Tim consistently hit all the right spots, and even as his rhythm started to falter, the heat rose steadily inside Rory until he couldn't hold back anymore. It only took a fleeting touch of Tim's hand brushing over the head of Rory's cock to send Rory over. He bit into his hand to stifle the noise but almost broke skin. Tim followed close behind, his deep grunt signaling his climax before he collapsed on top of Rory, pushing both of them into the mattress.

They lay panting for several minutes. Rory enjoyed the warmth and heaviness of Tim's bulky frame on top of him and felt safe, cradled. After a while, the fact he was lying on top of Tim's hand became uncomfortable, and it only took a small shift for Tim to slip out of him.

"Hang on, almost lost the condom," Tim murmured, retracting his hand and reaching between them to take care of everything.

As Tim got up from the bed, Rory could see his gait wasn't entirely steady. He returned moments later with a washcloth he'd wet at the small washbasin behind the wardrobe, but by that time Rory was sitting on the edge of the bed, getting ready to crawl back into his sleeping bag.

"Stay here," Tim whispered in Rory's ear after sitting down next to him and handing him the washcloth. "My bed's warmer."

Rory didn't know what to say. He wasn't used to the cuddling, the sleeping together. Part of him wanted to, but another part just wanted to hide away in his sleeping bag.

"Please, Rory."

Rory dared to look at Tim's face, and what little he saw of it in the pale light shining around the curtains was all good. Tim's expression was soft, caring, seductive even. He was leaning against him and kissing his ear, and Rory felt all warm inside. As foreign as the idea was to Rory, Tim obviously wanted him to sleep beside him.

"Okay," Rory said with a croak in his voice. They crawled under the covers, and Tim wasn't too hesitant to lead Rory's arm around his shoulder so he could settle lying against Rory. For a long time, Rory stayed awake as Tim's soft kisses against his temple stopped and Tim became heavier in his arms, as his breathing became shallow. It was almost morning when Rory fell asleep himself, still unable to fathom how many feelings Tim had awakened in him.

—12—

RORY woke up just before daybreak. He didn't feel like he'd slept at all, but he didn't mind, because every time he inhaled, he caught Tim's scent. They were still entangled, naked as the day they were born, and huddled under warm blankets. Tim was sound asleep and snoring lightly. Rory couldn't resist smiling. The only time he'd ever slept close to another man was to keep warm, and then the snoring was annoying, but now it made Rory feel connected to Tim. The room was cold, but under the blankets it was positively scorching, so it didn't matter that they were naked. Rory wondered why he never knew how amazing it felt to lie skin to skin.

The feeling of bliss didn't last long. A piercing flash, lighting up the entire room, immediately followed by loud thunderous rumbling, made Rory take notice of the rain outside. He listened to it for a moment or two and then slowly tried to disentangle himself from Tim's embrace. Although Tim was still sound asleep, his grip on Rory was tight, and Rory was afraid he was going to have to wake his lover up, so he easily relented and went back to enjoying Tim's closeness.

"Tim, wake up," Rory whispered when he heard knocking on the door. He didn't dare answer it himself since he was afraid it would give away too much.

Tim lazily opened his eyes only just enough to look at Rory in the dim light of his room, aided by the occasional lightning strike.

The next voice came from outside the door. "Wake up, Tim. I know I can fire up a cannon next to your bed, but since you have a roommate I'm not risking barging in there."

"Hugh!" Rory said in a voice as subdued as he could manage. He shook Tim for greater effect.

"All right, I'll be right there," Tim croaked as he got up to sit on the edge of the bed. He looked at his naked body and sighed, then wiped the sleep from his face with his hand before grabbing his jeans from the chair next to the window and putting them on. Rory noticed Tim looking at him briefly, probably to check whether he was decent, before going to the door and opening it just a bit while Rory scrambled out of bed, afraid to be caught by Hugh.

"It's raining cats and dogs, and the ground is so dry the water is streaming down the mountain. We need to get about thirty horses away from the valley meadow in case we get a flash flood," Hugh announced.

Tim nodded and started closing the door. Hugh's hand snuck inside to hold the door open. "Wake Rory up as well. If any horses get into trouble, we'll need someone who can take care of them while we get the others away from danger."

As soon as Tim had closed the door, Rory started dressing. They didn't speak until they were both kitted out to leave the room and start work.

"Hugh knows," Rory stated quietly.

"He doesn't care," Tim was quick to reply. "Correction. He does care. He's my brother. Of course he cares, but only because he wants me to be happy."

Rory wanted to ask Tim whether he was happy but didn't dare. Instead he called his name and made Tim look at him. "Be careful out there, okay? It sounds like it's storming pretty badly."

Tim smiled, and Rory was somewhat reassured. "Nothing we haven't dealt with before. I just hope we don't lose any horses."

"Or wranglers," Rory added.

Tim winked at him. "As long as the ranch hands don't get in the way, we'll be fine."

Rory wanted to give Tim a hug, but Tim was holding the door open for them to leave the room, and that would put them out into the busy hallway where other ranch hands were getting ready to walk out and help as well, so Rory just threw Tim a half smile and walked past him to the stairwell.

Once outside, the full impact of the storm was visible. What had been a quiet, sunny meadow yesterday was now a field strewn with broken-off branches. Heaps of leaves had been blown against anything in the way of the fiercely cold wind blowing over the unprotected range. Rory followed the wranglers into the horse stables and helped them saddle their horses. He lost sight of Tim almost immediately, but there was enough work to be done, even once all the riders had left. Most of the other ranch hands started their morning chores, but Rory figured there were more urgent matters to attend to first. On the tour Rory had been given his first day, Tim had shown him a large barn that was mostly unused, except for Bernie's dressage practice. It had a dirt floor and enough light to take a decent look at any horses brought in with injuries. Rory figured this barn had been used for such purposes before, so he started moving some of the extra bales of straw there. Coop Nelson caught him and obviously thought it was a good idea since he helped him to load and unload them. Despite the fact Coop had been a lawyer in a previous life, he was a man of few words, which Rory didn't mind.

Once the barn was more or less kitted out, Rory ran through the gusty wind to the main homestead and knocked on the kitchen door.

"Rory, come on in!" Christy said, gesturing at Rory to urge him inside. "The weather's hideous. You're soaked."

"Yeah, and I've been inside getting the barn ready. I can only imagine what it must be like for the guys out there in this rain."

"Sit," she commanded, pulling out a chair. "I'll get you some coffee."

Rory didn't sit down. In fact, he didn't move from the mat near the door, because he didn't want to drip all over the kitchen floor. He just took off his cap and ran his hand through his wet hair. "I can't. I have to go back to work, but I was wondering, since the guys all left before breakfast, if you could make sandwiches for them, and maybe coffee too, so when they come back with the horses, they could grab a quick bite to eat."

Christy didn't reply immediately. She just smiled enigmatically, making Rory uncomfortable. "That's very thoughtful of you, Rory," she said eventually.

Rory had the distinct impression she had wanted to say something else but had chosen the more polite reply. He didn't know how to react, so he just remained standing near the door when Beth, Hunter's mother, walked in.

"How's it going out there?" Beth asked Rory.

"No idea, ma'am," Rory replied, casting his eyes down. "I prepared the big barn just in case some of the horses need shelter and care."

"He came with the suggestion of making sandwiches and coffee for the men when they returned," Christy added.

"Excellent, Rory," Beth replied. "We'll get right to it. We'll give you a call when they're ready, and then you can bring some of the ranch hands to help you carry it over." She turned to the larder, and Christy smiled at Rory.

Christy started gathering bread and butter and jam. "Tim always said you were good at organizing. The guys are going to love knowing they're well taken care of."

Rory didn't know what to do with such praise, so he just stared at the table. "I better go," he said eventually.

"Rory?"

Rory looked up at Christy's kind face. "You haven't had breakfast either, have you?" She didn't wait for an answer. Instead she put a good smear of jam on a piece of bread and added another on top before giving it to Rory. "You can eat it on the way to the barn. At least you won't keel over before you get there."

"Thanks, ma'am," Rory said, accepting the gift.

"Christy."

"Christy," Rory replied with a shy smile. He put his cap back on his head and bit into the bread before nodding at Christy and walking outside.

Rory ran through the flood of rain, trying to keep his sandwich dry. He hadn't realized how famished he was until he started eating; by the time he reached the foaling stables, he'd finished his bread. When he returned to the big barn about thirty minutes later, Christy was there setting up a table with food.

"I thought you were going to call me to help?" he asked Christy, looking at everything she'd whipped up in such a short time span. There were stacks of sandwiches, all neatly buttered, with egg and cheese and ham, and there were thermoses of coffee and tea and a basket of apples, oranges, bananas, and bars of chocolate.

"Go ahead. Grab one," Christy said, pointing at the chocolate and ignoring Rory's question. When Rory didn't immediately take her up on it, she grabbed a bar of dark chocolate and gave it to him. "This is Tim's favorite." She rummaged through the rest. "You look more like the nutty type." She handed him a mixed nut bar. "Unless I'm wrong?"

Rory smiled. "As long as it's sweet and melts in my mouth, I'm good."

Christy smiled warmly. "I'll have to remember that!"

At that moment the big door rolled open and Coop walked in, closely followed by two more ranch hands. "They're on their way with two horses and a foal they rescued from a bog. No idea what state they're in."

Moments later the barn door opened again and two unsaddled horses stormed in, veering off in different directions. Coop and the other ranch hands tried to direct them to run into the makeshift stalls Rory had built out of bales of straw so they could calm down and the men could rub them dry.

Rory waited for the foal, knowing Tim would be taking care of the little one. He pulled some straw out of the bale and started rolling it up, just to have something to do. When the doors opened again, it was to let Grant and Hugh come inside. Rory looked at them expectantly as they dismounted.

"All the horses safe?" Rory asked Grant with some apprehension.

Grant didn't answer. "Tim not back yet?"

"Maybe he's had to carry the foal?" Hunter suggested, joining them.

"Guys," Rory intervened, "he's a strong guy, but even he can't carry a one-year-old."

"Wasn't a one-year-old," Hunter answered. "It was one of the last foals. Practically a newborn. Don't know how it got out there. It's supposed to be with its mother. It's still suckling, for heaven's sake. I just got back from seeing a frantic mare in the foaling stalls."

Rory's mind raced. Had he forgotten to close the barn door? Had he left a half door to a stall open? He admitted to being a little careless with the wrangler's horses because they never ran anywhere, but he knew to be careful with the foals because new mothers tended to be easily spooked, and the foals followed them everywhere. That's how little ones got into trouble.

Rory looked at the two dripping cowboys and their semi-dry boss and knew he had to go look for Tim, so he ignored the fact he was only wearing a worn-out fleece jacket that sucked up every raindrop and ran outside. The weather was even worse than when he came into the barn. The wind was sweeping the rain into his face, and he could barely see in front of him. Although it was supposed to be daytime by now, it looked like dusk. All Rory could think about was that Tim was out there alone and that he was most likely to blame. If he'd been more careful, Tim would have returned with Hunter and Grant.

Time seemed to last forever as Rory continued his frantic search for Tim. He had no idea where to look but knew he couldn't give up. Purely by chance, as he rounded one of the outer barns and the wind stopped blowing for just a moment, he saw a dark form stumbling, and he ran to it.

"Tim?"

Tim nodded, resting his hand on Rory's shoulder so he could get up. He said something that Rory couldn't make out, so Rory dragged him behind the barn and out of the wind.

"Need a blanket. Can't carry the foal anymore." Tim repeated. "Had to leave it behind."

"It's alive?"

Tim nodded again, clearly trying to preserve his breath. "But we need to be quick."

Rory lifted Tim's arm around his shoulders and supported him back to the big barn. As soon as they entered, Hugh and Grant ran to them.

"The foal?" Hugh asked Tim rather gruffly, Rory felt.

"Alive, but barely. Need a blanket to transport it. It's barely moving, but I can't carry it all the way back here," Tim said, needing to take breaths in between talking.

"Grant and I'll go. Where is it?" Hugh asked.

"Under the thick brush at the back on the north meadow, behind the last barn. It was pretty spooked. So spooked it wouldn't move. The broken leg didn't help either."

Hugh nodded, and Rory was happy to see him smile at his brother. "We'll get it. Rory? Ask Hunter to call the vet and then get the mare in here. She'll want to see her little one."

"Tell him to be careful," Grant added. "It sounded like she was pretty rowdy."

"I'll get her," Rory offered, but Tim's hand held him back.

"Stay here. We'll get two stalls ready for them so they can see each other but not get together. The foal needs to see its dam, but putting her with an injured foal is asking for trouble."

Rory nodded, secretly happy that Tim wanted him near. "I'll just go tell Hunter."

When Rory returned from talking to Hunter, he found Tim sitting on a straw bale looking utterly exhausted. He'd taken off his duster, but his shirt was still soaked. Rory had brought some towels Hunter had given him. He handed one to Tim and then went back to get coffee. He wanted to pull Tim close and tell him how glad he was that he was okay, but he settled for crouching in front of him to hand him the cup.

"The two horses seem fine. They've been rubbed dry and they've had water to drink. Now take care of yourself before they get back with the foal."

Tim threw Rory a questioning look, but it turned into a faint smile soon enough. "Thanks."

Rory smiled back, rubbing Tim's thigh. As soon as Tim rested his hand over Rory's, Rory withdrew it. He wanted to confess that it was his fault the foal got out, but couldn't. He didn't want to see Tim's face when Tim realized how unfit Rory was for working the ranch. Rory noticed Tim reaching out for him, but he let his hand grasp thin air. Luckily, at that moment the barn door rolled open and wind and rain swept in, closely followed by Grant and Hugh carrying an eerily still foal on a blanket between them.

"Is he still…." Tim asked, veering up from where he was sitting as if he'd caught his second wind.

The other men knew what he meant. "He's alive," Hugh replied. "But very cold and paralyzed with pain. Bill here yet?"

"No," Hunter answered, running in from the other side of the barn. "He's been called elsewhere. Seems there are more ranches with animals in trouble."

"I'll splint the leg," Tim offered. "Keep it safe until Bill can set it. Foal's quiet now anyway. As soon as it warms up, it'll try to get up, and we'll need to make sure it doesn't harm itself then."

Hugh nodded, giving his baby brother an encouraging pat on the shoulder. "So you have a stall made up for this one? Where we can also bring the mother in?"

"This way," Rory replied. "It's just bales of straw so they can't hurt themselves. They'll be able to look at each other, but not get together."

"Good thinking, Rory," Hugh said, grabbing the blanket and looking at Grant to coordinate their movements. The encouragement from Hugh helped Rory set aside his feelings of self-doubt, and he followed the men into the makeshift stall, keeping his eye on Tim.

—13—

TIM was drained, cold, and wet. The last two could be remedied by a nice hot shower, but he knew he had work to do.

The makeshift stall looked nice, and Tim couldn't help but smile, thinking Rory was responsible for all the work in the barn. He was a fine ranch hand, and Tim didn't doubt he'd make a fine wrangler too. Whether that meant Rory had found his niche and would stay beyond the terms of his parole was another thing, but Tim knew he'd deal with it when the time came. There was no use fretting over something he couldn't possibly know about right now; besides, he was too tired to do much thinking. The horses in the threatened meadow were safe, and they'd found the three strays who had broken loose because of the violence of the thunderstorm, so all was well. Tim had no idea what time it was, though. He only knew he was famished, but that it would have to wait until the foal was out of the woods.

When he walked into the stall, Hunter arrived with the medical kit, which was a large box full of everything Tim used in the foaling stable and then some. Grant and Hugh were sitting around the foal, rubbing it dry with soft, gentle strokes, using rolled up straw covered in rags to make it softer. The foal wasn't even quivering. It lay still, its breathing barely visible.

"Will it be okay?" Rory whispered just behind Tim.

"I don't know," Tim replied equally softly. Tim sat down nearest the foal's injured leg and took it in his hand. He felt along the leg, pressing it at regular intervals to try and find the break site. "It's broken through the growth plate."

"Is that good or bad?" Rory asked, crouching down next to Tim.

"Could go either way. If we can keep the foal calm and it can rest enough then it should heal. If it flails around too much waking up, the break could shift, and they usually don't operate because it could damage the growth plate and then he'd end up with a shorter leg. Then we might still have to put it down." Tim looked up at Rory as he felt Rory's hand on his shoulder and saw the worried look on his face. "Time will tell. We have to get him warmed up first and then hope his lungs hold out. That's no weather for a three-month-old."

"So what can I do?" Rory asked.

"Hand me the swaddling there," Tim asked, pointing at the box.

"You should have been a vet," Rory said, smiling kindly as he handed Tim the rolled up bandage.

Tim shrugged. "I don't have a head for books. Besides, I'd never have wanted to be away from the ranch for so long. Jack did the studying for all of us." He looked at Hugh, who nodded.

"Did Jack teach you how to do this?" Rory asked while he held up the foal's leg so Tim could wrap it up.

"I watched the vets do it. This isn't the first foal to come up lame. Sometimes they get kicked at by older foals or other breeding mares. Sometimes when the dam's inexperienced she gets nervous around her foal and hurts it that way. We see a bit of all that. Sometimes when the foal's badly injured we need to wean it, but this little colt is too young." Tim finished the bandage. He looked up as Hunter brought the clearly excited mare into the next-door stall.

"So we bring the mare in here?"

"Not until the colt is better. We'll probably have to milk her," Tim said. "You want to try it?"

Rory threw him a stunned look. "No, thank you!"

Tim chuckled as he continued gently rubbing the colt. "Don't worry. It takes practice to get the hang of it. You take my place with the little one and I'll milk the dam." Tim heard Hunter trying to soothe the mare by talking to her quietly. She was snorting and stomping, though. Although the colt had been eerily quiet until now, he now seemed to react to his dam's presence. His eyes seemed to look for her and his ears were moving as well. "Try to prevent him from getting up," Tim instructed Rory. "But don't injure yourself."

Rory took Tim's place, soothing the colt while Tim went to where Hunter was trying to keep the mare in check. When Tim arrived in the box, carrying his milking supplies, the mare was calm, and to his surprise Chase, the docile gelding Tim had used to teach Rory to ride, was in the stall with them.

"Good thinking," Tim said to Hunter. "If he can't calm down a distressed horse, nobody can."

Hunter was tying both horses close together against the side of the barn. "I figured this way I could try and make sure you don't get kicked while you milk her."

Tim smiled, crouching in what was possibly the most precarious position around an excited horse: near her back hoofs. To his surprise, once she got used to Tim's ministrations, she calmed down, and once he had a nice amount of milk, he got up and took out a bale of straw so she could look into the next stall. He admitted it was only partially for the mare's benefit. Tim wanted to make sure Rory was doing okay with the colt.

When the mare whinnied, the foal lifted its head, and Tim knew he'd be ready to drink.

It was still a bit of a struggle to get the little colt to drink from the teat, but once he got the hang of it, he drank until he was too tired to drink any more.

"So this is good, right?" Rory asked hesitantly, still gently rubbing the colt's belly.

"Yeah, but I'll have to keep vigil. A lot of things can still go wrong. But Mom next door has company, and I'll stay here with the colt."

"I'll stay with you," Rory said.

"You better go to the crew house and get some food."

Tim watched Rory retreat reluctantly. The colt was quietly sleeping, and Tim hoped his mother's milk would be enough to rehydrate him for now. Occasionally he'd see the dam's head pop over the wall of bales, and he'd click his tongue at her to reassure her. It wasn't until now that he realized how tired and hungry he was. He rested his head against the wall behind him.

"Bologna or strawberry jelly?"

Tim opened his eyes and saw Rory standing over him, brandishing a paper plate with sandwiches. "There wasn't much variety left and I didn't want to ask Christy for more. She did so much work for the wranglers today."

Tim smiled. "Right now I could eat just about anything." He took the top sandwich and bit into it. To his surprise when Rory's other hand appeared from behind his back, it was filled by a shiny canister. "Coffee, too?"

Rory smiled. "Figured you'd need rehydrating about as much as the colt." He took the cup off the top and filled it with steaming liquid. "Here." He handed the cup to Tim and put the plate on Tim's lap.

"What about you?" Tim asked.

"I only have two hands. I have to go back for my food."

"No, stay, Rory. We can share." He scooted a little closer to the colt so there was space for Rory to sit between Tim and the bales of straw. Tim was too tired to try to interpret the insecurity in Rory's face. He just wanted Rory close, wanted to feel his warmth next to him and his scent under his nose.

Rory sat down and leaned against Tim, so Tim pulled him close. "So, bologna or jelly?"

"You know I have a sweet tooth," Rory said quietly. Tim handed him the next sandwich, which had red edges from where the strawberry jam had soaked into the bread.

"Thirsty?"

Rory nodded.

Tim offered him his cup. "You can put sugar in if you want."

Rory drank a big gulp and then handed it back. "'S okay. Bread is already sweet."

They ate in silence for a little while. Tim felt very relaxed sitting there with the sleeping colt on one side and Rory on the other. Somewhere around the time they finished the food, Tim pulled off Rory's cap and kissed his hair, inhaling Rory's scent of rain and sweat. "Want to stay here and keep vigil tonight?"

Rory didn't answer right away.

"I'd like you to," he murmured against Rory's scalp. "We can get some blankets and some more bedding straw."

"Somebody will see us if we fall asleep here," Rory said, but Tim didn't think it sounded like Rory was going to refuse.

"Hunter or Grant will check in on us. Maybe Hugh or Izzie. They all know anyway." Tim kissed Rory's temple again, and this time Rory leaned back and offered his mouth. It was a sweet kiss, and Rory tasted of strawberries.

"But what if it's Johnny?"

Tim knew if anyone ever mocked their bosses' relationship it was Johnny, so his finding out that he and Rory where sleeping together would probably be worse, since Tim wasn't the one signing the paychecks. He wasn't going to hide for Johnny's sake, though. He'd never been terribly open about being gay, not even after it became clear that Grant and Hunter were an item, but then, he'd never felt any need to be. Now that he had Rory to think of, he found he didn't want to circumnavigate the subject anymore. "I think we can handle Johnny," Tim said after a long pause. "The last thing he can get away with at this ranch is being a homophobe. He's entitled to an opinion, but he'll find few people sharing it here."

Rory nodded but didn't say anything. He didn't move away from Tim either, so Tim contented himself with that one small victory.

—14—

TIM and Rory were just unsaddling their horses after a short riding exercise when Hugh walked into the stable.

"You two, we need you at the house." He was gone before they could ask why.

Rory looked at Tim and Tim shrugged. "Don't look at me. I didn't do anything."

"You think they saw us, you know… together?" Rory asked.

Tim raised an eyebrow. "They might have, in the barn when we were looking after the colt, but Grant and Hunter wouldn't make a big deal out of it. The worst I'd expect is for Hunter to tell us to tone it down in public, but it would surprise me if that's what warranted a summons to the big house." Tim could tell Rory wasn't completely at ease, but since he didn't know what was going on any more than Rory did, all he could do was tell himself it was probably nothing bad. "I'm sure it's nothing, Rory. Don't worry."

They finished with the horses, washed their hands and faces, and walked together toward the biggest of the houses. Tim noticed Rory's unease because Rory looked at him every five steps or so. The closest he could get to comforting his man was by touching his shoulder as they walked up the steps to the main house.

Everyone was in the sitting room, it seemed, but there was one man Tim didn't recognize.

Hunter got up from his seat. "Come in, guys. This is Mr. Emmanuel. He looked into Old Mac's estate for us. Apparently Mac left a will."

"I didn't even know he owned anything," Tim said before walking to the notary to shake his hand.

"Are you Mr. McCown?" Mr. Emmanuel asked.

Tim shook his head. "I'm Tim Conroy." He gestured at Rory. "This is Rory McCown."

"Just the two men we need."

Tim and Rory sat down on the sofa, neither of them relaxed enough to sit back.

"As you may have gathered, Mr. Mackenzie left a will. In fact he left two, but only one of them is legal. He didn't own much, but in his possession was a cabin situated on Mr. Krause's land. The actual land it is sitting on of course comes with the cabin, but everything surrounding it is legally Mr. Krause's. Now about that cabin. Mr. Krause found scribbled notes in what was left of Mr. Mackenzie's possessions asking that upon his death, the cabin should be handed over to Mr. Tim Conroy and Mr. Rory McCown, shared equally among them."

Tim looked at Rory with big eyes, and Rory, barely noticeably, shook his head.

"However, this document is not legal, because it was not signed by witnesses. Mr. Krause asked us to look into a real will and we found one, filed with the county clerk's office. It's about fifteen years old and states that the cabin should go to Mr. Tim Conroy. I'm sorry, Mr. McCown."

Rory shook his head more clearly now. "I wouldn't know what to do with it anyway."

The man turned to Tim. "Mr. Conroy, with your permission, I'll draw up the papers, and all you need to do is pick them up from the county clerk's office and the cabin is yours."

"Ehm, yeah, sure."

They all shook hands, and Mr. Emmanuel left after being seen out by Hunter.

"Congratulations, Tim," Grant said. "Now you and Rory have a place of your own."

"Yeah, I suppose we do. But as I recall, the cabin is barely standing."

Grant nodded. "Hunter and I checked it out after we found the scribbled notes. It's truly a cabin. Three rooms and an outhouse, that's all. No running water or other plumbing, and no heating except for a fireplace in the living room and one in what I suppose was a bedroom."

"Sounds like paradise," Tim sighed sarcastically. "I think we'll stay at the crew house for the time being."

Hunter joined them again. "It needs work, but we'll help out." He put his hand on Grant's shoulder. "We haven't forgotten all the work you did at our house. We'll gladly chip in—put in a pump for the well so you have running water. And a hot water boiler. And a toilet instead of a plank with a hole in it. The back room has this antique bath on legs in it. Needs a good cleaning, but I'm sure it'll be useful."

"The walls are sturdy," Grant continued. "But the roof leaks like a sieve and there's debris everywhere."

"I suppose we could work on it in our spare time," Tim said, looking at Rory but not getting much of anything in the form of a reaction. "It's not like we don't have a place to stay already. There's no rush." That seemed to relax Rory somewhat, and Tim wondered if the idea of living together really freaked Rory out so much. Maybe he was getting ahead of himself. After all, they were only living together in his room out of necessity and had only fucked once, so it wasn't like they were planning a wedding yet.

At that moment, the doorbell rang. Since Tim and Rory were about to leave anyway, they all filed into the hallway. When Grant opened the door, Mr. Emmanuel was standing on the porch, soaking wet.

"I'm sorry to bother you, but it started raining, and I can't get my car started."

"I'll call the garage for you," Hunter suggested, gesturing for the man to take shelter inside the house again.

"If you want, I can take a look at it," Rory suggested out of the blue. Everyone looked at him at once. "Might be something minor, since he drove his car up here this afternoon. Would save him a lot of money if he could drive it to the garage instead of getting the tow truck out here."

"Sure," Hunter replied. "Do you know anything about cars?"

Rory nodded. "Worked in a garage in Georgia for a while before heading out here." He pointed at his cap. "I liked it."

"Let's go see what can be done, then."

Since it was raining cats and dogs, Hunter, Grant, and Tim stayed on the porch to watch as Rory and Mr. Emmanuel walked over to the car. It didn't take Rory long to figure out that water had gotten a little too friendly with the spark plugs, and after wiping them off with a cloth, the car started like nothing had happened.

"I'd get it looked at by a garage, sir," Rory suggested. "There's a slight crack in your distributor cap, and it's going to give you grief soon."

"Well, thanks, young man," Mr. Emmanuel said. He took out his wallet and gave Rory ten dollars.

Rory took it and put it in his back pocket. "You're welcome."

Soaked by the rain, Rory returned to the porch. "You staying for dinner?" Hunter asked.

Tim looked at Rory, who shook his head.

"There's soccer on cable tonight. Hunter and I are watching. You're welcome to stay," Grant added.

This seemed to sway Rory. "I don't want to be a burden."

"There's plenty of food, and you can explain the rules of soccer to us later," Hunter said directly to Rory.

"Well, if it's not too much trouble…."

Tim nodded a silent "thank you" at Grant. He'd asked Grant and Hunter shortly after Rory's return whether they'd be allowed to watch a soccer game on cable sometime, since they didn't show any soccer on the regular sports channels, and Rory had told him he was a fan. Now he was going to find out what the big deal was and possibly see Rory happy about something. And Tim would do just about anything to make his man happy.

Grant and Hunter went inside, but Tim stayed outside with Rory. "I didn't know you knew your way around cars."

"It's been a long time."

"You should get your driver's license back. We could use a good mechanic here. Right now we need to call the guy from the garage in town to help us out whenever one of the trucks gives us grief."

"I'm not a good mechanic. I just sort of know my way around a combustion engine, that's all. And it's been a long time. Cars have changed."

Tim put his arm around Rory's shoulders, ignoring the dampness seeping through the fabric of his shirt. "It doesn't matter. Like you said, if we can get the car to start so we can drive it into town, we don't need to pay the tow truck. Besides, you can learn on the job. And it would give you credit with the other ranch hands. Get them to see you in a better light."

Rory nodded, but Tim figured it was just so he would stop talking about it. Tim hoped it would lighten Rory's mood, but it didn't seem to. Rory stayed quiet all through dinner, though Tim figured it was just too rowdy for him, with all the kids running around and the adults talking across the table in multiple conversations at once.

After dinner, in the living room in front of the TV, it was just the two of them and Hunter and Grant. Rory seemed to relax a little, although the conversation still felt a little forced. Once the game started, the atmosphere cleared, and not even Hugh entering with beers changed that, although Tim knew Hugh wasn't Rory's biggest supporter.

"So who's playing?" Hugh asked, passing the beers around.

"Barcelona against Real," Rory answered.

"Never heard of them. Are they any good?"

"The best. They're the teams who always compete for the top spot in the Primera Division in Spain."

"Ah, Spain. I see."

Tim shot his older brother a warning look.

"What? I'm sorry I'm not up-to-date with the latest Spanish soccer."

"Hugh, stop it," Tim cautioned.

Rory pretended not to notice and kept his eyes on the screen. Tim figured that was probably the safest way to behave. In the meantime he was mad at his brother, who luckily didn't stay around. Hugh retreated to the kitchen, and Tim followed.

"What was that all about?" Tim hissed as soon as the door closed behind him.

"What?" Hugh asked innocently.

"Your tone. And your attitude."

Hugh opened the fridge, took out another beer, and closed it again. "I was just asking what you were watching. It's not exactly an everyday occurrence to walk into the living room and find a bunch of men watching sports. In case you haven't noticed, it's pretty much a woman's domain in here."

"What I've noticed is that you don't like Rory and you know we're in there watching soccer because of him," Tim replied, grabbing onto the kitchen counter to keep himself under control.

"Get that chip off your shoulder, Tim. I know you're the savior of lost causes and Rory fits right into that image, but I have nothing against him. He's a hard worker, and as long as he pulls his weight, I don't care who fucks him."

Tim launched himself at Hugh, and despite the fact Hugh was half a head taller than him, Tim easily pushed him against the counter. "Don't talk about Rory like that," he hissed.

At that moment Hunter walked into the kitchen and stopped when he saw the brothers. "What's going on here?" he asked cautiously.

Tim stepped back and turned away from his brother, then shrugged his shirt into place. "Nothing," he dismissed.

"It's almost half-time. Why don't we move it to our house so we can finish watching the game over there? We have beer in the fridge, and that way *the women* can have this house back." It wasn't lost on Tim that Hunter directed his speech to Hugh, but it was meant for Tim to get the two to stop going at each other.

Tim was glad Hunter had diffused the tension somewhat. He knew he'd have to talk with Hugh, both because he was his brother and his foreman, but he realized the emotions ran too deep for him to be able to do it now. He threw Hugh a stern look and walked out, closely followed by Hunter.

"You okay?" Hunter asked softly as he held Tim back in the hallway.

"Yeah, sure," Tim replied, sitting down on the bench underneath the coat rack.

Hunter sat down next to him. "Hugh's just being protective of his baby brother."

"He doesn't need to be. I'm old enough to take care of myself."

"Hugh knows that too."

"Then why does he insist on giving me grief about Rory?"

Hunter smiled. "Even Hugh has to admit that Rory's doing a great job. I guess he can't forget all the horses we lost."

Tim sighed. "And you? They were your horses."

"I think it was clear at the trial who the mastermind was, and it wasn't Rory. I thought we should give Rory a second chance, and I haven't regretted it yet. Despite the fact he very much keeps to himself, he's become a part of the team. That was very clear when we rescued those horses during that flash flood. We came back to a barn that was fully kitted out for what we needed, thanks to Rory. Christy said he even thought about making sure we had food and coffee when we came in. I have to say, finding out that he knows his way around under the hood of a car is a plus as well. Not to mention that you have pretty strong feelings for him, right? Isn't he returning them?"

"That's none of your business!" Tim snapped. Then he realized what he'd just said. He and Hunter grew up together, so Hunter would cut him some slack, but he was still his boss. He leaned forward, resting his elbows on his knees. "Sorry."

Hunter smiled and rubbed his jaw. "I just want you to be happy, Tim. You've always been the glass-half-full guy. Even when the foals were disappearing, you kept saying everything was going to be all right. Now people left and right tell me they've spotted you brooding over something at odd hours of the day. There's a reason your dad always called you Sunshine, but lately there have been clouds in your sky."

Tim didn't know what to say. He'd never realized he was so transparent.

"I know what it's like to fall in love with the wrong guy, Tim. Grant wasn't exactly a prize catch either, but I can't imagine my life without him anymore. People will come around."

"Now all I need is for Rory to catch up," Tim confessed.

"So he *isn't* returning your feelings?"

"He is. Sometimes."

"Maybe you should think of him as a skittish foal. Not used to being touched. Remember Rialto's foal last year? When we lost her to colic, that little colt was totally lost. Nobody could come near it, but you managed. You spent a whole day and night in that stall with him until he'd let you come near, and then you got one of the other breeding mares to let him suckle, and then he was fine."

"I think we're a little past that stage, Hunter."

Hunter raised an eyebrow. "So he's letting you come near, then?"

Tim eyed him sideways and saw the teasing look on Hunter's face. "We're two unattached gay men sharing a room. What do you think?"

Hunter laughed. "I think you need to fix up that cabin. Soon!"

—15—

RORY sat down on the bed. Tim's bed. He still couldn't think of it as *their* bed, at least not yet. And maybe he never would. He liked Tim in it, though. Dressed in just a T-shirt and boxers, or just boxers, or, like after they had sex, in nothing but his deliciously warm, naked skin. Except after that first time, Rory had always returned to his sleeping bag. Holding Tim, feeling his shallow, sleeping breath ghost over his own naked flesh until it gave him goose bumps, was just too much. He didn't sleep when he was in Tim's bed.

He'd only ever slept with one man before. Actual sleeping, even with a little cuddling. Charlie had begged for Rory to stay with him in his officer's quarters in the compound in Iraq right after they'd lost two of their platoon in an ambush. It was the night before the last day of their tour, and neither knew if they'd ever see the other again. Charlie was going home to his family in Virginia, and Rory was due some R&R in Guam before starting his second tour. They'd fucked like crazy, and just when Rory was ready to go back to his bunk in the soldier's hangar, Charlie had asked him to stay. It was after lights out, so Rory figured nobody would notice until early the next morning at roll call. They shared a narrow bunk that night, kissing and caressing, and fucking again before Rory snuck out at dawn.

"What are you thinking about?"

Rory looked up, a little surprised that he was looking into Tim's eyes and not Charlie's.

"Charlie," Rory said, figuring honesty would get him at least some brownie points.

"Your lieutenant."

"Yes."

"Where is he now?"

"Married to his father's best friend's daughter and raising a brood in Virginia," Rory said, not hiding how he felt about that. "Like it never happened. Like I never happened."

"So what made you think of him?"

"Sitting here, on the bed. Charlie was the only man I ever slept with until… you."

"I'm flattered."

"We slept, I mean…."

"Slept. Not had sex. Get it."

Tim was sitting next to him taking off his socks, and Rory had the overwhelming urge to wrap his arms around him and squeeze him tight. He didn't, though. Instead he just sat next to him, staring at the rug on the wooden floor. He was already in his T-shirt and boxers, ready for the night, but warring with himself about where he was going to sleep. He didn't feel confident enough to crawl under Tim's blankets, despite feeling cold.

"Hey." Tim nudged his shoulder. "Do you still miss him? Charlie?"

Rory shook his head. "It was eighteen years ago. I'm over him."

"But you miss the thought of him? His touch? What you shared?"

Rory swallowed away the lump in his throat. Why the hell did Tim have to be so perceptive? "Yeah, I suppose I do."

"We had fun, didn't we?"

Although he wasn't sure if Tim was referring to the sex or the soccer game, Rory was glad for the chance to change the subject but decided to play it safe. "Yeah, Hunter and Grant are great. It was really nice of them to let me watch soccer at their house."

"You're going to have to explain the rules to me one day. I get you have to kick the ball into the other team's goal. And you're not allowed to touch the ball with your hands. Or kick an opponent. I got that when the ref pulled out that dorky red card."

Rory smiled, but more to himself than directly at Tim. "You ran off. I explained it all to Grant, and he got the hang of it pretty quickly. I explained the offside rule to him and the field positions."

"Yeah, but Grant's a man of the world, like you. Hunter and I are just some redneck hicks from Idaho."

"You're not redneck hicks," Rory replied softly. "You just have to broaden your horizons a little, that's all."

"We do? That's it?" Tim turned around and grabbed Rory around the stomach, tickling him incessantly. "And who's going to help us? You and Grant?"

Rory chuckled under the onslaught but couldn't hold back for long, not even when Tim pushed them both down on the bed and crawled over him, touching him everywhere at once. Rory wouldn't stop laughing, not even when Tim did.

"I love you, Rory McCown. Always have. From the first day you walked onto the ranch."

Rory laughed until the words sank in. Before his brain truly kicked in, Tim kissed him. Long and hard. Invasive. Tim's weight made him sink into the mattress, and he was totally relaxed from laughing so hard. Panting too, especially when Tim stopped kissing him and moved down his body, getting rid of his nightclothes with practiced ease. And then Tim stopped.

"You're uncut."

Rory pulled away from Tim and drew up his legs to hide what felt like a shameful thing. Most of the men in prison didn't care about his cock. He was a hole to fuck, nothing more. Outside of prison, with those men who did want him for his cock too, he'd gotten mixed reactions. Some were fascinated by it, some barely noticed, but most were disgusted by it. Rory wasn't sure in what category Tim would fit, but he wasn't about to find out. "Listen, never mind, okay?" He got up off the bed, but Tim pulled him back.

"What's wrong?"

Rory shook his head.

"I don't mind, Rory. I've just never... had... an uncut cock."

Rory thought Tim looked a little awkward and uncharacteristically unsure of himself, but he didn't seem disgusted, so he sat down on the bed.

"Can I look at it again?" Tim asked tentatively.

Rory closed his eyes, feeling terribly self-conscious. He hated the scrutiny, but Tim looked so adorably unsure, he couldn't help returning the look.

"Didn't mean to make you feel shy," Tim said. He put his hand on Rory's naked thigh. "It's just a little unexpected. I still want to… you know." He moved his hand up toward Rory's groin, and Rory felt his cock stir.

Rory nodded almost imperceptibly and let Tim smooth him down to the bed. Tim kissed him lightly before resuming his way down Rory's body, and although Rory was still nervous, he let Tim's soothing touches calm him. He kept telling himself Tim wanted this, that he wasn't forcing him to do anything, and that if Tim pulled away, he wouldn't die of shame. Despite all Rory's apprehensions, he was still half hard, his erection lying in the crook of his hip as Tim licked the length and then took Rory's cock in his mouth.

"Fuck, Timmy," Rory exhaled more than said. He couldn't resist looking down, watching how Tim sucked him off. When he realized Tim's fascination with his foreskin extended to playing with it with his tongue, he could feel his cock filling even more. When Tim looked up at him, Rory just had to run his hands through Tim's floppy locks, wiping them away from his eyes so he could see the enjoyment in them. Tim was smiling, and Rory couldn't hold his gaze. It felt too intimate and the pleasure was too great, so he threw his head back and pushed it into his pillow, letting the feelings of ecstasy wash over him. He didn't want to come yet, but the laughter and the feeling of total acceptance that followed had made his resistance weak, and he couldn't hold back.

When Rory opened his eyes, Tim was hovering over him. "You didn't pass out, did you?"

"No. Almost," Rory admitted. "Are you going to fuck me?"

"Can't," Tim confessed. "You tasted so delicious, you made me come too. But give me a little time to recuperate and who knows?"

Tim settled half on top of Rory, their faces close together and the blankets pulled around them. "Unless you want to sleep?"

"Not yet," Rory whispered. "Later."

THE next morning when Rory woke, Tim was gone. He washed in the crew shower downstairs and dressed before going in for breakfast, only then realizing it was already late. He hurried to the foaling stables to check up on the little colt with the broken leg and to let the few other foals out, along with their mothers.

All through his morning work, Rory caught himself smiling. He'd had a great evening and an even better night. It had been ages since he'd watched a soccer game, and watching it with guys who didn't know the first thing about the sport hadn't diminished his fun. At night, he'd realized he was starting to feel comfortable enough with Tim to sleep soundly. The trust between them was starting to build, although he couldn't imagine feeling the same security Tim obviously felt. Who would have thought? Then again, Tim was a ray of sunshine. What was not to love?

Love.

Rory hadn't felt this way for anyone since Charlie, and after that betrayal, he didn't think he'd ever lose his heart again. Now it seemed he was definitely smitten. It made his stomach clench and his skin tingle at the same time. *Shit*, he was starting to become attached to his life here, and he couldn't have that. He couldn't pin all his hopes on everything staying the way it was and living the rest of his life here with Tim. Life just never panned out that way. Not for him. That had been the story of his life, ever since that fateful night in that Georgia gas station when his mother told him to be quick in the bathroom, and he'd fumbled with the zipper on his new pants and had taken so long his mother had left without him. Of course in his head, he knew his mother hadn't left him behind because he'd taken too much time taking a leak. A man had walked into his mother's life, and that man hadn't liked the fact that Ellie May had "a runt," so the runt had to go. She'd chosen her man over her son and had left him behind for the authorities to pick him up and put him in the system.

Although he had no illusions of a better life, Rory had often wondered what it would have been like if his mother hadn't left him then. They probably would have continued living like the first six years, in her car, traveling to wherever they could whenever she had gas money. Moving from one man to another until they got tired of her, and then they'd move on. It was nowhere near perfect, but most of the men didn't give a hoot about him and left him alone as long as he kept quiet. They'd spring for the occasional burger and rarely left him hungry, so that wasn't bad. It was better than when he'd have to stay behind in the car, all by himself, when his mother would go from truck to truck to "entertain" the men driving those monsters of the road. At six, Rory hadn't understood what his mother had done until he'd found himself earning a few bucks in exactly the same way ten years later. He'd even found an old picture of his mom in one of the cabs and had swiped it when the old trucker wasn't looking. It was the only picture he had of his mother.

Rory continued sorting out the straw on the stall floor, shaking his head to dispel the thoughts. He hadn't seen his mother in almost thirty-five years. For all he knew, she was dead, and if she wasn't, it didn't make a difference. She'd probably long forgotten she had a son.

From the corner of his eye he saw movement, and before he could identify it, he was pushed against the stall division and kissed. He smiled when he tasted Tim and managed to relax.

"You know, you're lucky I'm not as sharp as I used to be," Rory said when Tim let him come up for air. "I'm a trained soldier, remember."

"That was years ago," Tim teased, stomach remaining against Rory's so he could pin him in place.

"I was holding a pitchfork, a very formidable weapon in the right hands."

Tim raised an eyebrow and smiled, taking the "weapon" Rory was still holding from his hand and throwing it on the floor. "I just disarmed you, and I never saw an army barracks up close."

Rory looked Tim in the eye, and Tim stopped smiling. "You were so serious."

"Always am when I'm working," Rory replied, hoping Tim wouldn't ask him what he was thinking about. Tim wiped a strand of hair out of his eyes, and Rory leaned into the tender touch, craving its warmth and comfort.

"Why don't we take the afternoon off and go for a drive? Just you and me."

"I have work to do and so do you," Rory protested, although it wasn't wholeheartedly.

"Just for an hour or two. It's not that busy, and we can catch up afterward." Tim leaned closer so he could whisper in Rory's ear. "I just want you all to myself for a little while."

Rory could feel his body reacting to Tim's words, his tender touches, and his insistence. He always liked a man who knew what he wanted. "If you're sure?"

Tim nodded and kissed Rory quickly before pulling away. "Now I better get a move on. I'll pick you up around three at the crew house?"

Rory nodded and picked up his pitchfork to continue what he was doing before he was interrupted.

NERVOUS as he was, Rory had showered and dressed in clean clothes by the time Tim parked his truck in front of the crew house.

"Give me five minutes, okay?"

Rory nodded and drifted into the kitchen for a cup of coffee. To quell his nerves, he laced it with the contents of his hip flask and slowly felt a semblance of control return as the alcohol did its job. After finishing his cup, he poured himself another few swigs and then drank that in a hurry, hoping Tim wouldn't be able to taste the alcohol if he kissed him.

"Ready?"

Rory smiled at Tim and rinsed his cup before following him outside to the truck.

"Where are we going?" Rory asked after driving for a few miles and noticing they were heading into town.

"I'm taking you clothes shopping."

"Clothes shopping?" Rory parroted.

"Yes," Tim replied calmly. "I figured you could use a few pairs of Wranglers, a shirt or two, and a new pair of boots." He put his hand on Rory's knee. "These are going to drop off your ass one of these days, and no matter how enticing the idea of that is to me, the other people on the ranch might not be so enamored with it. Except maybe Grant and Hunter."

Rory eyed Tim suspiciously. "I can't afford that."

Tim's smile didn't wane. "Birthday present."

"How did you—?"

Tim turned into the parking lot, the tires spitting up gravel around the truck as he came to a halt. "Hugh told me. It's in your personnel file."

Damn Hugh. "He had no right."

"Rory." Tim sighed. "He figured I'd like to celebrate it with you."

"I don't go for that sentimental crap," Rory spat out, looking out at the mirror instead of at his lover.

"Well, I do. And I know there are things you need, so I thought I could buy them for you. It's not sentimental crap, Rory. I've been looking for a reason to help you out, and Hugh handed it to me. Just indulge me. It's once a year. And maybe Christmas."

Rory dared to look at Tim and saw his enticing smile. There was no pity in it, just the warmth he usually spread to anything within a mile radius, and Rory felt it warm him up too. Maybe Tim was right and he was just being silly.

"I don't like owing people things."

"They're presents. I could have bought them for you. I can probably guess your size, but I figured since your closet isn't exactly bulging with clothes, you'd appreciate being able to choose what you want to wear. And I'd like to see you in a pair of jeans that hug your butt."

Rory couldn't hold back a smile. "Pervert." He couldn't look at Tim's reaction.

"I know everyone else will be eyeing you too, but I don't mind sharing. As long as you end up in my bed at night."

Rory closed his eyes when he felt Tim's hand on his thigh. He wanted to turn into the warmth, let it envelop him, but he couldn't.

They were practically in public, and anyone wandering by could look into the truck cabin and see them sitting there, so he simply put his hand over Tim's and squeezed.

"Fine. If it'll make you feel better, you can buy me a pair of jeans."

"Two pairs. And two shirts. And a couple of T-shirts and a pair of boots."

"Don't push your luck," Rory said, but he couldn't hide his amusement, no matter how much he hated accepting things for free.

They exited the car and walked into the store, which looked plain and a little disorganized on the outside. Inside they were greeted by a bored-looking young girl with ratty dark hair that had purple streaks running through it. She was wearing dungarees over a very short T-shirt that barely covered her perky little breasts. Rory was amazed to see such a creature outside the city, since everyone he'd seen around the ranch was a lot less "out there."

"Timmy!" she cried out, launching herself at Tim and wrapping her arms and legs around him like a monkey. She started kissing him all over his face like he was a long-lost love, and Rory raised an eyebrow. He found it amusing that Tim simply underwent the treatment and barely reacted until she let go of him.

"Max, this is Rory."

"Boyfriend?" she asked boldly.

"Ehm, yeah," Tim answered with some hesitation.

"Cute," she asserted. "Could do with a haircut. I could do it if you like." She turned to Rory. "See, I used to work at a hairdresser's in Boise, but the hair salon here didn't want me because I'm a bit too avant-garde for them. What do they know?"

Rory smiled. "You look fine to me."

She turned back to Tim. "You sure he's gay?"

"Maxie," Tim cautioned.

Max rolled her eyes at him. "Fine. If he's with you, he's gay. I get it. So what can I get you boys?"

"The works for him," Tim said, pointing at Rory with his thumb.

"We have some really groovy underwear," she quipped.

"Don't push your luck, Max!"

Rory felt curiously relaxed, seeing his lover trade wisecracks with the store girl. He also admitted he liked her and that he'd never felt so at ease being labeled. She was a lot like some of the city girls he'd met on his travels. They wanted to stand out from the crowd and loved people who were "different" as well. They were always the ones who knew which side Rory's bread was buttered on and really didn't care. Max felt very much like that.

"Let's get your man dressed up, hey?"

—16—

THEY hadn't been in the store for very long, and already Max had brought in everything but the kitchen sink to find clothes Rory felt comfortable in. Tim perched on the counter, pointed at a few things, and smiled as Max kept handing Rory different kinds of jeans and T-shirts and button-down shirts, some more colorful than others.

"Give us a show, Rory," Tim suggested, knowing this was way out of Rory's comfort zone. "It's just Max and me here, and Max doesn't care, right, Max?"

Max snorted. "I've already seen him in his tighty-whities, Timmy."

Tim looked at Max and winked as he jumped down from the countertop and moved to the fitting room. Rory startled when Tim pulled back the curtain. He was facing the mirror in his underwear and a tight black sleeveless T-shirt, nothing else, and the sight made Tim's blood run south. Not even the crude tattoos near Rory's neck peering out from behind the T-shirt—something Tim wasn't a fan of, to put it mildly—could change that feeling.

"Looks good on you," Tim said softly as he caressed Rory's muscled shoulders while standing behind him. "Can't wait for summer so you can wear this for work."

Rory shrugged him away. "It's too tight."

"No, it isn't." To prove his point, Tim lowered his hands to rub Rory's stomach, and this time Rory let him. Tim put his chin on Rory's shoulder and gazed at their reflection in the full-length mirror. "You look dead sexy in this. Even if you're not going to wear it to work, I'm buying it for you to sleep in. Don't expect me to let you actually sleep, though."

Rory blushed, but at least he didn't pull away or deny anything Tim had said.

"Did you try on those jeans too?"

Rory nodded.

"Can I see?"

"Tim," Rory drawled. His blush spread to his neck and chest.

"Hey, I'm buying you this as a birthday present, and I like to know what I'm buying before I pay for it. Even if I am letting you choose it yourself." Tim turned his head slightly so he could whisper in Rory's ear. "Besides, I want to make sure those jeans fit nicely around your ass." Tim felt Rory tense up. "If they're too tight, everyone will stare at you, and I don't want just anyone to eye your ass." A faint smile reappeared on Rory's face, and Tim loved seeing it reflected in the mirror. He also couldn't miss the bulge in his lover's tight, white underwear. He didn't react to it but reached out to grab the top jeans on the pile instead.

Tim stepped back to give Rory a chance to step into them and only moved closer when Rory was zipping himself up. "I like these."

"The others are more comfortable."

Tim handed him another pair. "These?"

Rory was quick to change. Tim bit his tongue as he watched the new pair of jeans mold itself to Rory's slender frame.

"I think I can agree with you on these." Tim stood behind Rory again, his groin pressed against Rory's ass. The reason they fit together so nicely now was because Rory was barefoot and Tim still wore his boots. Tim let his hand slide to the band of the jeans. "Only problem is, they fit too snugly for me to push my hand inside." Instead he lowered his hand over Rory's considerable bulge and gave it enough of a squeeze for Rory to feel Tim wasn't exactly unaffected by the sight in the mirror. As he gently massaged Rory with his hand, Tim could see his lover's eyes cloud over. "Just let me take care of you," he whispered almost inaudibly.

"But we're out in the open," Rory protested, albeit very meagerly.

"It's just Max here, and she'll warn us if someone else comes in." Tim moved his hand some more and Rory let him, closing his eyes to let the sensations take over.

"She knows?"

"She knows." Tim wasn't worried about being overheard. As usual Rory was silent, breathing through his open mouth, but his growing arousal was more than evident in his body language. Tim decided there and then he wanted a big mirror in their bedroom once the cabin was ready. "She doesn't care," Tim continued in the same hypnotically soft tone, while he continued rubbing the growing package Rory was sporting. "In fact, she'd probably like it if you made some noise, and so would I."

Rory tensed up and opened his eyes.

Tim soothed him. "Relax. You're as quiet as always. *I* can't even hear you."

This time when Tim resumed his ministrations, Rory didn't close his eyes. Instead he looked straight into the mirror, and Tim wondered if he saw defiance in his man's eyes. In any case, it was better than the shyness and unease that always seemed to be around when they got close. This time was different, though. Now Rory was participating, grinding his jeans-clad ass against Tim's groin to the point where Tim thought he'd come from the combination of the friction, their reflection in the mirror, and the feeling of Rory's substantial cock in his hand. Tim moved his left hand to Rory's chest to steady his lover and saw him respond to Tim brushing his nipple. "You like that?"

Rory nodded, his eyes still focused on Tim in the mirror.

Tim rubbed the nipple again through the fabric of the black T-shirt while rubbing Rory's cock. Rory lost control, turning to putty in Tim's hands. Tim almost lost it too but tried to hold off, because he soon realized he was going to have to keep Rory upright. For a few moments they stood like that, Tim holding Rory, and then Rory seemed to regain his strength. He turned around and sank to his knees, making quick work of unzipping Tim and taking him in his mouth. It didn't take much for Tim to come. He moved his eyes from Rory's face to the sight in the mirror and almost lost his own footing.

With a broad smile on his face, Rory rose to grab Tim, and they stood holding each other until Tim's breath had slowed enough for them to kiss.

"Happy birthday, Grumpy," Tim said, giving Rory's lips one last lick before pulling apart.

Rory smiled.

"So will you let me buy these clothes for you?"

"Okay," Rory conceded. "But only what I need. No more. And no extras."

Tim smiled teasingly. He left Rory standing in the changing room and returned moments later wearing a Stetson. "You'll need these," he said, tossing Rory a six-pack of cotton briefs.

While Rory looked down to see what Tim had thrown him, Tim took the hat and put it on Rory's head.

Rory was quick to react. "That's too much, Timmy. I wouldn't feel comfortable." He took the Stetson off his head and replaced it with his garage cap.

"Fair enough," Tim conceded. "But I'm buying you the underwear, two pairs of jeans, and you better choose two shirts and a few T-shirts." He moved closer to Rory and hooked a finger underneath the T-shirt Rory was wearing. "Starting with this one."

Tim could tell Rory wanted to protest but didn't, so Tim quickly kissed him and then left him alone. When he walked over to the counter, Max was standing behind it with a knowing smile on her face.

"Don't say anything," Tim cautioned her, his voice barely louder than a whisper. "I'm paying for everything he chooses."

"That must have been one hell of a blow job." She mouthed those last two words.

Tim narrowed his eyes and shot her a poisoned look, but it didn't wipe the smile off her face.

She pointed at the Stetson Tim was holding. "Starting with that?"

Tim looked back at the changing room. "Nope, maybe next time. Need to make a cowboy out of him first, I think. He does need some decent boots to go out in the snow."

Rory appeared behind him, wearing his old clothes and carrying the jeans and T-shirt he'd been wearing as well as the opened package of briefs. He deposited them on the counter.

"Do you have another one of these jeans, Max?" Tim asked. "And a blue and a red plaid shirt in his size?"

"No red," Rory was quick to argue.

"Green?" Max suggested.

"Black?" Rory countered.

"Won't be plaid, but you'll look stunning." Rory looked at Tim, and Tim shrugged. "I told you; anything you want."

Tim paid for everything, and they walked out of the shop with two bags each, dropping them in the truck. "Now I'm taking you out to dinner."

Rory stopped. "No, Tim. This is enough."

Tim smiled, hoping to make his Grumpy feel better. "Don't get used to it. I'm only doing this because it's your birthday."

Once they were inside the truck, Tim turned to Rory. "How old are you, anyway?"

"You mean Hugh didn't tell you?"

"Nope."

"Big 4-0," Rory said with a sigh.

"Wow, you're old!" He laughed to make sure Rory understood he was joking. "Seriously. I never would have guessed. You don't look a day older than me."

"Funny you should mention that day, since your birthday is tomorrow," Rory teased.

"And is that something Hugh told you?"

"Nope, Izzie did."

Rory was smiling, and that made Tim happy. He wanted to kiss Rory, but he knew that wouldn't go down well, exposed as they were in the truck parked on the main street, so he settled for putting his hand on Rory's thigh and squeezing. "Let's get us a nice, juicy steak."

THE morning after Rory's birthday celebration, Tim woke up at the crack of dawn, like always. Instead of jumping out of bed, he leaned a little closer to the warmth of the man he'd fallen asleep with. He was quickly getting used to sleeping like this and hovered between waking Rory up for a quick romp and letting him sleep a little longer. Instead he snuggled closer against that long, lean back and buried his face in Rory's unruly locks, inhaling his scent. He figured that if he woke Rory up, it would be a nice way to start his own birthday celebration.

Rory didn't even stir, though, so after a while, Tim's hand traveled from Rory's smooth chest down to his almost-washboard stomach and into his soft, luscious pubic hair to encounter him half-mast. Tim couldn't resist the challenge, grinding his own morning wood against Rory's ass for good measure.

"Is that all you ever think about?" Rory grumbled.

Tim lifted his hand away from Rory's groin and pulled back. "Sorry, Grumpy."

This time the nickname didn't make Rory smile. Tim knew morning wasn't his lover's favorite time of day, but most of the time Tim could make it better. Not this morning, though, so Tim turned and sat up in the bed, staring down at his own erection, and resolved to either take care of it in the shower or let it die down by itself.

"Don't sleep too late, okay?" Tim said over his shoulder. "I'm going to go work."

—17—

BY THREE thirty that afternoon, Rory was in a much better mood when he announced he was done for the day and was ready to start celebrating Tim's birthday.

"You don't have to, Rory."

"After the gifts you gave me yesterday, I couldn't just let today pass, right? I'm not as rich as you, but I have something in mind. Could you drive us there?"

Tim shrugged. Why not? Work was done, and he knew Hugh wouldn't begrudge him a night away to celebrate his birthday. "Give me ten minutes to jump in the shower and change my clothes, and then I'll grab the keys to the truck."

"No need," Rory said, "for the shower, I mean. The keys, yes."

Ten minutes later they were on the road, and Tim followed Rory's directions until they stopped at a motel a little off the main road.

"It's not much, but I figured we could fool around here and nobody would care. Beats trying to be quiet in the crew house," Rory said, opening the door to the motel room.

The lighting fixtures were old and cast cold light around the room. The upholstery looked old-fashioned, to say the least, but the room didn't smell damp or rank; the carpet looked reasonably clean and so did the bedspread. Rory put the only thing they'd brought—a plastic bag—on the small round table and started taking off his boots while Tim closed the door.

"You got us a motel room for my birthday?" Tim said, trying not to sound too confused.

"There's a halfway decent diner next door if you want to eat first," Rory replied, sounding a lot less confident than moments ago when they walked through the door. "I couldn't just let the day pass without giving you something, and I know you like to fuck me, so I thought I'd give you a little more privacy and possibly some more time to do that and—"

Tim grabbed the lapels of Rory's coat and pulled him around, pushing him against the door, but not before he'd moved his right hand to cradle Rory's head, preventing it from crashing into the hard surface. Rory's eyes went wide as Tim kissed him, hard. Tim closed his eyes, feasting on Rory's curvy lips and soft beard. He'd never fancied himself much of a kisser, nor had he ever imagined he'd enjoy kissing a man with a full beard, but he loved to kiss Rory. One hand entangled in Rory's thick mane; he let the other caress Rory's cheek, while Rory let Tim's tongue inside his mouth. Tim liked to explore Rory's naturally perfect teeth and the one crooked one he had such a hard time keeping his eyes off of every time Rory smiled.

Although Rory was a little taller than Tim, he wasn't wearing his boots, so they were about the same height now. Tim easily held the more slender man pinned to the door, grinding their hard bodies against each other.

"Does this also mean I'm going to hear you while I'm fucking you?" Tim asked as they came up for air.

Rory shrugged and shook his head almost imperceptibly.

Tim leaned against him and whispered in his ear. "I want to hear you moan when I push into you, and I want to hear you shout when you come. Nobody who gives a shit can hear you here."

When Tim looked up, Rory looked insecure again, despite the clear arousal Tim could feel through two layers of denim. "Let this be my real birthday present," Tim suggested softly. "I'm not denying that I like to fuck you, but without sounding shallow, I really want to hear you moan, and then I want to hear the pitch change when I brush over that sweet spot inside of you. And I don't just want to make you see stars, I want to hear it when you do as well."

"Tim, I...."

Tim pushed himself away from the door and Rory. "I don't want you to do this because you feel you owe me a birthday present, Rory. If I want a piece of ass to celebrate the fact I'm another year older, I can drive into the city and get laid. The thing is, I don't want just a piece of ass. I want you. And with that, I want to know you're enjoying it too. I want… I *need* to hear you. Not just some fake, porny moaning, but the real thing. The kind of sounds you can't hold back. And if I don't do it for you in that way, then we might as well leave here and go home again."

For what felt like a long couple of moments, Rory didn't move. He didn't even look up at Tim.

"You *do* do that to me, Tim," Rory eventually said, hardly loud enough for the sound to travel between them. "It's just not easy to let go like that."

Tim sat down on the bed and gestured for Rory to join him. "Why not?" Tim asked softly.

"Because I've never really been in places where shouting out in ecstasy was something that was appreciated."

"Like in prison?"

Rory sighed and looked at the floor. "Army barracks, homeless shelters, alleyways, and yes, prison."

Tim bumped his shoulder against Rory's. "Hey, I know you've done time. And I watch TV. I can imagine that being an eager bottom gave you some leverage in there."

"It's nothing like on TV."

Tim put his hand on Rory's thigh, and Rory shivered, despite the fact he was still wearing his coat. Tim leaned a little toward him. "We've been working all day. Why don't we jump in the shower?"

Rory smiled and turned his head toward Tim without looking at him. "Together?"

"Of course," Tim said, feeling amusement bubble up inside him now Rory was responding. "Saves water and time."

"Well, that remains to be seen," Rory replied with a smirk as he got up from the bed and started to take his clothes off.

Tim couldn't stop himself watching, although Rory was playing it more for speed than entertainment. To see that slender but well-developed body appear from beneath layers of clothes was something Tim wished he could see every night. When Rory was only wearing his boxer briefs, Tim pulled him closer, kissing along the dark line that ran from Rory's belly button into the soft-worn cotton. Rory's stomach muscles contracted under his ministrations even as Rory tried to pull away from Tim's grasp. Tim wasn't about to give in, though, pulling Rory's narrow hips into his embrace and locking him there until Rory enveloped Tim's head with his arms. When Tim looked up, Rory's dreamy gaze made Tim feel all warm inside. Tim loosened his grip, and Rory used it to move back enough so he could start unbuttoning Tim's flannel shirt. Rory was just pulling it out of Tim's jeans when he slid down until he was straddling Tim.

"Want to feel your skin," Rory murmured before kissing Tim full on the lips and pushing him to lie on his back.

It felt strange for Tim to lie there with Rory that way. Usually they didn't cuddle much and kissing was just a prelude to a good, thorough fucking. Now they were lying face to face, Rory on top of him, grinding his almost naked body against Tim's clothed one and pushing his hands wantonly underneath Tim's shirt, trying to cover as much skin as possible. Tim, too, wanted to feel Rory under his hands. Of course, he had an easier time of it, but he couldn't resist pushing his hands underneath the cotton of Rory's briefs to squeeze his butt cheeks.

Tim's arousal grew together with Rory's, with Rory's breathing speeding up and Tim growing as hard as Rory already was, but it was definitely not as fast as he was used to feeling it. Were they taking their time? Tim let Rory unbutton his jeans and gasped when Rory inserted his hand and squeezed Tim's cock. Tim slipped from underneath Rory so he could get up and take some clothes off. Rory's worried look turned to interest when Tim took his time, first letting the shirt slip off his shoulder and then letting his jeans slide down his long legs.

"How about that shower now?" Tim suggested.

"Can I take the rest of your clothes off first?"

Tim nodded, since he was only wearing his shorts anyway, so Rory scooted to the side of the bed. He gave Tim a teasing smile and then pulled him between his legs so he could nuzzle his bulge. Tim swallowed, breathing harder than before through his open mouth as he watched Rory lick the cotton over his distended groin. Part of him wanted Rory to get on with it, but another part wanted to make it last. Who knew if he'd ever get a birthday surprise like this one again?

Licking his lips, Rory sat up and slowly pulled Tim's underwear down, letting his erection spring free. Tim wanted Rory's mouth on him, for he knew how good it was, but he also figured everything would be over soon if Rory did that, and they had all night. For a moment, Tim wondered if he could still have more than two or three orgasms in an evening like when he was a teenager, but then Rory got up and pushed himself against Tim's body, and all he could think of was that he wanted to fuck Rory right there and then.

And then Rory walked away toward the bathroom, and Tim heard the shower being turned on.

Dizzy with arousal, Tim willed his feet to move. Rory was standing under the spray with his back to Tim, wiping the water off his hair. Tim checked out the wash basin and found a small bottle of shampoo. He opened it and inhaled the scent, making sure it didn't smell too flowery, and then entered the narrow shower cubicle.

Rory looked over his shoulder at Tim.

"Can I wash your hair?"

Rory nodded, poking his head under the spray and then leaning back to let Tim lather him up. It felt curiously intimate, even when, halfway through, Rory turned around and wiped his hands over his hair to pick up some of the shampoo and rub it into his beard. Rory then picked the shampoo bottle off the little shelf in the wall and returned the favor, massaging Tim's scalp until the lather started drooping into Tim's eyes. As Tim stood under the shower head, letting Rory wash the suds out of his hair, he realized he may have had sex in a shower before, but he'd never had this sensual experience. He knew they'd end up fucking, but there was no rush, and Tim reveled in that luxury as he playfully hugged Rory and kissed his neck. Slowly he let his hands wander over Rory's arms, admiring the muscles born from manual labor stretched over his shoulders, appreciating his strong back and narrow waist, his firm buttocks. Feeling Rory's roaming hands on him made Tim's blood course through him as well. The thought that this was turning Rory on as much as it was affecting him was all Tim needed.

"Let's move this to a drier place?" Tim suggested.

"I'm just getting warmed up," Rory teased, moving closer for a kiss and at the same time taking both their cocks in his large callused hand.

The feeling of Rory's erection next to his was enough for Tim to push into the hand reflexively; the firm grip was enough to make him close to coming. With considerable force, Tim pushed Rory against the shower wall, only to press his own body against Rory's again.

"You're going to make me come like this," Tim groaned into Rory's ear.

"I thought that was the point," Rory replied.

"Not if you want me to fuck you." Tim wrapped his arms around Rory and very purposely aimed for his ass, kneading the cheeks and pushing a finger between them in search of the little rosette.

"You want to fuck that little hole?" Rory said with clear confidence. "I have what you want, Timmy."

"But I only want it if you want it too," Tim replied, trying to exude the confidence Rory showed as well.

"You've never said no to me before. Why start now?"

Tim shook his head and stepped out of the shower, turning his back on Rory to grab a towel. He inhaled sharply when he felt Rory fold himself against his back.

"Or do you actually want to be at the bottom? Is that what the birthday boy really wants? A good fucking until that little hole is all pink and puckered because it's not used to a good pounding?"

Tim smiled at himself in the mirror and watched Rory eyeing the two of them standing together. Rory looked like a drowned cat, so Tim twisted round and started rubbing Rory's hair with his towel. As soon as Rory's face came back into view, Tim kissed him.

"I said I wanted to make you moan. I don't doubt for a second that it's easier for me to do that when I'm inside of you than if it's the other way around. Am I right?"

When Tim stopped his onslaught, Rory opened his deer-brown eyes and smiled ever so slightly. Then Rory turned the tables on him, rubbing the now half-wet towel over Tim's hair, then his face, and then his chest.

"I can't say no to you either," Rory confessed softly as he stopped what he was doing to drop the towel. "I would think you would have caught on by now."

Tim tried to grab Rory again, but Rory got away, running back into the bedroom. As he was pulling the covers off, Tim tackled him, and they both ended up on the bed, half on top of each other.

"Fuck me, Timmy," Rory demanded. "Make it impossible for me not to moan."

—18—

TIM woke up on his stomach and had to remind himself where he was for the first few moments. The room was dark and smelled unfamiliar, yet there was also a more familiar aroma.

Sex.

Tim smiled when he remembered Rory's hesitant invitation, the seduction in the shower, and then the lovemaking on the bed, first slow and deliberate and then more intense, culminating in an earth-shattering shared orgasm. The memory was so vivid that Tim grew hard just thinking about it.

They'd ended up in a pile after Tim, unable to resist the enticing view of Rory's naked ass, complete with water drops from their shower still clinging to him, had tackled Rory to the bed. Rory was on his stomach and Tim was on top of him and Tim's cock fit so nicely between Rory's round ass cheeks he couldn't not push against him.

"Fuck me, Timmy. Make it impossible for me not to moan."

That's what he wanted. He wanted to hear Rory in the throes of passion. He wanted him to moan in ecstasy, not hold back like those other times when he'd come so silently they could have fucked in a museum if it hadn't been for Tim's feral growls.

"Just do it," Rory continued. "Condoms and lube are in the plastic bag on the table."

They both eyed the bag, but Tim didn't want to let go of Rory's enticing body. "Get on all fours," Tim ordered, feeling Rory's muscles flex under his hands.

As Rory got on his knees and pushed his ass up, Tim forgot he was halfway to the table and returned, needing desperately to feel that little pucker between Rory's round butt cheeks open up to his ministrations.

"Yeah," Rory whispered, coming close to a moan. He lowered his head to his folded arms and opened up even more for Tim, whose fingers were now running circles around Rory's hole while he palmed Rory's tight balls with his free hand.

Even after the shower, Rory still tasted very much like himself, and Tim inhaled his scent as he kissed his smooth skin. When he moved his hand down to Rory's cock, he found it just as hard as in the shower. He slowly rubbed it, then moved his hand up again, wetting his thumb before pushing it against Rory's entrance.

"Yeah, do it," Rory whispered. "Open me up, then fuck me hard."

Tim's thumb easily slipped past the first muscle, and Rory exhaled silently. Tim pushed the thumb side of his palm against the sensitive skin underneath the hole, and then Rory pushed back, letting Tim's thumb slip in a little further. With his left hand, Tim touched his own erection, feeling it fill up more as soon as he did. *Slow*, he told himself. *Don't rush things. Don't want to come as soon as I'm inside him. He deserves more than that.* Rory was fucking himself on the thumb when Tim focused again. Tim was leaking so hard he could spread it around his own cock by now. He just had to pull away, and to his surprise, that elicited a sound from Rory. It was a quiet whimper. A mark of protest. Still fairly quiet, but Tim heard it.

"Just getting the supplies," Tim said, and he realized he was already breathing harder in anticipation. "Turn over," he demanded.

Rory looked at him and didn't move.

"I want to look you in the eye when I fuck you."

Rory shook his head. "I'll moan, but I can't. Not yet."

Tim wanted it. He wanted so many things. He wanted to see Rory's face when he came. He wanted to hear Rory shout his name, or howl, or grunt, or something. And he wanted to plow into him so badly. Two out of three wasn't bad. He'd fucked Rory doggy-style before. He knew it would be good. Rory was eager enough to be fucked to make it better than good. And he'd promised to moan. Now all Tim had to do was deserve those moans.

Tim picked a condom out of the bag, opened it, and rolled it over his erection. Then he fished out the lube and squirted some over the condom, warming it as he rubbed it all around. All the while Rory was watching him, still on all fours, still hard. Tim wiped his hand around Rory's entrance, slipping one finger in to test the waters, and then knelt so he could line himself up. Rory pushed back as soon as the tip of Tim's cock brushed over the partially relaxed muscle.

"Fuck yeah," Rory exhaled more than spoke as Tim pushed in deeper.

Rory was tight, but Tim knew how easily he could take it as he slowly pushed in to the hilt. Rory lowered his head to his hands again as he pushed back, demanding Tim move.

Tim took it slow, repeatedly telling himself that if he set the pace his body was demanding of him, it would all be over in ten seconds flat.

"Tease," Rory groaned softly.

Tim pulled out about halfway and then rocked back and forth, guided by the hitch in Rory's breathing that, he concluded, signaled the head of his cock rubbing across Rory's prostate. With every push, Rory sank closer to the mattress, and Tim followed until Rory was flat on his stomach with Rory's erection trapped between the sheet and his belly.

"Knees getting weak, baby?" Tim asked, his voice a little strained from holding back.

"You have me pegged," Rory whispered, seemingly only to himself, but Tim picked it up anyway.

Tim moved a little higher, changing the angle of his thrusts, and canted his knees outside Rory's legs, which made Rory close his.

"Fuck, you're so tight now."

"Thought you'd like that."

Rory, stretched out underneath Tim, pushed up on his elbows and looked over his shoulder at the man fucking him. Tim leaned on his arms and just managed to nick the side of Rory's mouth with his lips while he kept up a slow rhythm.

"Does it feel good to you too?"

Rory smiled. "Hell yeah. This is… definitely… good for me… too."

Tim pulled out a little more and then pushed in again all the way. "Lemme hear ya."

Rory was biting his lip, and Tim pushed in again, a little harder this time but still keeping the slow pace.

"Nobody can hear us."

Rory's breathing sounded labored and choppy, but he was still barely making a sound, and Tim so needed to hear him. He bent down until he was resting on his elbows, just like Rory, but because Rory was narrower than him, he could envelop his lover in his embrace, lining up their arms and placing his hands over Rory's.

Rory moved into the touch, pushing his back against Tim's muscled chest and his ass against Tim's belly.

"You feel so amazing," Tim whispered in Rory's ear. "Talk to me." He continued slowly thrusting into his lover, pushing Rory down against the mattress every time. "Just for my ears, Rory."

Tim kissed Rory's neck, and Rory let his head fall between their entwined hands. Tim continued kissing him between thrusts, and small sounds started reaching Tim's ears. They were just whimpers at first, then muffled grunts, always in time with their combined movements. Tim wanted to say something about how amazing it was to hear Rory's reactions, but he didn't dare, afraid Rory would stop, and the sounds, however small, were turning Tim on more than he could have predicted. He made his movements more deliberate and even slower, although his body demanded the opposite, until Rory threw his head back and wailed. He was shuddering underneath Tim and left no room for speculation. Tim could feel Rory's climax through every fiber of his being, and it didn't take more than a few more thrusts for Tim to join him.

As they both fell to the side, neither spoke. Tim wanted to revel in the feeling of sated bliss as long as he could, holding Rory close and taking in his scent, but all too soon he felt himself drift off.

WHEN he woke again, the room was dark and Rory was gone.

Although it had been one hell of a birthday fuck, Tim felt cold. He'd hoped that Rory would stay with him through the night: that they would talk a little, maybe kiss some more, and that Tim would get a chance to explore more of that long, sinewy body he liked so much. Instead he was lying alone in a strange bed.

Tim was just reaching for his watch when the door opened and Rory walked in, carrying a well-filled plastic bag and a brown paper bag which looked like it had liquor in it. He turned on the light without asking, and Tim squinted at the brightness.

"Sorry," Rory apologized, switching on the bedside lamp and flicking off the overhead light. "I thought you'd still be asleep. You were out for the count."

Tim moved forward so he could touch Rory as he sat down on the bed. "I'd hoped to wake up with you still in my arms."

"I was hungry," Rory stated matter-of-factly. "They had a rib special at the diner. It's not much of a birthday dinner, but I hope you'll like it anyway. It smells really garlicky, but I figured if we both ate it, it wouldn't be a problem."

Despite his low voice, Tim thought Rory sounded like a teenager. He wanted to brush the insecurity away and recall the confidence Rory showed while he was seducing Tim earlier, simply because he wanted Rory to be at case around him.

"It smells great," Tim said, rubbing Rory's back. "Come here and let me feed you. You can use a little more bulk." He tried to tickle Rory, but Rory got up and took the food to the table. He was unpacking it when Tim got out of bed to follow.

Tim could see Rory eyeing him. He wasn't really the bashful kind, so the fact he was in his birthday suit while Rory was fully clothed didn't bother him. In fact, the faint enjoyment in Rory's eyes made him feel like he should flaunt it a bit. If he were the flaunting kind. He wasn't, but that didn't mean he was going to hurry to cover himself up. He walked to where Rory was sitting and reached into the box of ribs Rory had taken out of the bag.

"They smell delicious. I don't mind garlic."

Rory looked at him without shame. "You are delicious too. Can't believe you're still hard after what we did earlier."

Tim looked down as he licked the sauce off his fingers. "That's not hard." He chuckled. "But I woke up and you weren't there and then I remembered what happened last night and—"

"It's still last night," Rory interrupted. "It's still your birthday."

"Which means I still get to call the shots." Tim wiggled his eyebrows and walked back to the bed. "Take your clothes off, come back to bed. And bring the food. I'm hungry."

After stepping out of his clothes, Rory was clearly less confident about his nudity, despite his earlier flaunting under the shower. Of course, then Tim wasn't lying on the bed watching Rory's every move and not hiding how he was feasting his eyes. As soon as Rory came close enough to the bed with the box of ribs, Tim pulled him closer. For a moment Rory froze up, and then he relaxed again.

"It's just me. You know me by now," Tim whispered in Rory's ear as he settled the slighter man against his chest. "I'm a big lug, but I'm harmless."

"I know," Rory said. "So you want to eat here?"

"Only place you should eat in bed is where you don't need to wash the sheets," Tim said with a chuckle.

Rory sat up, and Tim wished he'd relax a bit more. He let Rory get comfortable, though, and nicked another rib from the box, biting into it and letting his appreciation be known with a moan. He settled next to Rory, his back to the headboard of the bed, and continued eating the meat off the bone. Occasionally he looked over at Rory, who still seemed uncomfortable.

"What's wrong?" Tim asked.

"Nothing." Rory shrugged.

"So relax."

Rory smiled, and Tim got a sideways glimpse of Rory's crooked tooth again. He couldn't resist leaning over Rory and kissing him. To his surprise, the insecurity returned.

"Rory, what's wrong? Would you rather be somewhere else?"

Rory shook his head.

"Then what? Don't shrug it away. One moment you're happy and flirty and all over me, and another moment I feel like I'm keeping you here against your will."

"I'm just not used to this, okay?" Rory replied, showing his frustration.

"*This* being what? Talking? Sharing food in bed?"

"Both. I don't know how I'm supposed to behave. I've never had a friend who also fucked me. I mean, I've had friends and I've had… well… lovers is too strong a word. Men I had sex with."

That explained quite a bit, Tim thought. Not that Tim was all that experienced in that particular combination either.

"I know what you mean," Tim said. "I have friends at the ranch, but most of them don't even know I prefer men, let alone have firsthand experience. When I want sex, I drive for an hour and go to the Handle Bar. It's kind of nice to know I don't need to drive all the way out there anymore."

Rory stared at their feet, signaling to Tim that wasn't what Rory wanted to hear.

"What I mean is, I kind of like it that the man I sleep with is also a friend. I was sort of hoping that he'd relax a little more so I wouldn't feel like a one-night stand, awkward and a little anxious about what he expected from me, but I'm sure he'll get there eventually."

Rory nodded and then smiled at Tim. This time Rory initiated the kiss, and it was so hesitant and shy that Tim felt like a teenager again. He tried to be less impatient than he'd been in his younger years, giving Rory the time to explore. They didn't progress much, and after a few pecks, Rory sat back again, so Tim took a rib from the box and waved it in front of Rory's face. A little drop of juice slid off it and onto Rory's bare chest. Tim tried to pick it up with the rib, purposely making it worse so he had to lick it off. He circled one of Rory's nipples and licked that off too.

"You should eat more. You're too skinny," Tim said, trying to make it as teasing as possible while he rubbed the greasy piece of meat over Rory's lips.

"I thought you liked my body the way it was? At least that's what you keep telling me whenever you're fucking me."

Tim cocked his head. "I do. I do like your body. But I don't like eating alone, and I'm still hungry."

Tim kept enticing Rory with food, and occasionally Rory would bite into it, but mostly it was an excuse for Tim to paint and lick Rory's chest and arms. Eventually what was left of the dinner was discarded and they just kissed. Tim could tell Rory was starting to feel more comfortable, until suddenly Rory stopped and gently pushed Tim away.

"Need a drink. Are you thirsty?" He didn't wait for an answer and simply unearthed the bottle of cheap vodka from the paper bag next to the bed.

"I don't drink much," Tim said. He took the bottle from Rory anyway and took a small sip. It burned down his throat, and he grimaced as it slid down to his stomach.

Rory took a bigger swig, and then another one, like it was water. After that it didn't take Rory long to relax, and within no time he was his flirty self again. It didn't seem to make him drunk, at least not as far as Tim could tell, but it did make him more amenable, and Tim found he didn't mind the slight taste of the liquor in Rory's mouth. When Rory turned onto his stomach, Tim figured it was the sign they could start round two. The heat between them rose more quickly, and the lovemaking was more frantic. Rory wasn't as silent as before, either, although you could barely accuse him of being loud. Two out of three wasn't bad.

—19—

WHEN they returned to the ranch, on the surface, life didn't change that much. The difference stayed behind closed doors. Rory put out the air mattress every night but crawled into Tim's bed, and not a day ended without them having sex.

Rory realized he really liked his butch cowboy, not in the least because of Tim's positive, bright personality. Rory had the tendency to be quiet and brooding, never thinking the best of people or situations, but Tim made that impossible. Rory found himself smiling more and more when he was around Tim, simply because Tim's sunny disposition rubbed off on everyone within a mile radius, and everything seemed to go right when Tim was around.

One night, sleeping in Tim's tight embrace, Rory dreamed about taking a walk around the ranch with his lover. With every step Tim took, flowers would instantly sprout around his feet. Where he touched a tree, leaves grew, and when they crossed a fence to walk outside of the ranch grounds into the forest, a deer walked up to Tim and let Tim pat it.

When Rory woke, he remembered the images vividly, and he felt very silly, but he realized that was what Tim represented for him. Tim was one with nature and only saw the good in people. The horses instantly knew this, and especially the foals took to him as if they were meant to be petted by him.

Rory snuggled a little closer to his man and simply enjoyed the warmth emanating from Tim's naked skin. He carefully caressed Tim's taut pecs and tight washboard stomach and couldn't believe how fortunate he was to be loved by this man. There was no doubt in his mind that Tim loved him. Tim had told him so many times, although Rory couldn't bring himself to reciprocate. It wasn't that he didn't feel it too; it was just that he couldn't believe it. After the life he'd led, he simply didn't deserve a guy like Tim.

Tim continued sleeping, and the longer Rory stayed next to him, wide awake, the more the negative thoughts invaded his brain and the more he craved a drink. A few good gulps would make the voices go away. Rory knew that from years of experience. Tim's embrace and warm, naked body felt too good to leave, though. Plus, he'd probably wake Tim up, and his boyfriend needed his sleep.

Eventually thirst won, but like he'd predicted, as soon as he slipped away from Tim, his lover woke. Rory thought Tim looked adorable with his hair messed up and his sleep-drunk eyes seeming much smaller than usual. The smile was there, though, as Tim scratched his hair, then wiped across his face and rubbed his chest.

"Damn, I need to pee," Tim murmured. He crawled from under the covers and walked out the door to the communal bathroom, totally unruffled by the fact he wasn't wearing a stitch of clothing.

Although Rory couldn't wait for Tim to leave so he could take a swig or two from the vodka bottle he'd hidden among his things, he wasn't beyond admiring Tim's bulging muscles and half-erect cock. Maybe they could fuck before they had to get up for work?

LATER that afternoon, Tim was helping Rory muck out the foaling stables when he announced they were invited for dinner at Hunter and Grant's house.

"So why do they want to see us?" Rory asked with some reservation. "I don't remember there being any soccer on."

"Maybe they just want us over for a social visit."

Rory raised an eyebrow. "A social visit?"

Tim shrugged. "They have Gable and Flynn over for dinner all the time. Hugh and Izzie go over there too. Maybe they figured now we're a… couple, they should invite us over as well."

Rory didn't miss the hesitation with which Tim used the word couple. He knew it wasn't because Tim didn't like the word. In fact, Tim loved the word. He loved the concept even more. Tim had never kept it a secret from Rory that he wanted them to be a unit, a couple, mated for life like swans. Rory knew the hesitation was for him. It was Tim bracing for impact, wondering how Rory would react to his use of the word.

So Rory let it slide.

They were a couple, after all. They shared a room and a bed and worked together practically 24/7. They kissed and had sex, and although it had taken some time, Rory had gotten used to being with Tim and trusting him more every day. He'd even quietly entertained the idea of staying longer, if Tim still wanted him around after his parole was done.

"Too bad we can't invite them back," Rory replied after Tim returned with a wheelbarrow full of fresh straw.

"Don't think they care. I was just thinking it was a little weird to go over to the boss' house for a social visit. It blurs the lines even more. Not that it's that strict, but Hunter still owns the place, and he *is* the boss."

"But he's also your friend."

"We grew up together, you mean?"

Rory nodded.

"Nowadays everything is on a first name basis, but my dad never called Hunter's father anything other than Mr. Krause. He wouldn't have even contemplated calling him Matthew. And Hunter's mother is still Mrs. Krause, although when she's not in the room some people will call her Beth. Never to her face, though." Tim chuckled.

"I wouldn't dare to call her Beth either. She scares the hell out of me," Rory admitted.

"Hunter says she was never the warmest person. I bet he's intimidated by her as well."

"I bet he is," Rory concurred.

"So shall I tell Grant to expect us?"

Rory shrugged as he continued to spread the straw. "I suppose."

AFTER washing and putting on clean clothes, Tim and Rory walked up to the smaller of the two homesteads and knocked on the intricately carved front door.

Moments later the door opened and Hunter was standing on the other side of it, carrying his son, Matthew. "Come on in. It's still a little hectic here, but go on into the kitchen and Grant will get you a drink." He gestured to the other end of the room, where the lights were brighter than in the living room. "I'm going to try to get Matty to bed, and then I'll join you."

"Hey guys," Grant greeted them from behind the cooking island in the middle of the modern kitchen. "Sit." He gestured to the high table set for four, which seemed to be a part of the island, and Tim and Rory sat on the bar stools. "Beers okay for you?" He didn't wait for an answer but turned around to the huge refrigerator and took out three bottles. "Dinner's almost ready. How'd you like the sunshine today? Was a nice change from all that rain."

Tim looked at Rory before answering. "The sunshine was nice. I wanted to take Rory out for a riding lesson, but there was no time left."

"How's the riding going?" Grant asked Rory while he flipped the steaks.

"Okay, I suppose. You better ask the teacher."

"He's an eager student," Tim answered, and the pride he saw in his lover's eyes made Rory blush. Luckily his beard hid most of it.

"If anyone can make a wrangler out of you, it's Tim here," Grant said to Rory while he slapped his hand on Tim's shoulder. "We can always use another hand when it comes to mustering the herd, if you don't mind doubling up from time to time."

"I like working in the foaling stalls," Rory admitted, "but I guess it would be nice to be working outdoors more as well."

"You got the best of both worlds, just like me," Grant continued. "When I'm sick of the dust in the woodshed, I load stuff onto a tractor and go out there and fix some fence posts. And when that's all done, I get on horseback and find some more rotten posts that need fixing."

"I like you all sweaty and bare-chested in that woodshed," Hunter said, joining them in the kitchen and putting his arms around Grant, kissing his neck from behind.

Rory realized the unashamed display of affection gave him mixed feelings. On the one hand, he liked the idea that Grant and Hunter felt comfortable enough around them to be free with each other, but it also turned him on, just like it had the first time he'd seen them together on the porch while he was lurking in the bushes. The reaction it provoked in him made the voices from his past reappear. *Faggot. Dirty, dirty boy. Pervert.* And those were just the nicer names he'd been called because he liked looking at other boys and men and because he liked touching them, kissing them, fucking them, and being fucked by them.

Rory took a big swig from his beer, got up from his seat, and quickly excused himself to go to the bathroom. Luckily, he vaguely remembered where it was from the time they'd watched the second half of the soccer game in this house. Once inside, he realized the door didn't bolt, so he pushed his back against it and tried to breathe. *Faggot. Cocksucker. Fudge packer.* He shook his head, but the voices wouldn't stop. He knew what he needed. He exited the bathroom again and walked into the living room. Everyone was still in the kitchen, so he walked to the liquor cabinet. It was hidden next to the big screen TV he'd admired so much while watching the game. There wasn't a lot in there. Guess the guys weren't big drinkers either. He grabbed a half-empty bottle of whiskey and snuck back into the bathroom. Sinking down against the door, he opened the bottle and took a swig. *Better take a big one, boy, because otherwise this is gonna hurt.* Rory smiled. It didn't hurt. In fact he'd loved every minute of it, right after the burn had subsided. He took another swig. That was another burn that made him feel good. The burn of liquor. The burn of a good hard cock. As the alcohol started diffusing into his body, he started to relax. He could do it now. The voices were gone.

Rory stuck his head out of the bathroom and walked out. The living room was still deserted, and he put the bottle back in its place before following the roaring laughter to the kitchen. Tim was sitting with his back to him, and he couldn't resist mimicking Hunter's earlier movements and grabbing Tim around the waist and kissing his neck.

"Hey," Tim said softly. "Everything okay?"

Rory didn't let go, not even under the scrutiny of the other two men. Why would he? They knew he and Tim were lovers. "Perfect. Just had to make some room for all that delicious food." He winked at Grant and saw a smile break on the handsome cowboy's face.

"You'll need it, because Grant's a great cook," Hunter said, winking back at Rory.

"Nothing to it. It's just a steak, a salad, and some baked potatoes."

"It smells divine," Rory said before letting go of Tim and sitting down next to him. He couldn't resist squeezing Tim's knee before grabbing the dangerous-looking steak knife next to his plate and digging in.

—20—

A FEW days after the dinner at Hunter and Grant's house, Tim took Rory out for a ride. Rory was becoming more and more proficient, so Tim had given him Scooter, a young and eager buckskin gelding with black points who wasn't afraid of the snow. In fact, once they left the first gate and the snow became thicker, Scooter started to enjoy himself, and Tim could see Rory had a hard time keeping his horse in check. He didn't say anything and just let Rory handle it himself. The horse enjoyed prancing around from one snow stack to another, and Rory needed all his concentration just to stay in the saddle. Just when Tim figured Rory was finally relaxing, Scooter threw him off and then stood there waiting innocently until Rory had gotten up.

"Everything okay?" Tim asked, trying not to laugh out loud.

"Yeah, yeah," Rory replied, wiping the snow off his coat. He was smiling, though.

"Having a good time?"

Rory's smile grew as he walked to where Tim and his horse were standing, so as soon as Rory was within reach, Tim grabbed him by the shoulder, bent down, and kissed him.

"Yeah, I am," Rory whispered to Tim. "Despite the antics of that teenager over there," he said in a louder voice, directed at Scooter. This time Tim did laugh out loud and Rory joined him.

Rory adjusted the old oilskin Tim had lent him and took a few steps in the direction of Scooter with the intent to mount him again so they could continue their ride. Scooter kept the distance between them about the same, though, stepping aside as Rory came closer.

"He's toying with you, Rory," Tim said, still smiling. "Walk away from him."

"He won't run?"

"No, if he likes you enough to want to play with you, you just have to join the game and turn the tables. He's a young horse; he'll test you, and now's the time to teach him manners. Whatever you do, play by *your* rules, not his, and I'm sure you'll get along just fine."

Rory turned away from Scooter and immediately got his attention.

"That's right," Tim said in a soothing voice. "Come over here and give me another kiss."

Rory smiled and walked teasingly slowly over to Tim. They kissed again, languid and slow this time, and Tim noticed Rory was being pushed against him.

"Jealous bastard," Rory murmured against Tim's mouth.

Tim reached over Rory's head to grab hold of Scooter's bridle without breaking the kiss. "He's ready to work for you again, Rory. Let's go, we have some fences to check."

Rory reluctantly broke away, and Scooter patiently waited for his inexperienced rider to mount him.

Despite the cold of the winter's day, Tim felt warmed by the smiles Rory threw him from time to time. He remembered his promise from the day he picked Rory up from prison; he was slowly making it come true now Rory was smiling more. He'd always told himself they had a future together, but now he found grounds to believe it as well.

"Look, Tim." Rory was pointing in the distance.

Tim urged his steed to speed up to take a closer look at a break in the fence caused by a large collapsed spruce tree. "Looks like it died last summer and it couldn't bear the weight of the snow anymore."

"So what do we do? We need to fix the fence, right?" Rory asked.

"Yeah, I'll get on the radio."

Tim called Grant, asking whether he was interested in some spruce timber, and then radioed the ranch hands to give them directions to the site so they could bring a chain saw and a truck to pick up the bigger pieces.

By late afternoon, Tim and Rory had worked themselves into a sweat despite the cold weather. They'd fixed the fence, so the horses would be safe in the spring when they brought them up for grazing.

Tim had just sent the guys back to the homestead with the truck when his radio crackled into action.

"Tim?"

Despite the antiquated technology, Tim recognized Hunter's voice. "What's up, boss?"

"Can you come to our house as soon as you're back?"

"Sure thing. The guys are on their way back with all the wood we collected, and Rory and me will be coming back on horseback."

"We'd like to talk to you alone, Tim." Tim sensed the hesitancy in Hunter's words but tried not to let it worry him. If something was truly amiss, he was sure to find out as soon as he talked to Hunter, and there would be time enough to worry then.

"Everything okay?" Rory asked as he brought Tim's horse closer.

"Yeah, sure," Tim answered, trying to sound upbeat. He was sure Rory had overheard the conversation since sounds carried much further across the snow-covered terrain. "Boss wants to talk to me. Probably wants to discuss what needs to be done throughout the winter. It's likely nothing important." Tim knew he was saying this more for his own benefit than Rory's, because it wasn't like Hunter to summon him and make it clear that Rory wasn't welcome.

As soon as they returned to the homestead, Tim jumped off his horse.

"I'll take care of the horses. Go on and see what Hunter needs," Rory suggested.

Tim nodded his thanks at Rory and walked to Hunter and Grant's house. Although like with every other house there, the door was unlocked, Tim used the big knocker at the front door to announce his presence.

Grant opened the door, and the look on his face immediately worried Tim. He couldn't put his finger on why, though.

"Hey, Tim."

The softness and unease of Hunter's voice coming from over Grant's shoulder didn't soothe him either.

"What's wrong, guys? Why the summons?"

Tim could see Hunter looking at Grant. He couldn't read what they weren't saying to each other, and he felt anxiety creeping up on him.

"Sit down, Tim. You want a beer?"

"Sure," Tim replied, somewhat apprehensively. "I'm pretty much done for the day, so a cold one would be nice."

"You've been out all day," Hunter noticed. "I'll get you a nice cup of hot coffee instead, if you like."

"Yeah, whatever," Tim replied. *Just get it over with, guys!*

As Hunter left to get the coffee, Tim realized he'd never seen Grant so quiet. Grant was usually the life of the party, cracking jokes and making everyone feel at home, but this time the silence was uncomfortable, and not just for Tim. As soon as Hunter returned, Grant jumped up to take the mugs from his lover and handed Tim his. Hunter and Grant sat down next to each other on the sturdy dark leather couch opposite Tim. If he didn't know any better, he'd think they were ganging up on him.

"So will you cut to the chase, please?" Tim asked, showing just how worried he was getting.

Hunter took a deep breath and looked briefly at Grant before returning his gaze to Tim. "We've had a rather disturbing set of phone calls lately."

Tim's face must have spoken for him because Grant took over.

"You know that Miranda, Matthew's mother, abandoned Matty at birth?"

"Yes, but this is nothing new, right? And what does it have to do with me?" Tim asked, the comments not making any sense.

"Miranda is trying to get custody of Matthew," Grant said, as if he were trying to get it all off his chest in one go. "We got a message from some hot-shot lawyer in Boise who is representing her."

Tim breathed a sigh of relief when he realized Hunter and Grant had asked him over to tell him something that had nothing to do with him. "Oh my God, I'm so sorry. Who in their right mind would take Matty away from here? I remember when he first arrived. Tiny, sickly baby, and look at him now. He's thriving."

"I know," Hunter replied. "We've talked to our own lawyer, and the problem is, we need to make sure Miranda has no ammunition. The way it stands now, we can prove Miranda abandoned her son, but we'll need to prove that the environment he's growing up in is much better than anything Miranda could give him."

"That should be easy enough. All this fresh air, the horses, the way you've organized yourselves with Christie and your mom. Hunter, every kid should be so lucky to have all these aunts and uncles and two dads, and…." And then, as he saw Hunter and Grant's expressions, it dawned on him. Rory. They had a convicted felon, on parole, living near the kids. "They're going to use Rory's presence as ammunition?"

Grant nodded, avoiding Tim's gaze.

"He stole a couple of horses. And a car a few years ago. And there was a DUI from many more years ago…." Tim tried to recall what he remembered of Rory's rap sheet. All the other stuff was minor offenses, misdemeanors as far as he could recall.

"And he came close to being convicted of a sex crime in Georgia, Tim," Hunter added. "The charges were dropped at the last minute as far as our lawyer can gather, so it isn't on his rap sheet, but it was a case of statutory rape. It's all about perceptions, Tim. There was a minor involved, and Miranda's lawyers are going to use this against us. You have to understand."

"No," Tim said repeatedly. "No, it can't be. Rory isn't capable of anything like that. You know him. Hunter! Grant?" Both men were avoiding his gaze, Hunter by looking out the window and Grant by looking at the floor. "You can't do this to us! Do you have any idea what he's been through?" Tim got up from his seat and started pacing around the small sitting area. "He's finally found a home, a family. Someone to love him." Tim didn't care that his voice broke with that last statement. "He's been abandoned all his life, Hunter. By his mother when he was six, by all these people who claim they run foster homes, then by the military for falling in love with his lieutenant. I'm not abandoning him too."

"We're not asking you to, it's just…. He's a grown man, and this is about a helpless child who might be taken away from us, Tim."

"*Might be*, being the appropriate words. You don't know for sure."

Hunter sighed. "We can't take the risk. I'm sorry, Tim."

Tim felt the anger rise but knew it wouldn't do anyone any good if he blew his top. He scrubbed his hair with his hands, trying to keep his emotions at bay. "If his parole wasn't tied to him working at the ranch, I'd take him away from here, but I can't, because if he leaves, they'll put him back in jail. What do you want me to do? He can't go back there."

"We know," Grant said.

Tim jumped up from his seat. "For Christ's sake, this didn't just fall out of the sky. You must have known when you had us over for dinner earlier in the week!"

"We knew about Miranda trying to get to Matty," Grant replied.

"She called to tell me she wanted to see Matty," Hunter admitted, "but you have to believe me when I say we didn't know she'd taken on some lawyer, and we didn't realize that Rory's presence would be a problem."

Tim threw Hunter a desperate look.

"We didn't know until we'd talked to our lawyer."

Tim dropped back down to the chair, his hands shielding his face. They'd been doing so well. Rory was finally happy and content now that he'd found a home, and Tim was happy too, because Rory was with him. Now everything was caving in around them.

"When does he need to be gone?" Tim asked quietly.

"We'll help you find a solution," Hunter offered. "We'll call his parole officer to ask him to help us to find another place for him, and we'll make sure he knows he's been an exemplary employee."

Tim shook his head. "He won't help. The man's a bastard. Every time Rory has to go see him, he comes back so pissed off, he…." Tim didn't finish his sentence. Instead he focused on something else. "Rory's marking the calendar and knows exactly how many more times he has to go see him."

"We'll find another way, Tim."

Hunter's words didn't soothe Tim. "There is no other way." He got up from the seat again and walked two steps in the direction of the door before turning around. "I understand that your kid comes first, but for me, Rory comes first. I found him this job. I'll help him find another, but if that means I have to offer them my services as a wrangler as well, then I will."

"Tim, please," Hunter pleaded. "We're hands short as it is. We need you here."

Tim sighed. "I know, and I don't want to leave the only place I ever worked, but like I said, Rory comes first, and the way I see it, he needs me more than you do."

Tim could see the hurt look on Hunter and Grant's faces, but his mind was made up. Now all he had to do was find a solution before he was forced to tell Rory what was going on. He didn't like lying to his lover, but he understood that Hunter and Grant hadn't talked to Rory themselves because they knew it would break the man's heart to tell him he had to leave. And the last thing Tim wanted to do was watch Rory's heart breaking.

—21—

RORY was waiting in Tim's room when Tim returned. He'd had a shower, changed into clean clothes, and checked out what was for dinner. Christy had made them hamburgers with all the trimmings, and they could make their own fries in the crew kitchen. It was definitely the best kitchen he'd ever come across, and that included the army.

"Hey," Rory greeted his man as Tim walked in. He knew Tim had been worried about his talk with Hunter, and that worry was still visible on his face. "How did it go?" Rory asked with more than a little apprehension.

"Okay," Tim answered with fake perkiness. He sat down next to Rory on the bed. "He wanted to know how the fall foals were doing and if we needed the vet to come and look at the pregnant mares, but I said they were doing just fine."

Damn, Tim was a bad liar. Rory supposed that was a good thing. It proved he was right to trust Tim, because if Tim ever hid the truth from him, Rory would be able to tell. It left Rory at a loss, though. He hated seeing his man miserable, but since he didn't have a clue what was really going on, there was nothing he could do about it. All that was left was to show Tim he supported him, no matter what, so he snaked his arm underneath Tim's and rested his cheek against Tim's shoulder.

"Let's go grab some dinner. It's hamburgers and fries from Christy's, and we know that's way better than Burger King and Barnaby's combined, right?"

Tim smiled for just a moment, and then the sadness returned. "Can we just stay here for a few minutes?" He extracted his arm from Rory's grasp and wrapped it around Rory's shoulders, pulling him close and kissing his temple. "You know I love you, right? More than anything? And I'd do anything for you?"

Rory nodded, feeling his chest tighten. Any moment now, Tim was going to say they were over, that they couldn't stay together anymore, for whatever reason. Rory tried to keep his face neutral. He could do that. He'd had years of practice at that, so it should be easy.

"Let's just lie down for a moment."

It sounded like a question, a suggestion maybe, as if Rory would ever say no. He'd never do that, not even if Tim was cutting him loose. Rory desperately wanted to feel Tim's arms around him one more time. He wanted the memory and was going to do his best to remember all of it. Every detail.

They settled on the bed, Tim on his back and Rory on his side, so Rory could nuzzle Tim's neck and he could caress his man's chiseled chest. He inhaled Tim's scent. Tim hadn't showered after work, so he smelled quite manly, and Rory loved it. He was going to remember that smell for a long time to come.

Tim's hand entangled in Rory's hair was another favorite. Whenever Rory had the shakes, whenever he had nightmares, Tim would soothe him like that, and even now, it worked. As long as Rory didn't think about this probably being the last time, he was fine. When Tim's hand stopped moving, Rory put his head on Tim's chest and listened to his heartbeat. He often did that when he woke up at night and Tim was still asleep. He'd snuggle closer to Tim's back and just listen to the thumping, but it was better from the chest side, where he could rest his head and be softly rocked by Tim's breathing.

Rory looked up at Tim. There was a hesitant smile on his face, and Rory pushed the feelings of impending doom to the back of his mind. He was going to enjoy every minute of it for as long as it lasted.

They kissed, softly but without hesitation. It felt familiar and, now that Rory was allowing it, soothing as well.

"I've never loved anyone like I love you, Rory McCown."

"Me too," Rory replied, as if it wasn't the first time he'd admitted it.

This time Tim smiled for real. "You do?"

"Of course I do, you bastard." He thumped Tim's chest. "You think I just go around sleeping with guys left and right?"

"Well...."

"This is different from just sex, Tim."

"I know. You might be my first real boyfriend, but I *can* tell the difference, you know."

"Good." They kissed again, and it was just like earlier, but so different from their usual kisses. Most of the time, if they started kissing, the heat quickly rose between them as their interaction deepened and became more passionate. Kissing was just a means to an end; foreplay to end in fucking. Not this time, though. This time they were tasting each other, exploring without moving on. Rory didn't push, because he didn't want it to end, ever, and he knew that if he let the heat rise between them, it *would* end. But even the most magnificent fireworks wouldn't prevent him from regretting that end.

Tim stopped kissing and just nuzzled Rory, as if he too needed to stock his memory for later. "Are you sick?" Tim remarked. "You feel hot. Flushed."

Rory shook his head." I'm fine. It's been freezing cold for days. It's just a bit of a cold."

Tim put his hand on Rory's forehead and then smiled. "Let's go and eat something before the hamburgers are all dried out."

They got up from the bed, straightened their clothes, and left the room together.

The dinner hall was almost completely deserted, and they ate in silence. Rory couldn't stop looking at Tim, and then Tim took his hand, right there in public. Rory didn't say anything; he just tried to enjoy it and made a valiant attempt at pouring the feelings he had for Tim into the way he looked at him.

As soon as they'd finished their hamburgers, they went back upstairs and undressed each other. Even in bed, naked and exposed, close together under the covers, they had trouble getting started. They kissed, of course, and touched. Rory was still trying to map every inch of Tim's body, committing it to memory, and almost every touch was reciprocated.

Rory kept thinking this was not the Tim he thought he knew. Tim was always straightforward, unafraid, and now he was holding back, as if there were something he wanted to say but was afraid to. Rory wasn't much of a talker, though, and since he was naturally afraid of any confrontation, he just didn't have the nerve to call Tim on his change of attitude.

Their attempts at making out fizzled until they were just lying in each other's arms, both awake, but not talking or moving.

THE next morning, Rory woke up early from a fitful sleep. Neither of them had slept much, and so Rory wasn't surprised to feel Tim stir.

"I'll help you out with morning chores," Tim whispered, "but then I need to go into town to run some errands. I won't be back until dinnertime."

"Anything I can help you with?"

Tim shook his head. "It's nothing major. You're not due back at your parole officer's for another two weeks, right?"

"Right," Rory replied. As if Rory only needed to go into town for that. Tim was concealing something from him, and that was so unusual, it fed into Rory's insecurities until he couldn't even look at Tim. "Listen, I can do my own chores. You do what you need to do and I'll see you tonight." He hoped he didn't sounds too dismissive, but he needed to put some distance between them. And he needed a good, stiff drink.

Rory got up and put on some clothes before going to the crew house's mud room to get his boots and coat. The boots weren't the fancy ones Tim had bought him for his birthday; these were snow boots, and he'd bought them with his own money. The coat was Tim's, though. It was an old oilskin that was a little worn around the sleeves and too tight around Tim's shoulders. Rory was grateful for it, and since he was skinnier than Tim, it fit just fine. Rory wished it still smelled like Tim, but it didn't.

Rory had a vodka bottle hidden in the mudroom. Had Tim stumbled on it, and was that the reason for the standoffishness? Rory shook his head. Even if Tim had, it could have belonged to a number of people. In fact, Rory knew of at least one other bottle of liquor hidden in the mudroom that didn't belong to him. He took out his bottle and saw it was almost empty. He'd have to ask Coop for a ride into town so he could buy some more. Since Tim was going to be gone all day, he didn't have to find an excuse. Rory finished off the bottle and then dressed warmly to walk out into the still-dark morning.

On his way over to the barn, it dawned on him that his drinking was more habit than anything else. He hadn't felt a buzz from alcohol in so long, he wondered why he drank at all. Of course the answer to that was simple. He knew what would happen if he stopped drinking, if he just didn't talk to Coop about making a trip to the liquor store. He had no vodka left, so it would be a matter of a few hours before he got agitated, started feeling sick, and then inevitably, the shakes would start. How long would it take? The last time he'd dried out, they'd found him passed out on the floor of his cell and had taken him to the infirmary. He didn't remember how long he'd been there and hadn't bothered asking, because a few days later, he'd found himself a supplier among the prison guards. He was a married man with a taste for men, and Rory had gladly exchanged sexual favors for regular supplies of cheap liquor. Quitting the drink had its advantages, though. The one thing he remembered from his sober days was the clarity he'd felt then—clarity he hadn't experienced in years.

Rory started his morning work clearing out the foaling stalls, and as usual, it gave him too much time to think. Tim's distance had awakened an idea he couldn't shake. Did Tim deserve better than him? Rory shook his head and attacked his work with so much vigor, the mare positioned herself between Rory and her foal. Rory stopped and put his hand on her flank, calming her.

"It's okay, girl. Don't worry." He stroked her and felt her relax. Rory often talked to the horses and found them exceptionally good listeners, especially very early in the morning when it was too cold to put them outside in the meadow. He smiled when he realized the reason was that they didn't talk back and just let him ramble. It also helped that they seemed to like the sound of his voice, although Rory never cared for it that much.

The foal came out of hiding and nuzzled Rory's back as he was raking up the dirty straw. Rory turned around to look at the inquisitive youngster and his vigilant mother.

"Hey, boy," Rory said, holding out his hand to let the foal sniff it. "So what do you think? Would Tim like me better sober?" He'd only just uttered the words when his hand started shaking. He pulled it back and shook it, then held it out again and saw the tremor was gone. "It's gonna be hell, and I don't want him to have to go through it with me. I don't want him to see me like that. Then again, once it's all over, I'll be so much better. No more hiding, no more sneaking around." Rory closed his eyes. "Go away." This time he wasn't addressing the foal and mare, but the voices inside his head. *It'll never work, Rory. How many times have you thought about quitting? How many times have you drunk mouthwash because you didn't even have the money for a cheap bottle of vodka? How many times have you thought about quitting, only to lower yourself to stealing from other people or from gas stations because you just couldn't hack it? Weakling. You won't last past lunch time. Faggot weakling.*

Rory had almost forgotten about the voices. They'd be worse than usual. How long would he have to endure them? If he really set his mind to it, he could last a few hours, he was sure of that, but would that be enough?

By the time he was done with the foaling stalls, he was hungry, so he hurried back to the crew house and grabbed some sandwiches. He ate quickly, without really tasting them, simply because he knew he'd feel better with a full stomach, then he wiped the table with a paper towel and discarded it. When he looked at his hand, it was shaking again, and Rory knew it was getting worse. All he could think of was that he needed a drink, but his hip flask was empty and his hidden stash was depleted.

He had a choice. He could try and find Coop and either ask him to bring a few bottles from the liquor store or suggest they go together, since Coop usually didn't mind driving into town. Or he could find a place to weather the storm. Rory knew he couldn't go cold turkey in Tim's room. Tonight he'd be at his worst, and he didn't want Tim to find him all sweaty and shaking and not making much sense. He was going to have to lock himself up someplace safe.

After his late breakfast, Rory remembered that he'd promised Hugh to look at Old Mackenzie's truck to see whether he could get it running again. Rory liked working on engines, so it would be a good distraction. It was also parked in one of the old barns, so he would be sheltered from the icy wind. That was a good thing, because he was sneezing and coughing. He wondered if that was another symptom of his body's desperate need for alcohol or whether he was actually coming down with something.

Like Hugh had told him, the key was in the glove compartment, but the truck wouldn't start. Hugh had already charged the battery, and it didn't sound totally dead when Rory tried to get it to catch on, so he opened the hood. "Stop it," he told his shaking hands as he looked over the electrical connections of the old truck, taking out spark plugs, cleaning them, and putting them back. After all the cleaning, he got in and tried to get it to start it again. At first it seemed reluctant, and then it sprung to life. Rory couldn't resist smiling. He still hadn't lost his touch. All it needed was a little maintenance.

Rory got out to open the barn door after deciding it would be good to take the truck out for a spin. He knew he couldn't drive far because he had no license, but he figured he could take it around the ranch, so he drove it out around the homesteads and then toward the driveway. It had been a long time since Rory had driven a truck and it felt good, so he kept on driving, out the front gate and toward the road. It was just past noontime and the traffic was fairly busy, despite the snow covering much of the road. Suddenly Rory found himself in front of the liquor store, not really realizing where he'd gone until he was in front of it, still inside the truck.

All of a sudden, his mind was crystal clear. He couldn't go inside. If he wanted to prove to Tim that he was worthy of being his lover, he had to prove he could kick this habit. He shifted the truck into reverse and backed out of the parking lot, determinedly driving along. There was only one place he could go. It was a little out of the way, but it was a place with good memories: Tim's birthday celebration motel room.

Failure. "No I'm not," Rory answered the voices in his head before walking into the front office of the motel. He paid the clerk with the money he would have spent on liquor and was certain it was a good decision. As he used his key to open the room door he added, "I'm not letting you win again. I'm going to show you I'm not a failure."

Faggot.

Worthless faggot.

Rory smiled, despite the shakes becoming worse by the minute. The voices weren't very imaginative today. So what if he was a fag. It was the truth, after all, although personally, he'd use less colorful language. There was no denying that Rory loved a man so desperately he was going to do anything he could to keep him. So what if that meant he'd be called names?

Rory's nose was running, and he took out some tissues and blew it. A headache was forming behind his eyes.

Cocksucker.

Fudge packer.

He sank down on the bed and tried to close his eyes, then rolled into a fetal position as he started to feel cold.

Shit stabber.

"Stop it. Stop it. Please stop." Rory cradled his head, which was pounding, not just with the horrible words but with actual, physical pain. He was also cold, so cold he was shivering, and it felt different from the shakes.

Fairy.

Pillow biter.

Sausage jockey.

He stopped listening to the words. They no longer meant anything to him. He was all those things. He was a worthless little shit who liked to be fucked in the ass and who loved to suck cock. So what? It wasn't like he could change that. Not in twenty-five years had they been able to beat or rape that out of him. And even if they could, he wouldn't want them to.

Tim.

Battle stations!

Tim was the reason he was doing this. Tim was the reason Rory was okay with who he was, except for this one thing he hadn't been able to change about himself. That was all about to change now. And Rory was going through with it even if it killed him.

Full Battle Rattle! Get off your lazy asses!

His teeth were chattering now. He felt like he was in an icebox. He had to get warm.

With great difficulty he rolled off the bed and crawled to the bathroom. He managed to turn on the shower and waited until the water cascading over him was scalding hot. Slowly the chattering stopped and the tremors started to take over again. They were a nuisance too, but he'd weather through them. Breathing was hard, though, especially when he started coughing.

Sand storm! Take cover!

Rory was coughing his lungs out and shaking as he tried to wipe the sand, no… water off the top of his head. He had to get out. The water was too much.

Bo-HE-ka!

Rory crawled out of the bathroom, away from the cold tiles. He managed to find something to wrap around himself. A sheet? A blanket? "Embrace the suck." It became his mantra. That and, "A little longer. This too shall end." He couldn't say it out loud without coughing, though, so he thought it. It also shut out the voices. At least some of them.

Bend over, boy. You like taking it up the ass? There's a few guys here who'd love to oblige. And Charlie just loves to watch his boy perform. Right, Charlie?

Rory's eyes opened with a start. He'd forgotten about that. He'd forgotten all about what had happened after their CO had found them in bed together.

There was pounding on the door. The men were back. Men from their platoon. Men he'd trusted his life to, some whose lives he'd saved and who'd saved him. They all turned on him, hurt him like nobody had before. Hurt him like he'd only ever been hurt once before, when he was nine. He'd forgotten all about that one too, pushed it away, hidden it in the depths of his brain. Now it was back, and all he could think of was that he couldn't let that happen again.

They were almost through the door. He had to defend himself.

—22—

WHEN Tim returned to the ranch late that afternoon, Rory was nowhere to be found.

"Did you try the truck barn?" Hugh suggested. "A few days ago I suggested he take a look at Old Mac's truck. I figured that if he could get it to work, he'd have wheels of his own. It's really old and probably not worth the maintenance, but it's just gathering dust right now and—"

Tim shut his brother up by shaking his head. "Rory doesn't have a driver's license."

"He looked kind of happy when I told him about the truck. I figured it would be a good challenge for him, and since everything is snowed under, work is slow anyway."

Tim sighed. "I'll go take a look." He walked out into the failing light of the early evening. He had to pick up his mood before finding Rory, even after a disappointing day like today. He'd visited a few ranches in the neighborhood, trying to secure Rory another job, but nobody wanted the risk of taking on a convicted horse thief, not even after Tim explained how well he was doing. He even did what he'd feared he'd have to do and offered his own services as a wrangler in the hope it would make them bite. He'd received several work offers, but none of them extended to Rory, and he'd made it clear that they were a package deal, even if it meant advertising his more than friendly connection to Rory.

So he came home with no results to show for it and the dreaded feeling that he was going to have to lay his cards on the table for Rory, explaining that Hunter and Grant were asking him to leave the ranch. He had no idea how he was going to explain it to Rory without hurting him beyond repair. He hoped he could play it by ear.

As Tim neared the truck barn, he saw the door was open and the light was on. Despite the dread of having to bring Rory bad news, the idea of seeing his lover again made Tim smile. The smile quickly disappeared when Rory didn't answer to his name. Tim walked among the trucks and tractors and peered inside every one of them, but no Rory.

Then he noticed Old Mac's truck was gone.

"Damn, Rory," Tim murmured to himself. "Getting caught driving without a license might be enough for that bastard to revoke your parole!"

Tim walked out again and followed the tracks in the snow right up to the homesteads and beyond. He decided to jump in his own truck, knowing the tracks would get muddled as soon as he drove off the ranch but unable to just sit around and wait for Rory to return. He hoped he had a good enough recollection of what Mac's truck looked like that he would recognize it if he saw it around town. He had no idea where Rory could have gone. All he could hope was that he would find Rory before the cops did.

After unsuccessfully driving around for about an hour, he turned to the interstate and drove in the direction of the bar where their relationship had started. Although it was hard for Tim to believe that Rory would go looking for casual sex again, there was a little voice telling him that after last night's failed attempt at having sex and the brush off that morning, it wasn't entirely out of character for Rory to go there. Tim told himself that at least if he could catch Rory there, he'd be able to prevent him from getting caught drinking and driving. They could discuss the reasons for Rory going there later; after he'd found him.

He'd only just entered the interstate when he saw the exit Rory had directed him to on his birthday. It brought back memories of playful banter, a very relaxed Rory, and wonderfully hot sex. Before he consciously realized it, Tim had taken the off-ramp and was driving to the motel. He figured it would only set him back about ten minutes to drive through the parking lot and then continue on his way.

"Their" motel room was all the way in the back, but it didn't take Tim that long to recognize the old green Ford truck parked in front of it. He only just managed to cut the engine before jumping out, a mix of emotions running through him. Of course he was happy that he'd found Rory—or at least the truck he was supposed to have driven off with—but then he started wondering what Rory was doing there. Had he met someone else, and was this his go-to place to have sex? Or possibly worse: was Rory hiding here for some reason?

Tim knew there was only one way to find out. He looked through the window of the motel room, but the curtains were drawn. There was light on inside, though, and a small sliver of it shone through between the curtain and the side of the window. Tim saw a glimpse of a naked body and recognized the tribal tattoo on Rory's arm.

For a moment he contemplated doing the right thing and running to the office to get the manager, but then he figured he'd have to do some explaining, and the man would probably call 911. Rory wasn't moving, so valuable time would be lost. Tim made a split-second decision and forcibly planted his shoulder against the door. When it didn't budge, he ignored the pain in his arm and tried again. This time the door gave way and he burst into the room.

Rory looked up and then scrambled to his feet, as though shielding himself from an unknown enemy.

"It's me, Rory."

Rory didn't seem to recognize him, so Tim didn't push.

"It's okay, Rory. Are you cold?" Tim could see Rory's wet skin glistening in the light of the bedside lamp. He was shaking violently and didn't seem in control of most of his movements, so Tim grabbed the covers off the bed nearest the door and held them out to Rory.

Rory shook his head in short, spastic movements and tried to move back even more, tripping over something that was lying in his way. He never took his eyes off Tim, and Tim was almost certain Rory didn't know who he was. What was wrong with Rory? Had he taken drugs? Tim didn't pretend to be a man of the world, so he had no idea what could have caused this condition in his lover, but he knew Rory needed help, because Rory could barely stay upright and was shaking uncontrollably. Every step Tim took closer to him was met with the look of a caged animal. Tim tried to think what he could do. The only thing that came to mind was what he would do with a frightened, injured horse, but he was afraid to break eye contact. He spoke, using quiet, soothing tones.

"I'm here to help you, Rory. Don't be afraid. It's me, Tim. I've never hurt you before, remember? I was always your champion. I was always in your corner, right?"

Rory didn't answer, but he did seem to relax some.

"You need to stay warm, Rory, because I think you're sick, and you need more help than I can give you here. Let me take you to the hospital."

"No hospital," Rory rasped. His voice was raw, and the two words launched a coughing fit that made Tim's skin crawl.

"Okay, no hospital," Tim lied, just to soothe Rory. "But you have to let me take care of you, Rory." Tim took another step closer and Rory let him. He held up the blankets, and Rory scrambled back, but he was trapped against the wall, and Tim didn't move closer. "Take the blanket. You'll feel less cold." Rory didn't budge, but he seemed to settle, allowing Tim closer than he'd been before. Tim crouched down, getting on hands and knees. Although Rory kept watching him, they'd forged a stalemate. For a moment Tim looked over at the door. It was still half-open, and because of the cold, he contemplated getting up to close it, but he was too afraid Rory wouldn't let him approach again, so he didn't. Since the manager hadn't caught on by now, and they were all the way at the end of the long line of rooms, Tim figured they wouldn't get too many spectators.

After what felt like a very long time, Rory started losing the battle with his fatigue, and Tim saw the chance to crawl another bit closer. He was almost touching Rory when Rory startled awake. Tim launched himself at the more slender man, shielding himself with the blanket, but Rory was surprisingly quick, and with amazing power, his fist connected with Tim's face. Tim saw stars and stumbled back.

"Rory, please?" Tim pleaded, but Rory shook his head. There was confusion in his eyes, though, as if suddenly, Rory recognized him.

"T-Timmy?"

"Yes!" Relief filling his voice, Tim tried to get closer, but Rory shouted at him.

"No. Go away. Don't want you to see me like this!" Rory launched into another coughing fit, and Tim knew he was losing the battle. He also understood the urgency of getting Rory to a hospital. He had to call for help. He took out his cell phone and contemplated calling 911. The problem with that was that the police would be informed, and if Rory had taken drugs, it would land him back in jail. Even if he hadn't, the motel room was a mess, and they might conclude that Rory had a violent outburst and arrest him anyway. So 911 was out. Neither Grant nor Hunter wanted anything to do with Rory, so Tim didn't want to call them. He needed someone who could help him handle Rory, and if need be, use some necessary violence, so Calley or Izzie were out of the question, which left only one possibility. Tim knew Hugh wasn't Rory's biggest fan, but he was still Tim's brother and would come if he called. He'd deal with the explanations later.

As Rory was dozing off, propped against the wall, Tim dialed Hugh's number. He hoped Hugh would answer soon.

"Hugh?" he said as soon as the ringing stopped.

"Yeah. What's up?"

"Sorry, Hugh, but I don't have time for small talk. My friend… Rory's in trouble. I need to take him to the hospital but he won't let me and I need help."

"So call 911."

"Hugh, please. I can't involve the authorities. They'll send him back to jail. Just this once, simply help me out and don't be a hardass."

There was silence at the other end of the line, and Tim kicked himself for deciding to call his brother.

"Listen." Hugh groaned. "Where are you?"

Tim sighed with relief and gave Hugh the address of the motel.

"Okay, I'll be there in about ten minutes. Hang in there. Do I need to bring anything?"

Tim couldn't think. "Your muscle. I don't know, Hugh, just get here."

The phone went silent, and Tim looked at his lover, who was still lying against the wall. He slowly crawled closer and managed to put the blanket over Rory but didn't dare to do more. Rory looked small and even skinnier than he usually did. His skin was glistening, and while he seemed asleep, his breathing was raspy and irregular. Tim had the feeling they were running out of time.

After a while, Tim saw headlights and worried about cops, but then realized the lights weren't flashing and it was probably just Hugh.

Tim was beyond caring what Hugh would think. He'd deal with that later.

"So where's the troublemaker?"

"Ssh," Tim cautioned his brother. "He's just fallen asleep."

Hugh looked at him with concern. "And he did this to you?" He reached up to Tim's swollen eye, and Tim nodded.

"Don't worry about me."

"So what happened?"

Tim sighed. "I have no idea. Rory disappeared around noon, and when I found him here, he was a mess. He didn't even recognize me. I think he has a fever. His skin is clammy. He's coughing like he's gonna die."

"He's a skinny guy, Tim. How come he decked you?"

Tim shrugged. "He's a Gulf War veteran. I guess instinct kicked in."

Hugh cautiously approached Rory and crouched down next to him. He took Rory's wrist and waited, then felt his skin. "His heart is racing, and I think you're right. He's got a fever. We need to get this guy some medical attention." Hugh waved his hand in front of Rory's face and then opened one of his eyes. Rory didn't react. "You don't know what happened?"

"No," Tim answered, too exhausted to care.

"He on drugs?"

Tim snorted. "Not that I know of, but I must admit it crossed my mind."

Hugh looked up at Tim with concern all over his face. "Let's get this guy to a hospital so they can figure out what's going on."

As they tried to move him, Rory woke up and started fighting again, but Hugh was a tall, strong guy, and together they managed to get Rory wrapped into a blanket and then into Hugh's truck.

—23—

"SHIT, Timmy, what exactly did he do to you?" Hugh asked when he returned from picking his wife Izzie up from the homestead.

Tim shook his head at Hugh to stop fussing over his swollen eye. "Nothing. At least nothing worse than he did to himself."

"What are you talking about?" Hugh asked. "He decked you. I never thought he was the violent sort."

"He isn't. He may have been a thief, but he never used violence. This was instinct taking over."

"So have they told you anything more? What caused this?"

"They don't know. They're not telling me anything. I just know he had a fever and he was shaking and coughing and vomiting. He didn't recognize me, and when I tried to get closer to him, he hit me."

Hugh brushed aside Tim's hair and took another look at Tim's shiner, despite his brother's protests. "He beat you up?"

"Just slugged me. Once. It's not his fault."

"I think it's time you stopped making excuses for him, Tim."

"Stop shouting," Tim said a lot more quietly than Hugh had. He looked around the waiting room, where other people were staring at them.

"I'll stop shouting when my baby brother comes to his senses. Rory McCown is a criminal with anger management issues, and the sooner you come to terms with that, the better."

Tim pushed Hugh away from him. "When have you ever seen Rory lose his temper? Hell, you have a shorter fuse than he does, Hugh. He'd much rather walk away from a confrontation, and you know it."

"Come on, guys, let's go outside to talk this over. These people here don't need to hear this," Izzie said, trying to come between them with some caution.

Hugh looked at her and seemed to calm down. Tim knew she made sense. Izzie always made sense.

"Hugh, go find us some coffee. Tim and I will be just outside." She nodded at her husband and then ushered Tim out the emergency room doors.

"Okay, spill," she said as soon as they were outside the sliding doors. "What the hell happened?"

Tim shrugged. "Rory was nowhere to be found. He'd run off while I was gone, and when I returned nobody knew where he was. I found Rory at this motel room and he was sick."

"Back up for a moment," she told Tim, holding up her hand. "How did you know where to find him?"

Tim shrugged again.

"Was it a place where the two of you went together in the past?"

Tim swallowed but didn't answer.

"Tim, I'm not the *National Enquirer*. Or his parole officer. If you tell me something in confidence, it stays between us. I've always known you were gay, remember? Did I ever tell anyone? No! I let you do that. I've seen you and Rory together. I didn't tell anyone that either. Not even your big brother, who I don't like to keep secrets from, on account of him being my husband, you get that?"

"Hugh's always pretty much known too." Tim still didn't answer her question but threw her a cautious stare.

"So what's the problem, then?"

Tim took a long breath. "I love him, Izz."

"I know," Izzie said, a lot quieter. She gazed at him with compassion, which Tim really hated. "It's no big surprise, Tim. I've seen the way you look at him, and I've seen how he looks at you. Besides, he *is* sleeping in your room." She took Tim's hand and led him to a bench just outside the ER entrance. "And he can be a really sweet guy when you get to know him."

"You think so?"

She nodded. "He's a hard worker. You're a lucky guy."

Tim leaned against her and put his head on her shoulder.

"Now can you tell me what happened?"

At that moment Hugh walked up to them with three cups of coffee.

"Thanks, darling," Izzie said as she took two cups from her husband and handed one to Tim. "Could you maybe get me something to eat, too? I'm starving."

Hugh hesitated for a moment and then walked off again.

"You didn't have to send him away," Tim said to Izzie.

"Yes, I did," Izzie replied. "There's no way you're going to tell me anything with your brother here."

Tim nodded, silently agreeing with Izzie's assessment.

"So what happened?"

"Grant and Hunter know about us. But they're being sued by Miranda for custody of Matthew, and their lawyer thinks having a convicted felon living on the ranch will give her ammunition to get custody, so they asked me to tell Rory to leave."

Izzie shook her head. "I can't believe they did that to you, Timmy. Or to Rory."

"It's about Matty, Izz. I can't blame them, but I couldn't bring myself to tell Rory. This is the only family he's ever had. So I tried to fix it. Today I tried to find him another job so he could stay out on parole and wouldn't have to go back to jail. But nobody will hire him."

Izzie pulled Tim closer and kissed his hair. "You can't take the entire world on your shoulders, Timmy. Even you aren't strong enough for that."

Tim shrugged it away. "Anyway, I had the feeling he'd misinterpreted my horrible mood from the night before, so when he disappeared…. By sheer luck I found him at this motel we've been to before. He was sick, and I didn't know what to do. He didn't want to see a doctor, but he just got sicker and sicker, and he was shaking and sweating and coughing." Tim swallowed hard. "Then he finally fell asleep, and when I touched him, he woke up and then he slugged me. I called Hugh, and he helped me get Rory here. I thought he was going to die, Izz."

Izzie pulled him into another hug, and at that moment, Tim's cell phone buzzed in his back pocket.

"Tim Conroy," Tim answered. "Yes, I do. I'm right outside. I brought him in. I'll be right there."

Izzie looked at him, puzzled.

"That was the doctor. They want to talk to me. Apparently they found something in his pocket with my number on it, and that makes me the closest thing to next of kin." Tim grabbed Izzie's hand and dragged her inside. After some negotiating, the triage nurse let them back inside the ER.

"You're the person I called regarding Rory McCown?"

"Yes," Tim said with a quiver in his voice.

"Let's go in here and talk," the doctor said, gesturing to a small office. He didn't offer either of them a place to sit but instead started talking as soon as they entered.

"May I ask what your relation is to Mr. McCown?"

"I work with him," Tim said.

"My husband's his foreman, and my brother's his boss," Izzie elaborated.

"Does he have any family?" the doctor asked.

"I don't know," Izzie answered.

"No, he doesn't," Tim corrected her. "I'm the closest thing he has to family."

"And you're his…?" the doctor fished.

"Partner," Izzie was quick to answer, eliciting an angry stare from Tim.

It worked, though, since the doctor now addressed Tim. "This won't be easy to hear. Are you sure you want her here for this?"

Tim looked at Izzie and then nodded at the doctor.

"We'd like to admit Mr. McCown, but we need to know if he'll be able to foot the bill," the doctor said coldly.

"I'll vouch for it," Izzie said before Tim could say anything. "My brother owns one of the largest horse ranches this side of Idaho. I'll sign for it if I need to."

"What's wrong with him?" Tim asked, unable to wait any longer.

"He's going through severe alcohol withdrawal."

"What?" Tim asked. "I thought he was sick. A bad cold or something?"

"He's got severe bronchitis too, but he's already responding to the antibiotics we gave him, so that won't be our chief concern. I'm sure you must be aware of his drinking?"

Tim couldn't believe what the guy was saying. "Rory drinks, but no more than me."

"Listen," the doctor said, opening his hands. "This isn't his first time he's tried to quit, but the problem with chronic alcoholics like him is that every time they try, it gets worse. The shaking, vomiting, and even the fever are signs of physical withdrawal, of his body having to go without. The violence and the lashing out, that's a psychotic episode. Some people see pink elephants, some people go totally paranoid. That's what he's going through now." The man seemed a bit more sympathetic all of a sudden. "Did he do that to you?" He pointed at Tim's eye.

Tim shook it away. He was too devastated by what the doctor had told him and didn't know how to react. "I thought he was sick."

"Oh, he is. He's a very sick man. What he needs right now is medication and rest. What he'll need in two days' time is a rehab facility, but I should warn you that in cases like his, the chance of relapse is almost a hundred percent. Like I said, this isn't his first time. He's been through this before, and for all we know, he's been sober for stretches of time. He needs a place where he can learn to live without alcohol, and afterward he'll need an environment where he's supported and cared for. This is not going to be a walk in the park."

Tim tried to process all the information but found he couldn't fathom it. "Can I see him?"

The doctor shook his head. "That wouldn't be a good idea. As soon as the payment papers are signed, we'll have him admitted and start treatment. We'll see tomorrow."

"Can you at least ask him to call me?"

The man hesitated, then nodded. "I'll suggest it to him, but depending on his state of mind, he may not be ready for that for a while."

"Could you just make sure he has my number, in case he does want to call?"

The doctor nodded. "It's in his personal effects, and he'll get those back as soon as he can be trusted with them."

Tim thanked the doctor and followed Izzie to the admissions counter to sign the necessary documents. He couldn't get what happened over the last forty-eight hours out of his head. He was used to Rory's mood swings by now, but he'd never seen him like that before. Could it all be attributed to alcohol? The doctor had called Rory a chronic alcoholic, but the only time Tim recalled seeing Rory drunk was when he'd knocked a few back himself. And come to think of it, Tim had felt the effects of the alcohol, but Rory had still looked pretty sober. Surely the doctor was wrong.

It wasn't that Tim didn't know what an alcoholic looked like. There was a reason he barely touched the stuff, and Hugh was pretty wary of alcohol too, unlike their middle brother who sometimes drank enough for the three of them. Their mother had been the classic drunk, and when she died, they'd all reacted differently. Tim was the youngest and missed her most, even though Hugh reminded him that they'd never really had a mother and that their dad had always taken on most of the parenting, despite being foreman of a thriving ranch.

Tim remembered his mother mostly asleep. In the mornings, she'd never get up when the boys had to do their chores before breakfast, and even after that, it was always their dad and later Hugh who fixed them sandwiches and made sure they wore clean clothes to school. By the time they came back from school mother was "not to be disturbed," which meant she'd shout when they made too much noise but rarely came out of her room. Their dad usually slept on the sofa, and on the rare occasion that their mother made an appearance, it was to shout for another bottle, and she always looked disheveled and didn't make a lot of sense.

The dubious honor of finding their mother had fallen to Jack, who had been dragged back to their cottage by Tim because he hadn't heard any noise all day. Jack was fourteen at the time, and he had asked his sixteen-year-old brother to help him clean up before the doctor arrived. They'd kept Tim out of the room by telling him to fetch their dad.

To Tim, the memories of seeing the number of empty bottles his brothers cleared out of that room, together with what his mother looked like, lying in a puddle of her own disgusting-smelling vomit, was what an alcoholic looked like. Despite what had happened in the last twenty-four hours, he couldn't reconcile that image with how he saw Rory.

Rory was a hard worker, up at the crack of dawn every single morning. His work was neat and accurate, and he took responsibility. Yes, on more than one occasion Tim had seen Rory sneak a drink from what looked like a small hip flask, but he'd never called him on it and had never even wondered, because it never affected his work. Tim had kissed Rory more than a few times, and he loved how Rory tasted. The only time Rory had tasted of alcohol was on Tim's birthday, when he'd brought a cheap bottle of vodka to their room and had taken a large drink right in front of Tim, but that was a celebration. Surely the doctor had made a mistake in calling Rory an alcoholic?

—24—

"TIM, what brings you here?" Gable said, holding on to the door he'd just opened.

Tim swallowed before answering. "Can I come in?"

Gable took a step back, clearing the way for Tim to walk into Gable and Flynn's modest homestead.

"I'll go check to see if the horses are good for the night," Flynn said as he passed between the two other men to walk outside.

Tim saw Gable and Flynn exchange a look, and he felt grateful for the silent understanding between them and Flynn's giving them some privacy. He waited to speak until Gable had closed the door.

"I need an understanding ear. And some advice. Possibly."

Gable raised an eyebrow, smiled slightly, and walked into his kitchen where Tim followed.

"Coffee?"

"Sure." Tim sat down without being invited to do so. He didn't come to Gable's house that often, but he knew Gable well enough to know the man didn't stand on ceremony.

"So what brings you here?" Gable asked, although Tim had already told him.

"It's Rory."

Gable nodded and handed him a mug of strong, black coffee.

Tim took a sip and almost squirmed. "Got any sugar?"

Gable chuckled, reached into an overhead cabinet, and unceremoniously plopped a container of sugar on the kitchen table before sitting down opposite Tim.

"Never knew you took sugar in your coffee."

Tim smiled. "Call it Rory's bad influence."

Gable smiled back and added a spoon of sugar to his as well.

"So what's with Rory? Is he in trouble?"

"No. Yes."

"Which is it?"

"He's not in trouble with the law, but...." Tim didn't finish. All of a sudden it all seemed trite.

Gable put his hand over Tim's, and although Gable was a man of few words and even fewer gestures, especially toward other men, the warmth flowing between Gable's hand and the hot coffee mug infused into Tim's entire body. It helped him to relax and made the uneasy feeling he got from Gable's intense stare abate a bit.

"He's an alcoholic. And I didn't know," Tim confessed.

Gable raised both eyebrows and squared his jaw. "I thought you and him—" He gestured with his head as if Rory was just upstairs.

"That's why I'm kicking myself so hard."

"Because you never noticed."

"Because I didn't *want* to notice."

Gable didn't say anything, but Tim could tell he wanted him to continue. At his own pace, because that was the kind of guy Gable was.

"After Mom, you'd think I'd know better," Tim said after a few moments of silence.

"What does your mom have to do with it? Rory works all day. From what Hunter's told me, he's a real asset to the ranch. Now if he'd fallen down on the job and you hadn't noticed, then I'd question your judgment, but have you ever seen him drunk?"

Tim looked straight at Gable, surprised at the amount of words that had flowed out of Gable's mouth. He wasn't used to his friend being this talkative.

"Well?"

"I've seen him a little buzzed, when we go to the Barrel Run. In fact, if I drank what he does, I'd be blind drunk and you'd have to carry me home. He just seems a little...."

"More loose?" Gable eventually suggested.

"Yeah."

"Like when he kissed you three years ago and made you fall in love with him?"

"I didn't."

"No, he just made you pine for him for three years, and now he's back. And not just on your ranch, but in your bed."

"Gable!" Tim cautioned.

Gable chuckled. "You were never any good at keeping secrets from me, Timmy."

"Well, I'm not a seventeen-year-old virgin anymore."

"No, you're a grown man who's worried about his lover."

Tim opened his mouth to reply and then closed it again. He wanted to protest Gable's use of the word "lover," but he couldn't deny it. Not to Gable, the one man who knew what that meant to Tim.

"I don't know how much advice I can give you, Tim. I may have been known to sink a little deep myself in the past, and there is a reason why I'll never offer you a beer and Flynn goes without alcohol as well in this house, but that doesn't mean I'm an authority. Unless you drag Rory kicking and screaming into a hospital to dry out, he's got to want to kick the habit himself."

Before Tim could answer, Flynn walked through the door, and they both looked at him.

Flynn, clearly aware he was walking into a difficult conversation, hesitated only for a moment and then walked over to stand behind Gable, putting his hands on his lover's shoulders.

"Horses are fine and all settled in for the night."

Gable looked up at his man. "Why don't you go soak in the tub? I'll be up in a little while."

Flynn smiled lovingly at Gable, and Tim felt his stomach go warm. He knew he was envious of what Gable had found with Flynn and could only hope that one day he'd have the same with Rory. He watched how Gable's eyes never left Flynn until Flynn had disappeared upstairs.

"He's in the hospital right now," Tim said quietly as soon as he heard the water running upstairs. "I had to take him there earlier this week."

"Oh?"

"He tried to quit on his own. I found him in our motel… a motel room," Tim was quick to correct himself, hoping Gable hadn't caught on. "I thought he was going to die, Gabe."

"Well, at least he's getting help."

"He can't stay there. Besides it being hideously expensive, he can't let his parole officer find out, and the longer he stays there, the bigger the chance that asshole will catch on. The guy is just looking for an excuse, any excuse, to tell the judge Rory isn't doing a good job toeing the line. I need to bring him home so we can at least pretend he's working, and—"

"Bringing him home when he's not ready isn't going to be easy, Tim," Gable interrupted. "The only thing that kept me off the sauce after my accident was the fact I couldn't drive into town and Calley refused to bring me liquor."

"That's what worries me. At the crew house, there's booze everywhere. Hell, most of the guys there can't even contemplate an evening without drinking. And there's another thing…."

Gable nodded at Tim to urge him to go on.

"Hunter and Grant want him off the ranch. They're being sued for custody of Matty, and their lawyer thinks they'll use Rory's presence as ammunition to show the kids aren't growing up in a safe environment."

Gable whistled. "Although you and I both know there's no better place for those kids than with Hunter and Grant, outsiders might see it differently, and these days, perception is everything. So how about that cabin you inherited?"

"It's a dump. The only source of heating is the fireplace, and there's no running water. Besides, I can't lock him up, and when I'm working there's nobody to keep an eye on him. I don't know what to do, Gabe."

Gable sighed. "Listen. I'll have to talk with Flynn about this, and I can't pay him much, but if you want to bring Rory here…. As soon as he feels up to it, he can putter around the barn, maybe ride some of the younger horses. Just until you fix up the cabin, all right?"

Tim nodded. "Thanks, Gabe."

"I still need to square it with Flynn, so don't be disappointed if I have to withdraw my offer, but I'll plead your case with him."

"Gable," Flynn singsonged from upstairs.

Gable cracked a smile. "Now you better go home, because my man is waiting for me upstairs, and I do need to seduce him into having a boarder."

Tim got up and held out his hand to Gable. Gable took it, but instead of shaking it, he pulled Tim into his embrace. "Take care of your man, Timmy. He's going to need all his courage and yours too, but knowing someone cares for you makes a world of difference. I should know." He gestured upstairs.

Tim squeezed Gable tight before letting go. He wanted to thank Gable again but felt he'd sound like a broken record, so he just nodded at him, smiled, and walked out the door without saying another word.

Outside in the truck, Tim ran his hands through his hair, hoping to arrange his jumbled thoughts. Gable was right. Rory was going to have to battle his own demons, but Tim was going to be right there to support him. He knew how much Flynn's love had done to help Gable get his life back on track. Flynn had been barely more than a stranger when Gable had almost died after losing his foot, but he'd stuck around when Gable was recuperating, and now they were a solid couple and Gable's ranch was thriving. Tim could only hope that his own future somehow had Rory in it.

THE next morning, after a fitful sleep, Tim arrived at the hospital. After a week of waiting, he was finally going to be allowed to see Rory. That is, as the therapist of the substance abuse program had explained to him, if Rory wanted to see him. When he reached the floor, the nurse told him they were expecting him and showed him into a waiting room. Tim walked in, expecting to be alone. To his surprise, Rory was sitting in one of the chairs. He looked worn out and dead tired, but calm—at least a lot calmer than the last time Tim had seen him.

"Hi, Timmy," Rory said, standing up.

"Hey, Grumpy," Tim reciprocated. He was afraid of walking further until he saw a smile breaking on Rory's face. Then all he could do was fling himself around his boyfriend's thin frame. To his contentment, Rory hugged him back, and they stood holding each other for what felt like a long time. Finally Tim let go because he just had to look at Rory's face.

"So how are you doing?" Tim ran his hand through Rory's brown hair so he could see his dark-circled eyes.

"Right as rain, can't you tell?" Rory quipped. "Drugged up to my eyeballs, but I suppose that passes for fine."

"Drugged?" Tim took a step back.

"Valium. And a few other things as well. I wasn't doing so great when you brought me here."

"Well, that's an understatement. I thought I was going to lose you."

Rory hesitantly lifted his hand to caress Tim's cheekbone, which still bore some color from the night Tim just wanted to forget about. "Did I do that?"

Tim nodded. "Hugh would have chewed you a new one if you hadn't been so—"

"Totally out of my mind?"

"Yeah. I told him you didn't mean to hit me."

"I was seeing things, Tim. And they weren't pink elephants." He hesitated. "I thought I was back in the army and you were trying to kill me."

"I know, you told me."

"I did?"

"You said you were a soldier and you'd been trained to kill and that you wouldn't hesitate to kill me if I threatened you."

"I didn't know what I was saying." Rory sat down again, and Tim took the seat next to him. "I didn't mean what I said, Tim."

"I know. That's what I told Hugh. He's still pretty pissed off, though."

"He's not exactly a member of my fan club."

"He just wants to protect his baby brother."

"Only his baby brother doesn't need protecting," Rory said with an absent-minded smile. "He can take care of himself, and his boyfriend, just fine."

"Especially his boyfriend," Tim said with a sideways smile.

Rory grew serious. "Maybe Hugh was right, Tim."

"About what?" Tim tried hard not to let the feeling of dread sink in.

"About me. And about you deserving something better than a felon and a drunk."

"Let me be the judge of that, okay?"

Rory smiled, but this time the smile didn't reach all the way up to his eyes. "I've barely been sober a day since I was discharged from the army, Timmy. What makes you think I'll beat it this time?"

"You have something to live for this time," Tim answered with more confidence than he felt.

"Like what?"

"Like a job you like. A cabin to live in. Me."

"I can't let my life be dictated by you, Tim. I can't depend on you for everything."

"You don't."

"It's your cabin. And I work on your ranch."

"It's half my cabin. The other half is yours. I'm sure old Mac had a reason for putting it into his will like that."

"That was just his scribbles. The official will said it was to go to you. All of it."

Tim sighed. "That was the legal bit. Just because Mac hadn't gone back to his lawyer to get it fixed before he died."

"His lawyer being Coop Nelson, who never managed to pass the bar again after his suspension and now works as a ranch hand."

"That doesn't matter, Rory. Mac wanted us to share that cabin. He wanted us to fix it up and live there together."

"I never told him about you and me, you know."

"He knew. He was always telling me to pursue you."

"He what?"

Tim laughed at the total surprise in Rory's face. "I would check up on the foals and he'd be leaning on his pitchfork, smiling that nearly toothless smile of his and telling me not to let you get away. Like you were a girl and it was the most normal thing in the world."

"Maybe to him it was. He used to live in the city when he was young, you know."

"I didn't know that."

Rory nodded. "He told me, that first night I slept in the crew house. When you brought me home from prison. He sat next to me in the crew kitchen after everyone had moved to the TV room, poured me a Scotch, and gave me the third degree. For the longest time he was the only one who'd talk to me. Except you, of course."

"He was probably the only one who didn't give a shit what the others thought."

"I was surprised about the cabin. That he owned such a thing."

Tim shrugged. "All I know is that when Hunter's father bought the land from Mac's family, the only stipulation was that the cabin remain in the family. It wasn't in a great location, and the Krauses were only interested in the prime grazing land anyway. The cabin itself isn't that great. There's a well, but no running water, and there's no heating except for a fireplace that hasn't been used since it was still occupied. I'm surprised it survived the last storm, to be frank. It'll need a lot of work if we're going to make it habitable again."

"So let's forget about it, then. It's not like I had any money before I was taken in here, and I sure as hell don't have any to fix that cabin."

"I do. And the hospital bills are covered. Worker's benefit."

"Tim." Rory sighed. "I can't take that."

"You can and you will. As soon as you're well enough to leave, I'm taking you to Gable's. At least at his house there's no alcohol, since he can't be trusted around a bottle of hard liquor either. We'll fix the cabin up and move in there as soon as we know it won't collapse around us at the first sign of heavy winds."

"Gable's?"

"Well, taking you to the crew house is like letting you sleep in a bar, Grumpy."

Tim was glad to see the nickname still made his boyfriend smile. Seeing Rory's crooked tooth made him want to kiss him, and he leaned closer, but Rory didn't reciprocate.

"You can help him out on his ranch, and once you're feeling a bit better, you can come work at ours. And in our spare time, we can fix up the cabin. You're good with your hands and so am I. We can do a lot of it ourselves. Hunter said we could use some of the leftover wood from their house, and Grant said the woodshed was full of useful stuff too."

"And they're just going to give it to us?"

"I'm practically family, Rory. Besides, it's welcome. We'll have to invest in some decent plumbing and put in electricity, so I'm not going to say no to a few handouts."

"I can do the electricity," Rory suggested a little hesitantly.

"You can? What are you doing mucking out stables if you can fix cars and electrical stuff?"

"With my record, nobody'll hire me, Tim."

Tim pulled his boyfriend closer and kissed his hair. He didn't know what to say. Rory was right. He'd found out firsthand that nobody was jumping to hire Rory, no matter how desperate they were.

Rory leaned back in his chair and stared straight ahead, as if he needed time to let it sink in.

Just when Tim thought it was probably better if he left, Rory shifted and leaned against him, letting his head drop to Tim's shoulder.

Tim had to swallow away the emotions that surged up inside his chest.

Rory wasn't pushing him away.

—25—

TWO days later, Tim picked Rory up from the hospital. Rory still looked like he hadn't slept in days, but Tim had barely started driving when Rory was asleep next to him on the truck bench.

As soon as he knew he'd be allowed to bring Rory home, Tim had called Gable. It had taken some persuasion, but Flynn had finally conceded in letting Rory stay with them for a little while. Flynn's only stipulation had been that they start work on the cabin, and that he and Gable would help to make it habitable as soon as humanly possible.

As a goodwill gesture, Tim had started working on it already, sweeping out the rooms, fixing a broken window, and changing the rusty lock on the front door so they could secure the building, since it wasn't hidden from the highway like most of the other ranch houses. For now it was okay to work in it, even if the weather outside wasn't all that predictable, but there was no way they could stay there overnight yet.

Until then, Tim would stay at the crew house and Rory would live at Gable and Flynn's place. Since Rory didn't own much and Tim had packed all his clothes so he could wear them at the hospital, they didn't need to swing by the crew house to pick up Rory's things.

"We're here," Tim said as he shook Rory awake.

"Uh? Oh." Rory stretched to crack his back as he woke. The look he gave Tim melted his heart, and Tim pulled Rory into his arms and kissed him. "Maybe you should stay here too," Rory suggested.

Tim smiled. "I think one house guest is enough for these two. Remember, they're used to having the place to themselves."

"Which means that if I hear sex noises in the middle of the night, I'll know who it is, as opposed to at the crew house when it could be just about anyone."

"Exactly." Tim nodded with a smile.

By the time they got out, Gable was on the porch to meet them.

"Tim. Rory." He raised his mug of coffee by way of greeting. "I hope both of you are staying for dinner, because Flynn made a roast big enough to serve an army and I hate leftovers."

Tim looked at Rory and caught him smiling. "A good roast is hard to resist. And I've heard Grant rave about Flynn's cooking, so I won't say no."

"I'll show you Rory's room first," Gable said, walking inside without checking whether they followed.

Tim walked upstairs behind Gable and noticed him still limping slightly. He figured it could just have been a tiring day.

"This is my room," Gable started the tour. "And Flynn's, of course." He pointed at the door opposite the stairs and then at another one at the end of the corridor. "And that's our guest room. Rory's for now. Until you can move to the cabin." There was no malice in Gable's words, and Tim checked Rory's expression to see how he would take Gable's turn of phrase, but Rory simply walked past them into the room.

"Nice room," he said to Gable, dropping his duffel bag on the bed and looking around. It was a simple room, a bit like the one Rory first got at the crew house but smaller, with a single bed, a night stand, and a wardrobe. "Thanks for letting me stay here."

Gable nodded. "I better go help Flynn downstairs. Dinner will be ready in about ten."

Rory sank down on the bed and looked around.

"You'll be okay," Tim said as he sat down next to Rory. "It's only temporary."

"You sound like that movie where a mother brings her son to the orphanage and soothes him by saying she'll be back for him. Only she never comes. The boy waits for his mother until he's too old to stay there, and then when he's all grown up he finds out she died in an accident the day she left and they never told him."

Tim put his arm around Rory's shoulders and kissed his temple. "I promise that if I get flattened by a falling tree, I'll make sure someone comes here and tells you about it."

"Bastard."

"This is for you, Rory. Because you didn't want rehab."

"I can't afford rehab, Tim. Do I look like some spoiled-rotten movie star or a washed-up country singer? I can't even afford to pay last week's hospital bill!"

Rory's voice sounded way too loud in the small room, and Tim saw Rory cringe when he realized it.

Tim tried to stay calm, even if Rory couldn't. "I know. And don't worry about the bill. I made sure it got paid."

"Yeah, right. I'm your charity case."

"Come on, Rory, you know that's not true."

Rory got up off the bed, and Tim followed him with his eyes as he moved his duffel bag from the bed to the one chair inside the room without making a move to unpack it.

Tim got the sneaking suspicion Rory was going to make his getaway as soon as he saw the opportunity and tried to push the dreaded feelings away.

"Rory, sit down."

"Dinner will be ready, and we shouldn't be late."

"Just for a minute."

Rory sat down again, and Tim bumped him with his shoulder. "You know I love you."

"Yeah."

"We'll have a place of our own soon."

"A leaky cabin."

"Beats sleeping rough."

"True."

"And you won't be alone."

"You'll be there."

"Yup."

"Where are we going to find the money for a stove? And a bed? And a sofa?"

Tim smiled. Rory was making plans, and he loved it. "They replaced the stoves in Beth's kitchen last year, and one of the old ones is still in storage. She said we could have that. It's ancient, but it works, apparently. And they have a sofa too. We can just move my bed from the crew house to the cabin. In fact, we can move all my furniture. So we'll have two wardrobes too. Grant's making us a kitchen table and chairs. Hunter says Grant's tickled pink that he can make us furniture, because Hunter wanted store-bought stuff for their house and he still hasn't lived that down."

"So how much work will this cabin take?"

Tim shrugged. "Maybe a week or two. Or three. Then we should be dry."

Rory moved closer and put his head on Tim's shoulder, just like that day in the hospital, and for the first time, Tim figured they were all right again.

—26—

THE first few days were tough. Rory still had to take his meds, and they made him feel tired and restless at the same time. He tried to stay busy helping out around Gable's ranch and enjoyed that Gable let him ride some of his horses, but he often had to rest and he still had a cough that wouldn't go away, so that slowed him down as well. He'd hit it off with Gable right away, because he was kind of quiet and didn't crowd him. Flynn was another thing altogether. Tim had told him that Flynn had needed the most persuading, and so Rory was a little wary of him. It got on Rory's nerves pretty quickly that the younger of his two hosts kept hovering around him, as if he was checking up on him. Rory knew better than to say anything, since he was there only because of the friendship between Tim and Gable, and he knew that would sour quickly if he blew up in front of Flynn. That didn't mean he had an easy time of it.

After Rory mucked out the stalls of Gable and Flynn's riding horses, he turned the corner with his wheelbarrow and practically ran over Flynn. Unable to hold his temper, he dropped the barrow and briskly walked the other way.

"Everything okay?" Flynn asked behind him.

"Everything is fine," Rory hissed between clenched teeth. He took a deep breath and grabbed a broom, trying to calm his nerves. "I'm sorry if I ran into you."

"You didn't," Flynn replied.

Rory knew he had to say something and hoped Flynn wouldn't take it the wrong way. "I just… I know how to muck out stalls and rub down horses. I know what to feed them. I've been doing this over at the Blue River Ranch for a while now."

"I know," Flynn said casually. "I just wanted to be around in case you had questions."

Rory didn't reply right away. He was a little surprised that Flynn hadn't become mad yet. Usually when Rory spoke his mind, he was misunderstood and it would ruin everything.

"I'm crowding you." It wasn't a question. "Gable tells me I do that." Flynn chuckled. "In fact, he told me to give you some space just this morning."

Rory looked at Flynn and saw him smile. He still wasn't totally at ease, but some of the tension was gone.

"It's not that I don't trust you. I'm just a bit of a stickler for details. I need to learn to let go."

"That's okay," Rory replied.

"No, it isn't, but I'll learn. Just tell me to lay off your case and I will."

Rory bit his lip. "I can't tell you that. You're the boss."

Flynn laughed. "Gable is the boss, actually. And you and him are a lot alike. I know how to handle him, so it should be easier with you, but it isn't. Let's make a deal, okay?"

Rory nodded while he continued sweeping the floor.

"If you have any questions, ask. Either me or Gable."

"Okay."

"And I'll try to leave you alone."

Rory nodded. His nervousness didn't abate completely until Flynn left. When he retrieved the wheelbarrow, Flynn wasn't around either, and Rory started to relax. After that, Flynn was straightforward with Rory, telling him exactly what he expected of him. After their initial confrontation, Rory realized he liked knowing where he stood.

WHENEVER Rory took a moment to catch his breath or rest his aching muscles, the thoughts he hated came back to him. Although he tried to resist them, he found himself thinking of ways to leave the ranch and go into town. He knew where the guys kept the truck keys, and he knew when the mailman came. Whenever Calley came to the ranch, he was tempted to ask her to bring him a bottle of something stronger than water, but he knew it would be counterproductive, so he didn't. But boy, was he tempted, every moment of the day and night. He hoped it would get better eventually, just like Lamar, his sponsor at the AA meetings, had promised.

Every evening, Tim came by the ranch to see him. Sometimes he brought food and joined Flynn in the kitchen to prepare it, but most of the time Tim just joined them for dinner and then took Rory into town for his meeting. Rory always felt guilty that Tim had to wait for him in the truck, but it showed Tim's dedication—not that Rory needed any proof of that.

Nights were the worst. Although the constant fatigue made Rory long for his bed as soon as they got back from town, it took him forever to fall asleep, and every little sound woke him again. He was grateful that Gable and Flynn weren't the type to go at it all night long, because the walls of the ranch house were paper thin.

It was those moments in the evening or just before daybreak, when he heard the whispered terms of endearment and the soft moans coming from the other room, that he knew what was missing. Although Rory had slept alone all his life, he realized he missed sleeping next to Tim. He missed it more than the sex, although when he was listening for the stifled grunts and other evidence of sex going on next door, and he took himself in hand, he wanted nothing more than for that hand to be Tim's.

Over the weekend, they'd agreed to work in the cabin, and Rory got his first look at where Tim wanted them to live. It was truly a dump, with roots growing through the steps up to the door and water damage in more than one corner. Rory could see they'd have to replace at least two walls, and probably the entire roof. Tim was annoyingly positive, though.

"Grant says the foundation and the wood skeleton are solid. He's jumping at the opportunity to help out, Rory. Hunter and Grant built their own house, and we all helped, so this should be easy. The cabin is much smaller, and everyone promised they'd help out, so in a few weeks, we'll have a place of our own—"

Rory shut him up with a kiss, and it felt so good he could feel his groin stir. When Rory pulled away, Tim opened his mouth to speak and then closed it again. Then he smiled. "I missed you."

"So come with me tonight, or let me sleep in your room," Rory said, trying not to make it sound too much like begging, although obviously, it was just that. "I miss you too."

Tim didn't get to answer, because the front door flew open and Hugh stormed through it, closely followed by Izzie and their two little girls. Just moments later, Grant and Hunter followed with Danny, Hugh's ten-year-old son, in tow.

"Let's get started," Grant suggested.

"I don't know if having the girls here is such a good idea," Tim stated. "They could hurt themselves, and—"

Izzie, carrying her youngest on her hip, came closer to Tim and kissed him on the mouth. "Don't fret, Timmy. I'm just here to see what you need. I'm going shopping, and it looks like you could use some more cleaning stuff." She walked into the area that was once a kitchen and opened some of the cabinets. "Looks like these need work too, Grant," she called out to her brother-in-law when she couldn't get the cabinet to close again.

"Everything needs work here, but we'll get it all done," Grant replied, smiling at Tim and Rory. "Right now it looks like a tornado hit it, but it isn't nearly as much work as our house was. Give it a few weeks, and then the guys can have all of us over for dinner."

"You'll need to give them cooking lessons, Izzie," Hugh quipped, throwing a teasing look at his baby brother. "Don't think Timmy's ever cooked anything in his life."

Izzie snorted. "You know I just sit down at the table and eat too, Hugh. Between Mom and Christy, I don't get to cook either!"

"I'm sure Christy won't mind teaching them the basics, Izz," Grant said.

"Guys, please. We'll be fine. We'll figure it out," Tim intervened.

"That's the fun of starting out together," Hunter said, putting his arm around Grant's shoulder. He winked at Rory, and Rory smiled just a little. "Now let's stop talking and start working. How about we make a cleaning crew who can start mucking out and a handyman crew who can start measuring and figuring out what needs replacing? Grant's the carpenter, and I heard Rory is pretty good with his hands too, so how about you two being the handymen, and Tim, you can tell the rest of us where to start cleaning."

Rory was glad that Hunter was taking charge. He could tell he was used to doing that, and it came quite naturally to him. Rory also appreciated being called to do some of the handy work. He'd worked a building crew in his distant past, and although he'd mostly done electrical work, he knew a thing or two about woodwork as well. It was nice to feel useful.

By dinnertime, Rory was amazed how much better the place looked. He and Grant had figured out how much wood was needed to replace some of the walls and that the roof would indeed need to be replaced completely. Grant had drawn some rough plans, which included the addition of a porch and an extra storage-slash-mudroom, and Rory was happy to see his lover's eyes light up when they told him about their plans.

"The cabin will be twice as big," Tim remarked with a wink directed at Rory. "Now come and see what we did."

Tim took Rory through the rooms, and Rory was amazed about what had been accomplished. "I wanted to get the bedroom ready first. I figured if we fix that, we can move the bed, and then we can move in." He pulled Rory closer and kissed his temple. "I can't wait."

Rory smiled. "Can I stay with you tonight?"

Tim kissed him full on the mouth this time. "Can't wait for that either. Go tell Gable he has his house all to himself tonight."

"I'm sure Flynn will be thrilled."

On the way over to the crew house, Rory realized he hadn't thought of having a drink all day. Tonight would be a test, though. There would be alcohol at the dinner table, and he knew he couldn't have any of it, not even a sip of beer. He also knew where most of the men hid their stash, and it would be all too easy to slip away from Tim to have a drink. Rory tried to push the thoughts away, replacing them with something more alluring, like he'd been taught in group. He tried to focus on what was going to happen afterward, when he had Tim all to himself in Tim's room. It felt like months since the last time they'd had sex.

"Look what the cat dragged in," Johnny said with clear disdain in his voice as Rory and Tim walked into the crew house kitchen. Johnny was never one of Rory's biggest fans, and that was aggravated by the fact that he too had been forced to vacate his room after the fire that killed old Mac. Only Johnny didn't get to sleep in the crew chief's room.

"Drop it, Johnny," Tim cautioned him.

Rory threw Tim a warning stare, silently asking him not to run to his defense. It was bad enough the news had spread that Rory had been in the hospital and that he was now working at Gable's. Most of the other workers had helped out at Gable's ranch at some point when Gable was recovering from his accident, and there was no doubt in Rory's mind that some of the ranch hands thought Rory had landed a cushy job at the much smaller ranch. Add to that the fact that most of them noticed his closeness to Tim, and Rory wanted to run. He tried to ignore the stares, hoping the men would soon retreat to the TV room and leave them to eat in peace.

When Rory turned toward the stove to check what was for dinner, he felt Tim's hand on the small of his back and shrugged it away.

"What's wrong?" Tim whispered.

Rory shook his head, not answering. He filled his plate and sat down in the farthest corner of the dining room, eating with deliberate movements in an attempt to get Tim to not say anything.

"Stop fighting for me, Tim," Rory whispered as soon as he was sure no other guys could hear them.

"I'm not."

"Yes, you are. You told Johnny off. He was just toying with me, and you made it worse by coming to my defense. It isn't bad enough that I've been banned from working here, but now your actions and words will give them something else to gossip about."

"I didn't realize—"

"No, you don't realize what it's like. When I arrived here, I wasn't just the outsider, Tim. I was also the convict and the drifter, but I didn't care. It was not so different from the other places I'd worked at. The difference here was you. As long as nobody knew about us, it didn't matter, but thanks to you always coming to my aid and not treating me like you treat the other guys, the whole crew has caught on that I'm special. Special to you."

Tim sighed and withdrew. "I'm sorry, Rory, but I'm allowed to love who I like. They have no right to judge you by it."

Tim's calm helped Rory to settle down as well. Tim always had that effect on him. Rory was used to rubbing guys the wrong way—and more often than not did it on purpose. Then they would retaliate, which made it abundantly clear to Rory that people just didn't like scum like him. Even during Rory's first stint on the ranch, Tim had been different. Tim was patient, calm, and, in Rory's eyes, at least, unshakeable. Rory drew on that strength, and although it gnawed at his self-sufficiency, it drew him to Tim in ways he'd never been drawn to anyone.

"They still do," Rory replied. "They still judge me for it, just like they judge you." His voice was a little raspy, and he knew it betrayed years of hurt, but he couldn't hide that from Tim. He also didn't want to hide it. They'd shared a lot these past months.

Tim took his hand and Rory let him, despite the fact they weren't alone in the crew kitchen. The other group of men was old-timers, Coop among them. Coop was a man of the world, a disbarred lawyer who'd indicated to Rory more than once that he didn't care about Rory's past or about his friendship with Tim. Coop threw him an accepting smile, nodding at him to indicate he was glad Rory was back, and his smile didn't go away when he saw Tim and Rory holding hands. Even then, Rory didn't want to pull away.

"Let's clear our plates and go upstairs," Tim suggested.

—27—

TIM had both looked forward to and dreaded the first time they would be together after rehab. He'd badly missed Rory, but Rory had been even more quiet than before, and Tim really didn't know what to expect. After the strained dinner conversation, they'd made their way upstairs, and once they were in the privacy of their room, Tim took out the T-shirt and boxers he still kept for Rory to sleep in.

Rory took them without talking and changed into them while Tim changed into his own night clothes, quietly hoping they wouldn't be wearing them for long. He couldn't help noticing that Rory looked downright skinny, his ribs and hip bones showing. When Rory sat down on the bed, Tim walked to his side and sat next to him. After a few tense moments, he took Rory's hand in his. "I'm glad you're staying. It was getting pretty lonely in here."

A shiver racked Rory's frame, but he didn't pull his hand away.

"Why don't we crawl under the covers and get warm?"

Rory nodded and did just that.

Tim had to admit it was warmer under the covers, but Rory was on his back, staring up at the ceiling as Tim got in next to him. He might as well have crawled into bed with a sheet of ice. Tim desperately wanted to feel Rory's skin against his. "Want to come a little closer?"

Rory shrugged.

"Listen, I'm sorry about what happened in the kitchen. I'll talk to Johnny tomorrow."

"You didn't listen, did you?" Rory threw Tim a menacing look. "Stop fighting my fights. He wasn't giving you a hard time, he was aiming at me. If I feel he needs talking to, *I'll* talk to him."

Tim nodded, kicking himself for saying the wrong thing again. How was he ever going to get his Rory back?

"Okay, I get your point. I won't say anything," Tim said as softly as he could. "It just hurts to see someone treat you the way they do because of prejudice or malice. It hurts to see anyone treat someone I love badly." When Tim looked up, Rory had a compassionate look on his face.

"You're such a softy."

"I am when it's about people I love."

"And animals."

"Yeah, animals too. I can't fathom how people would tie a dog to a post to let it die. It's cruelty." When Tim looked at Rory, Rory was smiling.

"Softy."

"Don't mind if I am," Tim replied, rolling to his side so he was facing Rory. Rory looked at him with such love, Tim thought he'd melt.

"I don't mind either."

Tim put his hand on Rory's stomach and felt just how tense his boyfriend was. He snuggled closer and rested his head in the crook of Rory's neck so he could smell him. Slowly Rory relaxed.

"I'm sorry about blowing up like that. I know you mean well," Rory eventually said, turning his head to rub his nose through Tim's hair.

"I love you," Tim said for the umpteenth time. He knew it sounded cliché, but he meant it with all his heart. And he was sure Rory loved him back, although he'd never actually heard Rory say it.

THEY must have fallen asleep like that, because when Tim woke up, it was dark in the room with no light creeping around the drapes. Rory was still next to him, breathing slowly. He'd turned away, facing the door, and Tim snuggled closer so he was spooning him. He wasn't sure, but he thought he felt Rory leaning into the touch. He was soon asleep again. The next time he woke up, it was dawn and Rory was getting dressed.

"Morning," Tim greeted his boyfriend, subconsciously rubbing his stomach down to his morning wood. Damn, he'd really looked forward to sex with Rory, and now he seemed to have squandered his chances. "What are we going to do today?"

Rory smiled. "I figured we should put in some more work at the cabin."

Tim leaned half out of bed and grabbed the top of Rory's jeans. "Just stay here for a little while longer."

Rory resisted for a moment and then let Tim pull him onto the bed, where Tim buried his face in Rory's long hair. "Just for a moment. I missed you, Grumpy."

"I missed you too," Rory admitted. "I liked sleeping here."

"I was hoping you'd want to do a little more than just sleep."

Tim saw Rory hesitate, but then his shy smile was back. "Let's work on the cabin so we can be together every night soon."

Tim couldn't argue with that, but what difference would an extra fifteen minutes make? Reluctantly he let go of Rory and watched him put the rest of his clothes on.

THEY worked hard that morning, and after lunch Grant, Flynn, and Gable joined them, tearing down a wall and part of the roof and then covering it with a large building tarp. The rest of the cabin was pretty much gutted. Tim was glad that Grant seemed to know what he was doing, and Rory mostly agreed with Grant's plans.

Grant was checking whether the tarp was sturdy enough when he invited them over for dinner.

"There's enough food, guys, everyone can come over."

Flynn and Gable thanked Grant for the offer but declined, so Grant turned to Tim. "We'll see you in about an hour?"

"No, we have dinner covered, thanks," Rory answered, much to Tim's surprise.

Grant took it in stride and said his goodbyes.

"What was that for?" Tim hissed after Grant left. "You know there's no dinner at the crew house on Sundays."

Rory was clearing up the last of the tarp and dropping it in a corner of what was going to be their living room. "I thought it was obvious, Tim."

"What? It was just a dinner invitation. Grant knows it's each to his own on Sundays."

Rory turned to Tim, his face tense. "If I'm not good enough to work their ranch, then it's surely not safe for me to be in their house, around their child."

"I can't believe you're holding that against them. They didn't want you gone. It's their lawyer who didn't think it was safe for Miranda's lawyer to find out you were on the ranch. Do you think Grant would be working here to fix the cabin if he thought you'd ever harm Matthew?"

"Oh, Timmy, sometimes you're just naïve. He's fixing the cabin for you, not me. And this is farther away from the homestead than the crew house, so if I'm here instead of with the crew, then I'm farther from their son. They can pretend I don't live there because of the road separating us from them."

Tim was stunned into silence. He couldn't believe what Rory was saying. He knew Hunter and was pretty sure he could read Grant as well. There was no way either man would actually believe Rory was a threat to the wellbeing of little Matthew. Besides, Grant would never invite them over to dinner if that's how they felt. Still, if this was what Rory was thinking, he'd have to find a way to persuade Rory he was wrong.

"I'm going to Gable's," Rory said dismissively. He threw down the cloth he'd used to wipe his hands on and walked out the door before Tim could react. Tim was still standing in the middle of the room when he heard the sound of a truck engine being started and had to remind himself that Rory used Mac's old truck to drive between their cabin and Gable's ranch. It took a few moments for Tim to realize that the truck had driven the wrong way, and by the time he was outside and in his own vehicle, the old green Ford was nowhere to be seen. Tim drove around for a few miles and then decided to head over to Gable's to see whether he'd simply heard wrong. The only truck there was Gable's, standing under the apple tree. Tim didn't need to look further, since

Gable didn't have a garage. He headed back to the road into town, hoping he'd spot the truck, or Rory, somewhere along the way.

At Calley's shop, Leah, Calley's shop assistant, hadn't seen Rory, so Tim headed along the strip mall, driving through the parking lot. He had to find Rory, because he still didn't have his driver's license, and if a cop pulled him over, Rory would be taken back to jail, since any brush with the law would be seen as a parole violation.

"Damn, Rory, you've come this far. Don't blow it now just because you're frustrated."

As Tim drove on, a feeling of déjà vu crept up on him. The last time he'd gone looking for Rory because he was out driving, he'd found him delirious in a motel room. This time, not as much time had passed, so Tim hoped when he did find Rory, he'd be in better shape, and hopefully still sober. Tim stopped at the liquor mart, but didn't go inside. He decided that even if the attendant had seen Rory, it would be unlikely that Rory had told the man where he was going, and if Rory had been inside, it would only make Tim more apprehensive about Rory falling off the wagon.

Would Rory go to the same place? It wasn't that far away, so Tim decided to risk it. The meeting hall where Rory went to AA was on the way, so he could hope the truck would be parked there. To his considerable relief, Tim spotted the old green Ford in front of the hall, and he smiled as he sat waiting for Rory to come out. It was a relief that when times were tough, going to a meeting was still Rory's staple, although Tim was sure he'd have arrived late. Looking around as he waited, Tim spotted a white sheet of paper tacked to a light post and noticed the black-and-white picture on it looked familiar. He got out of the truck to take a closer look and recognized Rory. The caption on the sheet said, "Pedophile among us. Working on the Blue River Ranch. Keep Your Children Safe!"

Tim ripped the paper off the post and then spotted some more a bit farther down the street. He collected about twenty tacked up all around outside the hall before he ran inside. He'd never gone into a meeting, had always diligently waited outside for Rory to finish, though he'd met Lamar, Rory's sponsor. So when everyone came flooding out of the hall, Tim spotted the chubby African American.

"Lamar."

Lamar eyed him with some suspicion before it seemed to dawn on him who Tim was. "You're Rory's boyfriend."

Tim nodded.

"He wasn't here, I'm afraid, if you're looking for him."

"I am. Thanks anyway. I usually drive him here, but he left all by himself and I don't know where he went. His truck's here."

Lamar patted Tim's arm. "He wasn't inside. I'm sorry, I can't help you. If he calls me, I'll ask him to call you. I'll tell him you're worried and that you came looking for him."

Tim nodded again, feeling defeated. Then again, if the truck was here, Rory couldn't be far. He would have had to walk, and he hadn't gotten that much of a head start. The hall had a large parking lot behind it, and Tim decided to investigate. He was just about to give up when he heard retching sounds coming from the back. Rory was bent over, puking his guts out, so Tim ran over. He could smell the alcohol when he got closer, and as Rory stood up and wiped his mouth with the back of his hand, he could tell Rory had recognized him.

"I see you've found the flyers."

"Are you okay?" Tim asked, ignoring Rory's statement.

"Obviously not," Rory replied, turning away to vomit again.

"Are you sick?" Tim realized his voice sounded cold, although he really didn't want it to.

Rory swallowed. "I'm a drunk, Tim. When are you going to realize that?"

"You've been doing well for almost a month now. I know it isn't easy, but you've come this far…."

"It's the meds. They make it easier, but they also make me sick if I have a drink."

"But only if you drink." Tim could see Rory fighting his emotions. He just wanted to take him in his arms and tell him everything was going to be okay, but he remembered the warning the substance abuse counselor had given them. Even one drink could be fatal for Rory, and judging from the bottle leaning against the tree next to Rory, he'd had a lot of alcohol in a short period of time. "You had a close call last time, Rory."

"I know," Rory said after swallowing again. "Please help me," he added, the words barely audible.

Tim took two big steps to get closer to Rory. He ignored the smell of liquor and vomit and dragged Rory into his embrace. "I'll take you home, get you cleaned up and into bed. You need rest. And then tomorrow I'll ask for a little time off and we'll work on the cabin. Just enough so we can live there. The bedroom should do, right?"

Rory nodded, staying close to Tim as they made their way to Tim's truck.

"We'll pick up your truck in the morning. You really need to get your driver's license."

"Don't see why," Rory replied.

A little stunned, Tim looked at his boyfriend. "So that if you run off, and the cops stop you, you won't get thrown into jail again."

Rory smiled. "But then you won't come looking for me."

Tim laughed, relieved to hear a sense of humor coming back into the conversation.

AT THE crew house, Rory went into the showers as Tim ran upstairs to get towels and soap. Once downstairs again, it didn't take him long to spot his boyfriend, deliciously wet and naked under the spray. "Mind if I join you?"

Rory looked around, wiping the water off his hair and beard. "Sure. Take your clothes off first, though."

Tim brought the shower gel, and after getting naked, he started spreading the suds over Rory's skin.

"Feels nice," Rory purred. He let his head fall back so the water filled his mouth, and he spit it out before turning around and kissing Tim. "Most of the alcohol came up again, but I still feel a little buzzed. Weird, that."

Tim knew Rory was right. He was his gregarious old self now, so far removed from the dark, broody man he'd been since he came out of rehab. Tim was scared that was what Rory was really like, and the flirty, up-for-anything man was only there after he'd hit the sauce. Tim knew he wouldn't allow himself to give up on Rory, though. He loved this man, which meant he had to cut him some slack. He couldn't run for the hills at the first sign of trouble. He simply had to stick by him, through thick and thin. Like the wedding vows, through sickness and in health, and Tim was sure Rory was still sick.

"I scared you, didn't I?"

Tim looked up at Rory and realized he'd been miles away. "Yeah, a little bit."

"I'm sorry."

"Just don't do it again. You know what your counselor at the hospital said. You could die—"

Rory stopped Tim with a searing kiss as he flung himself around Tim's bulky frame. "I'm alive, Tim," Rory said as he came up for air. "Now, will you fuck me, please?"

"Let's go upstairs then," Tim suggested.

"Fuck me right here," Rory demanded.

—28—

RORY knew he hadn't ingested that much alcohol. His sides still hurt from heaving as the medication he was taking made him expel most of the whiskey he'd tried to drink. It had been a long time since he'd felt any effect from alcohol, though. To his detriment, he'd felt the craving for more reach dangerous heights. Tim was right. If he didn't stop drinking, he'd kill himself, and as Tim liked to point out, he had something to live for now.

That something had his hands all over him as they stood under the spray of the crew house shower. Rory knew they could get caught there. One of the men could wander in for a late clean-up and catch them naked together, sharing a stall. If Rory could get Tim more aroused, they could even be caught fucking. Rory had to admit to himself it had a certain appeal. For once, the definite prison feeling didn't put him off.

"Come here, Timmy," Rory murmured, pulling Tim closer and enveloping both their cocks in his hand. "Want you inside me. Want you to fuck me until I scream."

Tim smiled. "You won't scream. You won't even moan. Especially not here where someone might catch us."

So Tim had caught on. Rory felt brave, though. "If you fuck me here, I promise the whole house will hear."

Tim snorted but kissed him anyway. Rory still felt a little buzzed from the alcohol, but also relaxed, and braver than usual. He started kissing Tim's jaw, then his neck, and felt more than heard Tim moan. He pushed him away from the spray and against the wall of the cubicle before licking his way down Tim's smooth, wet chest to his nipples. It wasn't terribly warm in the shower room, but the spray was still cascading over Rory's back, and that kept him from shivering. Tim's body heat provided the rest.

"Oh God, yeah," Tim moaned as Rory flicked over a nipple with his tongue. Tim's cock twitched in Rory's hand, and Rory sank down so he could take it in his mouth. At that moment, the lights conked out.

Tim giggled. "Fuck. I hate how dark it is in here. Can't see you now."

Rory got up from his crouching position. "Better?"

Tim laughed. "It's fucking black. No windows, nothing. I can feel you and that's about it."

"Not enough, hey?" Rory whispered in his ear. He knew just how hard and eager Tim was. He also knew Tim liked the visuals, but he couldn't tear himself away from Tim's warm body, so he grabbed his own half-hard cock and enveloped it together with Tim's in his hand. When he moved back and forth, the friction felt heavenly. Rory remembered how Tim had been so fascinated by his foreskin and the fact he wasn't cut. Would Tim let him surprise him?

As they continued kissing, Tim's hands around his face, Rory lowered his left hand to their combined cocks. It took some fiddling in the dark, but he aligned them and pushed his foreskin over the head of Tim's cock, enveloping it with the excess skin.

"Fuck, that feels amazing!" Tim gasped. "What are you doing? I want to see!"

"Later," Rory murmured as he tried to continue the kiss. Tim pulled away, though, and his cock slipped out of Rory's hand. Rory moved under the spray as the heat of Tim's body disappeared. He had a pretty good idea what Tim was going to do, but he still startled when he heard the thump and then the lights came on full blast.

"Come here," Tim demanded as he returned to the shower and pulled Rory close. "Now show me what you were doing."

Rory wet his hand under the spray and then resumed his ministrations. The fascination on Tim's face amused him. "This is why I like not being cut." Rory realigned their cocks, head to head, and then pushed his foreskin forward. The purple head of Tim's cock disappeared almost completely, and he rubbed his thumb over it for good measure.

Tim's breathing sped up, and he pushed forward into Rory's heat. Rory sucked his lips between his teeth in anticipation of seeing ecstasy wash over his lover's face. He leaned his forehead against Tim's. "Feel good?"

Rory had to close his eyes, because feeling Tim's cock brush against his more sensitive head was enough to make him lose it and he really wanted Tim to come first. He opened them again just in time to hear Tim grunt and feel the hotness squirt out underneath his skin, bathing him with warmth. It was enough to make his spine tingle and send him over as well.

"I think that's the hottest thing I ever saw," Tim said, panting, "or felt, for that matter." He kissed Rory, invading his mouth with his tongue, and Rory gladly gave into it.

The alcohol buzz was wearing off, and Rory felt tired all of a sudden. He pulled away from Tim and rinsed off the sweat and semen under the spray of the shower. Tim hugged him from behind, and they stood like that for a while, until the light flipped out again.

"I've got to have that timer checked out," Tim said with a chuckle. "No way was that fifteen minutes."

Rory turned off the water and felt his way around to the towel he knew he'd left on the bench.

HOURS later, Rory woke up in Tim's bed, shaking. The spot he'd slept in was wet with sweat, and he felt agitated, so he swung his legs out of bed and sat up.

"You okay?" Tim asked.

Rory kicked himself for waking Tim up. "Yeah, fine," he replied, but his shaky voice betrayed him. Within moments, Tim was behind him, trying to embrace him.

"Don't," Rory said, shrugging Tim off. "I'm all yucky."

Tim chuckled and got out of bed before turning the bedside light on. He rummaged around behind Rory's back and then walked to where Rory was sitting. "Arms up." Rory complied and Tim pulled Rory's soaking shirt off. He just sat there as Tim wiped him with a towel and then helped him put on a clean T-shirt. He instantly felt better, although he still couldn't stop shaking.

"Did you take your meds last night?"

Rory shook his head.

"Did you bring them?"

Rory nodded. "My jeans."

Tim got up again and brought Rory his pants, then filled a glass with water and gave it to him.

"I don't want to be a burden, Tim."

"You're not," Tim said without a single hint of recrimination.

"You told me about how your father had to take care of your mother all those years, and now you're doing it for me."

"Yes, I am," Tim replied. "You're my partner. That's what partners do."

"I'm a drunk. So was your mother. You know what will happen."

Tim crouched down in front of Rory, resting his hands on Rory's knees. "Yes, you're an alcoholic."

Rory cringed at hearing Tim put it so blatantly, although he'd said it himself numerous times at meetings.

"But you're working at getting better."

"I fell off the wagon."

Tim smiled. "I fall off the wagon all the time."

"You?"

Tim rolled his eyes. "I'm a slob. I tell myself you'll never want to live with me because you'll have to contend with dirty socks and bunched-up underwear and me not having any clean clothes to wear, and then for a day I do laundry and take care of everything, because I don't want you to be disgusted by me."

Rory couldn't prevent a smile from breaking out over his face at hearing Tim ramble. "It's not quite the same, now is it?"

"Hey, Grumpy. I know you try. Nobody would have bet money on you lasting a month without drinking. But you did it."

"That's all shot now." A violent shiver racked Rory's skinny frame.

"No, it isn't. You get right back on that horse."

"Wagon," Rory corrected him.

"You're on a horse ranch now, dude," Tim replied.

Rory chuckled.

"Now come to bed. I'll warm you up. We'll have to share my side until your side dries up, though."

Rory was starting to feel the effects of his medication. It always made him feel tired, so he nodded and let Tim tuck him in before he turned off the lights. Rory just wanted to sleep, but Tim seemed to want to talk.

"Rory?"

"Yeah."

"Did you see the flyers?"

Rory nodded. He swallowed against the feelings of dread when he recalled the words that were written underneath his picture. "I didn't do those things, Tim."

"I know. Do you have any idea who might have put those up?"

Rory sighed. "Only one name I can think of."

"Delco." It wasn't a question, and Rory knew Tim was right.

—29—

IT JUST wasn't Tim's day.

On the way to bringing some of the adult herd up to a higher range, they'd encountered three fences that were down and a collapsed lean-to, although Tim had inspected the fields two days before to check everything was in place and the herd's drinking water was no longer frozen after the long winter.

"Don't worry about it, Timmy," Hugh said, patting his baby brother on the back. "I'll call Grant to bring some wood and a few workers and they'll have it fixed in no time."

Tim grunted and rode off while Hunter approached his foreman. "What's with him?"

Hugh shrugged. "Man trouble, I assume."

Tim overheard them and directed his horse closer to the other two. "Butt out, okay?" He knew he was out of line, but he was in a pissy mood and he didn't care who got the full load. Especially not if it was Hugh. Trust his brother to make a remark like that. Of course, his mood had to do with Rory, but it wasn't Rory's fault.

That morning, Tim had swung by the sheriff's office to report the flyers and had been told this wasn't the first time Rory had been slandered. After some digging, the new deputy showed Tim an equally shabby photocopy of the same picture with the text "Rory McCown. Horse thief. Beware. Works at Blue River Ranch" underneath. The sheriff's office hadn't taken much notice of it and had simply filed it in Rory's folder. When Tim suggested Delco could be behind it, the deputy called in the sheriff, who simply shook his head and replied that he "didn't know the little shit was back."

In any case, Tim walked out of there even more frustrated than before, because the sheriff had made it clear they didn't have the manpower to pursue a case of "littering." By the time Tim was back in his truck, he was fuming, because he felt powerless to do anything about the defamation of Rory's character. He knew how hard it was for Rory to change his life around and how much slander like this gnawed at what little self-esteem he had, but he also knew he had to keep Rory from doing something stupid, like violate his parole to get back at Delco.

Tim was startled when he heard knocking on his window. He rolled it down when he recognized the new deputy.

"Listen," the man said, looking through the opened window. "I know he said we didn't have the manpower," he gestured at the sheriff's office with his head, "and we probably don't, but that doesn't mean I can't keep my eyes open. Is this Delco guy harassing you?"

"Yes and no," Tim said with a sigh. "I haven't seen him in years, but my... friend...." Tim paused, fighting with himself about how much to divulge to the man he'd just met and deciding to play it safe. "The guy on the flyers works on my ranch. He's on parole, but he's doing a really great job walking the line. I'd like to keep it that way. The smear campaign isn't helping, though."

The deputy nodded. "Like I said, I'll keep my eyes open, but I can't promise anything." He shook Tim's hand and then went back to the office, leaving Tim still frustrated.

Now the broken fences and Hugh's off-color remarks made an already bad day even worse.

Hugh left him to grumble for a good twenty minutes and then rode alongside him again. "So what's eating you, Grumpy?"

"Don't call me—" Tim started to snarl, but then he held it in. "Grumpy," he added, a lot calmer after a long exhale. He chuckled, more to release the tension than to laugh. "Grumpy's my nickname for Rory."

Hugh smiled. "I can see why."

"He's not grumpy all the time. He just hasn't had an easy life, and it gets him down sometimes. He's trying, though, Hugh."

"I know," Hugh replied, adjusting his seat atop his large gelding. "It can't be easy for the two of you now he's living at Gable's, either."

"All I want is for people to understand that the only thing I need is to be allowed to be with the man I love. It's no more difficult than that."

"So what's holding you back?" Hugh asked, much to Tim's surprise. He thought Hugh would be the last person to sympathize with him, given the fact he really didn't like Rory.

Tim took a deep breath in, stalling for time. Hugh was his brother. Hugh had confided in him when he was leaving Lisa, his first wife, for her sister Izzie. Maybe it was time he confided in Hugh now. After all, he was family. "Delco is back in town. Last week he plastered the whole area around the AA meeting hall with photocopies of Rory's picture with the words 'Child Molester' written underneath. Rory saw them. He was on his way to a meeting, but after seeing them, he went to the liquor store for a bottle of whiskey instead."

"So he fell off the wagon," Hugh remarked. "I guess he'd exceeded everyone's expectations by staying sober that long."

Tim threw Hugh a vitriolic stare and then kicked his horse's flanks, making it shoot away. He galloped past the herd in the hope of calming his already on-edge nerves and was just thinking that it was helping when Hugh came alongside him.

"Stop running, Timmy."

Tim pulled on the reins to slow his horse down. "Why? So I can take crap from my own brother for sticking by the man I love?"

"So you'll listen to the truth."

"Your truth, my truth, or Rory's truth?"

Hugh sighed. "Listen. You're my brother. I never gave you a hard time for being gay. Frankly, I don't give a damn who you sleep with. But when I see how much you've changed in these last weeks, how you've turned from a glass-half-full to a glass-always-empty guy, then yes, I worry. Because this isn't the Tim who told me everything would work out if I just stayed true to myself and told Lisa about Izzie. You are no longer the man who firmly believed we'd catch the guys who stole our foals. You're not even the guy anymore who begged me to hire Rory, although you knew it was a long shot. So forgive me for wanting my happy-go-lucky brother back."

Tim knew Hugh was right. He silently watched his brother urge his horse on to go after Danny, his son, who was being outnumbered rounding up the adult horses on one side of the herd. It gave him an excuse not to answer, because he wasn't ready to grovel yet. His side of the group of horses was docile and calm, so he had time to think about what he was going to do about it.

By the time the horses were safe in one of the higher fields and all the fences were mended, Tim knew what he had to do. Instead of going home, he went to Hunter and Grant's house and let himself in.

"How quickly can we get the cabin habitable?" he asked Grant, who was peeling potatoes, without even saying "Hi."

"We just demolished a wall. And half the roof. Depends what you consider habitable, I suppose," the older man said calmly.

"Hey, Timmy," Hunter said, joining the two of them.

"Tim wants to move into the cabin," Grant said.

Tim could have sworn it was accompanied by a sigh and a dismissive look, but he couldn't really see Grant's expression.

"I think you'll both be more comfortable, not to mention warmer and a lot dryer, where you are. Don't you think?" Hunter suggested to Tim.

"They want to be together, Hunt," Grant interjected. "You of all people should understand that."

Hunter replied by putting his arm around Grant and kissing him. "Yes, I do." Hunter turned to Tim without letting go of his lover. "So what can we do, Grant?"

"You could give me time off to start on their roof."

"Guys," Tim intervened, "spring is coming and work is picking up. We can't just take time off from the ranch to build the cabin."

"We can if everyone chips in," Grant replied. "It would mean putting in a few hours every evening, say between four and seven, light permitting."

Tim shook his head. "Forget I asked. I'll figure something else out." He stormed out of the house, feeling no better than when he got up that morning.

When he drove Rory to his meeting that evening, Rory picked up on his foul mood too. "What's wrong, Tim?"

They were a little early at the meeting hall, and Tim had cut the engine. He took Rory's hand. "I want to move into the cabin with you. We can fix it up while we're in there."

Rory chuckled. "Reality check? We're missing two walls and most of the roof. We have no running water, no kitchen to speak of, no electricity, and no heat."

"I know." Tim sighed. "But I miss you. Making out in the car before or after your meeting is getting old. I don't just want to take you to Gable's in the evening, I want to take you home." He leaned over Rory and kissed him, hoping Rory would agree to his suggestion. Rory didn't react, and Tim felt a little deflated.

Later that evening, after bringing Rory back to Gable's, Tim picked up some stuff from the storage room of the crew house and drove to the cabin, where he bunked down and tried to sleep. It was bitterly cold and more than a little drafty in the one room that still had four walls. He resolved to look for excess wood and try out the fireplace the next day.

—30—

IT WAS freezing in the cottage as Tim was trying to light the fire in the fireplace. He watched Rory, who was sweeping the floor in the coat he'd given him, and wondered what had possessed them to move in here before the cabin was finished.

Old Mackenzie's cottage still felt kind of dirty and inhospitable and it only just kept them sheltered against the snow and icy winds. Tim had no idea if the chimney still worked, and for all he knew they'd end up with a house full of smoke. He knew they'd have to make do, though.

Tim startled out of his thoughts when he felt Rory's hand on his shoulder.

"Chimney seems to be working. You're a good boy scout, getting that fire going. Should be warmer in here by the time we go to bed."

Tim put his hand over Rory's and got up from his crouching position until he could look Rory in the eye. Rory's hand was cold, and Tim enveloped his lover's hands with his, transferring his warmth.

"It'll take some time to make this home, but yeah, at least this room will be warm enough to sleep in. I hope," Tim said with a smile on his face.

"I'm sorry for the mess," Rory said softly.

"You've cleaned it up nicely. Tomorrow after work we'll see if we can get my bed out here, and we're all set. At least we have this old sofa that the Krauses gave us."

Rory shook his head. "You have to live like a vagrant because of me, Tim."

Tim could tell Rory was having a hard time of it. He pulled the more slender man into his embrace and squeezed him tightly before kissing his temple. "I love you. All the rest is superficial. Window dressing. We'll fix this place up, and then we'll have our own little home. It's not like we have a brood walking around and we need a mansion like Hunter and Grant." Tim pulled back and placed his hands at either side of Rory's head, forcing him to look straight ahead. "I have a little money stashed aside. We can put some real heating in here and hot water and a small kitchen. What more do we need? For now we can shower and eat at the crew house."

"We can't put in heating before the walls are back up and the roof is fixed. You had it good before I arrived. Now...."

"Rory, stop it." Tim sighed, feeling powerless against Rory's attitude of defeat. "I chose you. I pursued you even. I knew what I was getting into. You threw me a few curveballs, but we survived. I knew it wouldn't be easy, but I'm not backing down. I'd live on the street with you if that were necessary."

"That's stupid."

"Yes, it is, because we wouldn't have to. Even staying here is better than sleeping rough, and it will be *our* place. Yours and mine. We'll turn it into a real home where we decide what it will look like. I remember when Hunter and Grant built their house and how important it was for them to do it their way, despite how much Beth Krause wanted to interfere."

"We don't have anyone to interfere with us. Neither of us have any parents left."

"Trust me," Tim said with a smile. "Izzie will try to, and don't discount Beth. Remember, she mothered me for a number of years after my mother died. I think Christy will know better than to say anything to our faces, but you can bet she'll have an opinion."

"In that case I'm glad it's just you and me who need to decide, because we don't have the money for all the women's fancy ideas."

Tim took Rory's hand. "We'll make it work. We're both employed. It'll take some time before we can start saving again, but just think: this is our home!" Tim looked around the bedroom of the dilapidated cabin. It was definitely going to take quite some manual labor, but he'd never been afraid of that. And Rory knew his way around tools as well. They'd install a pump for the well and a water heater that would take care of hot water. There was a fuse box and a connection to the mains outside, and Rory would be able to make good on the experience he had wiring building sites, so the electricity was taken care of as well.

Over the weekend, Grant and Rory were going to replace the wall and get started on the porch and the roof.

Sitting here together on the old couch in front of the roaring fire definitely lifted Tim's spirit. They'd been in stasis, not going back and definitely not going forward, and Tim needed to move his life forward. Tim wrapped his arms around Rory's shoulders as Rory leaned against him when he pulled his knees up to his chest.

"The only way is up now, Rory," Tim said with a sigh. "I'm happy you're going to be sleeping next to me again."

"I'll need to if we're not going to freeze to death."

"At least we'll die happy."

Rory elbowed him, and Tim pretended to be hurt, which made Rory laugh. Because it rarely happened, Tim tried to commit Rory's uninhibited laughter to memory.

Later, they slept in most of their clothes, huddled underneath a scrambled assortment of bedding. Their lovemaking felt more like the fumbling attempt of two teenagers, but Tim didn't care. He had his Rory back in his arms and in his house. The bed would surely follow.

The next day after work, they moved Tim's bed to the cabin and plugged up a few draft holes in the bedroom wall. That night the room felt much warmer, and thanks to a lack of other amenities, they spent most of the evening snuggled up together in bed, talking.

"So are you convinced we'll be happy here now?" Tim asked Rory just as they were drifting off to sleep.

Rory nodded. "I've never had a place to call my own, so yeah, I'm sure we'll be okay."

Tim smiled. "Good. And I'm sure Hunter and Grant will come to some agreement with Miranda, and then there won't be any reason left for you to work at Gable's. You can work with us again. Me."

Rory didn't say anything but instead buried his face against Tim's neck. Just moments later, Tim knew he was asleep.

IN THE middle of the night, a loud thunderclap made Tim wake with a start. He immediately felt around and found the bed not only empty, but cold as well, although the blankets were tucked neatly around him.

"Rory?"

No answer.

Tim repeated his lover's name a little louder. It was a small cabin, so the fact that Rory didn't answer meant he'd either fallen asleep on the couch—which, given the cold, wasn't likely—or he wasn't inside. Tim jumped out of bed and into his jeans and grabbed a T-shirt and sweater before walking out. He was wearing them by the time he entered the living room. No Rory. A quick scan of the only other room—the bathroom—revealed the same. Rory simply wasn't there. Kicking his sleepy brain into gear, Tim tried to think where Rory could be. He instantly discarded the idea that Rory had run off. Last night's conversation about how good Rory felt on the ranch dispelled that idea right off the bat. So where was he?

One look out the window into the dark night gave Tim a pretty good idea. The rain was coming down in sheets and, like the weatherman had predicted, most of the winter's snow was gone. The meadow running alongside the house was flooded, which meant the small meandering river that flowed through it was totally saturated.

Tim tucked his T-shirt into his pants and donned a sweater before putting on his duster, boots, and Stetson and venturing out. Both his truck and Rory's were still parked next to the house, so Rory must have walked wherever he'd gone. Tim figured his best bet was the main house or the stables. Maybe Rory thought the horses would be in danger.

The unpaved road between their cabin and the house was full of potholes and hard to navigate on a good day in broad daylight, but right now it felt like driving through molasses. Luckily the four-wheel-drive truck had a strong engine, and now that Rory had tuned it, it no longer complained too much. The main homestead was dark, so Tim drove past Hunter's house and saw a faint light on in one of the back rooms. From there, he could see that the stable block was fully lit up.

He parked around the side and walked in to see Grant and Hugh saddling their horses. "What's happening?" Tim asked, shaking the water off his hat.

"Rory said the river by your cabin was flooding the meadow," Grant answered. "Before I could react, he'd saddled a horse and went out to see what the meadows look like upstream. Hunter's gone after him, because Rory's not experienced enough to do that on his own in the middle of the night and during a torrent like this, but he was gone before we could saddle another horse. I brought Matty to Christy and woke Hugh up to come and help."

"He left me to sleep," Tim said, feeling confused about Rory's irresponsible actions.

Hugh threw his baby brother a compassionate look. "Let's hope those riding lessons you've been giving him pay off."

Tim went in search of his own horse and passed another empty stall. It was where Amarant, Danny's new gelding, was usually housed.

"Hugh, did Danny ride out with Hunter?"

"No, why?" Hugh asked as he approached Tim. "Oh, shit," he said when he saw the empty stall. "Will he ever learn?" He turned around to walk over to Grant. "Danny's out there on Amarant. So we have two liabilities in this weather."

Tim could tell Hugh was worried about his son, but he could also sense his annoyance. Hugh was right. The last thing they needed was to babysit a ten-year-old with too much bravado and an adult man with a hero complex who'd only just learned to ride. Tim understood the mix of worry and responsibility he shared with Hugh.

Tim saddled his horse and walked it over to the other two who were about to head out. "You think they rode out to where we had to rescue Danny three years ago?"

"Rory doesn't know where that is. We can only hope they're together and can keep each other out of trouble," Grant replied. "At least Danny knows his way around." He fished a small handheld device out of his coat. "Here, take the GPS and call us on the radio if you find something. We're all experienced enough to ride alone and radio for help if we need it."

Tim nodded. There wasn't much he could say. He hoped they'd find them, before there was trouble. Then all they'd recall later was a very short and very wet night.

—31—

RORY was soaked to the bone by the time he was well on the way upstream. He'd figured not even Tim's oilskin would keep him dry in this weather, but he was already regretting the decision to wear his threadbare coat. Not only was he wet now, but he was bone-weary cold too. He'd grabbed a set of wrangler's gloves from inside the stable block, and those kept his hands from getting waterlogged, but other than that, he was starting to see visions of warm showers and dry clothes pretty quickly. His mission was clear, though. The river that passed through the land surrounding their cabin also ran through Gable and Flynn's land, but more upstream. If the soil was waterlogged where they lived, it wouldn't be much better where Gable's adult horses were. Rory had just helped move them there a few days ago. He figured by now they'd be standing up to their knees in water.

As Scooter slowed down on a particularly slippery patch, Rory took a deep breath. Reminding himself that Tim had told him horses could sense their rider's anxiety and would become anxious themselves, Rory tried to survey the landscape to calm his beating heart. The night was pitch-dark, and since it was raining cats and dogs, thick rainclouds were obscuring the moon. It didn't give him a lot of confidence. He could follow the river, though. It was a glistening, black, writhing mass, and he could hear the sound of all that melting water coming down the mountain. As he stopped Scooter to get his bearings, Rory thought he heard a faint voice.

"Uncle Rory?"

Rory tried to make out where the voice was coming from and for a moment hoped he wasn't hearing things again, but then he saw a soaking wet boy emerge from the darkness. He was leading a calm tan gelding and looked miserably cold but otherwise didn't seem scared to be out here on his own in the middle of a torrent and an out of control river.

"Danny?"

"Yes, Uncle Rory. I need your help."

His original mission forgotten, Rory jumped down from his horse. Realizing how much taller he was than the ten-year-old boy, he crouched down in the mud. "I think I should get you back to your dad. He's going to be worried sick."

"He doesn't know I'm gone. And I've done this before. Three years ago Uncle Grant came to find me." Danny looked kind of smug admitting that, Rory thought.

"I still think you should go back to the homestead instead of being out here. It's not safe."

"We need to break the beaver dam," Danny said with clear determination.

"Beaver dam?"

"Robbie and me were playing there the other day, and we saw they'd made such a work of it that the river found another bed. That's why the river is closer to our homestead than it should be."

Rory hoped that also meant that Gable's horses were safe. It wasn't like he could leave Danny to his own devices to go chasing after Gable's herd. He looked back in the direction of the main houses, but it was too far to see any of them. There didn't seem to be any hope of the Krause men finding them, either, so Rory saw only one course of action: help Danny with the beaver dam.

"Okay, boy," Rory said. "Show me where the dam is. And after we fix that, we're going straight home!"

"Yes, sir!" Danny said with a laugh and a mock salute.

Rory was glad Danny seemed to know his way around, because by now, Rory was questioning his own sanity for venturing out into the dead of night. When they reached the beaver dam, Rory could see Danny's point. Occasional flashes of lightning showed there was a huge mass of branches and old leaves sticking out over and under what looked like a fallen tree. Only a little water ran underneath it, but most of it cascaded down the slope to their left. This was the river Rory had followed to the spot where Danny had found him. Now he thought about it, he had noticed the river didn't have a very deep bed and that it seemed to meander through the fields, finding the path of least resistance. He had no idea how to break the dam, though.

"Danny, we need help. We can't shift the tree by ourselves."

"No we can't, but we can break up some of the stuff that's cluttering up the river. Once that's gone, the water can flow through again."

Rory wasn't so sure, but Danny looked determined. Before Rory could react, Danny had dismounted and taken a flashlight out of his saddle bag. He was climbing the construction like a monkey.

"Danny!" Rory shouted, feeling his heart skip a beat.

"It's okay," Danny shouted back. "Robbie and me played on it for days, and it's really sturdy." He picked up something long. "I brought a shovel to dig into it, but I'm not strong enough."

Rory figured he wasn't going to be able to stop Danny, so he tied up his horse and tried not to fall into the water as he climbed up on the dam. "Hold the light. Show me where to dig." At one side of the dam the water was high, and every time Rory moved his foot, it seemed to end up in the water. He was practically digging blind, not because of the dark—since Danny was holding the flashlight—but because of the pool of nearly still water that had formed upstream from the dam. He stabbed at the water, trying to feel where he hit the half-submerged tree trunk and where he missed it, hitting soft mulch and half-rotted leaves and branches. After a while the softer part of the dam seemed to give way, and after a few more stabs, Rory lost the shovel. "Damn!" he cursed, and only then realized he was in the company of a very impressionable minor. "Don't repeat that," he added with a chuckle, but a stabbing pain was becoming evident in his ankle.

"Look!" Danny shouted, pointing his flashlight over the dam. "You did it! The river's flowing again!"

Rory could feel the ice-cold water streaming over his foot, and it made him slowly lose sensation of the pain. He wasn't sure it was a blessing, though. Danny skipped off the dam toward the horses and then looked back.

"Come down, Uncle Rory. We did it!"

"I know," Rory said, raising his hand at the youngster and immediately bringing it down again to keep himself from toppling into the ice-cold water. He waited a few breaths and then called for the youngster again. "Danny? Can you ride back alone?"

"You said you were going to bring me back," Danny protested weakly.

"I… I can't. I'm stuck."

"Oh my," Danny replied.

Rory thought he could hear clear apprehension in the youngster's voice. He couldn't blame him. It was cold and still pitch dark, the flashlight their only source of light, and even for someone who knew the terrain, like Danny, it wouldn't be easy getting his bearings because of how the river had changed their surroundings. If he was honest with himself, he also didn't want Danny to leave him alone. He had to think of Danny, though. He didn't know what was best: telling Danny to stay where they could keep an eye on each other, or asking Danny to ride back in the hope that the kid could get someone from the ranch to rescue him from his predicament.

"Danny?" Rory said again. "Danny, come here." The kid climbed back on the dam until Rory could see his wet face in the glow of the flashlight. That's when Rory decided. If Danny thought he could find his way home, at least the kid would be safe. "Do you think you can find your way back to the house? Right now?"

"I don't want to leave you. Dad always says you don't leave your friend if he's hurt."

"We don't have a radio, so you have to get help."

"But you're hurt!"

A little apprehensively, Rory put his hand on the youngster's slender shoulder. "Danny, you can help me more by getting your Dad and Uncle Tim out here than you can staying with me. I'm okay, but you need to find someone to help me get unstuck, okay?"

Danny didn't immediately respond.

"You needed my help because I was stronger than you, right?" Danny nodded. "I'm not strong enough to get myself out of here." And the longer they waited, the more melting water was coming down that mountain.

Danny seemed to think about it and then looked up at Rory. "I'll go get Dad out here. I can do it."

Before Rory could react, Danny flung his arms around Rory's neck and hugged him tight. He then let go and jumped down from the dam onto the soggy ground.

"Go get him, buster," Rory shouted, trying to sound stronger than he felt. The cold was creeping up on him, and it seemed every minute he had to hold on tighter so he wouldn't fall. He had no idea how much time had passed, but he couldn't feel his feet anymore. He knew he had to stay awake, though. He tried to dislodge his foot again, but pain shot into it and he cried out, so he stopped moving.

He knew Danny would be back with his dad and Grant and probably even Tim. Rory had to stay awake. He had to keep with it for Tim.

—32—

"RORY! Danny!" Tim kept shouting their names until his voice was hoarse and stinging from the cold. He heard a helicopter overhead and was blinded by its floodlight for a moment, and then it was dark again. Tim checked the GPS to make sure he was still going in the right direction, then tucked it back into his oilskin and took out his radio. "Hugh?"

"Here," Hugh answered.

"Anything?"

"No."

"Did you see that helicopter?"

"Yeah, I didn't call for it. I didn't know the sheriff's office had a chopper, so maybe we should tell him what we're out here for. Two people missing and all."

"Hunter? Can we call the sheriff?" No answer. "I'll find Hunter, Tim."

"Okay, I'll keep looking."

A few moments later the radio crackled again. "Hugh? Tim?"

"Yes!" they both answered almost simultaneously. It was Hunter's voice.

"Sheriff just called in a possible sighting. You know where the river curves back on itself? Near our north border?"

"Yes." This time Tim was quicker to answer.

"There's a fallen tree across the river, and they think they saw a red and black checked coat."

"Shit." Tim sighed, knowing that could well be Rory. "I'm closest to that area," Tim replied into the radio.

"I'm joining you there," Hugh replied.

Making his way on horseback and on a slippery slope, progress was slow, but Tim estimated about ten minutes had passed when he saw Hugh emerge from the darkness. To Tim's surprise, he wasn't alone.

"Danny found me right after we got the call. He knows where Rory is."

Tim breathed a sigh of relief. "He's okay?"

"Uncle Rory hurt himself breaking the dam, Uncle Tim."

"Breaking the dam?"

"Danny, you can explain later. Show us where Rory is."

Danny directed Amarant out front, and Hugh and Tim followed.

"He's hurt?" Tim asked his brother, not able to hide his apprehension.

"Danny says it's just his foot. He didn't seem all that worried."

Tim didn't know whether that put him fully at ease, but at least they'd know soon. As soon as they rounded the bend, Tim knew something was wrong. He could just make out the red in Rory's coat, and when the helicopter flew overhead again, he could see Rory slumped forward over the fallen tree trunk. Without thinking, he jumped down from his horse and ran over to the dam, climbing on top of the slippery tree trunk to get to Rory.

"Tim, be careful!" Hugh shouted over the sound of the helicopter rotors. "The last thing we need is both of you hurt!"

As soon as Tim got close enough to touch Rory, he pulled off Rory's cap and saw he wasn't responding. "Call the sheriff and tell him we need to get Rory to the hospital!" Tim shouted back. "Then help me get him out of here. The water's freezing!" Tim shook Rory, but Rory's head fell back and he was limp in his arms. He tried to feel around Rory's body to see if he could figure out if it was just the cold or whether something else was wrong and soon realized he couldn't move Rory's left leg.

When Tim looked up again, Hugh was climbing on the tree with him, and Hunter and Grant had arrived as well. "Do we have any tools? His foot is lodged in the debris, and I can't get it out."

Hugh nodded and left again to converse with Hunter. When he returned, he was carrying a spade. "Hunter's calling the sheriff to arrange for an ambulance."

"Be careful with that," Tim said, nodding in the direction of the tool Hugh was wielding.

"You hold on to him, I'll take care of his foot," Hugh replied.

Tim grabbed Rory and pulled him into his arms, hoping he could somehow transfer some of his body heat into Rory's limp form. He let go of Rory long enough to unzip his coat and tried to wrap Rory into it as he pulled the lifeless body to him. And he talked. Nonstop. It helped him forget the cold and made him feel he was doing something for his man.

"Tim? Can you move him that way?" Hugh asked, gesturing for Tim to pull Rory away from him.

Tim nodded and tried to move Rory. At first he couldn't, and he saw Hugh hacking away at something. The resistance disappeared so quickly that, if it hadn't been for Hugh grabbing Tim by the collar of his coat, both of them would have landed in the water.

"Gotcha. Hold on, we'll get him out of the water."

Hugh and Tim managed to get Rory off the fallen tree and onto drier land. He still wasn't showing any signs of waking up, although Tim had felt for a faint pulse.

"How's he doing?" Grant asked.

"We need to get him to a hospital. He's so cold."

Hunter nodded. "Kelly Freed, the new deputy, was the one flying the helicopter. They're ready for Rory at County Medical, but we're too far from the road for the ambulance. Kelly offered to take him in his chopper so we'll get there quicker."

Supported by Hugh, Tim moved one arm underneath Rory's legs and picked Rory up off the ground. Halfway to the clearing, they were approached by the scruffy blond-haired man Tim had met at the sheriff's office on his last visit.

"I'll fly you to County," Kelly shouted over the sound of the rotors. Tim could see the worried look on his face. "Is he breathing?"

"Barely," Tim replied.

"I have rescue blankets in the back. We can wrap him in those and conserve what little body heat he has left."

It wasn't a huge helicopter, but Tim figured it would do. Like Kelly had said, there were blankets on the floor, and he used them to try and make Rory comfortable, but it wasn't easy moving Rory's unconscious form around the tiny space. As soon as the chopper took off, Tim was just happy to hold on and forget his apprehensions about flying for the first time by taking care of Rory.

Tim heard Kelly converse over the radio to relay his time of arrival, so a gurney was waiting on the helipad the moment they touched down. Tim tried to explain what had happened but was all but ignored by the doctor and nurses who transferred Rory to the gurney and wheeled him in. He followed and was directed to a waiting room where Kelly joined him some time later.

"Any news?"

"They won't tell me anything," Tim replied, nodding at Kelly to sit down next to him.

"Don't think we've been properly introduced. I'm Kelly Freed. I'll be running for sheriff when Hanson retires."

Tim shook Kelly's offered hand. "Tim Conroy. Wrangler at the Blue River Ranch."

"And the guy we flew in is your partner," Kelly added. It wasn't a question.

"Yes," Tim replied anyway. "He's Rory McCown." He had no idea what Kelly meant by the word "partner," but he really didn't feel like exploring how homophobic the next sheriff was.

"I know," Kelly replied. "He's a parolee. From the flyers you brought in a while ago? His time is almost up. He's done well. Can't be easy with his history, so he can probably credit you for keeping him walking the line."

Tim shook his head. "Rory's done it all himself. The crimes *and* the rehabilitation."

Kelly smiled at Tim but didn't say anything. Maybe he was a good guy after all.

For the umpteenth time, a doctor came into the busy waiting room, but this time he walked straight up to Kelly. "Officer Freed? You brought in the hypothermic?"

Kelly briefly looked at Tim and then at the socially inept intern. "If you mean I brought in Rory McCown with symptoms of hypothermia, then yes." He grabbed Tim's elbow. "This is his partner, Tim Conroy. He'll want to see Rory."

The doctor turned to Tim and looked uncomfortable. "I see, well, yes, we're still treating him for the hypothermia—"

"Meaning you're trying to warm him up," Kelly interrupted.

"Yes," the intern said, looking at Kelly. "He's got a sprained ankle, but it doesn't appear to be broken, and other than the hypothermia, I mean the fact his core temperature, his temperature was too low, he seems fine. We put him under a Bear Hugger and gave him warm fluids, so as soon as he's warm again, you can take him home." The intern didn't stick around.

"Can I see him?" Tim called after the doctor.

"In a minute," the man said, glancing back. "A nurse will come and get you."

When Tim looked at Kelly, the tall deputy was smiling. "I'm sorry, I have a way of making people feel uncomfortable. It's just—"

"He deserved it."

Kelly chuckled. "Yeah, he did. I can't stand it when doctors show up spouting jargon. How hard can it be to just talk English?"

"I bet he won't know what we're talking about when we talk horse wrangling either," Tim said.

When Tim was taken to Rory, he insisted Kelly come along. "Rory'll want to see the guy who rescued him."

They were shown to a cubicle where Rory was still on a gurney. He was covered with an air-filled blanket that lightly hovered over him, and there was an IV bag hanging from a stand next to him. He seemed to be asleep, but as soon as Tim touched his shoulder, Rory opened his eyes. "Hey."

"Hey yourself," Rory answered. "What happened? They said something about me falling in the river?"

"You didn't fall in." Tim stuck his hand underneath the blanket, and when he found Rory's, he felt it was toasty warm. "You got your foot stuck in a beaver dam, and you were up to your waist in glacier water from the thaw."

"How did I get stuck in a beaver dam?"

Tim squeezed Rory's hand. "Danny had something to do with it, apparently. Don't you remember?"

Rory shook his head, apparently confused. "And who are you again?"

Tim felt his heart stop. Rory didn't remember him? "Rory, I'm…." Tim stopped when he saw a smile spread across Rory's face.

"Sorry, Timmy, I couldn't resist. The look on your face was priceless."

Tim breathed a sigh of relief to see Rory was joking, and when Rory laughed, he chuckled too, still holding Rory's hand underneath the warming blanket. Then he realized they weren't alone behind the curtain. He looked over his shoulder at Kelly. "Rory, you probably owe your life to this man. Deputy Kelly Freed."

Rory's eyes drifted to the blond-haired man. "Never thought I'd say thank you to anyone from law enforcement, but thank you. What did you do?"

"I flew you to the hospital in my chopper."

Rory looked from Kelly to Tim and back to Kelly. "You mean to tell me I flew in a helicopter and I don't remember?"

"I guess so," Kelly replied. "Then, I have to take the chopper home anyway, so I can give you a lift."

"You'd probably have to wait too long," Tim interrupted. "The paperwork will take a while, even if they discharge him right now."

"Don't worry about it." Kelly shrugged. "I wasn't on duty anyway, so it's not like I need to get back to work."

Tim looked at Rory. "So are you all warm again? Shall I ask them if you can go home?"

"Home would be good," Rory said.

—33—

BY THE time they got home, the weather had miraculously cleared up. The sun was even shining, and although the grass was still glistening with moisture, the ground seemed less waterlogged than the night before.

Rory made his way up the rickety steps to their cabin on crutches, his left ankle heavily bandaged. He tried not to get nervous at Tim's constant fidgeting.

"If you want, we can stay at the crew house," Tim suggested. "It's probably warmer there and possibly more comfortable."

"Your bed's here, remember?" Rory said, one eyebrow raised.

"Right. So no going back."

"Having regrets already?"

Tim put his arms around Rory's shoulder and hugged him to his chest, almost making him lose his precarious balance. "Not for a second."

"We'll manage," Rory said determinedly. He meant it too. He'd decided while he was waiting for Tim to rescue him that he'd make a real effort at accepting everything Tim did for him, because he knew Tim did it out of love. He'd never felt this loved before, not even by Charlie. The way Tim loved him was on a whole different plane. While Charlie had loved to fuck him, Tim seemed to want his company, seemed to like his sense of humor and his attitude as well. Yeah, Tim liked to fuck him too, but it was more the icing on the cake and less the means to an end. And he liked Tim, too. For his warmth and strength and for how Tim made him feel wanted and cared for. For the first time in his life, he felt like he had something to look forward to.

OVER the next few days they continued work on the house. Grant and Hunter and sometimes Flynn and Gable would come and help them. Even Coop dropped by one Sunday, and he brought along a few of the newer ranch hands to lend a hand.

In the beginning Rory was frustrated that his bruised ankle prevented him from helping Grant work on the roof, but Flynn was fearless up there, so Rory sawed planks while keeping the weight off his injured foot. Gable wryly joked that he could give Rory some pointers on how to work around his injury, so all in all, they had fun while making the house more habitable.

Rory was still going to AA meetings almost every night, and Tim still drove him and waited outside in the car. On his six month anniversary, Rory had arranged for something special, which made him nervous. Rory usually didn't say much at meetings unless he had something to celebrate, but his sponsor had convinced him it was a good thing to share, so he'd done his very traditional "Hi, my name is Rory and I'm an alcoholic" speech a few times now. Today was different, though. He'd been given permission to bring Tim, because there were certain things he wanted to tell him but couldn't tell him face to face. Tim would just be allowed in to hear Rory speak and would then leave the hall again. Lamar, Rory's sponsor, would get Tim from the hallway as soon as it was Rory's turn. All the other members of the assembly had agreed that this was the way they were going to do it, so as soon as Lamar nodded in Rory's direction, he knew Tim was within earshot, although to preserve the anonymity of the meeting, he wasn't allowed to see the other members.

"Hi, my name is Rory and I'm an alcoholic."

"Hi, Rory."

"I've been sober for six months today, and although I'm the one fighting the fight every day, I have one person to thank for getting me through the very first day and every day since then, and that is my partner, Tim, who is sitting just outside the door listening in. I was very good at hiding my drinking from everyone, and I'm not just saying this to boast, but even Tim didn't know. He just thought I had mood swings, you know."

The group laughed.

"Tim figured I was not a morning person, when the truth was that I needed a drink, and as long as he was in the room with me, I couldn't. I was always in a better mood after he'd had his shower. So one day, he was in a really crappy mood and I thought he'd figured out that he was living with an alcoholic. That tells you something about how selfish we can be."

More laugher from the group.

"Anyway, I still don't know what was wrong with him that day, because the next time I saw him, I thought he was trying to kill me and I decked him, gave him quite a shiner. I was going through DTs, and he bore the brunt of it. He found me and got me to a hospital. The doctor later told me that I could have died because the alcohol deprivation was aggravated by me having bronchitis, and that's why I not only blacked out but had a few seizures as well. I hope I'm not freaking Tim out now, because he doesn't know the half of what went on in the hospital. I haven't found the nerve to tell him this face to face, so that's why he gets to listen in on what I'm telling all of you."

TIM felt his eyes fill with tears. He had to prevent himself from bursting into the meeting hall because he had the overwhelming need to grab his boyfriend and give him the tightest hug he could manage; he knew that would have to wait. He'd get his chance later.

"I know I'm supposed to take all the credit for staying sober for the last half year, and I know Lamar keeps telling me that it's not good to depend on Tim too much, but if it hadn't been for him, I wouldn't have been able to do it. You see, since I was twelve, there hasn't been a day that I hadn't drunk alcohol in some form or another. Sure, I've tried to quit before, and maybe lasted for a day or two, but even then I was kidding myself and lying to the people who were trying to help me. That's the downside of never looking or acting drunk. Even with half a bottle of vodka in my system, I could still tell people I was sober. I even went to meetings like that a few years ago and went through all the motions but kept on drinking. It's so different now, but I hope people will forgive me for all the lies I told in the past. I've tried to make amends with everyone I could find, but most of all, I need to make amends with Tim.

"Anyway, back to Tim and what he means to me. He's my family, you see. The only family I have, if you don't count his family, who are all great. He's the reason I want to stop lying, stop covering things up. I haven't told him about the voices in my head telling me I'm worthless and no good. I haven't told him about how hard it was to accept myself for who I am, and for who I love, because you see, he's Mister Positive. He always sees the best in people, doesn't just think, but actually believes that everything will work out in the end and that people only want good things to happen to you. I used to think he was naïve and hadn't lived out in the real world, but living where we live now, I'm starting to understand his way of thinking. It's actually rubbing off on me, and that's what's given me the strength to tell those voices in my head to buzz off, because they're lying. I think the voices are getting the message too. They're only bad some of the time now, when I'm a bit anxious or don't feel too great for some reason."

Rory took a deep breath, and Tim had to swallow to keep the emotions down.

"I've talked to Lamar about this, and I agree that I'd be really screwed if I ever lost Tim, but he keeps telling me he loves me. I wish I could say it right back, but he beats me to it every time, and then I just shut down. I can only hope that he knows."

"Well, he knows now," someone in the group replied, with laughter following from the rest.

TIM sat in the back of the hall, away from everyone else, and he had to wipe the tears from his face as Lamar approached him.

"You okay?"

Tim nodded. "Yeah, I'm fine. I just wish I could tell him right now that he's got nothing to worry about."

Lamar smiled. "He knows, but it's always good to hear it from the people who mean the most to you. Rory's a great guy. He's still got a long way to go, but he seems to be in a really good place right now, and that's the reason he's doing okay."

Tim nodded, unable to add anything to that.

"Rory'll be out as soon as the meeting finishes, but I need to ask you to go back outside so we can wrap up."

"Yeah, of course," Tim said. "I usually sit in my truck and wait for Rory there anyway."

"That's commitment," Lamar said with an appreciative nod. "Don't get me wrong, but it's also control. He might be ready to be trusted with going to a meeting alone. He told me he'd gotten his driver's license back recently."

"I just wanted him to know I support him every step of the way."

Lamar smiled. "He knows. I'm not telling you how to lead your life. I'm just saying: talk about it. Ask him if he feels up to coming alone. He might not, but then again...." Lamar didn't finish his sentence. He patted Tim's shoulder and then gave him a nod.

Tim knew that meant he really needed to go.

WHEN Rory walked outside, it was like déjà vu from the day he'd walked out of prison.

Tim was across the road, wearing jeans, a plaid shirt, and a Stetson and leaning against his parked truck. Just like that last time, Rory felt his heart jump, and then apprehension took hold. This time it was because he'd opened his heart to the group, and Tim had heard those confessions too.

"Hey, Grumpy," Tim greeted him.

"Hey, Sunshine."

Tim's smile lit up their surroundings as far as Rory was concerned, so he'd definitely earned his nickname. He saw Tim raise his hand and throw something, and out of reflex, Rory caught it. Car keys.

"You want me to drive?"

"I figured now that you'd gotten your license back, you could get rid of the chauffeur."

Rory took a step closer, but Tim wouldn't budge from his place against the driver's side door. Then he reached out for Rory and pulled him closer by his belt buckle.

"Don't you have something to tell me?" Tim whispered in Rory's ear.

"Tell you? I did a whole speech in there." He gestured with his head toward the hall where they'd had their meeting.

Tim leaned closer again. "I'm just dying to tell you something, but you asked me not to beat you to it."

Rory felt his heart race. "I...." He felt like such a doofus, not being able to say it. "You heard the whole thing?" Not to mention they were standing on the street, and they were so close together there was no denying the intimacy. Any passerby could see them.

"Of course I did," Tim answered softly. He stopped talking, and underneath his hands Rory could feel the tension in Tim's chest.

"I.... You're the best thing that ever happened to me, Tim."

"I love you too," Tim replied and then he kissed Rory, right there in the street.

—34—

OVER the course of several weeks, they added a porch to the cabin, extended the roof, and rebuilt the two walls that had sustained too much water damage to survive. Rory put in electricity, so they had light and Tim could plug in his laptop. All that time, Tim and Rory had more or less camped out in their cabin, where only the bedroom was fully equipped.

Once they were wind- and watertight, they'd moved Beth Krause's old stove to the kitchen and installed a water heater and pump so they had warm running water. Those two things made the cabin more habitable.

To their surprise, one Friday night, Hunter and Grant showed up with a large sturdy table and six chairs, all of them handcrafted by Grant.

"Wow, guys, thanks!" Tim said, admiring the handiwork.

"We promised you the dining room set," Hunter replied. "Besides, the table and two of the chairs were already made."

"Only Hunter wanted store-bought ones," Grant added, poking his lover in the ribs. "I hope you like them."

Rory sat down behind the table. "They're great. Usually chairs are a little low for me, but these are perfect."

"They were made for us slightly taller men," Grant agreed. "And since there are no women here to protest...."

Tim laughed from his chair. "Izzie might feel like a child sitting in this. My feet barely touch the floor."

"Well, shorty, you'll just have to grow some more," Rory joked, his hands on Tim's shoulders.

"Seriously, thanks, guys. It's starting to feel like home now."

"That was the idea," Hunter replied. "Now we're going. We have a birthday party to set up for tomorrow."

"Matthew?" Tim asked.

"Yes," Grant answered. "I hope next year we can invite you, after everything is settled."

"With Matty's mother, yes, we know," Tim continued, looking at Rory and happy to see it didn't seem to affect him.

After they'd gone, Rory lit the fire in the living room.

"I hope they settle everything with Matty's custody soon," Tim said, plopping himself down on the old sofa.

"I'm sure they will," Rory replied blankly. "It can't go on forever. No doubt his mother will run out of money for lawyers before Hunter and Grant do."

"Would be nice if you could just work here again instead of going out to Gable's every day."

"I like working at Gable's. They're nice people, Tim."

"I know." Tim let his arm rest on the back of the sofa so he could put it around Rory's shoulders as Rory sat down next to him. "But Hunter and Grant are nice people too."

"Only your brother doesn't like me."

"He's okay with you, Rory. I'm sure Hugh knows by now you make his baby brother happy, and if he doesn't, Izzie just hasn't done a good job whipping her husband into shape."

Rory just shrugged.

"In any case, we're still short of wranglers, and I'm sure by now you've had plenty of practice riding. Gable said you're doing well and he's letting you ride the horses that are about ready to be sold."

Rory nodded. His silence made Tim wonder how much Hugh's silent disapproval was still bugging Rory, though.

Tim tried to keep both their spirits up and let out a contented sigh. "In any case, I'm glad we're starting to turn this place into a home. Christy wants to make us curtains, so I said we'd go into town and buy rods to put them on. Want to help me pick out some fabric?"

"I don't know about those things, Tim."

Tim snorted. "You think I do? We'll have to figure it out as we go along. Same with the cooking thing. But I want us to figure it out together, okay? It could be fun. We can fail together." Tim chuckled, but Rory remained impassive. The only reassurance Tim got was when he put his hand over Rory's hair. Rory rested his head on Tim's shoulder and leaned into the kiss Tim placed on top of his head. Tim knew he had to give Rory time, but the insecurity was gnawing at him.

"I'm tired," Rory announced. "Can we just go to bed?"

TIM felt he'd barely slept when a loud thunderclap woke him. He checked the nightstand for his watch and got confirmation that it was still the middle of the night. Rory wasn't in bed beside him, though, and Tim rolled his eyes at his boyfriend's constant disappearing act. "Rory?" No answer. Tim got up and slipped into his jeans without bothering with boxers. It was cold in the bedroom since they hadn't lit the fireplace the evening before, so he put on his flannel work shirt as well before venturing out into the main room of the cabin. With no Rory anywhere, Tim grabbed his coat from the hook by the door and noticed Rory's old red-and-black coat was gone as well. With a deep sigh, Tim stepped into his boots, opened the front door, and saw Rory standing in the pouring rain outside the porch.

"We've been through this, Rory," Tim shouted over the torrential rain. "Come inside so we can talk."

Rory blatantly ignored him, and Tim couldn't make out through the sheets of rain and in the faint light from the cabin illuminating the dark night air whether it was intentional or whether he just hadn't heard him. He knew how stubborn his lover could be, and for a moment he thought it best to just let him stew and leave him out in the rain, but he knew Rory would be a lot more stubborn than he could ever be, so Tim grabbed his hat and stepped out of the cabin. When he came alongside Rory, he could see the strain in his lover's clenched jaw. He was going to have to tread on eggshells.

"I know you're upset about something, and for all I know it's something I said or did, but this isn't solving anything. You need to tell me what's wrong."

Rory didn't even flinch.

"Fine. Have it your way." Tim turned back to the cabin and shook the water off his coat and hat on the porch before taking off his boots and going inside. He looked outside again to see whether Rory had moved, but he was still there, in his threadbare coat, getting soaked to the bone. Tim walked into their makeshift kitchen and started cleaning the stove that had been brought in the day before, knowing he'd have to keep himself occupied unless he wanted to go out there, grab Rory's arm, and yank him inside like a petulant child. He knew Rory well enough to know the effect that would have, so he kept himself busy until their tiny kitchen looked spotless. This time when Tim looked outside, Rory was gone. He grabbed his coat again and opened the front door, then felt around in his coat pocket for his truck keys.

"I'm here," Rory said, sounding closer than Tim expected.

Rory was sitting on the floor of the tiny porch, his back against the cabin wall and his knees pulled up to his chest so his feet wouldn't get wet. Not that it really mattered, since he looked like a drowned cat, but Tim figured the cold had finally gotten to his lover.

Tim sighed. "Come inside and get warm before you catch something," he said, trying to sound as unaffected as possible. He didn't think he'd succeeded completely. Until then, he hadn't noticed how scared he'd been, and now he knew why. Rory's parole was coming to an end, and with it, Rory's attitude had changed. Not by a lot. Tim knew from Gable that he was still a hard worker and could still be relied upon to do the job he was assigned to do, but he stayed even more in the shadows than usual and clearly kept his head down, which wasn't an easy feat for a tall guy like Rory. The problem was he also hid in plain sight around Tim, avoiding him as much as possible. It had only been a few days, and Tim was used to giving Rory space, so it hadn't dawned on him until he realized he was afraid Rory was going to take to the road and run off.

Rory didn't answer, so Tim sat down next to him, mimicking Rory's posture. "Were you thinking of leaving next week after your last parole hearing?"

Rory shrugged. After what seemed like a very long time, he took a deep breath in. "Yes."

Tim swallowed, hoping to keep the emotions at bay. "Please don't."

For the first time that evening, Rory looked at him. "I wanted to cut my losses. You're not responsible for me anymore once my parole is over, so I figured you'd expect me to find somewhere else to stay."

"Rory, come on!" Tim called out, exasperated. "I can't believe you don't get it. Or maybe you don't *want* to understand what you mean to me. I thought you felt the same."

Rory didn't respond; he never did when things got emotional.

Tim couldn't sit down anymore, so he pushed himself off the floor and paced the narrow strip of dry porch. They were opposites where this was concerned. Although he had no problem staying tight-lipped around strangers, to his loved ones, Tim was an open book. Tim had never hidden his feelings for Rory and had told him early on he loved him, because that's how he felt. Rory had never reciprocated, but Tim had always been sure that at least some of his feelings were returned. Now he felt betrayed, as if Rory was telling him he'd only slept with Tim because it gave him job security and a way of waiting out the end of his parole time. Or because it won him sympathy from the others around the ranch. Tim leaned his outstretched arms against the side of the cabin in an attempt to stretch the pain out of his tensed-up muscles. As soon as the pain ebbed away, he realized he had only one recourse. He wanted some answers, and the only way he would get them was to lay himself totally open.

"I love you, Rory. I loved you four years ago when you came here to work those three weeks, and despite of everything that has happened since, I couldn't get you out of my mind. That's why I asked Hugh to hire you again and why I picked you up when they let you out."

"And you just assumed I'd love you back?"

Tim couldn't look Rory in the eye. "No. But I had to sort out my own feelings, because three years is a long time to pine for someone. I had to know whether you'd return my feelings, and if you didn't, then it would be easier to get you out of my mind. I figured a year was plenty for that. I didn't expect you to jump in my bed right away. I just wanted to know."

"I didn't want you to pine for me, Tim," Rory said in such a soft voice, the rain drowned out most of it, so Tim wasn't sure whether he'd actually heard it or imagined it.

"It's not like I had a choice, Rory."

"I know."

Tim crouched down next to Rory, soothed by Rory's calm, quiet voice and soft words.

"I kept thinking about you when I was in prison. It was the one thing that kept me going in there. The idea that I could look you up once I got out was enough. Of course, I would never actually have had the nerve, but when I walked out and I saw you there, I just wanted to jump you right there and then."

"You could have fooled me." Tim sat with his elbows resting on his knees, and he let his hand dangle close to Rory's. To his surprise, Rory took it, and they sat like that, holding hands, without talking for a little while.

"I don't allow myself to be happy, Tim, because in a heartbeat it can get snatched away, and then the only way I can move on is if I didn't get invested."

"That's no way to live, Rory."

"I loved Charlie and he betrayed me. Before that, I loved my mom and she left me at a gas station when I was six. Who leaves a six-year-old boy at a gas station, Tim?"

Tim didn't know how to answer, but he did feel overwhelmingly like he needed to comfort his boyfriend, so he got up and used the momentum to pull Rory to his feet and into his arms. To Tim's surprise, Rory didn't fight him. Strangely, Rory didn't feel as tall as usual, and Tim easily cradled Rory's head and pulled it to rest on his shoulder. Rory wrapped his arms around Tim's bulkier frame and squeezed him tight. It felt good, as if it was Rory's way of saying Tim was right and his love was returned.

"Let's get out of the cold and inside to get warm, okay?"

Rory nodded against the side of Tim's neck. He didn't let go, though, and Tim wanted to walk inside but found he couldn't move. "Rory?"

Rory looked up and straightened his back, making him look taller again. "Sorry." He let go of Tim just enough to walk inside with him. It was a tight squeeze to get through the door, and Rory led Tim to their one couch.

"I'm sorry about your mom," Tim whispered as he took his coat off and dropped it on the floor, just as Rory launched himself at him. Rory was soaking wet, and Tim felt the water seep through the fabric of his shirt, but he didn't care. Rory was kissing him with abandon, and although Tim knew this was Rory's way of avoiding the confrontation, he had to admit it felt good to think they were okay again.

Instead of pushing Rory away, Tim decided to get Rory out of his wet clothes. Subsequently it was no surprise that when Tim eventually did push Rory away from him—somewhere between sliding the shirt over his shoulders and unbuttoning his trousers—the look on Rory's face was somewhere between panic and confusion.

"You're cold and wet. Let me run you a bath so you can get warmed up."

LESS than five minutes later, they were both in the large, free-standing bath-on-legs with Tim sitting behind Rory and Rory's legs dangling over the side, because it really wasn't a bath made for two full-grown men. This was the first time they'd been able to enjoy the comfort of running water in their bathroom, and the hot water felt heavenly. Tim felt Rory slowly relax as he warmed up, and he enjoyed caressing his boyfriend's nearly hairless chest while Rory's hands rested on Tim's knees.

Tim moved his hand up to Rory's head and kissed his temple. "You know you can trust me, don't you?"

Rory nodded.

"I won't leave you."

Rory looked at the wall and didn't respond.

"I can't leave, because I live here."

"You can ask me to leave."

Tim heard the coldness in Rory's voice and squeezed him into a hug. "I'm not promising you happily ever after, Rory, but I know I've never felt for anyone what I feel for you, and if I have a say in it, it can last forever. Nothing would make me happier than to grow old with you. I can totally imagine us ten or twenty years from now."

Rory shivered almost imperceptibly, and for a moment Tim wondered if he'd imagined it. Then Rory raised himself up and turned around, hands resting on the curved sides of the bath. Water sloshed over the sides with the suddenness of his movements, and when Tim looked up, he saw Rory's cheeks were wet. Judging from the redness of his eyes, the bathwater wasn't to blame. Tim had only just reached up to touch Rory's cheek when Rory dove down and pressed his lips against Tim's. When Rory bent his arms, their bodies lined up, albeit a little awkwardly because of the shape of the tub, and Tim pulled him closer.

"I love you with all my heart, Rory," Tim whispered into Rory's hair when Rory finally broke the kiss.

"I love you too," Rory murmured, and Tim's heart took flight.

A little while later, both of them dried off but still naked, they were on their bed, tucked underneath the covers. Rory's skin felt warm now, and they lay wrapped around each other. To Tim's surprise, there wasn't the usual sexual tension between them. Tim didn't remember if they'd ever just lain like this without it ending in a passionate exchange of bodily fluids, but now neither of them was aroused, and it didn't feel necessary, either.

From time to time, Rory would look Tim in the eye as if he needed to reassure himself that Tim hadn't changed his mind, but other than that, Tim felt completely content to be lying there, skin to skin with his boyfriend. Rory was still a lot more emotional than Tim had ever seen him, and he was surprised how Rory revealed that by kissing his eyelids and eyebrows and caressing his stubble with his hand. Their kisses were soft too, barely exploring, but Tim reveled in the fact that Rory initiated them too, as if he couldn't get enough of Tim's mouth.

Tim knew it was just a matter of time before they'd start to make love, and he knew it was going to be special again. They'd crossed another hurdle, and Tim wanted somehow to acknowledge that, but for the first time since they'd gotten together, Tim knew they had all the time in the world.

—35—

RORY liked working on Gable's ranch. It was a small affair, and he worked alone most of the day. Occasionally he'd ride out to the herd with Gable and Gable would explain things to him about the horses, teaching him basic stuff about how horses behaved as a group and how that affected the way you could train them. Rory sucked it all up, enjoying the calm presence of the older rancher and his unassuming manner.

Each day Rory returned home after work, his apprehensions lessened as well. Usually he was there before Tim, so he'd go to their bedroom to make the bed and pick up the clothes Tim, as a self-confessed slob, had left strewn around. Sometimes there were cups on the living room table and occasionally dishes in the sink, and Rory would wash those and put them away. More and more, it started feeling good to be able to care for Tim in that way.

That day, when Rory returned to the cabin, the front door was open. It wasn't warm enough for that yet, so Rory felt fear creeping up his spine. The lock had been forced open, and as Rory walked inside, he saw the stove was banged up, their new table and chairs hacked to bits as if they were firewood, and the cover of the old sofa ripped to shreds. When he walked into their bedroom, the bedding was torn up and Tim's old bed was hacked apart, just like the rest of their furniture.

"Tim?" Rory called out, despite knowing his boyfriend wouldn't be there yet. Rage started building inside of him as he fished for his keys and got into his green Ford truck. There was only one man who could have done this, and a part of Rory hoped he'd never find him, but he also knew where he hung out, so revenge was part of his plan. He didn't care if it got him in trouble with the law again. He drove to Gable's ranch, knowing neither Gable nor Flynn would be back at their homestead yet, and retrieved the rifle Gable kept in the back of the hallway closet. He hid it underneath the seat as he drove back out to the highway.

Rory tried to stay calm as he drove, but a familiar sort of unrest was mixed into his anger. Seeing their home so messed up, so violated—the home he had built with Tim—and knowing Tim would be walking into the same devastation, gutted him to such an extent that, although he knew going after their vandal would get him into trouble, he also knew he wouldn't be able to let it slide. This was too much. This hurt him and Tim on such a basic level that it warranted retaliation, and he didn't care if it landed him right back in jail.

Rory had seen the battered old truck Delco was still driving a few times around the Chester area. He'd even seen Delco inside it one time. It took Rory a few passes around the town to find the dilapidated house he'd seen Delco drive to that one time he'd spotted him. The truck was there.

His heart was pounding in his ears and he was dizzy from the adrenalin, but he knew he couldn't chicken out. He grabbed the rifle from underneath the seat. Despite his frequent brushes with the law, Rory wasn't all that used to handling guns. One of his foster fathers had taught him to shoot, but that had been a lifetime ago, and even the armed robbery he'd been convicted for hadn't required him to handle any weapons. He'd just driven the getaway car. He had to do this, though. He had to get Delco out of his hair once and for all.

Rory knocked on the door, and when it opened, he pointed his gun. He startled to see a petite redhead gasp at him and then step aside, her back against the hallway wall.

"Delco?" he asked, with surprisingly little quiver in his voice.

She looked at the door to the rest of the house, and Rory didn't wait for an invitation.

"Delco, you bastard, where are you?" Rory shouted as he advanced inside. He kicked open a door, but the room behind it was empty so he walked further down the hallway, his rifle still pointing ahead of him.

The third door he entered led outside, into the back yard. Rory's breath hitched when he saw the short rodeo cowboy standing by the barbecue, flipping hamburgers. Delco didn't look all that impressed with the rifle Rory was carrying, although he was eyeing it carefully.

"Look what the cat dragged in," Delco said with much bravado. "Call the cops, honey," he shouted over Rory's shoulder.

Rory turned around and pointed the gun at the woman. "Don't. Stay here. Nobody's calling the cops." He didn't wait for her reaction but saw the terror in her face before turning around to face Delco again. "Stay where you are. Call her to you, so you're both standing together."

Delco chuckled. "No way. You don't have the nerve, McCown. You always were a coward."

Rory gritted his teeth and almost blindly grabbed at the woman, pulling her to him without losing eye contact with Delco. It was surprisingly easy. She was shorter even than Delco and skinny too, and because she was clearly frightened, she didn't fight back. As soon as he felt that, he pushed her in Delco's direction. "Stay where I can see the both of you."

Delco chuckled again, making the rage inside Rory flare up. "Stop," Rory said with surprising command in his voice. "You've had enough fun for one day."

"What are you talking about, man?" Delco said.

"I'm talking about trashing my cabin."

"You mean that rundown shack where you run off to take that cowboy's dick up your ass? It's barely got four walls and a roof. Why would I be trashing that?"

"I know you did it," Rory said through gritted teeth. "Just like I know you put up those posters and called the sheriff on me more than once. Or did you think I wouldn't know who clued in my parole officer about all those things I didn't do?"

"Come on, Rory, we both know you're no saint. And we both know that if it wasn't for your stupidity, I would never have had a criminal record."

"It was your own stupidity," Rory rebutted. "You wanted to steal those horses because you had a buyer for them. I was just stupid enough to fall for your promises."

"Maybe I should have promised to fuck you up the ass instead of paying you and you wouldn't have gotten us caught."

Rory raised the rifle he'd let lower again. "It was only a matter of time, and you knew it. I told you to go to other ranches and not just the Blue River, but you wouldn't listen."

"I still think you squealed to your boyfriend."

Rory took a step forward and pushed the rifle into Delco's face, making him pull back. Out of the corner of his eye, Rory could see the woman had tears streaming down her face, and he wished he could just let her go, but then she'd call the sheriff and he'd be in trouble for sure. At least now he had some chance of getting out of there, although he didn't really have a plan.

"Tim wasn't my boyfriend then," Rory replied, his voice sounding a lot calmer than he felt. "And I didn't squeal on you. I had a lot more to lose than you did if we got caught."

"And here I thought you wanted to get caught. Back to jail. Three square meals, getting plugged in the showers, lots of free cock to suck."

"Stop it!" Rory shouted, pushing the barrel of the rifle against Delco's nose. "You have no idea what goes on in there."

"Oh, but thanks to you, I do. Thanks to you I got to sample prison life."

"For eleven fucking months," Rory hissed. "I got three years and parole."

"Which you are violating big time now."

Delco's arrogance was grating on Rory's nerves. For a guy who'd supposedly never had a brush with the law before his conviction four years ago, he wasn't easily frightened by the rifle or the home invasion. Rory knew he'd have to change his approach, so he lowered the gun. "Why couldn't you have left well enough alone? We both did our time."

"I have you to thank for soiling my clean record and for eleven months of my life going down the drain. What did you think? I was just going to let you get away with that? I was just going to let you set up house with your horse wrangler and live happily ever after? Life doesn't work that way, Rory. Life comes back and bites you in the ass. Call it karma. Then again, you probably like it when it bites you in the ass." Delco laughed, and Rory's already speeding heartbeat raced even more. He was seeing red. He'd come here to get Delco to stop harassing him, but Rory now knew that wouldn't happen, because it meant he'd have to take responsibility for his actions, and Delco would never do that.

Rory raised the rifle again. "Leave this town. Leave us alone. I don't owe you a single thing."

"You'll never shoot me. You're too much of a chicken. You wouldn't even carry that gun I gave you when we went out to steal those horses. Oh no, you couldn't because *someone could get hurt.*" Delco said those last words like a five-year-old would, mocking Rory's apprehension.

Rory cocked the rifle.

—36—

"RORY, I'm home," Tim singsonged as he walked through the open cabin door. The image before him made him stop in his tracks. Instead of finding Rory in their newly set-up kitchen, he saw the devastation of a ransacked cabin. Tim quickly walked through all the rooms, and when he couldn't find Rory, he panicked. He'd found it strange that Rory's truck hadn't been parked out front but hadn't thought much about it until he'd seen the state of their home.

Tim got back in his truck and drove up to Gable's ranch.

"Rory still here?" he asked Flynn, who was just walking up the porch to the main house as Gable walked outside.

"He left about half an hour ago, maybe a bit more," Flynn replied, looking at Gable.

"Probably more," Gable agreed. "What's going on?"

"The cabin's trashed. I was hoping Rory hadn't seen it."

"He didn't say anything about running errands, so I think it's a safe bet to say he saw it. He might have gone to the sheriff's office to report it."

Tim nodded and got back in his truck. He didn't think it was likely that Rory would seek out help from the law, but he feared he knew what Rory would do instead. He just wished he knew where Delco lived and hoped Rory didn't know either.

Driving off the ranch and into town, Tim's cell phone rang.

"Tim, this is Gable. Rory took my rifle."

Tim threw down the phone and cursed loudly. That meant Rory was seeking revenge, and that he knew where to find it. Tim tried to think, but he couldn't get his thoughts in order. He had no idea where to look for either Rory or Delco; he just knew he had to prevent Rory from getting himself into trouble. His only chance was the new deputy and the hope he'd been true to his word and kept his eyes open for Delco. Maybe Tim could wing it and persuade the guy to tell him where Delco lived without giving away why he wanted to know. It was his only chance.

TIM stormed through the front door of the sheriff's office and was stopped by the girl who manned the phones. Tim remembered her being a few grades below him in school. "Tim, you can't go in there. It's not—"

"It's okay, Jennifer. Let him through," Kelly interrupted. "What's wrong, Tim?"

Tim realized he hadn't thought it through. "Can I talk to you alone?" he asked to stall for time.

"Sure, step in here."

Tim followed Kelly Freed behind the counter and into an office. He rubbed his hands over his jeans-covered thighs to hide his nervousness. He hated lying, but he didn't know Kelly well enough to tell him the truth. Then again, Kelly hadn't even looked away when he'd seen Tim kiss Rory while he was unconscious on the hospital gurney, so Tim pretty much knew Kelly was aware of the fact they were in a relationship. He figured the rest of the truth would surface sooner rather than later anyway. Maybe telling Kelly the truth would work. Maybe Kelly would understand he only wanted what was best for Rory. When Tim looked at the deputy, he knew the man was trying to remain patient, but that he wanted to know why Tim was there.

Tim took a deep breath and decided to go for broke. "To cut a long story short, our cabin was ransacked today, and I think Rory's gone after the guy who did it."

"John Delco?" Kelly asked.

Surprised by Kelly's fast answer, Tim nodded. "Do you know where Rory could find him?"

Kelly cocked his head. "I don't know if Rory knows where he lives, but I do."

Tim gave him a questioning look.

"We could pay Mr. Delco a friendly visit." Kelly took out a key and opened a drawer, taking out his gun belt.

"You said friendly."

Kelly smiled. "Sadly, guns command respect in this neck of the woods. Wouldn't do for a deputy to make an official visit unarmed. Even if it was friendly."

"Okay."

"And I'm going to do my utmost to keep this friendly."

They walked outside. "Follow me in your truck. When we get there, stay back and let me do the talking. If things turn sour, go back to your truck and call the office for backup. Do *not* interfere. You can come with me only because Rory might be involved, but I don't want you in the thick of things, understood?"

Tim nodded. He knew he could do all those things, providing he was sure Rory was okay. If anything happened to his boyfriend, he didn't know if he could do what he promised, though.

Following Kelly's car, Tim was a little surprised to be taken out to Chester. He was even more surprised to see Rory's truck parked outside of the rundown house Kelly stopped at.

"Remember what I told you," Kelly said to Tim.

"That's Rory's truck," Tim said, gesturing at the dark green Ford pickup.

"I was afraid of that," Kelly said with a sigh. He took out his gun and checked it before putting it back in its holster. "Stay here."

"Like hell I will," Tim replied.

"I can't take you with me, Tim," Kelly cautioned. "I'll get Rory out of there as fast as I can, but you need to stay out here."

And then a gun blast sounded, and they both ran around the side of the house.

When they rounded the corner, they found Rory with a rifle in his hand standing in front of Delco, who was clutching his forehead. Blood was running down the side of his face, and he was pushing a woman away from him.

"Miranda?" Tim said as soon as he recognized the woman. "What are you doing here?"

She didn't answer. She looked frightened and frantically worried about Delco, who kept telling her to leave him alone. It was only as Tim looked at Delco that he noticed Delco was holding a large caliber handgun.

"Drop your weapons," Kelly said. "Both of you."

Neither man did as he was asked, and both Tim and Kelly kept their distance.

Rory was standing with his back to them and the rifle lowered. Delco was pointing the gun at Rory while his other hand covered the slowly seeping wound over his brow.

"He tried to kill me," Delco said. "I'm not taking any chances."

"Rory?" Kelly said.

Rory didn't let on he'd heard him, so Tim repeated Kelly's plea. This time Rory rolled his shoulders, but he didn't turn around and didn't let go of his gun.

To Tim's surprise, a smile formed on Delco's face.

"Well, Rory, now the law is here, you're going back to jail. You shot me, and that is a violation of your parole."

"I didn't shoot you, Delco," Rory said in a surprisingly calm voice. "You grabbed my rifle and tried to wrestle it away from me. You hit yourself in the head with the butt."

"Details," Delco said, acting as if Tim and Kelly weren't standing in the yard with them. "Who's going to believe you?"

Rory didn't answer.

"I was this close to getting you out of my hair, but you kept coming back for more. I got you thrown off the Blue River Ranch thanks to this little lady's son and the fact we whispered about your track record with little boys into the Krause lawyer's ear, but you just couldn't get enough, could you?"

"You used me to get back at Rory?" Miranda asked, suddenly finding the courage to speak up.

"Shut up, woman," Delco hissed.

"You told me you wanted to get me my baby boy just to get back at Rory?"

"You wanted to get back at Hunter just as badly, Mir."

"No, I didn't," she replied desperately. "You used me."

Delco lowered his gun just long enough to slap her upside the head, viciously and with the flat of his hand. She covered her jaw with her hand and sagged to her knees in the yellow grass.

Tim looked at Kelly, and just as the lawman moved, Delco raised his gun at Rory again, which made everyone stop in their tracks.

"Why didn't you just pack your bags and leave like all those other times? I figured they'd pin that escaped foal on you during that storm, but they didn't. Oh, right, you have a sugar daddy at the ranch!" he said, as if the interruption with Miranda never happened.

Tim inhaled sharply to say something, but Kelly stopped him by holding up his hand. Delco didn't seem to have noticed.

"Almost got you drinking again, too. Rory McCown, Horse Thief. Rory McCown, Child Molester. You know what my next flyers would have said? Rory McCown likes to take it up the butt. Rory McCown is a pederast. A deviant. A pillow biter. A sausage jockey. A fudge packer."

Delco said those horrible words with such clear amusement that Tim felt the bile rise, not only because of the power of those ugly words, but also because Rory had told Tim about the voices that crowded his head and called him those vile names. He wondered if Rory had told Delco about those voices and if Delco was now using that knowledge against him. The problem was that Tim was powerless to do anything. He could see that Rory's hand, the one holding the rifle, was shaking slightly, but other than that, Rory didn't seem all that affected by Delco's vitriol. Still, Tim wanted to take Rory away from this hurtful and relentless man, but Delco was still pointing the gun at Rory, and he knew acting now would be suicide. He looked at Kelly, who was keeping his cool but had little beads of sweat clinging to his forehead.

"You didn't have to trash our home," Rory said softly. "Did you really think that would make me leave Tim? It won't. Tim was there for me all through my time in jail. He'll wait for me now as well. He'll still be there when I get out, because you see, he loves me and he knows I love him. I bet that's something you can't even begin to fathom. You use people, Delco. And then you wonder why they turn on you."

Miranda sobbed from where she was sitting on the ground, but nobody took notice of her. Tim saw Delco's face turn cold, and in a split second, he saw Kelly shoot out like a lightning bolt. Before Delco could squeeze the trigger, Kelly had pushed his hand up, and the shot rang through empty sky. Tim looked over at Rory and saw him sag down to the ground. In an instant he was next to Rory, cushioning his fall.

"Rory, look at me. Did he shoot you?" Tim didn't think so. He was pretty sure Kelly had reached Delco before he'd pulled the trigger, but seeing Rory lose his footing made him reconsider. After all, they'd heard a gun blast before they ran into the yard, and if Rory hadn't been the one to shoot, it had to have been Delco. Tim couldn't see any blood on Rory, but Rory's eyes stared out blankly and his body was completely limp, despite the fact he was breathing. "Rory, talk to me. Rory, it's over. Everything's okay." Tim looked over at Kelly, sitting on top of Delco and cuffing his hands behind his back. The handgun was lying between them in the grass. Tim looked down again when Rory turned toward him and started shaking. All he could do was pull Rory into his arms and rock him.

"I didn't shoot him, Timmy. Please believe me?"

"I believe you," Tim replied. Over and over again.

—37—

KELLY let Tim drive Rory and Miranda to the station, and then put them in separate offices while taking Delco into the one interrogation room the sheriff's office had.

Tim was told to wait in front of the reception area. He contemplated calling his brother but didn't feel like getting another lecture about how Rory was no good and how this proved it once more. It was therefore a surprise when Gable sauntered into the reception area and sat down next to him.

"I've come to claim my rifle," Gable said matter-of-factly.

Tim nodded, and they sat together for a while. Then Gable put his hand on Tim's shoulder. "Is he in trouble?"

"I don't know yet," Tim replied honestly. "He says he didn't shoot, and I believe him."

"I keep just one bullet in the rifle, so if that's still in there, it's easy enough to prove. He didn't take any extra."

Tim looked at Gable, who was giving him his most compassionate grin.

"I like your man, Tim. He's a bit quiet, but he knows how to work hard and he's interested in picking up new things. He's also got a way with horses, although he'd never boast about it. And if the horses like him, what's not to love?"

Tim smiled. "I'm keeping him. But technically, stealing that rifle is a parole violation. So he'll probably go back to jail."

Gable squeezed Tim's shoulder. "So you'll wait for him. You did it before."

"Yeah, I'll wait for him."

Gable didn't let go of Tim's shoulder when Kelly walked into the reception area. "Rory wants to see you."

"I can go in with him?"

Kelly nodded.

"Is he free to go?"

"Not yet. Fremont County Prosecutor is on his way, but I'll plead Rory's case with him. If he says it's okay, then Rory can go home with you, but he might not."

"Okay, thanks," Tim said, getting up from his seat. When Tim walked behind the reception desk and into the office he'd seen Rory being taken into, Rory was sitting with his head bent down and his hands covering his head.

"Rory?"

Rory looked up and launched himself into Tim's arms, kissing him as if his life depended on it. "I'm sorry. I didn't mean to get into trouble, but I saw what he'd done to our cabin, and I had to do something to stop him. I couldn't live with the taunts anymore. He wasn't going to stop."

"I know," Tim said, rubbing his hand over Rory's silky hair. "It's okay. Kelly's going to put a word in for you with the prosecutor."

"They can revoke my parole for my carrying a rifle alone, Timmy. But I swear I didn't shoot it."

"I know."

"I just wanted him to stop. When I saw what he'd done to the cabin, *our* cabin... Tim, after all the work you put into it—"

"*We* put into it," Tim corrected Rory. "You put in all the electricity, not me."

"I just wanted him to stop."

"I know," Tim repeated. He pulled Rory down to the chairs again and allowed Rory to lean against him, knowing both how much Rory needed the closeness and how little of that closeness might lay in their future. If the prosecutor was in a bad mood, he could decide that, with Rory's track record, the only thing he could do was send him back to jail to finish his sentence.

Tim had no idea how long they sat there before Kelly walked into the room. He didn't like the look on the deputy's face.

"You want the good or the bad news first?"

"Bad," Rory replied at the same time as Tim said, "Good."

Kelly's face softened. "The prosecutor wants to talk to Rory's parole officer before making a decision, and he can't do that until tomorrow."

"So I have to stay here until tomorrow?" Rory asked.

"No," Kelly answered.

"County jail?" Tim asked.

"Nope," Kelly replied. "County jail is all full."

"State?" Rory asked with clear apprehension in his voice.

Kelly smiled and addressed Rory. "No, I managed to persuade the prosecutor that you were less of a flight risk than Delco. Also, we determined that the rifle wasn't fired, so although you carried a weapon, which according to the terms of your parole is not allowed, you have no priors involving weapons. He knows you were just the driver in the armed robbery, and you served your time for that. None of your other crimes were violent, and the prosecutor was impressed by a few things Gable Sutton told him about how you're turning your life around."

"So what are you saying?" Tim asked nervously.

"I'm saying that if Rory signs papers that he'll present himself at his parole office tomorrow at noon, you can take him home for the night."

Tim let out a relieved sigh, but Kelly raised his hand. "I'm not saying everything is settled. The prosecutor's going to talk to your parole officer and then determine what will happen."

"Okay," Tim said. "But we can go home?"

Kelly nodded. "For the night."

Tim got up and pulled Rory to his feet. "Let's go. I'm taking you home, baby." He dragged Rory into the hallway.

"We don't have a home, remember?" Rory reminded him. "Delco made sure of that."

"We'll stay in a hotel room for the night, if that's okay?"

"As long as we know where you are," Kelly agreed.

They signed the papers, and the stern-looking prosecutor reminded Rory to show up at his appointment the following day. Tim couldn't get his boyfriend out of there fast enough. He drove them to the motel that held both great memories for them and some pretty sad ones too. Tim didn't care. He was going to make the most of it.

Tim forked out the money for the best room in the motel, and they took a shower together before drying off and settling in each other's arms in the king size bed. They had kissed some under the spray of the walk-in shower, and Tim had taken his time washing Rory's body, but he could tell Rory was withdrawing, and it scared him. It was likely that they'd be apart for a while after tomorrow, and Tim didn't want to waste any time. Rory didn't seem in the mood, though. He held Rory close and tried to give him time.

Then he thought of something that might persuade his boyfriend. "What was your first time like?" he asked.

"First time?" Rory parroted, looking Tim in the eye.

"You know, with a guy."

"First blowjob I got a guy paid me twenty bucks," Rory replied flatly. "And the first guy who fucked me drove me from Georgia to Tennessee in his truck, so that was my way of paying him."

"Oh, Rory," Tim sighed, squeezing his boyfriend tightly.

"It's okay," Rory replied, emotion still far from his voice. "You'd be surprised how easily some truckers accept sexual favors as payment. It's kept me from starving or being beaten to a pulp more than once. It's not always easy to get guys to use condoms, especially in jail, but being able to take it up the ass without too much fuss is definitely an asset."

Tim couldn't hide his emotions like Rory could. He buried his face in Rory's hair and inhaled his scent, wanting it to calm him. It worked to a certain extent, but he still felt he somehow had to make it up to his boyfriend. Tim had made it clear before that he didn't have a problem with Rory's past, at least not the physical side. Emotionally, it didn't mean he could just brush it under the carpet and pretend it had never happened. For the umpteenth time, Tim felt fortunate that his first time had been almost perfect. His first lover had been older, more experienced, more patient, and infinitely more kind than he imagined

Rory's first time had been. Suddenly, Tim realized how he could make it better.

"Rory?"

Rory looked up. His face was soft and didn't display any of the hurt Tim imagined behind his eyes.

"Do you think I can show you what your first time should have been like?"

Rory snorted. "Right. And how are you going to do that?"

Tim wasn't taken aback. "The man who took my virginity was very patient and took it slow. He made me feel like nothing else mattered and like there was nobody else in the world for him. I was young, and he made me work hard for it. Legally I wasn't old enough to have sex, but I seduced him. He was the only other gay man I knew, and I wanted another man's touch so badly." Tim smiled at the memory. "At the time I had no idea there were bars I could go to or that there were other men like him and me who preferred male company. It wasn't like he advertised, but I guess I saw it because I was in tune with those feelings or something."

"You're talking about Gable, aren't you?"

Tim nodded. "Yeah."

"I can imagine he was good to you."

Tim looked at Rory and raised an eyebrow.

"I lived at his place, remember? I'm 'in tune' with those feelings as well. I see the looks he exchanges with Flynn, the little casual touches. Other people may choose to ignore them, but I was trying to get my life back on track and I kind of missed you, so lying in bed alone thinking of what was going on down the hall wasn't always easy."

"You missed me?"

Rory thumped Tim with his elbow. "No, I was tempted to join them." A little later he added, quietly, "Of course I missed you. Just like I'll miss you if I need to go back to jail."

"I'm going to try my best so you won't have to miss me, Rory," Tim replied without hesitancy. "I'll persuade that parole officer and the prosecutor that you did this for me. I'll make them understand you only tried to defend what was ours."

"They won't care."

Tim took Rory's face in his hands and kissed him, trying hard to put as much love into the kiss as he could manage. "I love you, Rory McCown, and if they make you go back to jail, I'll wait for you. I waited three years for you to be released and I'll wait another three if I have to. I'll just fix up the cabin again, and when they release you, you'll have a home to come back to."

Rory nodded, and Tim could see he was holding back tears, so he kissed him again until they both needed to come up for air. Then Rory started kissing Tim's neck, his beard tickling him as he slowly made his way down. Tim pulled Rory's face up again so he could make their lips touch, and he realized it was so much more about the intimacy than the sex.

—38—

RORY didn't know what to do. He was terribly turned on by the prolonged foreplay and by Tim's reluctance to up the ante. Tim's hands all over him, and his mouth covering all the spots the hands missed, were enough to drive Rory crazy with desire. He'd pulled Tim on top of him while they were kissing and was squeezing Tim's butt cheeks to increase the friction on their cocks rubbing alongside each other, but it was simply not enough. Exasperated, he pushed himself away from the bed, and with some effort, flipped them both over until he was lying on top of Tim's buff frame. Rory raised himself on his arms and saw Tim's contented smirk. Somewhere in that past hour, the dire mood from when they started had faded, and now it was all about making the time count. Who knew how long he'd have to miss this again?

"You're enjoying this, aren't you?"

Tim nodded.

"You're enjoying this too much."

"Why?" Tim asked playfully. "Is there such a thing as too much pleasure? Come here." Tim pulled Rory down and kissed him hard.

Rory pulled away. "Will you fuck me already?"

"I'll fuck you. Later. Don't want it to be over so soon. I'm enjoying it too much."

"You're a fucking tease."

Tim laughed. "I'll take that as a compliment." He pulled Rory to him again and locked their lips in another searing kiss.

It wasn't that Rory didn't like kissing. He did. He actually loved kissing Tim, who had a plump bottom lip and a thinner top lip and a perpetual smile that always made Rory feel happy. He just wanted it all. He wanted Tim inside him, fucking him hard. He wanted to sit in that parole office tomorrow with his body still humming. He wanted to feel Tim for as long as he could, because the odds were stacked against him having this again tomorrow night.

"I wasn't kidding that I want to show you how it should have been that first time, Rory," Tim murmured against Rory's mouth as they stopped kissing.

"We had. Our. First. Time. Remember?" Rory said, interlacing his words with kisses. "I know how tender you can be. I also know I want you to fuck me. Right now."

Tim shook his head and smiled. "Patience, my man."

Rory pushed himself up again and rubbed his groin against Tim's, teasing their cocks together. He could see the pleasure in Tim's face, and he spread his knees, pulling them up one after the other until he was sitting on Tim's hips. "Got a condom?"

Tim groaned. "Fine. Have it your way. Turn around. All fours."

Rory sucked his top lip into his mouth, trying not to look too smug at his small victory, and did what Tim asked, looking over his shoulder to watch Tim preparing himself. To his surprise, Tim didn't grab a condom or the tube of lube. Instead he spread Rory's ass cheeks and dove in. Rory gasped at feeling Tim's tongue near his entrance. For a moment he was grateful that they'd taken a shower just before going to bed, and then the sublime feeling of being thoroughly rimmed stole just about any conscious thought from his mind. Feeling the vibrations of Tim moaning against the slowly relaxing muscle made the rest of the world disappear. Just when he thought Tim was going teasingly slow again, he felt some pressure, and then something entered him. It wasn't very large, so it was probably Tim's finger. Rory pushed back, trying to impale himself on it, and then he felt Tim's tongue again, circling around the invasion.

Tim kept teasing the muscle, even when he pushed in another finger.

The stretch didn't hurt one bit. In fact, Rory welcomed it. "Fuck, Timmy. A little more."

"Show me how much you need it," Tim teased.

Rory could almost see Tim's smile and the way his eyes went all beady when his mouth went wide. So he pushed back while Tim kept his hand still. He fucked himself on Tim's fingers and didn't feel the least bit slutty about it. He even managed to move in such a way that Tim's callused fingers rubbed over his sweet spot, and he knew he was moaning. He stopped for a moment when he caught himself and then realized he didn't need to. Tim liked to hear him moan. He'd said so many times, and now it felt right. "Need more, Timmy," Rory said with a strained voice. "Need you inside me."

"I am inside you," Tim replied.

"Not with…," Rory sighed in frustration and upped the frequency of his movements until Tim pulled back his hand. "Fuck, Timmy! That's not what I meant." Almost as soon as Rory voiced his frustration, Tim's mouth was on him again, and he didn't think of protesting. It felt too good. He felt too accepted, as Tim's tongue brushed over his now-relaxed entrance, to utter anything more than incoherent babbling. Rory was almost on his stomach, his knees spread wide, hands against the headboard and face next to the fluffy motel pillow, when Tim reached his hand between his legs and started rubbing Rory's engorged cock while he continued rimming him. Tim's fascination with Rory's foreskin was always a turn-on for Rory, and this was no exception.

"Timmy, stop!" Rory managed to shout when the dual sensation became too much, but it was too late. He couldn't stop the rush and bucked into Tim's hand as ribbons of semen shot out of him. His breathing was still choppy as Tim moved higher and pulled him into his arms, cradling him from behind as he pulled Rory to lie on his side. Rory felt warm, cared for, and most of all safe, lying there in Tim's protective embrace until the twitching stopped and coherent thought was possible again.

"You didn't stop when I warned you."

Tim chuckled behind him, sending more shivers through his oversensitive body. "It was too amazing to see you lose it. I love it when I can get you to moan and plead, and hey, you even shouted."

Rory opened his eyes and looked over his shoulder at a very amused Tim. "I wanted you inside me when I came. I wanted you to come too."

Tim hugged him closer and kissed his hair. "I wanted to show you how unselfish love could be. And I do love you. No matter what happens."

Rory snorted. "Yeah, right. We're men, Tim. We fuck. And that means we want to get off."

"I'm sorry you feel that way," Tim replied without letting go of Rory. The words sounded dismissive, but Rory was still held tightly. "But I love you, and I'm sorry you've never felt that before, but that means I want you to come first. Pun entirely intended."

Rory smiled, just a little, and then Tim put his hand on his cheek and kissed him. From that moment on, Rory believed him. They continued to cuddle and kiss, slowly shifting their positions until Tim was lying mostly on top of Rory. Rory could feel Tim's erection dig into his hip, and he spread his legs.

Tim never lost eye contact with Rory when he eventually dug into the bag he'd dropped on the night stand and unearthed a condom and lube. Rory was relaxed by now, and little preparation was needed before Tim could slide into him. They didn't talk, but Rory couldn't stop looking at Tim, as if he needed to commit these moments to memory. He had no idea how long it would be until they'd be allowed to do this again. As Tim continued his slow, deliberate movements, Rory closed his eyes and tried to just let the sensation take him and hoped it would banish the thoughts of losing Tim.

"Don't cry. Rory, please, don't cry," Tim said softly. "I'll wait for you. However long it takes."

"I'm sorry," Rory said. He wiped his hand over his face. He hadn't even realized he was crying until Tim told him. "I'm sorry I can't seem to stay out of trouble."

Tim shushed him. "I would have done the same if I'd known where he was."

Rory pulled Tim closer and kissed him again, hoping they'd stop talking about real life long enough to continue their lovemaking. And then he knew what he wanted. "Timmy?"

Tim didn't answer, but he stopped kissing and looked at Rory with the slight smile that always hit Rory right in the heart.

"Take the condom off, Tim. I want nothing between us." As soon as the words left his mouth, Rory wanted to kick himself. They'd never talked about ditching the condoms, and he knew he was in no position to ask, given his history, but to his surprise, Tim put his hand between them and did what Rory asked. He lubed up again, and when Rory felt Tim push inside him, he was overcome with emotion. He pulled Tim closer to give him a searing kiss, just to hide the tears that were streaming down his face again. They were face to face, slowly moving together, perfectly in sync, and now there was nothing separating them. Rory never wanted this moment to end.

When Tim moved his hand to envelop Rory's erection, Rory knew Tim wouldn't last much longer.

"Can you come with me this time?"

Rory nodded, wanting nothing less, but Tim didn't speed up their movements. He continued slowly rocking back and forth, his hand on Rory's cock keeping to the same languid pace, until he used his thumb to pull back the foreskin from the head of Rory's cock. A few well-aimed rubs across the underside of the head and Rory came with a quiet moan against Tim's mouth. Just moments later, Tim stilled on top of him, and Rory felt the heat spread throughout his groin.

They continued to lie together for a long time until they were both dozing off. Tim startled and pulled away.

"Don't leave."

"Just going to get us cleaned up a bit. You'll appreciate it in the morning."

Rory nodded reluctantly as he watched Tim disappear into the bathroom. Tim returned with a warm washcloth, and Rory let Tim clean him up before crawling back into bed with him.

Although Rory wanted to stay awake, he found he couldn't. Tomorrow would always come too soon.

TIM knew he hadn't slept long when he woke up from feeling Rory move behind him. Ever since he'd had the feeling Rory might be taking to the road as soon as his parole was over, any movement coming from his lover would rouse him.

"You're awake, aren't you?" Rory whispered.

"Yeah," Tim answered lazily. He didn't open his eyes, though. He was too comfortable for that. Rory was snuggled up behind him, arm wrapped possessively around Tim's chest, and he could feel the soft tickle of Rory's beard against his neck and his soft breath behind his ear. It was his favorite way of waking up and something that didn't happen often enough in Tim's opinion.

"Been awake long?"

"A while," Tim replied, reaching back to pull Rory even closer.

"We should get up," Rory said, but Tim could tell there wasn't much conviction in his voice. He wondered if he could entice Rory for a little more than a cuddle. Not that he didn't like the cuddles. They were probably the biggest perk of sleeping together. Next to waking his lover up for sex, of course.

As Tim wiggled his ass a little, he could feel Rory move closer and felt the evidence of his man's morning wood. Suddenly he had the uncontrollable urge to feel Rory inside him. Tim realized it was the first time. From the early beginnings of their relationship, it had always been Rory at the receiving end, and Tim had never questioned that. There wasn't a single doubt in his mind that they fit perfectly that way, and Rory clearly enjoyed it, so there was no reason for them to turn the tables. They'd gotten to sleeping in a spooning position, though, usually with Rory behind Tim. There was no clear reason other than that Rory was taller than Tim. They somehow fit more snugly that way, and Tim loved the warmth against his back.

"Wanna fuck me?" Tim whispered, momentarily hoping Rory wouldn't hear him and then wishing he had.

"What?" Rory asked as if he'd just now opened his eyes.

Tim looked over his shoulder at his lover's adorable bed hair and smiled. "I figured I could just reach for the lube and we'd already be in position."

"I don't fuck you. You fuck me," Rory stated as if it was the most normal thing in the world. And maybe it was.

"I thought maybe we could try it the other way around."

Rory threw Tim a questioning look.

"I know we've never done it that way, but why not?" By now Tim was almost on his back, and he could see Rory contemplate his choices.

"I just never thought…. You're not the bottom type."

Tim chuckled. "And you are?"

"Well," Rory started but didn't finish. He was smiling, though, more inwardly than for Tim's benefit.

Tim caressed Rory's beard with his hand and let his thumb brush over Rory's lips. "I love you, all of you." Tim thought Rory was blushing, but it was a little hard to tell in the pale morning light and with so much of Rory's face covered in facial hair. "Even if that means you won't fuck me."

"I'll fuck you," Rory said casually, leaning against Tim and kissing him deeply while grinding against him for good measure.

They broke the kiss so Tim could raise his arm and wrap it around Rory's shoulders. This way he could pull his man on top of him and continue kissing. It became clear soon enough, though, that Rory's statement wasn't a promise. He didn't make a move toward deepening their interaction, not even when Tim spread his legs to let Rory slide between them. Tim wasn't totally disappointed, though. Feeling Rory lie on top of him, their cocks sliding together and Rory's hands all over him, was making the heat rise a lot more quickly than he'd intended, and within no time they were rutting up against each other and fighting for breath.

Rory was relentless, his fingers entwined in Tim's hair to facilitate their passionate exchange, and Tim gave in to it gladly. Rory might not be fucking him, but he was definitely in charge, and Tim couldn't have been happier about the change. He was hovering on the brink of orgasm but hoped he would last a little longer. While he'd been the passive one until now, simply reciprocating when Rory made a move, Tim decided to fight Rory a bit more, not to make him stop— because, Lord knows, this was an amazing bit of early morning sex— but to take his mind off just how mind-blowing it was.

As Tim pushed himself away from the bed in an attempt to flip them both over, Rory looked at him. For a moment, Tim thought he'd broken the spell, but then a smile appeared on Rory's face, and it made Tim's heart flutter.

"What? I thought you liked what we were doing?" Rory asked, pushing Tim back down.

"I do," Tim admitted with glee. "It's pretty amazing. I was just wondering if you'd go back to being the passive one if I resisted, or whether it would make you even more determined to get me off at any cost."

"Not at any cost," Rory said with a teasing expression on his face. "Get you off I will. But never at any cost."

"I'm touched," Tim joked.

Rory hesitated for a moment, and Tim waited anxiously. Then Rory grabbed both of Tim's wrists and pulled them over his head. He held them there as he dove down to kiss Tim until Tim felt he couldn't breathe anymore.

"Fucking hell," Tim panted.

"Not done with you yet," Rory replied, equally out of breath.

"God, I hope not," Tim murmured. He knew he was stronger than Rory, who was less muscled but could still hold his own. Tim didn't want to use his weight to his own advantage, though. He wanted to see what Rory had in mind for him, so he didn't fight as Rory kept Tim's arms secure with one hand and reached for their cocks with the other. Tim couldn't stop looking at his lover, determination all over his face as he thrust his cock into his hand, creating some delicious friction— not to mention great visuals—for Tim.

Tim slowly felt his control slipping, and as Rory also started fisting both their cocks and steady leaking became short, strong bursts, Tim felt the hot semen trickle all over him, and they lost it together. Rory collapsed on top of him, and Tim finally flipped both of them over so he could snuggle into Rory's embrace. After they regained their breath, they started kissing again, this time much more tenderly.

"You make me happy," Rory suddenly whispered, as if saying it out loud would break a spell.

Tim looked up, his head still resting on Rory's chest, and Rory nodded to acknowledge that what Tim had heard was real.

"You make me happy too," Tim reciprocated.

They didn't fall asleep again but simply lay there, in silence. Tim could feel Rory's heartbeat, and it soothed him. "Does this mean you're staying even after you no longer have to?"

"If you'll have me," Rory said quietly.

"Of course I'll have you. I'd marry you in the blink of an eye if they'd let us." When Rory didn't reply immediately, Tim thought he'd fucked up again by asking Rory for a commitment, but then Rory lifted his hand and caressed Tim's hair, and Tim closed his eyes so he could very simply enjoy their closeness.

Tim knew impending doom was looming over them, but he decided he wasn't going to let it ruin the last morning they might have in a long time.

—39—

ALTHOUGH Tim had tossed Rory the keys to the truck, Rory got in on the passenger side. Tim figured Rory was too nervous to drive them safely into town, and Tim hoped he wasn't just as bad.

Tim had driven to their ransacked house for clean clothes while Rory was in the shower, but he'd resisted bringing Rory's duffel bag with his belongings, stating those were the only clothes he'd found clean enough to wear. In truth, Tim wanted to feed his conviction that he'd be allowed to bring Rory home with him that night. He had to believe that. He couldn't contemplate seeing Rory brought back to jail, and he figured as long as he told himself it wouldn't happen, they'd be okay.

They arrived almost forty-five minutes early, and Tim parked the truck in front of the parole office.

"Can you park down there, please?" Rory asked, pointing at another spot in front of the clothing store.

Tim moved the truck. "Want to stay here for now? Wait it out in the car?"

Rory nodded, then got out anyway. Tim followed. "I needed the fresh air," Rory explained.

"It's okay," Tim said, putting his hand on Rory's shoulder but quickly withdrawing it when he saw an older couple coming their way on the sidewalk. "Let's walk."

Rory shook his head, waiting for the couple to pass, and then sat down on a bench in front of the diner. Tim sat down next to him.

After a long pause, Tim couldn't keep quiet anymore. "I'd be lying if I said I wasn't nervous too, Rory, but we have to face up to the music."

"That would be me facing up to the music, Tim."

"Yes, but I'm right here with you. You and I are together, which means I share in this too. Through thick and thin, sickness and health, that sort of thing."

"We're not married."

Tim swallowed away the emotions that came after hearing Rory's cold statement. "No, we're not, but we might as well be. Rory, we live together. We share a life. The law might not see me as your spouse, but I do."

To Tim's considerable surprise, Rory inconspicuously took his hand and held it. Right there in full view of everyone in town who cared to look. Tim watched their clutched hands for a long time. "Do you still hear those voices?"

"Sometimes," Rory replied.

"Are they still saying those nasty things?"

"Sometimes."

"Do they say nice things too?"

"No."

Tim squeezed Rory's hand, and Rory looked at him. "Sometimes I can just tell them to fuck off."

"Did they tell you to get the gun and shoot Delco?"

Rory closed his eyes, and when he opened them again, he shook his head. "That's not how it works."

"So tell me how it works, then."

"Why?"

"Because maybe we can use this in your defense."

Rory snorted. "So they'll throw me into the psych ward instead of jail? I'll take jail, thank you."

"I don't want to think of you in jail."

Rory gave him a stare as if he felt sorry for him and then returned his gaze to a spot somewhere in the middle of the road. "The voices don't tell me to go kill Delco. They tell me I'm useless and I can't even take care of my own home and that you don't deserve me because I attract trouble like a magnet."

"You know none of that is true," Tim said softly, trying to sound unemotional as it sank in what Rory had to deal with on a day to day basis.

"I know," Rory replied, surprisingly upbeat. "They're not as bad as when I quit drinking. I couldn't tell them to stop then. I thought I was back in Iraq. I thought you were trying to kill me."

"So that's why you hit me."

Rory sighed. "I'm sorry about that. I didn't know what was real and what wasn't. Now if I hear the voices, I know they're not real and I can tell them to take a hike. I hope it stays that way. I can deal with them when they're like this. Can't promise it won't go bad again someday."

"Just tell me when they get worse, okay?"

Rory nodded. "The voices didn't make me go to Delco, Tim."

"I know."

Rory got up from the seat, and Tim reluctantly let go of his hand. "We better go inside. Better to be early than late, and I want this over with."

Tim nodded and got up with Rory, walking alongside him. They entered the parole office and were told to wait. Through the half-shuttered windows, they could see Kelly inside the parole officer's office. The man was sitting behind a desk and kept shaking his head at anything Kelly was, quite passionately, telling him. From time to time he'd reply to something Kelly was saying, and they could see Kelly's disheartened look. Tim started feeling his stomach tie up in knots.

When the outside door opened, they both looked up.

"Cooper Nelson, what are you doing here?" Tim asked, getting up from his seat to shake the ranch hand's hand.

"Johnny was saying something about Delco ransacking your cabin and Rory stealing Gable's gun to go after him and, well, I thought I could help."

"You're not a lawyer anymore, Coop," Tim said, feeling grateful nevertheless that they seemed to have some friends over at the ranch.

"I know, and I can't represent you in an official capacity, but I can give you advice, if you want it. For free, of course."

Tim looked at Rory and Rory nodded.

"So what happened?"

Rory and Tim gave Coop Nelson the short version, and the weather-beaten man nodded thoughtfully. "We'll see how it goes," was all he supplied.

After another short wait, the inside office door opened and Rory's parole officer looked at them. "Mr. McCown, please enter."

Tim and Cooper followed Rory inside.

"And who are these people?"

Rory fidgeted, and Tim wished he could just touch him to show him he supported him.

"This is Tim Conroy, my partner. You met him the first time I came to see you. And this is Cooper Nelson, my law… here for legal advice."

The parole officer threw Coop a disdainful look. "You are disbarred, Mr. Nelson. You cannot legally represent Mr. McCown."

"I know," Coop replied with more confidence than Tim had ever seen in him. "But that doesn't mean I don't remember the law, so I'm simply here to offer advice. They know I will not charge them for anything, but I want to make sure Mr. McCown's rights are not violated. He has been an upstanding citizen for the last three hundred and sixty days, has barely missed a day of work, and has kept his nose clean. His record shows only non-violent crimes. He was protecting what was his from a man who has been taunting him without retribution for the entire time he has worked at the ranch. Now that man invaded his home and destroyed everything Mr. McCown has worked for this last year. He knows Mr. Delco better than most of us and knows he is capable of violence not evident from Mr. Delco's criminal record, so he knew it would be dangerous to go to him without means to defend himself. It is our right to bear arms—"

"Not if you are a convicted felon," the parole officer cut in. "And Mr. McCown was convicted of armed robbery. That constitutes a violent crime."

"We both know he drove the getaway car. He never carried a weapon. That's why he got a lighter sentence than his cohorts."

"You're wasting my time, Mr. Nelson. You should be giving this speech to the judge."

Cooper Nelson chuckled. "You and I both know I won't be allowed to do that. And we also know that since you're Rory's parole officer, the judge will follow your recommendations. If you tell the judge that Rory is no good and a worthless human being, he'll throw Rory in the slammer for another year."

Rory almost gasped, and Tim put his hand on Rory's back to steady him. Even Kelly looked at Rory.

Coop's eyes moved from Rory back to the man behind the desk. "But if you tell the judge that Rory's been an exemplary parolee and he simply did what you and I would do in the same situation; if you explain to him that his only crime was to do this five days before the end of his parole and not five days after it, when he wouldn't be your responsibility anymore; then I'm sure the judge will follow your recommendations." Coop leaned over the desk. "Emmett, the jail is crowded enough as it is, and you don't need to add to that. Keep the space for John Delco, not Rory McCown."

Emmett looked at Kelly, then at Rory, and then back at Cooper. They stared each other down for a long time, and then a smile broke on Emmett's face. "You know, Coop, I'm glad you never got down to taking that bar exam again, because you were always the best lawyer this town ever had, and I want to win some of my cases at least." He then turned to Kelly. "Officer Freed, I'd like to go over this case with you alone, please."

Rory looked at Tim, and Tim could tell he was confused.

"Mr. McCown? You can go home, but I'd like you to remain available at a moment's notice. After the judge makes his decision, you may well be called in to present yourself."

Once outside, Cooper Nelson's confidence from inside the parole office waned. He looked like the ranch hand they both knew. Tim figured he must have been a handsome man at some point, but his clothes were ragged, and his hair and stubbled jaw were unkempt.

"Good luck with the judge's decision," Cooper said, extending his hand to Rory. "You deserve a break, and I think Emmett knows that too."

"Thanks for your offer of help," Rory said, shaking Cooper's hand firmly. They walked back to the truck, and just before they got inside, Tim pulled Rory into his arms.

"They can see us, Timmy."

"I don't care," Tim said, not letting go of his lover.

"You think they're going to send me back to jail," Rory said flatly, and Tim felt his heart sink.

"No," Tim replied with more confidence than he felt. "I think they'll see you had no other choice."

Rory smiled. "You're such an optimist."

"Let's go back to the motel," Tim suggested.

"Let's go home. We have a house to clean up."

"Are you sure?" Rory nodded, so Tim took out his cell phone. "Kelly? We're going to the house to clean up the place, so if you need us, we'll be there until after dinner. Okay, thanks." He pocketed his phone and turned to Rory. "Let's go."

—40—

RORY cringed when he walked into the cabin. It was like his guts were ripped open a second time. Some of the debris was already cleaned up. The kitchen was empty, and their chairs and table were gone. The ripped-up sofa was still in the living room, but Rory could tell that some of the shreds of fabric had been picked up from the floor. In the bedroom, the mangled mattress was gone and Tim's old bed stood against the wall, disassembled.

"They were here. I suspect Izzie and Hugh cleaned up most of it."

Rory looked at Tim and took his hand. "What are we going to do?"

"Go and buy a new mattress, a table, and chairs so we can sit down to eat."

"Sheets," Rory added with a sigh. "You poured all your money into the water pump and the heater."

Tim shrugged. "Not much else I need it for anyway. We'll be okay, Rory."

"Hey, guys," Izzie greeted them. They turned around to face her. "Hope you don't mind that I tidied up a bit."

"Hey Izz," Tim replied, letting go of Rory to hug his friend. "We came to survey the damage."

"Luckily there wasn't much of your stuff here yet," she replied with a sigh.

"That's because we don't have a lot of stuff. I just moved my room here, and what Rory has fits in a duffle bag. Guess we both travel light."

"Maybe it's time you change that? Jack's coming back to the ranch to finally make things legal with Lisa, and Hugh said we should combine the shopping we'll do for their wedding gift with some stuff for this house."

Tim looked flabbergasted. "Why would he do that?"

Izzie smiled. "Because you two are practically married too, I suppose. And what goes for Jack goes for you, too."

"Did Hugh say that?"

"Not in so many words," Izzie said with a snort. "But I know my man. That's what he meant. And he meant it, Tim. He may not tell you, but you're his baby brother and he just wants to see you happy. He gets that 'happy' means 'with Rory' for you."

"Just tell him to hold off on the buying for a while," Rory interjected.

"Why?" Tim asked.

"Because I don't know where I'll be in the foreseeable future."

"I'll testify on your behalf if need be, Rory," Izzie said. "I know Delco up close and personal, remember. I know what a bastard he can be."

"That's okay, Izz. It's in the hands of the judge now. I violated my parole, and if I need my parole officer to put in a good word for me, then I'm screwed."

"Not necessarily."

Three pairs of eyes turned to the door to see a lanky young man standing there in an off-the-rack suit with a briefcase in his hand.

"I presume this is the residence of Rory McCown?"

"Yes, it is," Rory said with some apprehension. "And you are?"

He extended his hand and looked as nervous as Rory felt. "Sean Goddard, public defender."

"Oh," Rory replied while he shook the offered hand.

"Cooper Nelson called me. He's a friend of my father's and a bit of a legend in our house. He filled me in on your case, and I sort of winged my way into the prosecutor's office by saying you'd asked me to represent you. I admit I don't have a lot of experience, but a guy's gotta start somewhere, and I have Mr. Nelson to help me out. He can't legally represent you since he's disbarred, but—"

"We know," Tim stopped him.

"Mr. McCown needs legal representation. Otherwise he's flying blind, and at the mercy of our local parole officer, who we both know isn't a big fan of rehabilitation, so—"

"Will you cut to the chase, please?" Rory said nervously.

"Okay," Sean said. "I think you should plead guilty to trespassing and possession of a rifle, which, if my sources are correct, is what you did."

"Possibly," Rory replied. He knew these young lawyer types. He'd been represented by enough of them, since he never had the money for anything better.

"County jail is chock-a-block full. The prosecutor thinks you did a pretty good job staying on the straight and narrow until now, and he believes that with everything Mr. Delco did, you were more than a little provoked. So if you plead guilty and agree to testify against Mr. Delco at his trial, he thinks he can get you off with community service."

"But the parole violation would be on my record?" Rory asked.

"Technically, yes. But on the other hand, if the judge agrees, you will be sentenced for it, and you can only be sentenced for the same crime once."

"And then it will all be over?"

Sean nodded at Rory.

"Do it," Rory replied determinedly.

"Rory?"

"I know, Tim, but another thing on my record won't matter. It's an arm long anyway. And then it'll be behind us."

Tim looked unconvinced, and Rory turned and took him in his arms. "You know I love you. I just want it all to be over."

Tim nodded and buried his face against Rory's neck. Rory saw Izzie standing to the side, looking concerned. He extended his hand to her. "It'll be okay, Izz."

SEAN GODDARD left, and since neither Tim nor Rory felt like braving the guys at the crew house, Tim picked up food from there and brought it back to the cabin. They ate sitting on the sofa, which Rory had covered with a blanket to hide the ripped-up fabric. Although it wasn't all that cold, Rory had also lit the fireplace, and they were sitting together staring at the flames when they heard two cars stop outside the cabin.

Rory's heart raced when Tim opened the door and they could see Sean Goddard and Kelly Freed standing outside. Rory thought Kelly looked really concerned and Sean looked guilty.

"I'm afraid I need to take you in, Rory," Kelly said from the porch, his voice carefully controlled.

Rory bit his lips and looked at Sean. "Didn't go like you planned, did it?"

"The judge didn't go with the prosecutor. I'm sorry. Your parole officer told him you skipped out on your last parole, and the judge figured you a flight risk."

Rory turned to Kelly. "How long?"

"Just the remainder of your original sentence. I believe that's four days. If I take you in tonight, then this is your first day. Tim can come and pick you up on Saturday."

Rory saw Tim's eyes traveling to Kelly's waist. "You're not even wearing your gun belt."

Kelly smiled. "I was sure Rory would come with me without too much fuss." He turned to Rory. "Right?"

Rory nodded. For some reason, the trust Kelly had put in him because of that little thing felt really good. "You're not even going to cuff me?"

"Nope."

"Can I pick up some underwear?"

"Sure you can," Kelly answered. "You don't have a back exit, do you?"

Rory laughed and then saw Tim's concerned face. "I'll be out on Saturday. It's barely worth it to process me, so it's not that long, Timmy."

"I know," Tim said, still looking very concerned. Rory kissed him quickly and then walked to their bedroom to get the things he'd need. He went with Kelly quietly and only looked at Tim briefly when the car took off.

—41—

TIM was almost more nervous about picking Rory up than he'd been four years earlier. Then he'd had to drive out to the state prison; now it was just the county jail. And it had been four days and not three years since he'd seen his lover. He didn't understand why he was more nervous, because this time he knew Rory would be thrilled to see him. He knew Rory loved him. He knew he'd be taking Rory home with him and they'd share a bed tonight. Yet he was almost shaking in his boots, and the county jail officials didn't seem in much of a hurry to let Rory out.

Almost an hour after Tim had parked his truck across the road from the jail, Rory emerged, looking a little dazed. Tim raised his hand and smiled, and Rory smiled back. He looked almost the same as a year ago, in his red-and-black coat and battered jeans, wearing the garage cap that seemed to be welded to his head.

Tim pushed away from the truck and took a step closer to the road, watching as Rory waited to cross until the traffic slowed. Once he was within an arm's reach, Tim forgot they were out in the open and pulled Rory into his arms. "Fuck, it's good to see you."

Rory nodded and pulled away as a truck honked its horn in a long, drawn-out sound. He raised his hand at the driver in a half-hearted apology. "Just take me home, okay?"

Tim nodded and got in the truck. As Rory got in beside him, he was greeted by such loud barking, he almost jumped out of the truck again.

"What's this?" Rory asked.

"Down, Quiche," Tim said in a commanding voice. The dog barked once more and then whimpered as she sat down on the bench and Tim pulled her to him. "Sit down, Rory. She'll be okay."

"You got a dog?" Rory asked, still eyeing the strange-looking half-sized mutt suspiciously.

"She's a rescue dog from the pound. I figured we could use one to guard the house."

"You called her Keesh?"

"That was the name she came with. I tried calling her other things, but she responds to that. And she's good. She sleeps in the living room on a rug, and she doesn't chew things up or pee in the house. When we get home, you should feed her so she gets that you're part of the family."

Rory nodded, one eyebrow still raised. Tim hoped he'd warm up to her, because he couldn't exactly bring her back.

"So what did I miss?"

Tim ignored the question. "Was it okay in there?"

Rory shrugged. "Not too bad. I mopped floors in the offices and was kept from the general population. I think Kelly asked for better treatment or something. All things considered, they were nice to me."

Tim nodded, feeling bad for Rory all the same.

"I did sort of miss the perks of jail, though."

"What?" Tim asked, looking at Rory.

"Watch the road, driver," Rory said with a smirk, taking over petting Quiche so Tim could use his hands to drive. "You know, gratuitous sex. Being groped in the shower. Having to suck off a fellow inmate after lights-out. That sort of thing."

Tim looked at his boyfriend for a brief moment and then back at the road, since the Saturday traffic wasn't exactly light. "It's not funny, Rory."

"Nothing happened, Tim. Lighten up, please? I don't want to rehash everything right now. I've done my time, my parole is up. I'm a free man again."

Tim nodded. The idea was sinking in. Rory was free indeed. He hoped it also meant that Rory was free to stay with him, but they'd had that conversation. Obviously Rory had every intention of staying.

"Of course, I'll have to go to court when Delco's trial comes up, but I've been humiliated before on the stand, so one more time won't make a difference."

Just when Tim wanted to look at Rory again, Rory took his hand. "Take me home, okay? How's everything at the ranch?"

"I have a lot of news, actually."

"You do?"

Tim nodded. "We're invited to Grant and Hunter's tonight for dinner."

"Why?"

"You'll see."

"Oh, come on, Timmy, don't keep me in suspense. Their dinner invitations are rarely just social."

"It's probably to help plan Jack's wedding. I told you he was going to marry Lisa, right? And he wants to do it at the Blue River, since they're both really attached to the ranch. Hunter's agreed to host the celebrations if they don't make too much of a media circus out of it."

"Why would there be…. Oh, because of Jack's music career? But that's in Nashville."

Tim nodded. "But since he won that Country Music Award and couldn't pick it up because he was in rehab, the paparazzi feel everything he does is news. Lisa just wants a quiet family wedding. That's why they're doing it as far from Nashville as they can get and still have family with them."

"Should be interesting," Rory said with a smirk.

"So can I tell Hunter to expect us?"

"Just as long as I can have a good long bath before we go. Prison showers still give me the creeps."

Tim drove them home, and they barely made it through the front door without undressing each other. Tim was glad they didn't have to climb any stairs to get to the bathroom and that he'd given the claw-foot bathtub a good scrub before bringing Rory home. He ordered Quiche to her rug and pushed Rory into the bathroom before closing the door. Tim could feel the urgency in Rory's need for him, and they fucked hurriedly and without ceremony while they waited for the bathtub to fill. It was all over in a matter of minutes, but Tim knew they both needed it.

Afterward, they were lying in the bath, water up to the rim, Tim behind Rory and Rory's legs dangling over the edge. It was nice and warm in the bathroom since Tim had turned the heater up before leaving to retrieve Rory, and they were both wonderfully relaxed.

"So is this the start of the rest of our lives?" Tim asked with some apprehension while he wiped the hair off Rory's forehead.

"Well, we certainly made it a start to remember. So when are Hunter and Grant expecting us?"

"In about an hour."

"Can you get it up again before that?" Rory asked cheekily.

"I can if you can," Tim replied as he started to feel more relaxed.

THEY arrived at the newest homestead half an hour late, and to their surprise, it was Izzie who opened the door. "Hi guys! We're in the kitchen. You're just in time for dinner." She leaned closer to Tim. "You're late! Stud."

Hugh was sitting at the counter with a glass of red wine, and Hunter and Grant were in the kitchen putting the last touches to dinner.

"Hi, guys. Everything okay?"

"We're fine," Tim replied. He looked at Rory, who seemed more at ease than he was.

"Sit," Hunter said. "Can I get you anything? We've opened a bottle of wine, but we can get you a soda or coffee, maybe?"

"I'll have a Coke," Tim replied. He looked at Rory.

"Yeah, me too."

Hunter took out the drinks and poured them into glasses. As he put Tim's glass in front of him, Tim nodded at Hunter and Hunter looked at Rory. "I'll just drop this on you, Rory. We want to clear the air."

"Clear the air?" Rory parroted.

Hunter looked at Tim, and Tim returned a pleading look, wishing Hunter would get on with it.

"The aftermath of the whole Delco business helped us resolve Matthew's custody. Apparently Delco had convinced Miranda that it would be a good idea to ask for more time with Matthew—and to get a judge's decision on it—because she'd get financial support from us that way. Now with Delco gone, she admitted she didn't really want to be a part of her son's life. At least, not to the point where she wants to sue us for custody. She's going to come see him from time to time, but the whole lawyer thing was blown out of proportion by Delco with the sole intent of getting you off the ranch."

"And it almost worked," Grant added. "We're sorry for that, Rory."

Rory nodded, and Tim could tell he didn't really know how to react to what they'd just told him.

"So does that mean it's okay for Rory to start working here again?"

"Yes," Hunter said with conviction. "Rory, we'd like you to come back here to work. As a wrangler, even."

"But I like working at Gable's," Rory replied, much to everyone's surprise.

"We can pay more than Gable can," Hunter said.

"I know," Rory said. "But I really like Gable's ranch, so if he'll have me, I think I'd like to stay there. To work. I'm living at the cabin; that won't change. And I'll help out when you need me. Your men are always helping Gable out, so I don't think they'll mind if I come over here when you need an extra hand from time to time."

Hunter smiled compassionately. "Whatever you like, Rory. We'll discuss it with Gable. He might not need you full-time, and then we can share you."

"Guess it's nice to be in demand," Rory said, looking at Tim.

"Let's eat," Grant said, inviting them to the end of the counter where the table was set.

AFTER dinner, Tim went to the bathroom, and when he came back, he saw Rory standing by himself. "What are you—" Tim stopped midsentence as he saw exactly what Rory was looking at. It was a balmy evening, and the French doors at the end of the living room were wide open. Outside on the porch, Grant and Hunter were swaying together to the soft jazzy vibe drifting out from the house.

"I've never seen two men dance," Rory admitted.

"Not even in jail?"

Rory shook his head. "They wouldn't dare. You could hear the sex noises at night, or during the day in the showers, but no man dared to dance with another. That would imply feelings. And even in jail, you only fucked another man because there were no women around."

Tim wrapped his arms around his lover and kissed his neck. "So do you want to dance?"

Rory shrugged. "I wouldn't know how."

"I can show you," Tim whispered.

Rory turned around. "I don't know if I'm that gutsy."

"Nobody's watching. Izzie and Hugh are making out like teenagers in the kitchen, and our bosses are way too into each other to care."

Rory turned around, and Tim wrapped one arm around Rory's shoulders. With his other hand, he grabbed Rory's and kissed it. Rory hesitantly put his other hand on the small of Tim's back, and Tim smiled at him.

"I still don't know what to do," Rory admitted.

Tim could tell he was uncomfortable and hoped he could persuade him to relax. "Just let the music sway you."

Little by little Tim felt Rory ease into him. Rory's cheek was resting against the side of Tim's temple, and it felt curiously intimate. What Tim hadn't told his boyfriend was that he didn't have any experience dancing with another man either. It wasn't the sort of thing they did at the Barrel Run. Even The Handle Bar, the only place Tim knew of where men could be open about their sexuality, was the place where you went to get drunk or laid, not to dance. Focusing back on Rory, Tim moved his hand to the back of Rory's head and gently kissed him. That seemed to help him relax even more, and they slowly started moving. It didn't have a lot of rhythm, but Tim didn't care. All that mattered was that they were moving together and tenderly kissing, and Rory seemed to be able to let go of some of his apprehension. When Tim opened his eyes, he could see Izzie looking at them with stars in her eyes. She was nudging Hugh to look at the two of them, and Tim turned a little so Rory had his back to the other couple. The last thing he thought Rory needed was to realize they'd garnered some attention.

The song ended, and Rory looked at him.

"That wasn't so bad, now was it?"

Rory shook his head, smiling shyly. "Was nice, actually."

Just as Rory was pulling away, another song started. This song was a bit faster, less mellow, and Tim pulled Rory closer, taking the lead. Rory didn't follow easily, and they stepped on each other's toes. Tim was glad to see Rory smile.

"This is going to take some more practice," Rory admitted.

Tim pulled Rory closer but didn't start dancing again. "I'll practice with you anytime you like," he whispered, leaning his forehead against Rory's.

Their little intimate moment was interrupted by the hand Tim felt on his shoulder. He looked up, and Rory stepped back.

"Didn't mean to break you two apart, but we're leaving," Hugh told his brother.

Tim saw Izzie standing on tiptoes to whisper something in Rory's ear, and Rory blushed crimson. He didn't say anything to Izzie, so Tim was left guessing about what she'd said.

By the time they'd said their goodbyes to Hugh, Grant and Hunter had come back inside and Tim had missed the opportunity to satisfy his curiosity. His only chance was to get them out of there and on their way home as soon as possible.

Luckily, Rory felt the same. He looked at Tim and then at Hunter. "We better leave too. Can we help you clean up first?"

Hunter shook his head. "Don't worry about it. Not that much to clean up. We'll see you on Monday. Enjoy the rest of the weekend."

Tim and Rory walked home in silence. The cabin was just on the other side of the main house, and it usually took them about ten minutes. Although they both knew the path, there was no moon out and it was pitch dark, so they were navigating by the light of Tim's flashlight.

As soon as they were out of earshot of both houses, Tim couldn't contain himself anymore.

"What did Izzie say to make you blush so much?"

"Nothing," Rory said.

"Nothing?"

Rory sighed. "She told me to take my man home and spoil him."

"And that made you blush?"

"Tim," Rory sighed. "You may be used to Izzie saying things like that, but it feels strange, like she gets off on what we do in the bedroom or something."

Tim took Rory's hand. "It's just her way of supporting us, baby." Rory winced, and Tim just made it out thanks to the reflected light of the flashlight. He couldn't take back the endearment Rory disliked so much, though. "If you were a woman, she'd tell you the same."

"But I'm not a woman."

"That's the point." Tim stopped just before they entered their cabin. "To her, it doesn't make a difference whether I love a man or a woman as long as it makes me happy, and she knows you make me happy. She should know. She's seen me miserable."

"That's hard to imagine. You *always* smile."

Tim opened the door and let them in. They both crouched down to pet Quiche, who'd come quietly to greet them. "We grew up together, and she'd figured me out by the time we were about fourteen. Even before I'd figured it out myself. She didn't ask; she just told me. Don't know how she even knew it was possible for two men to love each other. Lord knows, I didn't have a clue. I just figured that I'd grow out of it and would meet a girl I'd like enough to want to kiss. I didn't know any other gay men. I didn't even know the word. How naive was that?"

"How did she know? About you, I mean."

Tim shrugged as he hung up his coat. "Took me years to get up the nerve to ask her. She said she'd seen the way I looked at her brother."

"Hunter?"

"Yeah. He was a popular guy. Everyone liked him. The girls were dropping at his feet and he had a ranch. He didn't go to school like the rest of us."

"So you could have ended up with Hunter," Rory said more than asked. Tim thought he looked amused by it.

"He wasn't gay then."

"Oh, come on. He may have been in the closet, but he was gay, even then. You just have to look at him with Grant and you know there's no way this guy was straight."

Tim smiled. "He conceived Matty the old-fashioned way. Before Grant came along, there was no indication he even swung that way." Tim could tell Rory didn't believe him. "Even Izzie took her time figuring him out. She knew I had my eye on him when I was younger and made it very clear that he was off-limits."

Rory chuckled. "Would have been funny, though. Izzie and Hugh, Lisa and Jack, and you and Hunter. All the Conroy boys in love with a Krause."

"Yeah, I suppose there's something about that family," Tim replied, looking at Rory sideways. "Then I wouldn't have met you. What a loss that would have been. Guess you need to thank Gable for setting me straight, so to speak."

Tim saw Rory retreat, and he put his arm around his lanky lover. "I'm not joking, Rory." He kissed his man's temple and inhaled Rory's sweet scent, which never ceased to turn him on. "Now will you do what Izzie told you to do? It's been a long week. I'm looking forward to spending some quality time with the man I love."

—42—

THEY had one more thing to do around the Blue River Ranch before everything returned to normal and they could bunk down for the winter. Just before the first snowfall, Jack Conroy, the middle of the Conroy brothers and the one to make a name for himself in country music, was returning to the ranch to marry Lisa Krause, formerly Conroy as well, since she was Hugh's ex-wife and the mother of Hugh's son, Danny.

With the happy couple came a whole media circus. The agreement with Hunter was that the media would be allowed a little time with the couple in between the wedding itself and the party afterward, but that everything else was to remain private. Jack and Lisa happily agreed.

Since the Blue River was still a working ranch, Rory knew Tim had to finish his chores before running back to the cabin for a quick bath and to don his wedding suit. Rory was waiting for him in the back room of the main homestead, where they were supposed to gather before the ceremony. He was dying of nerves, because it would be the first time Tim saw Rory in a suit.

"Fuck, you look…."

Rory turned around to face Tim. "Old?"

Tim exhaled, and then the smile he was always wearing broke all over his face. "The word I was looking for was… beautiful."

Rory felt uncomfortable in the rented suit, although he knew it fit him perfectly.

"Not what I was aiming for," Rory said with a hint of a smile on his face.

"Well, you clean up mighty nice. Is that better?"

A little hesitantly, Rory nodded. They were standing close together, and Rory could feel body heat radiate off him. He rubbed his chin over Tim's like he'd done so many times because Tim liked the softness of his beard, but now the beard was gone. He waited for Tim's reaction, all of a sudden wondering if shaving off his beard was such a good idea. "The whisker burn is going to be ten times worse, you know," Rory said with a smile, hoping to break the tension.

"I don't care," Tim whispered, letting his lips ghost over Rory's cheekbone, then down to his jaw and the corner of his mouth. "I'm not waiting to kiss you until that beard grows back."

"Won't take long," Rory said softly, turning slightly so their lips touched.

"How about shaving for a while?" Tim suggested. "You know I liked your beard, but I have to say I like you all smooth too."

"Won't be smooth for long. By tonight I'll have stubble again."

"Just give it a try. If you don't like it, well, like you said, won't take long to grow again."

Tim was looking at him, and it was making him feel self-conscious. He knew Tim loved him, and seeing the total acceptance in Tim's eyes was reassuring, but he didn't allow himself to get too attached to that feeling. Rory still expected it to go away, even after all this time. Rory didn't always allow himself to see how much Tim loved him, but right now it was pouring out of Tim, and Rory couldn't help but soak it up.

"I haven't *not* had a beard for so long, I feel naked." Rory chuckled, but didn't move out of Tim's personal space.

"I'm going to have the most handsome man in the whole world with me today."

"You haven't looked at Hunter and Grant lately," Rory said. "And that guy on Gable's arm, although really not my type, isn't bad either, in case you haven't noticed. And then there's the straight ones. You have two brothers who could pose for the horse breeder digest. And then there's you. There will be a lot more handsome men than me out there today, trust me."

Tim looked at Rory for what felt like an eternity and then kissed him. Not like when he wanted sex and stuck his tongue down Rory's throat, but more chastely. The kiss was soft and lingered. There was no tongue, no biting, just Tim's soft breathing against Rory's skin while their lips were pushed together, and Rory felt Tim's warmth infuse into him. Or could it be his love? Although Tim told Rory he loved him all the time, now Rory felt it too, and there was a little voice inside his head singing it. It was a welcome change from the menacing voices he usually heard. And for once, it wasn't lust talking, or Tim would have had Rory out of his fancy clothes and bent over already.

"I don't care about the other men," Tim whispered against Rory's mouth. "I care about the one I'm holding right now, and I'm going to show everyone there today that we belong together."

"Tim."

"I know," Tim continued. "I know it makes you uncomfortable, but we'll wait until the reporters are gone and it's just family, and then I'm formally introducing you to Jack and Lisa as my boyfriend. I want you to be a part of my family, Rory. Because I want you around for a long time."

Rory felt his flight reaction kick in, but he couldn't run now. Tim was offering him so much of what he'd craved all his life, and he was offering it to him with just one condition: that Rory stick around. So he couldn't run. It wouldn't just be unfair to Tim; it would be unfair to himself as well. For the first time in his life, he was happy. For the first time, he didn't need to steal or lie for money. He had a roof over his head and people around who trusted him. Trusted him with their horses and their children and their hearts. He simply had to stay.

"Yes," Rory said with a croak in his voice.

"Yes?" Tim parroted. When Rory looked him in the eye, he saw those happy little sparkles that appeared whenever Tim was truly content about something.

Rory nodded.

"You want to be a part of my family?" Tim said as if he couldn't believe it.

"If they'll have me."

Tim chuckled. "They better. After the wife-swapping my brothers did, this is a small one. I'm just going to tell them I found someone I want to spend my life with. Hell, I just have to tell Jack. Everybody else knows already."

"They do?"

Rory could see the confusion on Tim's face and realized Tim didn't get that he was joking, so he winked at him, and Tim laughed. "I think you even grew on Hugh. Then again, Izzie is probably to blame for that one."

"Should I be jealous?"

"Of Izzie?" Tim asked, flabbergasted by Rory's question.

"Yeah. She's always in your corner. I remember even Delco had lots of nice things to say about her."

"She's known me since I was weaned off my mother, Rory. We're the same age. We went to school together. She's got leverage over me."

Rory smiled. "So if I need to know your secrets, all I have to do is ask Izzie?"

Tim pulled him into a tight hug. "You already know all my secrets."

Suddenly the door burst open, and Rory wanted to pull out of Tim's embrace, but Tim didn't let go.

"Damn, you're both fully dressed already," Izzie said behind Rory's back.

"Polite people knock before walking into a room where people are changing, Izzie," Tim replied, still holding Rory close. "Can't you see we're in the middle of something?" He sounded more amused than annoyed, which somehow relaxed Rory.

"I can see that," Izzie said with a big smirk. "Like I said: too bad I walked in too late."

"We're getting ready for Jack's wedding. It's not like we have time for a romp in the hay. So what was so urgent you needed to tell us this instant?"

"They're waiting for you," she deadpanned, turning away.

"You could have just knocked," Tim shouted, but she'd already closed the door behind her.

Tim quickly kissed Rory before letting go and helping him straighten his suit jacket.

"They're seriously going to leave us in charge of the kids?" Rory asked.

"Why not?" Tim said, smiling encouragingly. "I suppose it's the downside of us being the bachelor uncles. We get to keep the kids in check while Izzie and Christy make sure the caterer does his job. There'll be plenty of people there we can ask for help if they get out of line."

Rory noticed that Tim had included him in "the uncles," and he smiled. He wasn't good with crowds, but he supposed that as long as he could make himself useful, he would survive, and the kids were certainly going to keep them busy.

"So how do I look?" Tim asked, turning around so Rory could see all sides of him.

"Like the man I love," Rory whispered.

Tim didn't say anything, and that too made Rory happy, since Tim was rarely at a loss for words.

"I didn't mean to embarrass you," Rory said.

"You didn't," Tim replied. "I'm just glad we found each other."

"So am I."

Tim pretended to straighten Rory's lapels, although he'd done the same thing just moments earlier. "Seriously. I always liked you scruffy, but this." He grabbed Rory's shoulder and swung him around so he was facing the full length mirror standing to the side of the room.

Rory was happy that Tim was behind him, supporting him all the way. He tried to look at his reflection, but he barely recognized himself. The suit really did fit well, and it made him look like a lawyer, or a real estate salesman; someone who'd actually finished high school and gotten some higher education, not a man who'd lived either on the street or in prison all of his adult life. He didn't remember when he'd last had his hair this short, and to see his face so bare truly made him feel naked.

"Look at your eyes. I can actually see them. And those beautiful lips of yours." Tim caressed Rory's jaw and then pulled his head back so he could kiss him. "I'm going to have the hardest time not kissing you every time I see you today. I may embarrass everyone there."

"Don't," Rory said quietly.

Tim pulled him into a tight embrace. "Okay, I won't. But I'll really need to ravish you tonight, then."

Rory smiled. "I'll make it a deal if you don't drink too much."

"I'm not going to drink at all," Tim stated as if it was the most natural thing in the world.

"You can drink, just don't get plastered, because otherwise you won't be able to ravish me."

"I'm not going to drink a drop of alcohol tonight," Tim repeated.

"But you're supposed to drink at weddings! There will be champagne and wine and beer. You can't stand there with a glass of orange juice all night!"

Tim chuckled. "Where does it say that? That you *have* to drink at weddings? I don't need to. There will be flutes of champagne, but also flutes of ginger ale so we non-drinkers can *pretend* to get plastered."

"Tim, don't. Not on account of me."

"Give me one good reason?" Tim looked defiantly at Rory. "I haven't had a single beer since you came back from the hospital, and you know what? I don't miss it. I can't even imagine drinking anything alcoholic right now. Not when it's such a struggle for you to stay off it."

Rory felt his eyes fill with tears, and he turned away from the mirror.

"Rory, it's no sacrifice. I never saw the appeal of alcohol anyway. The only thing it did for me was make me a little less self-conscious when I went cruising, and since I don't need to shop around to get laid anymore...."

Rory smiled, but just for a moment. "I don't want you to give things up for me."

"I'm not. Besides, we're not giving up the sauce for you. We're doing it for Jack. He's on the wagon too, remember?"

Rory nodded, still not looking at Tim.

"So we've all agreed that the only drinks coming our way are going to be non-alcoholic. And the flutes we toast with are going to contain ginger ale."

"Who's we?"

"Lisa and Izzie and Bernie and me and Hugh and Gable and Flynn and Grant and Hunter. Oh, and Mom and Christie. It was unanimous. And besides, this way the kids can pretend to be drinking champagne too."

"Can't believe you would all...."

Tim smiled contently. Rory did feel better knowing it wasn't all about him. "Told you we're doing it for Jack, so to help him, will you drink ginger ale with us too?"

This time Rory smiled at Tim. "Yeah, I suppose I could do that."

"So let's go see what a big-ass Conroy wedding is supposed to look like," Tim said. "After all, we need to know what to do and certainly what *not* to do once it's our turn."

Rory stopped dead. "Our turn?"

Tim smiled and dropped to one knee. He took a stunned Rory's hand. "Rory McCown, will you marry me? Will you make a decent man out of me?"

Rory swallowed hard.

Tim chuckled. "Just turn me down if you want, Rory, but put me out of my misery. This floor is hard."

"We can't get married, Tim. They don't let us here. It won't be legal."

Tim got up but didn't let go of Rory's hand. "I don't care. I want to have a party like this to show everyone how important you are to me."

"A party like this?" Rory looked demonstratively at the wedding favors stacked high in the corner.

Tim rolled his eyes. "Okay, not exactly this elaborate. I want something like Hunter and Grant had. A family picnic or something. Everyone we care about will be there, and they'll sit around and joke and eat and just be merry. It will be our celebration. And I'd like you to change your name to Conroy. Or if you don't want to do that, I'll change mine to McCown. That way we'll have the same name like married people."

"I don't know, Tim."

Tim pulled Rory to his chest. "I know it's too much show for you. We'll figure something out." Tim let go of Rory, and Rory felt guilty for the ice-cold reception.

"I'll do it for you, Tim."

Tim smiled at Rory. "It's okay, Grumpy. I know you love me."

"No, I mean, I'll change my name. It's not really mine anyway. It's not like I have family like you have. Rory Conroy. Sounds good, actually. But I'm not dancing with you."

Tim pretended to be hurt, and Rory instantly felt guilty again. "Maybe not at this wedding, but at our wedding I want to dance with you," Tim said determinedly. "Although I wouldn't be surprised if Hunter and Grant danced."

Rory shook his head, but he had a hard time not smiling. "Are you going to dance with Gable?"

"I might," Tim joked, quickly kissing Rory. "If Flynn lets me."

Rory smiled broadly. He could see himself growing old with Tim, with or without a wedding. And it was the first time he'd ever dared to look into the future.

ZAHRA OWENS was born in Europe just before Woodstock and the moon landing and was given a much less pronounceable name by her non-English-speaking parents. Being an Aquarian meant she would never quite conform, and people learned to expect the unexpected.

She started writing fairy tales in first grade; the same year she came into contact with her first group of English-speaking friends, a group which would eventually grow to include people from all over the world. On the outside she was a typical only child, accustomed to being with adults most of the time. On the inside, she sought ways to channel her wild imagination.

During the daytime she earns a living as a computer analyst, but it's her former career as an intensive care nurse that tends to seep into her fiction. Maybe this has to do with her weak spot for flawed characters and imperfect bodies, or maybe it's just her sadistic streak coming through. You be the judge.

Visit her web site at http://www.zahraowens.com/ and blog at http://zahra-owens.livejournal.com/.

Don't miss Gable and Flynn's story in

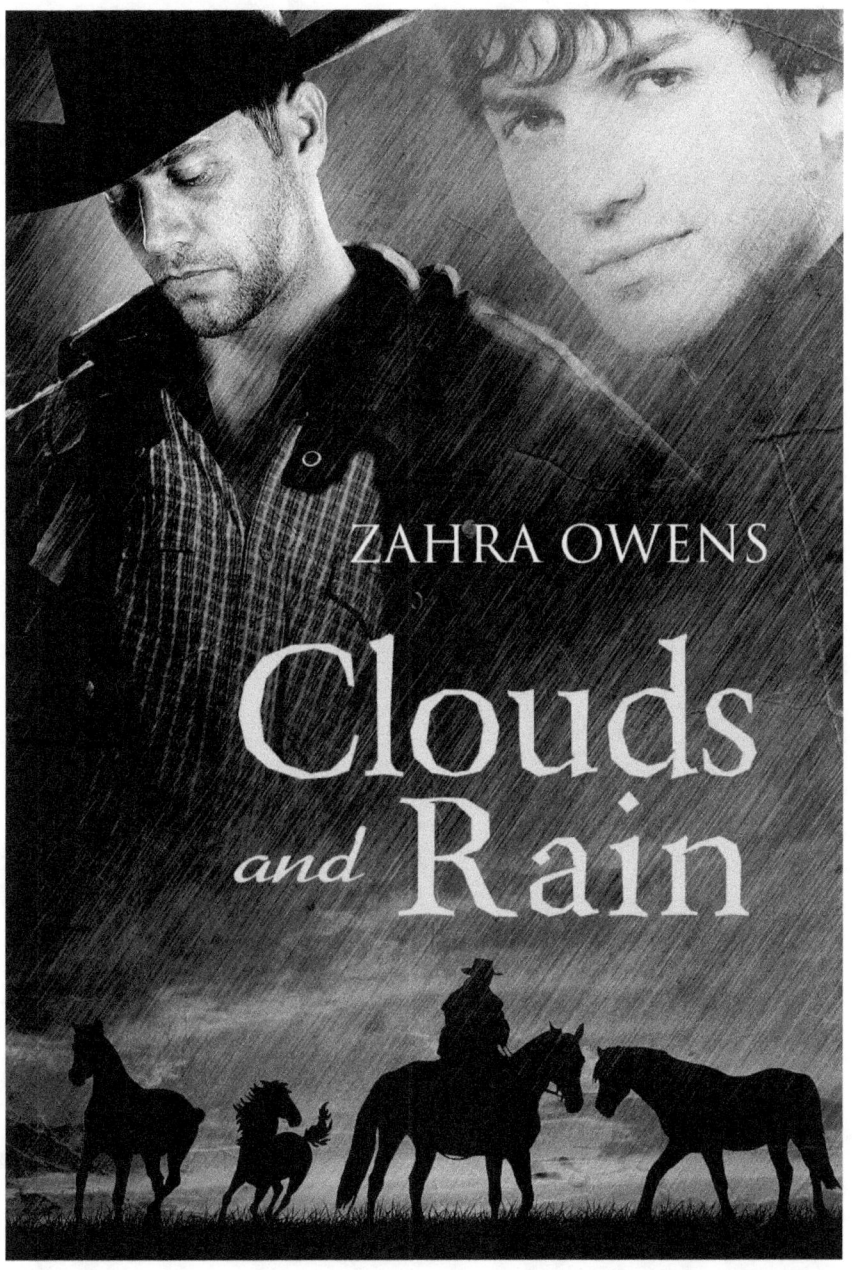

ZAHRA OWENS

Clouds
and Rain

http://www.dreamspinnerpress.com

Read Grant and Hunter's story in

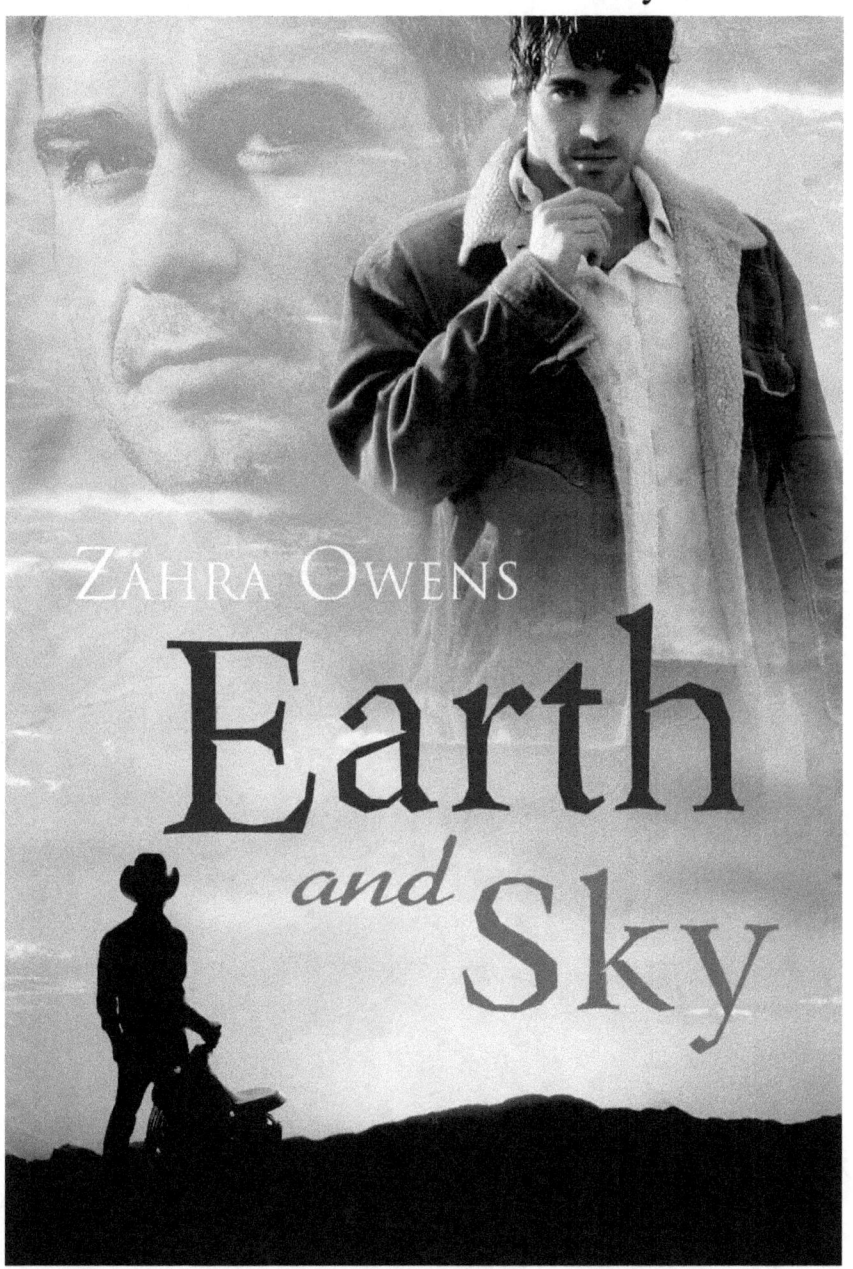

ZAHRA OWENS

Earth
and Sky

http://www.dreamspinnerpress.com

Also from ZAHRA OWENS

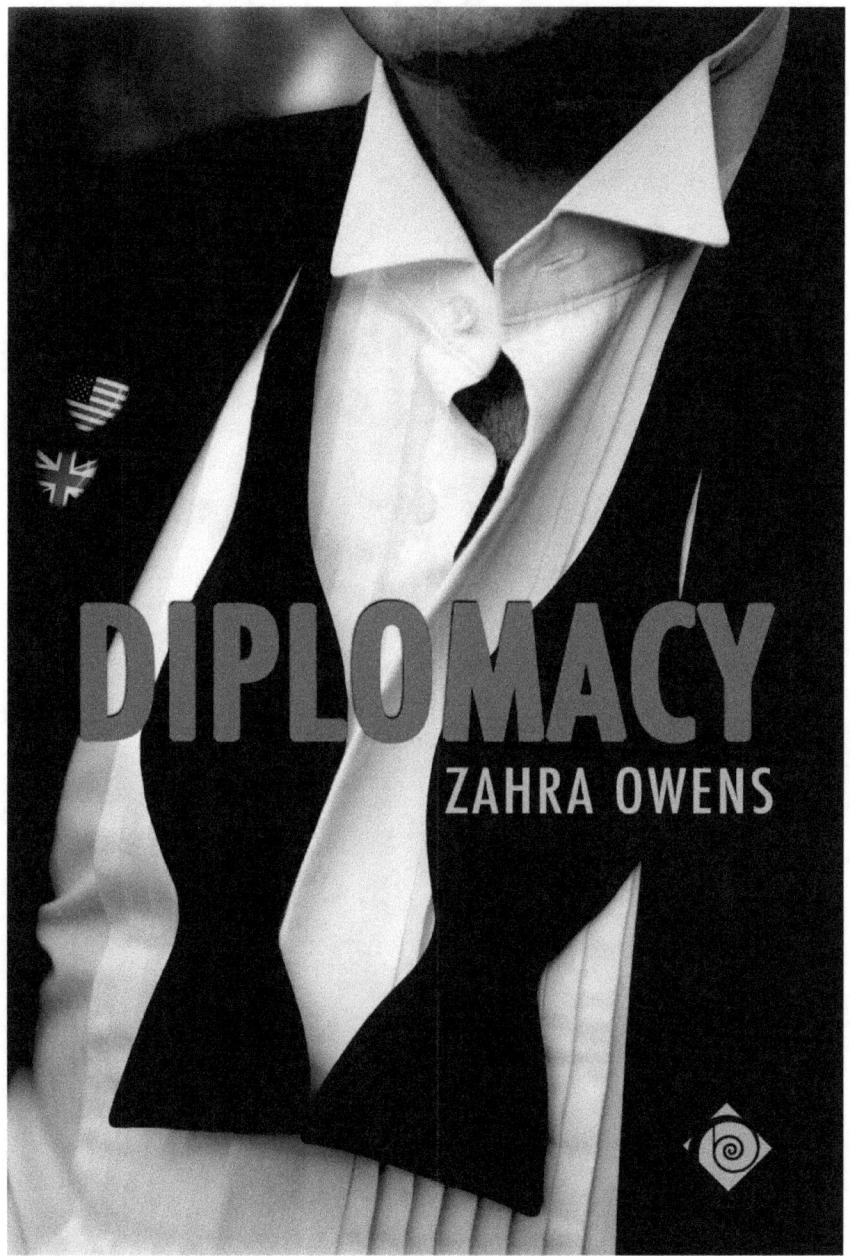

DIPLOMACY

ZAHRA OWENS

http://www.dreamspinnerpress.com

Also from ZAHRA OWENS

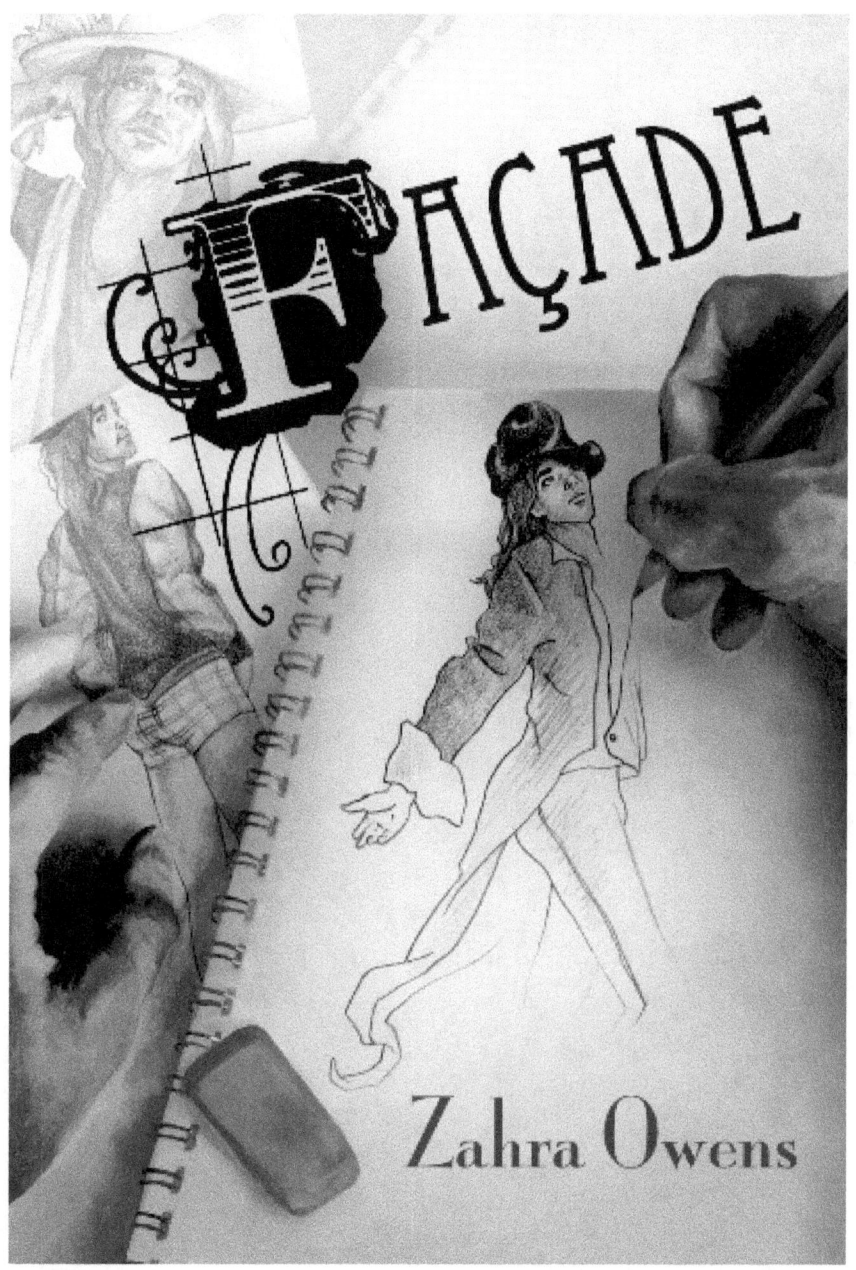

FAÇADE

Zahra Owens

http://www.dreamspinnerpress.com

Coming Soon: *Clouds and Rain* in Spanish

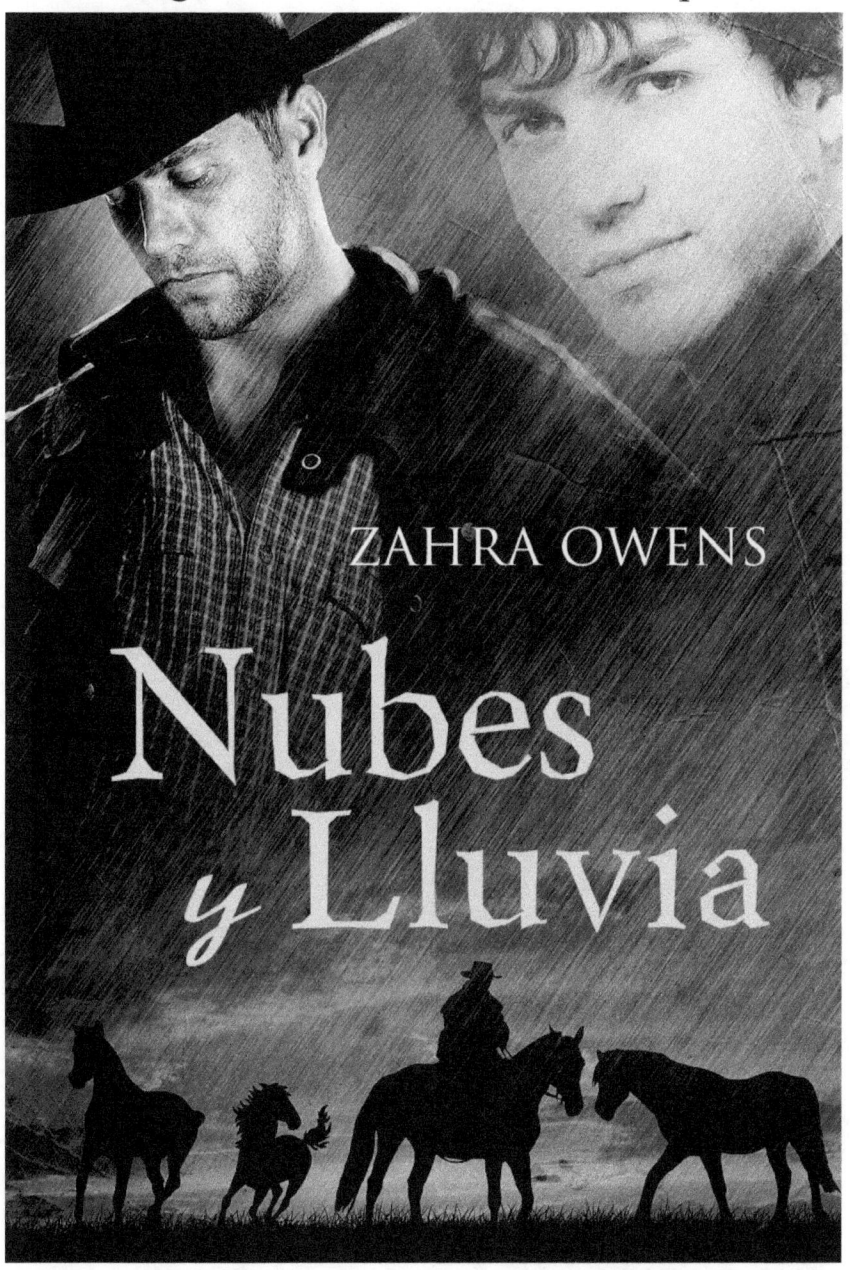

ZAHRA OWENS

Nubes y Lluvia

http://www.dreamspinnerpress.com

Also from ZAHRA OWENS

http://www.dreamspinnerpress.com

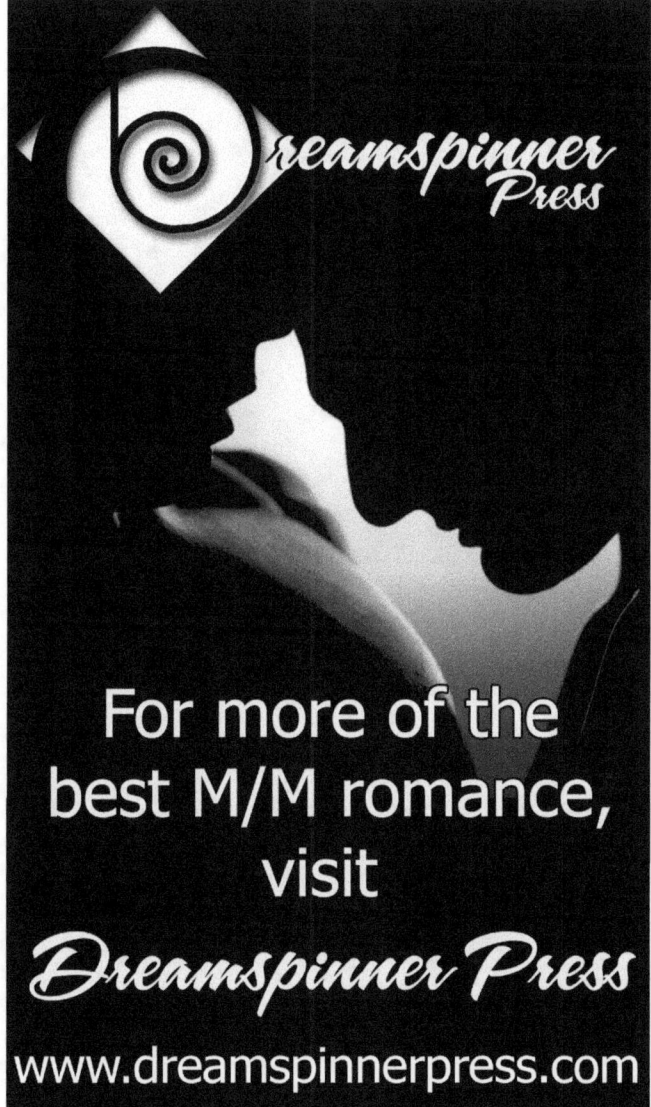

For more of the
best M/M romance,
visit

Dreamspinner Press

www.dreamspinnerpress.com

www.ingramcontent.com/pod-product-compliance
Lightning Source LLC
Chambersburg PA
CBHW070056030726
47506CB00002B/490